...ok Prize), ... La... ...pse, *The Earth Made of Glass*, *Elysium*, *In Desolate Heaven*, *The Sword Cabinet*, *The Book of the Heathen* (shortlisted for the 2001 WH Smith Literary Award), *Peacetime* (longlisted for the Booker Prize 2002) and *Gathering the Water* (longlisted for the Booker Prize 2006). His latest novel, *In Zodiac Light*, is now available from Doubleday.

Acclaim for:

Gathering the Water

'*Gathering the Water* belongs with a group of his (Edric's) novels whose artistry and resonance constitute one of the most astonishing bodies of work to appear from a single author for a generation'
Daily Telegraph

'*Gathering the Water* is a small novel but one that packs a mighty punch. Stylistically it is superb . . . above all though, it is in his marshalling of his themes that Edric proves himself such an accomplished novelist. At one level a book about loss and guilt, loyalty and ambition, madness and reality, *Gathering the Water* in fact ranges even further in its concerns, contrasting the immutability of nature with the similarly crushing immutability of money and business . . . a power-packed, stunningly crafted novel'
Sunday Times

'Booker judges take note'
Guardian

'*Gathering the Water* is an admirably serious novel, written in prose as spare as its setting. Its lament for the death of the community is subtle and powerful'
Daily Mail

'A compelling story . . . Robert Edric writes with a steady rhythm that, like the flow of the diverted dam waters, fills in a picture of horror and loss with a sustained and unrelenting force'
Times Literary Supplement

Swan Song
'Every bit as vigorously plotted as its predecessors . . . Edric creates
a fine crescendo. Reading his closing chapters is like being gripped
by a grungy, police-issue leather driving glove'
Mail on Sunday

'Bristles with confrontational conversation and drips with
atmosphere . . . absorbing'
Evening Standard

'Edric's spare, unflashy prose creates a very effective picture
of the contemporary city'
Spectator

Siren Song
'Subtle and intriguing. Edric is a considerable writer and
we are lucky to have him'
Literary Review

'The second volume, *Siren Song*, builds on the success of the first,
taking Rivers into even darker realms of the human psyche . . . Edric's
labyrinthine narrative is played out against a stifling Northern summer
and the sultrily evoked Hull settings strangely suggest the brilliant
American crime writers James Lee Burke and Dennis Lehane, who
may be the inspirations for Edric. Like his American peers, Edric is
anything but parochial: the Northern presented here is English
society seen through glass darkly'
Sunday Express

'In this superior, self-deprecating thriller, the workings of the plot
are secondary to the elegiac realism of the story'
Daily Telegraph

'Robert Edric has taken many of the ingredients of the classic
mystery to provide a realistic and convincing plot'
Natasha Cooper, *The Times Literary Supplement*

'Edric is a terrific storyteller but he also provides a pretty accurate
picture of modern-day crime and the way that it affects so many people.
Impressive stuff'
Observer

Cradle Song
'Deeply intelligent novel . . . it is refreshingly anchored to recognisable
realities and is infinitely the more powerful for that. The vertiginously
devious plot twists all close like a fist around the throat of the reader.

Peacetime

'There aren't many novelists whose new book I would read without question (Banville, Marias, Proulx) but I would read a new novel by the Yorkshireman, Robert Edric, even if its blurb told me that it was about a monk calculating how many angels could dance on a pinhead . . . If other novels deserve this year's Booker Prize more than *Peacetime*, then they must be very remarkable indeed'
John de Falbe, *Spectator*

'*Peacetime* has a seriousness and a psychological edge that nine out of ten novelists would give their eye teeth to possess . . . it will be mystifying if, 50 years hence, Edric isn't taught in schools'
D.J. Taylor, *Sunday Times*

'A marvel of psychological insight and subtly observed relations . . . Why Edric has not yet been shortlisted for the Booker Prize is a mystery'
Ian Thomson, *Guardian*

'Edric is one of those immensely skilled novelists who seems fated to be discovered insultingly late in a productive career when caught in the arbitrary spotlight of Booker nomination or television adaptation. Booksellers take note: this is a writer to put into the hands of people looking for "someone new" '
Patrick Gale, *Independent*

'This is a novel of ambition and skill, at once a historical meditation, an evocation of a disintegrating society and, perhaps most strikingly, a family melodrama . . . *Peacetime* deserves the recognition that Rachel Seiffert's Booker-nominated début received in 2001'
Francis Gilbert in the *Statesman*

'A gripping read, full of meaningful conversations and bleak introspection'
Sunday Herald

'Edric's evocation of far horizons, tumultuous seas and drifting sands is masterly . . . There are many memorable things in this novel . . . Edric has cleverly created a microcosm to represent a world still haunted by its terrible past and uncertain of its future'
Francis King, Literary Review

The Book of the Heathen

'The best historical fiction has something to say about the present as well as the past. Edric has demonstrated this in his previous novels and does so again, with accomplishment, in this latest work . . . Edric, prolific and critically acclaimed since his prize-winning debut in 1985, has struck an especially rich vein of form of late . . . the writing is as clear

and intelligent as ever, without being showy, and achieves the vital unities of theme and story, past and present, personal and political. Europe's colonial grip may have relaxed since Victorian times, but Edric offers a characteristically subtle counterpoint to the relationship between men, and between the strong and the weak in today's global economy'
Martyn Bedford, *Good Book Guide*

'Edric is a prolific and highly talented writer whose books give historical fiction a good name. They are distinguished not only by their formal skill and wide-ranging subject matters, but by their hairless, unshowy prose. In *The Book of the Heathen*, he uses suspense and thriller techniques to telling effect. His linguistic minimalism can also be effective – his low-key description of a hanging is quite the most harrowing I've ever read'
Sukhdev Sandhu, *Guardian*

'Many respectable judges would put Edric in the top ten of British novelists currently at work . . . as a writer, he specialises in the delicate hint and the game not given away . . . the territory Edric colonises is very much his own'
D.J. Taylor, *Spectator*

'Relentless . . . an impressive and disturbing work of art'
Robert Nye, *Literary Review*

'More disturbing even than Conrad in his depiction of the heart of darkness . . . out of the pervading miasma of futility – conjured up with Edric's usual atmospheric masterfulness – loom cameos of savagery and heartlessness. Their subjects sometimes recall George Orwell's writings. So does the terse, trenchant unforgettableness with which they are conveyed . . . rendered in prose whose steadiness and transparency throw the dark turbulence of what is happening into damning relief. Admirers of Conrad will soon spot affinities between this book and *Heart of Darkness* . . . but where Conrad leaves "the horror" at the centre of his story unspecific, Edric gives his a hideously charred and screaming actuality that sears it into the memory. It will be surprising if this year sees a more disturbing or haunting novel'
Peter Kemp, *Sunday Times*

'All the characters are memorably described. No less vivid is the author's depiction of the landscape, whose treacherous rivers and menacing tracts of wilderness provide a suitably unstable backdrop to this tale of shifting loyalties. Here and elsewhere in his fiction, Edric writes compellingly about relationships between men'
Christina Koning, *The Times*

The Kingdom of Ashes

ROBERT EDRIC

BLACK SWAN

TRANSWORLD PUBLISHERS
61–63 Uxbridge Road, London W5 5SA
A Random House Group Company
www.rbooks.co.uk

THE KINGDOM OF ASHES
A BLACK SWAN BOOK: 9780552774178

First published in Great Britain
in 2007 by Doubleday
a division of Transworld Publishers
Black Swan edition published 2008

Addresses for Random House Group Ltd companies outside the UK
can be found at: www.randomhouse.co.uk
The Random House Group Ltd Reg. No. 954009

The Random House Group Limited supports The Forest
Stewardship Council (FSC), the leading international forest
certification organisation. All our titles that are printed on
Greenpeace approved FSC certified paper carry the FSC logo.
Our paper procurement policy can be found at
www.rbooks.co.uk/environment

Typeset in 11/15pt Giovanni by
Falcon Oast Graphic Art Ltd.

Printed in the UK by
CPI Cox & Wyman, Reading, RG1 8EX.

2 4 6 8 10 9 7 5 3

For Paul Armitage

You think this is the past? This is not the past.
This is not even the present. What we sit to consider
here is a cold wind blowing so far into the future
that it will outlast us all.

General Nikitchenko
Russian Judge
Nuremburg

Trial Transcript 21 November 1945

Part One

Rehstadt, near Hanover
The British Zone of Occupation

Late Spring, 1946

1

Alex Foster leaned forward and looked down at the corpses. The slab of fractured concrete on which he was standing rocked slightly, and the man beside him held Alex's arm as the ground beneath them settled. Alex thanked the man and then turned back to the bodies. Rods of rusted and twisted metal protruded from the edge of the concrete; elsewhere, this reinforcing mesh had already been cut away and discarded.

He counted fourteen bodies, adults and children, including two much smaller ones who might have still been babies.

Upon his arrival at the exposed cellar, the corpses had been covered, but at his approach the men clearing the rubble had drawn back the tarpaulin to reveal what lay beneath. At the far side of the hole two ladders stood propped against the shattered floor, causing Alex to wonder why he'd been directed to this side of the cellar. He searched for a path through the mounded rubble, but none revealed itself to him. The man beside him went to join the small crowd already gathering on the street below.

Alex also wondered what was now expected of him. He called down to the men in the cellar. They were German labourers, many of whom had been working unsuspectingly on the floor above when the loosened joists had collapsed to reveal the unexpected chasm and mortuary beneath. Several of them had fallen, clinging to the boards and joists as the wood had settled, but none of these had been seriously injured.

Two men sat against the cellar wall, one with a bandage on his hand, the other with his arm in a sling, both dressings vividly white through the unlit gloom of the hole and the rapidly falling dusk.

The ground beneath Alex shifted again, and he turned to see Dyer coming cautiously towards him, a soldier on either side of him holding his arms.

'Too many,' Alex called to him, waving him back.

'What?' The anger and irritability in Dyer's voice were plain to hear.

'There are too many of you,' Alex called. 'Come forward alone. The ground's unstable.' He indicated the slab on which he stood.

'What – you think it's going to fall in?' Dyer shouted up to him. He pulled himself free of the two men and made standing alone at the base of the rubble seem like an act of defiance, of bravery almost.

'It's a possibility,' Alex said, realizing that Dyer was now looking for an excuse to turn back.

The two men had been together at the Institute when news of the discovery had reached them from the town. At first, Dyer had dismissed it as another false alarm, and then as a matter for Rehstadt's civil authorities, angry at the insistence of the man who brought the news that he, as the Senior British Officer, should go and see for himself. Consequently, he had sent Alex ahead of him, clearly hoping to hear that his own presence there was not required.

Alex had waited for him before climbing the rubble to look down at the corpses. After half an hour, and convinced that Dyer was not following him, he had gone alone to his unsteady vantage point above the cellar. He regretted the delay, primarily because of the audience which had by then formed to watch his every move, and also because of the tales and rumours of the discovery which would already have begun their unstoppable journeys through the small town, growing and changing as they went in accordance with whoever was repeating them. If he and Dyer had arrived together, sooner, then everything might have been contained; as it was, they had waited too long, and the speculation surrounding the discovery had already moved beyond their control.

'I'll wait here,' Dyer called to Alex. 'I don't want to put you in any danger.'

Alex smiled at the remark. If he'd been taken to the side of the hole where the ladders were propped, then he might have gone down to the bodies and examined them more closely. The people gathered behind Dyer could see nothing, but on the far side of the cellar, where the ground floor of the demolished building remained largely intact, a few dozen locals stood at the rim and looked down.

'Who are they?' Dyer called to him, meaning the corpses.

Alex raised his arms in an emphatic shrug.

'Then ask somebody,' Dyer said angrily. 'For Christ's sake, *do* something. Find out. This isn't any of our business. Get the proper authorities here. Let *them* sort it out.'

Alex said nothing in reply to this barrage of vague instruction. Checking that the ground beneath him had stopped moving, he leaned forward again.

It was immediately clear to him that the bodies had been placed in the cellar after death, and that they had not been killed in the position in which they had just been found. The tallest corpse had been placed against the side wall, and the remaining bodies had been laid against this in order of decreasing height, leaving the two smallest children at the far end of the line, and giving the whole row a faintly ridiculous appearance.

'Order,' Alex said to himself, convinced that others in the watching crowd already knew precisely how and when the corpses had come to be laid out like this. He was convinced, too, that records would have been kept, a list made – names and dates and causes. All he needed to do now to satisfy Dyer was to find someone amid the locals who could explain all this to him, whereupon their own involvement in the matter might be drawn to an official and convenient close.

He guessed that the men, women and children had all been killed at the same time – presumably during an air raid in the final months of the war – and that the cellar had been used as a temporary mortuary. Perhaps the building above it had been bombed and the cellar rendered inaccessible. Perhaps someone somewhere was waiting only for the collapsed masonry and timber to be cleared before coming forward to warn of what was about to be discovered. Or perhaps those people who knew — perhaps even those who had laid the corpses there – had been killed themselves, had left the town in the confusion of the war's end, or had simply chosen not to reveal themselves. He knew this last was unlikely, and expected that the bodies would be quickly identified and reclaimed by those already involved in their retrieval.

It struck him that because there were children in the cellar, then among the corpses there were entire families. And if that were the case, he regretted that the children had not been laid alongside their parents. He also found himself regretting that the younger children and the babies had not been afforded even the illusory refuge and security of being laid in their dead mothers' arms.

Looking down at the bodies, trying to discern individual features in the poor light, he was reminded of the bars of a toy xylophone he had possessed as a child.

The workmen in the cellar congregated at a shouted instruction and started to drag the corpses out of position.

'Wait,' Alex called down to them, uncertain who had instructed them; and equally uncertain why he himself had called a halt to the proceedings.

'What are you doing?' Dyer shouted to him. The man had moved in a circle around the rubble and now stood twenty yards to Alex's right, the two soldiers still beside him. 'Just let them get on with it. The sooner they get them out of there and out of sight, the better.'

Alex shook his head. 'It makes more sense to try and identify them where they are, together. Somebody here must know something.'

'I still think—' Dyer began.

'We need to do this properly,' Alex shouted to him.

Dyer, as angry now at Alex's interruption as at his insistence, said nothing for a moment. 'Then I'm washing my hands of it,' he said eventually. 'This is not why we're here. They can take care of this themselves.'

'We have a duty,' Alex said, but without any true or clear conviction.

'A what? A *what*? A duty? What we have a *duty* to, is what we're here for. Not sideshows like this. Don't make me tell you again, Captain Foster.'

Alex regretted antagonizing the man. Dyer revelled in the authority and the power he now possessed, and he was accustomed to being obeyed without dissent.

Before Alex could respond, someone lowered a cable into the cellar and a light was attached to this. A generator was started up, sending a thin plume of pale smoke above the rubble.

A man held the light above the bodies, and for the first time since his arrival, Alex was able to see their dusty faces. Other workers brushed and blew the sediment from the eyes and mouths of the dead, leaving them grey and stone-like, though suddenly human, and looking like carved effigies laid out on a tomb. A search was made of pockets and sleeves.

'Make sure that anything you find stays with the body on which you found it,' Alex shouted down in German.

Wallets, handkerchiefs, envelopes and papers were waved up at him and then laid on the chests of their owners.

The man holding the lamp crossed the cellar, casting shadows over everything. Alex called for the light to be fixed above the corpses and the man did this, looping the cable around one of the protruding joists.

'See,' Dyer called to Alex. 'They're going to have this sorted in no time. Wasted journey. We've got better things to occupy us, you and I, Mister Foster.'

Alex heard the cold emphasis he gave to the word 'Mister', and heard, too, the growing relief in Dyer's voice now that he had been proved right. 'I think you and I are going to have to have a serious talk about all this.' It was the final stamp of his authority on the matter.

Alex was about to say something in reply when he was distracted by excited shouting from below, and he turned back to the cellar to see several of the workmen leave the line of bodies and cross to the far side of the space. One of them returned for the lamp, pulling the cable behind him so that it ran over the corpses towards the far wall.

'What is it?' Dyer shouted. 'What now?' From where he stood, he could see nothing of what had attracted the men's attention.

Alex followed the light. The men had gathered at a mound of rubble, part of the collapsed floor. Several of them started to clear this, throwing the bricks and timbers into the space beside the corpses.

Alex watched without speaking, and Dyer continued calling to him, demanding to be told what was happening.

After several minutes, the work below ceased, each of the men falling still as though at a single, unspoken command.

Alex saw the tangle of buried limbs revealed by the light.

'There are more bodies,' he called to Dyer.

The light showed a mound of corpses piled one upon the other, perhaps the same number again as those laid out in their orderly, respectful row.

'Who are they?' Dyer called to him.

A murmur passed through the watching crowd, few of whom could now see what was happening. A woman standing close to Alex crossed herself and lowered her head in prayer.

The men below continued clearing the timbers until the bodies were fully revealed. It was an unsteady mound and there was a small panic as a corpse on the top of the heap slid unsettled from its position and landed at the feet of the workmen.

The man holding the light ran backwards a few paces, briefly darkening the cellar.

'There are at least twenty more,' Alex shouted to Dyer, regretting now that he had not come closer to him. Beside him, the praying woman fell silent, glanced at him and then walked away.

'In a pile?' Dyer shouted. 'Why weren't they laid out with the others? Find out who they are. This changes nothing. Make no mistake about that – ten corpses, a hundred, a thousand, it's all the same. None of our business – *theirs*, not ours. I'm not going to tell you that again, Foster.'

'No, Sir,' Alex said to himself.

One of the workmen arrived directly beneath where Alex stood. He wore a black beret and had a cloth fastened over his mouth. He lowered this and spat heavily at his feet.

'We found this,' he said. He held up a piece of clothing.

'What is it?' Alex asked him in German.

'Prison uniform.' He shook the dirt from the jacket and held it against his chest. Vague stripes were revealed.

'Any other identification?'

The man searched the jacket and shook his head. 'Perhaps they'd been brought in to help clear the rubble,' he suggested. 'Or perhaps they were just unlucky and got caught down here in the raid.' There was little true concern in his voice.

'Perhaps,' Alex said, unwilling to speculate openly in front of so many others, and with Dyer still listening to everything that was being said.

'What do you want us to do?' the man asked him.

'Take the mound apart; lay them out.'

'Foster,' Dyer shouted to him. 'This is where you and I turn around and walk away from all this.'

'And if they're prisoners of war?' Alex said, turning to face him over the mound of bricks. The smoke from the generator threaded across the ground between them.

'Meaning?' Dyer said, the word both a question and a cautious threat.

'I mean that if they *are* prisoners of war, then until we can positively identify them, perhaps we *do* have some responsibility towards them after all.'

Dyer considered this.

Around him, the watching crowd fell silent. Few could have understood what Alex had just said, but it now felt to him as though everyone knew precisely what was happening.

They know exactly who all those corpses are, Alex thought to himself. He looked slowly around at the towns-people. Some held his gaze; others turned away from him; a few began low conversations.

'So what do you suggest?' Dyer said, aware now that the circumstances had changed and that he could no longer publicly deny all responsibility in the matter.

'Leave it to me,' Alex said, knowing it was what Dyer wanted to hear.

'You'll need to liaise,' Dyer said immediately, raising his voice.

'With the proper authorities,' Alex said.

'Exactly. In fact, the people you need to see are probably already here. News like this travels fast.' He looked around him as he spoke. 'Find who you need, let *them* have a closer look. And if any of this starts to smell bad, then I want *them* standing closest to it when

27

that happens. This might have come as a surprise to you and me, Foster, but it'll be no surprise to them, I can assure you of that. Liaise. And then come to me with everything you get.' Dyer turned and walked quickly back to his waiting driver.

Alex watched as the men below dragged the corpses from their mound and laid them against the fallen timbers. He counted twenty-six more bodies. Most wore the same striped jackets and trousers, and some were naked from the waist up.

The man to whom he'd spoken returned to hold up other items of clothing for Alex to see. 'Some numbers,' he said. 'It might help.'

'Are they English?' Alex asked him. 'American? Forced labour?'

The man said he couldn't tell. He was approached by another, who spoke to him and then withdrew.

'What?' Alex asked him.

The man was reluctant to answer him, and as he considered his words, Alex knew exactly what he was going to say.

'Tattoos,' the man said. 'Numbers. Some of them have tattoos.' He slid back the sleeve of his jacket.

'It will all help,' Alex said, knowing how unfeeling the words sounded.

'Shall we cover them up?' the man asked him.

Alex looked to where the rearranged corpses lay on the floor or were propped against the fallen timbers, some of them now in a near-sitting position, their legs splayed, their heads slumped forward, and looking to him in that poor light as though they were living men taking a short rest from their labours.

2

Leaving the rubble, Alex made his way back through the dispersing crowd. The discovery of the corpses would remain the main topic of conversation in Rehstadt for days to come. As he walked, he expected the locals to pester him with questions, but few approached him. An old woman held his arm and asked him when the bodies would be removed, and where she would need to go to identify and claim her relatives. Others, he guessed, would already be making the same unhappy calculations.

The corpses, he told her, would very likely be taken to the town hospital. For some reason the answer disappointed her, and she released her grip on him. Rehstadt, he knew, had suffered only infrequently over the past years, and its few missing inhabitants were still remembered, still listed and sought.

The old woman continued to walk alongside him. When would she be able to retrieve her relatives? He guessed the following day, or the one after, and upon hearing this she turned from him and shouted the news to a group of nearby women. Alex regretted having put this spark to the fuel of their expectation.

As he left the centre of the small crowd, pausing to watch Dyer depart, a second jeep arrived and drew up behind him, and someone called to him. He recognized James Whittaker's voice. He turned and shielded his eyes against the glare of the headlights.

Whittaker came to him, searching around him in the darkness.

'It's up there,' Alex told him, indicating the mound of brick and timber blocking the view of the cellar.

'Our beloved leader called and told me to come. I take it there's no one actually requiring the attention of an exhausted, over-worked, highly skilled and otherwise-engaged-elsewhere doctor.' Whittaker lit a small cigar as he spoke and then drew hard on it, coughing as he blew out the smoke. He showed no inclination to approach the cellar. 'Can it wait until tomorrow?'

'I doubt they'll need you even then,' Alex told him.

Whittaker swore and picked flakes of tobacco from his tongue.

'I knew when Hauptmann Dyer called that I was coming for no good reason.'

'I think he just wanted a few more of us standing between him and the bodies,' Alex said.

James Whittaker was the Chief Medical Officer at the Institute. He had arrived there at the same time as Alex, four months previously, and they were billeted in adjoining rooms at the old Spa Hotel, their rooms opening out on to a shared balcony that looked out over the neglected gardens. They spent a good deal of their free time together. Whittaker was eight years older than Alex, in his early thirties, and was married with two young daughters. He wrote to his wife every morning and evening and posted these letters daily. Her own to him arrived in batches of half a dozen every week, and he had confided to Alex that he sorted these by date and extended his pleasure in reading them by opening only one each day. The table at the centre of his room was filled with photos of his wife and daughters.

'Anyone mention anything contagious?' he said to Alex in a low voice.

'After what, a year?'

Whittaker shrugged. 'You never know. Not very likely, but it's always a consideration.'

'Some of the workers had cloths over their mouths,' Alex said.

'Oh, well, there you go. No crucifixes or pomanders?'

'What did Dyer expect you to do?' Alex asked him.

By then, the small crowd had almost completely dispersed. Only a couple of the old women and a few men still waited on the cleared street, watching as the workers climbed out of the hole and drew up the cables and ladders behind them.

Alex indicated these watchers to Whittaker, who said, 'They must have known the bodies were there all along. Why didn't they tell anyone sooner than this?'

'Perhaps they thought the cellar had been filled with rubble, perhaps they were happy for it to remain a grave.' He told Whittaker about the prisoners.

Whittaker considered this. 'Hardly a surprise,' he said. 'The place must have been crowded with them at one time or another.' He turned and looked back at the jeep in which he had arrived, and only then did Alex see the young woman sitting there. She wore a man's heavy overcoat and a scarf fastened close to her head.

'Dyer thought I might need an interpreter,' Whittaker said. 'She was in Administration as I came through. I called, she answered.'

The two men walked back to the waiting vehicle. Its engine was still running, and Whittaker reached in to the steering column and switched it off. The few remaining onlookers turned at the sudden silence.

On the mound of rubble, the generator was also finally silenced, and as it shuddered and died, so too did the light it powered, casting the whole scene into darkness. Men still made their way across the bricks, calling to each other, shouting directions to those behind them. Reaching the cleared road, they gathered there.

'Ought you to go and talk to them?' Alex suggested.

Whittaker mimicked the phrase. 'And say what? Wash your clothes before tomorrow? Think twice before looting the dead?'

At this last, unthinking remark, the woman in the jeep said, in English, 'Oh, they would not do that.' She stopped abruptly and lowered her head.

'No, I know,' Whittaker said. 'My apologies. I shouldn't have said it.' He motioned towards Alex. 'This is Captain Alex Foster, another of Dyer's lackeys. Dyer sent him to prepare the way.'

Alex nodded to the woman and reached his hand out to her. The gesture surprised her, but she reciprocated, taking off her glove to shake his hand.

'Eva Remer,' she said. 'Your friend didn't know my name.'

'I barely remember my own some days,' Whittaker said, causing her to smile in acceptance of his apology. He, too, held out his hand to her, and she took it.

She removed her headscarf, revealing her vividly blonde hair beneath, almost white in the darkness. She ran a hand through her fringe, then flattened this to her eyes. At the back and sides the hair was cut in a line below her ears.

'*Did* they know about the bodies?' Alex asked her, indicating the last of the dispersing crowd.

She looked hard at them. 'I imagine so. There were raids here on two consecutive nights. Two years ago, longer. They said at the time that we were a "Target of Opportunity",' – she smiled at the phrase and all it disguised – 'that bombers unsuccessful elsewhere – Hanover, Bremen or Hamburg, perhaps – had dropped their bombs on something they spotted below so that they would not have to fly home with them still on board. The authorities here were forever telling us that we possessed nothing of any military significance in the town, nothing that you might waste your bombs on.'

'Were there no real shelters?' Alex asked her.

'Only the cellars.' She indicated the one behind them. 'It was one of the largest. I think it was reinforced a few years before the war began. Perhaps the people you found there were sheltering elsewhere. I remember there were problems – so many false alarms – when the mayor and his officials refused to open up some municipal buildings to allow their cellars to be used. Mostly, people preferred the security of their own homes. Some left the town and went into the forest each night, especially towards the end. There were camps there.' She smiled. 'So you see, people still felt safer there, outside the town and all its non-existent targets.'

'Do you know any of the families who might have lost someone?' Whittaker asked her.

'Perhaps. Some of them. Though I recognize few of the people here today.'

'Were *you* in the town during the raids?' Alex asked her.

'I live with my father and brother three miles to the north. A village called Ameldorf. My father has his business there.' She looked and pointed in the direction of her home. 'During the raids elsewhere, we stood out in the yard and listened to the planes passing overhead. It came as a surprise to us to hear them drop their bombs here. We came into town the following day and saw the destruction they had caused.'

A distant clock started to strike, and she turned her head to listen to this. She unfolded the scarf in her lap and re-folded it over her head.

Alex guessed her to be in her early twenties, but with the scarf again covering her hair and her cheeks, and with the bulky overcoat still fastened to her chin, she looked suddenly much older.

One of the few remaining onlookers, an old man, approached the jeep and spoke to her in German. Alex understood most of what was said. To Whittaker, he said, 'He thinks we're going to take all the bodies away because of the prisoners.'

'Why?' Whittaker said.

'As punishment.'

Whittaker smiled. 'Dyer will just be happy to see them all evaporate in front of him, and then for you to file your two-page report, unread, in that big grey filing cabinet of his marked "Unwelcome Interruptions Along My Rise to Glory".'

Waiting until the old man had finished speaking, Alex told Eva Remer to explain to him that provision would be made as soon as possible for all the bodies to be identified and reclaimed. 'Tell him to tell everyone else concerned to bring identification, confirmation of who the corpses might be. To the hospital, or the town hall.'

Eva explained all this to the man, who listened attentively, and who then took her gloved hand in both his own and kissed it several times.

The gesture surprised both Alex and Whittaker, and they concealed their smiles.

Caught unawares herself by the man's grip, Eva pulled her hand free and pushed it into her pocket. She told him again to go and tell the others what to do. The man stood looking at her for a moment, his hands held out, almost beseeching her to allow him to hold her again, before finally lowering his arms and backing away from her, bowing slightly as he went.

'What was all that about?' Whittaker said to Alex.

Overhearing the remark, Eva said, 'Ten years before the war, when I was a girl and my mother was still alive, my father was the mayor here. Until 1933.'

'So you—'

'So I was the mayor's daughter, yes. He knew my father, remembers him, that's all.'

Alex heard the undisguised note of pride in her voice as she explained this. 'Then perhaps . . .' he began. He was about to suggest to her that her father might explain to the townspeople what was now likely to happen concerning the corpses.

Eva Remer understood this and interrupted him.

'My father was stripped of his authority because he was never the ardent Party member others wished him to be,' she said. 'The man who replaced him is our mayor still.'

'Ah,' Whittaker said. Both he and Alex had met him on the few occasions when Dyer had called for meetings which included the local authorities. The presence of the mayor had not always been required at these, but the man had always insisted, in his usual peremptory manner, that he be allowed to attend and to participate. He cast himself as the locals' spokesman, and because he was obsequious and, ultimately, compliant and predictable, it was a role Dyer was happy for him to adopt.

'You know him?' Eva asked Alex.

'Only too well,' Whittaker told her.

Eva swung her legs from the seat and stood beside them. She wore fur-lined boots to her knees, and both Alex and Whittaker looked at these.

'I bought them from a soldier,' she said. 'Russian boots.' She laughed at the words. 'They may not be flattering or feminine, but they are warm and waterproof.'

The distant chiming had ended. 'I need to go home now,' she said. She held out her hand, first to Whittaker and then to Alex. 'If you *are* responsible for reporting the consequences of all this to Colonel Dyer,' she said to him, 'then I'll let you know of anything I hear or discover. It shouldn't be too difficult to identify the townspeople.'

'And the others?' Alex said, immediately regretting the remark and all it implied.

Eva shook her head. 'I imagine there are many others, unsought, and either unmourned or long forgotten in every village, town and city in this country.'

'I know,' Alex said. Her English was precise and formal, and he guessed that she used this veil of a foreign language to disguise her true feelings.

She turned away from him, about to leave, and on impulse he held her arm and told her to wait.

'What is it?' she said to him. She made no attempt to free herself.

'We can give you a lift,' Alex said. 'A lift home. You said three miles.'

'Nearer four from here,' she said, smiling again.

'You can let go of her now,' Whittaker said to Alex, who looked at his hand on Eva's arm before taking it away.

'Sorry,' he said.

The apology amused her further. 'Two men grabbing my arm in only ten minutes,' she said. 'I must be a very desirable woman.' She looked directly at Alex as she spoke.

'Of course you are,' Whittaker said, sliding his own arm through hers and turning her back to the jeep.

Whittaker had spoken to prevent Alex from saying something embarrassing – another unnecessary apology, perhaps – and Alex knew this. He watched the two of them climb into the jeep, Whittaker in the driver's seat, Eva in the centre, close to him. She patted the space beside her for Alex to join them.

He climbed in and braced himself against the door frame, feeling her pressed tightly against him.

She gave Whittaker instructions, and as he drove, he showed off to her, calling out to the few other drivers blocking their path, sounding his horn, accelerating too quickly and braking too sharply. His cigar remained only half-smoked and he held this in the side of his mouth as he drove.

'He's showing off,' Alex said loudly enough for them both to hear him above the engine.

'Of course I am,' Whittaker said, and Eva laughed at the remark.

Leaving the town, Whittaker drove more slowly on the narrow, unlit road. They drove through trees, past increasingly scattered buildings, until they arrived at a crossroads, at which a marker constructed of whitewashed oil drums had been erected. Eva shouted for Whittaker to stop, and the instant he did this, she pushed against Alex for him to allow her to climb out.

'Where's the house?' Whittaker asked her.

'A further half a mile,' she said. 'Please, I would prefer to walk from here.'

'It's no trouble to—' Whittaker began.

'Please,' Eva said again. She looked briefly at Alex, who climbed back into the jeep beside Whittaker. He took one of the small cigars from Whittaker's pocket and gave it to her.

'For me?' she said and pretended to smoke it.

'I thought your brother. But if you—'

'I was joking,' she said. 'And my brother is sixteen.'

'So?' Whittaker said.

'Your father, then,' Alex said, anxious only that she accept the small gift.

Eva took the cigar from her mouth and held it between her palms. 'Then thank you,' she said to him. 'I'll tell him what's happened today, see if there is anything he can do to help you with the identification.'

'But only if it means treading on the new mayor's toes,' Whittaker said.

Eva smiled and shook her head at the remark. To Alex she said, 'Make sure he drives more slowly returning to the town. Follow the road, no detours, no forest tracks. There are no short cuts. Is that the proper expression – "short cut"?'

'Short cut,' Alex said.

She waved to them, turned abruptly and followed a lane leading to the right, a cobbled track with overgrown hedges on either side.

Whittaker turned the jeep in a tight circle around the oil drums and drove back into Rehstadt.

3

The Spa Hotel had been built at the turn of the century to capitalize on the vogue for fashionable health resorts. The spring still ran, channelled and contained, through a tap in a room adjacent to one of the hotel's three empty indoor pools. The local men who still worked at the place had explained to Dyer how this might easily be diverted and the smallest of the pools filled again. At their urging, and because of the prestige the project might afford him, Dyer had attempted this. But after refilling over a period of three days, the small pool had then drained empty overnight. An engineer was called and he suggested that the foundations of the pool must have dried out and cracked during the long period when it had remained unused. The cost of repair was prohibitive, and despite further entreaties, mostly this time from his own senior staff, Dyer had abandoned the project.

The spa water still ran from the tap, and was pronounced undrinkable by all who tasted it. An analysis was carried out and it was found to contain nothing harmful, only excessive levels of the minerals which gave it its sour taste and distinctive aroma. On warm days, the empty pool and its adjacent shower and treatment rooms smelled of the water.

Occasionally, people from the town arrived with containers, demanding that these be filled. The older residents still believed in the spa's health-giving qualities. All who came were denied access into even the outer compound of the Institute by Dyer. Later, following the intervention of the mayor and his council, containers were filled with the water and left at the junction of the driveway with the road into the centre of Rehstadt. The townspeople still complained that they were unable to secure the water at its source, but they came and took what Dyer offered them all the same. The local newspaper recorded the vote of thanks accorded to the mayor for what he had achieved on the town's behalf.

There had been an earlier structure on the site of the Institute, a hunting lodge, whose origins were obscure. Photographs of the current hotel in its heyday lined the walls of the officers' quarters and their conference rooms. By comparison, the lodge appeared to have been a primitive structure, built of massive black logs, and with a turf-lined roof. High stone chimneys rose at either end of the older building. The trees of the surrounding forest had then come much closer to the rear of the hotel, but these had long since been felled and cleared to provide the ornate and spacious garden of the later building. A display of large white skulls, bear and stag mostly, had been built into a diamond-shaped design above the entrance to the lodge, and some of those same trophies still hung on the wall above the fireplace in the hotel lobby.

Records showed that the hotel had once catered for two hundred guests, and that twice this number had applied to visit at the height of each summer. A great many of the townspeople had been employed by the place, and it was still a commonly heard complaint that not enough of them were employed there now, that their livelihoods had been stolen from them.

Ten years ago, the hotel had been closed for a year and had been refurbished, afterwards opening to only a hundred and twenty guests, but providing these new and wealthier visitors with a wider and more costly range of treatments and services.

Massage rooms had been built. Individual shower rooms were constructed in the new wings that reached out from each of the larger pools. Two new kitchens and three larger dining rooms were added, the latter overlooking the south-facing terraces, which led in turn to the tennis courts screened by newly planted yew and laurel hedges. Overall, the extended grounds covered almost two hundred acres, fifty of which remained afforested. Walks and drives were laid into these woodlands. Stabling for sixty horses was built on the eastern boundary of the Institute, arranged around a large cobbled courtyard, and with living quarters for twenty grooms, ostlers and farriers above the stables.

Holidays which had once lasted only a week stretched to months for the wealthy summer visitors. Fathers and husbands came and went from the hotel on business while their wives and children remained there. Rehstadt had benefited in many ways from its close proximity to the place, and from the wealthy people who had holidayed there.

Five years after its refurbishment, the hotel was taken over by the German Military Staff as a centre of rest and recuperation for its senior officers. There was no true hospital there, only provision for those who had been wounded and treated elsewhere to recover in comfort, a reward for their suffering and sacrifices. Simply being sent there, it was claimed by the townspeople, was a guarantee of full recovery.

After Stalingrad and the year of defeats which followed, the Institute changed again. Its renowned luxuries declined and its beds doubled in number. It was still a place of ease, calm and plenty, but after the spring of 1943 it was adapted to provide a more practical service: the new wings were converted into hospital wards, and a medical staff of eighty was billeted there permanently.

The townspeople had had little say in what was happening to the place, and consequently to them, and this was another grievance they had burnished and clung to, frequently repeating it to Dyer and his officers, almost as though they made no clear distinction between what had happened to them during the war and what was happening to them now, in the war's drawn-out and seemingly unchanging aftermath.

By the war's end, the Institute had been empty for two months, and much of it was boarded up against the elements and the bands of foragers and scavengers who came and went during those uncertain and unsettling times.

With the arrival of Dyer and the decision to reopen the Institute, there had been some hope locally that the place might be returned in some measure to what everyone invariably referred to as its 'former glory'. Their reasoning was simple: the war was over, the world was being built anew, and what had been good and strong and decent in the past would surely be needed now as a foundation for the future.

But everything the townspeople saw and heard of Dyer's occupation and refurbishment only disappointed them further. And when their complaints were made to Dyer at the first of the meetings he had attended in Rehstadt, he had risen from his seat, interrupted the otherwise orderly and formal proceedings, and had demanded to know how these 'disappointments' compared to *his* disappointment at finding so little of that 'former glory' remaining to him. The luxuries and facilities enjoyed by the German Army, he insisted, had been considerably greater than those enjoyed now by his own staff.

It was all Dyer could do, a clerk had afterwards told Alex, to prevent himself from pointing out to the hundred or so townspeople at the meeting who were the victors in the war and who the vanquished. It was only because Dyer had been warned by his own superiors, the clerk added, that he had resisted making the remark. Upon hearing this, Alex had repeated the word 'vanquished' to himself, knowing that it was precisely the word Dyer would have used.

Dyer had subsequently refused the town council the reopening of the stables; refused the replanting of trees where these had fallen or been illegally felled on the estate; and refused to consider the employment of more local people alongside his own staff. He had refused to attend the weekly council meetings as a matter of course, insisting that these were concerned with minor, inconsequential issues unrelated to the Institute and Dyer's work there now. He was above all these concerns.

In Nuremberg, the preliminary hearings and depositions were almost completed. It was the job of Military Intelligence in places like Rehstadt to deal with what were considered to be the lesser war criminals, all of whom, it was decided, needed to be interviewed and assessed by the prosecutors of those occupying forces with an interest in them. Rehstadt had been chosen for its location, for the security that could easily be created and maintained there, and for the self-contained nature and relative isolation of the Institute and its hotel.

There was considerable cross-questioning and transfer of prisoners between Rehstadt and similar centres, and across the various zones of occupation, including the Russian zone in the east. Less than there had been during the months immediately following the war's end, perhaps, but still enough for Alex and his fellow investigators to be frustrated by the sudden loss of a prisoner because someone elsewhere had presented a stronger case for prosecution. At least now there was a proper structure in place, more reliable timetabling, which allowed a procedure to be followed and prisoners to be released – either to other military authorities, into civil custody or into freedom – with due record of all they might have revealed about themselves and others, and where they might be found and reinvestigated should the need for this arise.

It seemed to Alex, and to the more unhappy of his colleagues, that the only trials that now mattered to the world were those underway in Nuremberg, and that the work being undertaken at Rehstadt and the places like it was of considerably less consequence. Everywhere he looked in the newspapers, he saw the words 'International' and 'Humanity', as though they alone were proof of a new moral conviction in the world. He knew what the prosecutors at these show trials were about to attempt, but he also knew that the guilt or evil, or whatever else the watching journalists wanted to call it, did not belong to those few men alone. He knew that he had sat opposite so-called 'lesser criminals' who had lied to him day after day about the equally heinous crimes they too had been accused of, that he had breathed the same air as these men, and that their cigarette smoke had filled his lungs and eyes just as it had filled their own.

Upon first encountering the display of skulls and antlers high above the fireplace in the hotel lobby, Alex had gone to the framed photographs in the officers' quarters and identified those few specimens which had survived from the old hunting lodge. He was particularly impressed by the skulls of the bears, wondering where the animals had been killed – the Schwarzwald or Bohemia, he guessed – knowing only that they could not have been hunted within five hundred miles of where they now hung.

He had tasted the spa water himself, had taken a bottle of it to Whittaker, who, upon drinking it without first smelling it, had immediately spat it out over his balcony, afterwards swilling the taste from his mouth with the whisky he kept by his bed.

Whittaker suffered from insomnia, and claimed that the drink helped him get what little sleep he achieved. Alex knew that he had spent two months the previous summer at the camp at Belsen, and during his own sleepless nights he occasionally heard Whittaker wake with a shouted start from his nightmares. After Belsen, he had returned home to Shropshire for six months before being sent back to Germany. He had confided to Alex that he wished he hadn't gone directly home to his wife and daughters, that he should have stayed away a short while longer. He said that when he woke from his nightmares he was simultaneously shivering with cold and bathed in sweat. It was as much as he had volunteered on the matter.

Upon their arrival, the two men had explored the grounds of the Institute together, walking to the abandoned stables, following the carriage rides through the trees, and tracing the outlines of the overgrown gardens. But they had learned little they didn't already know about the place, except that it was no longer the energetic, vibrant heart of the community it had once sustained. It was a survivor, Whittaker had announced, mimicking Dyer's own glib and melodramatic turn of phrase. A survivor – uncertain, exhausted and losing hope. Just like the rest of us, he had then added, his voice falling. Just like the rest of us.

4

Alex next encountered Dyer two days later. He was crossing the terrace in front of the Institute, walking from the hotel to his office, when Dyer called down to him from his first-floor window. At first, Alex couldn't see who had shouted, and then he looked up to where Dyer stood. He shielded his eyes as Dyer called again, adding an emphatic 'now' to the order for Alex to go to him. Alex signalled to let him know he was on his way.

He entered the building and went to the main staircase.

He paused at the foot of the stairs in the hope of seeing Eva Remer – either at the reception desk there, or in the room behind this.

He had passed through the lobby several times the previous day, and on each occasion he had waited there briefly in the hope of seeing her. It would have been a simple enough matter to approach the desk and ask for her directly – he did, after all, have a valid reason for wanting to see her – but each time, upon seeing that she wasn't at the desk or close by it, he had said nothing to the other German women there and had continued on his way.

As he climbed the broad stairs, he wondered if Dyer had learned of her involvement yet. He was in no doubt that it was in connection with the corpses that Dyer wanted to see him now. He checked the few files he carried to ensure there was nothing he was not authorized to possess.

The corridor to Dyer's office was as broad as the staircase, carpeted and furnished, and had clearly once been the access to the grandest of the hotel's rooms. Men came and went from Dyer's outer room. Alex paused at the door, fastened his top button and pulled up his tie. His trousers were creased and his shoes had not been polished for days.

He entered the outer room and told the sergeant who beckoned to him that he had been summoned by Dyer.

'*Colonel* Dyer is occupied,' the sergeant said. He ran his finger down a clipboard squarely positioned at the centre of his otherwise empty desk.

'He called down to me, insisted I come immediately,' Alex said.

The sergeant asked him his name. Alex had encountered the man before. He was renowned for being as officious and as unwavering as Dyer himself.

'If you could knock and tell him I'm here,' Alex suggested, hoping to convey to the man that he was not impressed by this unnecessary procedure.

'Colonel Dyer is presently engaged.'

'So you said. Perhaps it's why he wants to see me.'

The sergeant remained unperturbed. 'If everybody who wanted to see Colonel Dyer just came in here . . .' The predictable remark remained unfinished as the door behind the man opened and Dyer appeared. The sergeant rose immediately and stood to attention, giving a salute, which Dyer returned.

'Foster,' Dyer said to Alex, beckoning him inside.

'I was just explaining to Captain Foster—' the sergeant began.

Dyer looked at him briefly, nodded once to silence him, and then waited for Alex to go through into his office. He closed the door behind them.

Inside, a second man stood at the window, coming to join Alex and Dyer only when they were seated.

He was an American. Alex read his insignia. Another colonel.

'This is Colonel Amos Preston,' Dyer said. 'I think we might dispense with formalities and background.'

'Is it in connection with the corpses?' Alex asked him.

Preston drew closer to Alex and held out his hand. 'Corpses?' He looked at Dyer.

'Some trouble in the town,' Dyer said dismissively. 'They cleared a cellar and found a few bodies. Something for the locals to sort out.'

'German corpses?' Preston said. 'Civilians?'

'Possibly,' Alex told him. 'People sheltering from an air raid. Plus a few prisoners, as yet unidentified.'

At the mention of the word, Preston turned back to Dyer and said, 'POWs?'

Dyer shook his head and then shrugged. 'We still don't know. We're doing everything – I'm doing everything – possible to find out. If it's of any interest to you, I'll let you know as soon as we discover anything.'

It was clear to Alex that Dyer was angry at this diversion, but that he was in no position to reveal this to Preston. Taking advantage of this, Alex said to Preston, 'Were there ever any American POWs in the town?'

Preston thought about this. 'Not sure. But even now we still have a good number unaccounted for. I'm sure our repatriation people would be grateful to take a look-see at any names, numbers or insignia you turn up.'

He looked from Alex to Dyer, who nodded vigorously and said, 'You have my word on it.'

Seizing a second advantage, and knowing how much further this would antagonize Dyer, Alex said, 'There's a woman, Eva Remer, one of our clerical staff. Her father was the mayor. She speaks English. She seems to know better than most what happened during the raid and I think—'

'Then keep her looking,' Dyer said, making it clear to Alex that enough had been said on the matter.

Sensing something of the animosity between the two men, Preston said, 'Thanks anyway, John. Like I said, I'd appreciate hearing of anything of interest.'

In the whole of his time at the Institute, it was the first time Alex had ever heard Dyer called by his Christian name. Even Dyer looked surprised and embarrassed at hearing it.

'I'll make sure Captain Foster passes on anything he uncovers,' Dyer said to Preston. 'Now . . .'

'Apologies,' Preston said. 'You're both busy men. And I'm here to ask a favour.' He rose from his seat, reached across Dyer's desk and picked up a slender file.

Alex saw the sudden, involuntary movement Dyer made to keep his hand on the file, and saw, too, how he then stopped himself and drew back.

'May I?' Preston said, waiting for Dyer's nod. 'We'd like you to question a man for us,' he said to Alex. He opened the file to reveal several sheets of carbon-copied documents. 'His name is Captain Johannes Walther and he was a corps commander, First Panzers.'

'Is he accused of anything specific?' Alex asked him, already guessing.

Preston handed him the file and Alex looked at the photograph clipped to its inner cover.

'We think he was at Malmédy,' Preston said, confirming Alex's guess.

'At the shooting? Has he said anything?'

Preston shook his head. 'I doubt if he even knows we're looking at him. But he fits. Right time, right place, right tiny little piece of the German Army. We've questioned others. Walther's name came up too many times for us to ignore him or for him *not* to have been involved in some way.'

'Are you building a case?' Alex asked him.

Preston shrugged. 'Our prosecutors want this one done properly. We all know what's going to happen at Nuremberg. What *we* want is all the dirt and blood on this one. We want every man, every scream, every plea and prayer, every bullet and every finger on every trigger. Nuremberg might happily and conveniently confuse the line between responsibility and consequence and all those other grand and abstract notions; what happened at Malmédy was something else completely.'

Alex glanced at each of the few sheets. The scattered pages of an incomplete Army record: dates, places, units, paymaster notifications. 'There's unlikely to be anything here that would even begin to convict him,' he said.

'Of course there won't be anything *there*,' Dyer said.

'That's why we – why Colonel Preston – wants the man questioned more thoroughly.'

'The records – such as they are – only fix the times, places and commands,' Preston said. 'We know how little that is. But it's a start.'

'Why not take him and question him yourself?' Alex said.

'Because then he'd get wind of what was happening for sure and clam up completely. They know how serious we are on this one. We already have fifty men in custody with cast-iron cases against at least half of them. According to our prosecutors, that is.'

'He might refuse to talk when he knows what's happening,' Alex said.

'He might,' Preston said. 'Or he might not think you're as single-minded as we are. Please –' He glanced from Alex to Dyer and then back to Alex. 'I don't mean to insult you or to question your methods. It's just that he's here, now, in Rehstadt. He's been at complete liberty for nine months. For all we know, he might even believe he's left it all behind him, that too much time has passed, that fingers have stopped pointing. Perhaps he might even believe we've lost our appetite for this kind of thing.'

Alex noted the vagueness of all this, and he knew that Preston, and in all likelihood Dyer too, was keeping something from him.

'And he probably believes the British will be less

energetic in pursuing him, in getting him to confess anything?' Alex said.

'Maybe. Where Malmédy is concerned, perhaps. Ninety men were killed in cold blood at Malmédy. They were overrun, they surrendered. They were disarmed, taken to the side of the road, out of the way of all those racing tanks of the First Panzer Corps, and then they were made to kneel or lie face-down in the snow and the mud and they were shot. Most of them in the head or neck, a few in the back. We know most of what we know because some of those men – don't ask me how – actually survived. Some of them made it into the woods and were picked up later. And we know some more of what we know because a lot of those Germans who were there – but whose own fingers, surprise surprise, were never actually on the triggers – also told us what they saw.'

'Saving their own necks,' Dyer said, anxious not to remain excluded from this conversation.

Alex closed the slender file and held it with the others in his lap. He guessed that there was a great deal of other evidence that Preston was keeping from him. Perhaps all that was expected of him now was to extract a single, seemingly inconsequential piece of corroborative evidence from Walther.

'How convinced are *you* that he was involved?' Alex asked Preston.

Preston considered what he was being asked. 'I'm a gambling man,' he said. 'I'd take the wager.'

'Was he responsible?' Alex asked him.

Preston paused again before answering. 'I'd give you less than evens. But he was a captain and a corps commander. It carries authority. If he gave an order, plenty of others would have been only too happy to obey it.'

'And if someone told *him* to do it?'

At his desk, Dyer pushed back his chair. 'I think we can leave all this speculation until *after* you've discovered something,' he said to Alex.

'It's OK,' Preston said to him. 'I hear what he's saying.' To Alex, he said, 'If Walther was involved, then all our boys want to know is *how*. Was he there? Did he participate directly? Did he know about it at the time? Did he hear about it afterwards? It was a lot of men; there were a lot of executioners involved. It might have been snowing, it might have been December, but it was all done in broad daylight. What I'm telling you, Captain Foster, is that a lot of people saw what happened. If Walther *was* there, then others will do your work for you. And if he wasn't, then it's unlikely that he won't at least know *something* about the whole affair.' He paused. 'Or perhaps he might have had nothing whatsoever to do with it. He might have been – might *still* be – a nobody—'

'And it's the nobodies you're interested in?' Alex said.

'Nuremberg has its chiefs of staff and generals and industrialists, and all you have—'

'That's enough of that,' Dyer shouted.

Preston held Alex's gaze. 'In this instance, yes – we want the nobodies. The same nobodies who gave the order to the other nobodies with the machine guns to kill the nobodies kneeling in the snow and mud. Perhaps a man will always be a nobody to the man looking at the back of his head with a pistol pointed at it.'

'I didn't mean to—' Alex began.

'I know,' Preston told him. 'And forgive me. I'm a lawyer by profession. I have my own practice in Cincinnati.' He smiled. 'And I'm betting that no one in this entire building even knows where that is. I'm in grave danger of forgetting where it is myself.' He laughed.

'Naturally, Colonel Preston will need to be kept informed of your progress,' Dyer said. He motioned to Preston to say more.

'Our prosecutors want to proceed to trial in –' he fluttered his hand '– six weeks. Give or take. It might seem like a long way off, but they want everything done properly, above board, and all signed and sealed before they begin. I promise you, they'll do a thorough job.'

'Are you part of the prosecuting team?' Alex asked him.

Preston hesitated before answering. 'I am.'

Dyer looked up at hearing this.

'What was it the Russian judge said as Nuremberg got under way?' Alex said. ' "The sooner the trial starts, the sooner we can hang them"?'

'His exact words,' Preston said. 'The same judge who warned all those on trial against attempting suicide, saying that even if they succeeded in this, then he would hang their bodies alongside the others. And for which he was soundly rebuked by everyone else. You, us, the French, everybody. They won't all hang. Some of them won't even be found guilty or sentenced to prison.'

The remark surprised Alex, but he saw the conviction in Preston's face and said nothing.

'I'm sure they'll all get what they deserve,' Dyer said.

'And I'm sure millions will disagree and argue about what that might be for decades to come,' Preston said. 'The point about what happened at Malmédy is that we can uncover it in all its details. We can count the spent shells, follow the tank and tyre tracks. We can name the men, their wives and mothers and families. We can count the bullets in all those skulls. We can do everything. All we need to do now is to gather together and then to hang on to all those thousands of little pieces. We already have hundreds of names and hundreds of individual testimonies, all of which are starting to add up.'

'But until you get absolutely everything, until you can prove a man's guilt in every tiny part of what happened ten times over, then you won't be certain of the justification or true value of your prosecutions and sentences?' Alex said.

'Fifty times over, a hundred,' Preston said. 'I can see now why John recommended you.'

The remark was intended to flatter both Alex and Dyer. In all likelihood, Alex believed, his name had been chosen at random by Dyer, or perhaps because Dyer intended this addition to his already full workload to be some further punishment for his interference concerning the corpses.

'One of our finest interrogators,' Dyer said. 'Spoken German second to none.'

'We'd appreciate it if you could make Walther one of your priorities,' Preston said.

'Of course he can,' Dyer said.

'And if my report absolves him of all responsibility?' Alex said.

'Then so be it,' Preston said.

It was a lie, a convenient line drawn under these preliminaries, and all three of them understood this.

Preston rose and said he was expected elsewhere. 'I'll wait to hear from you,' he said pointedly to Dyer.

'Of course. As soon as there's anything to—'

'Some place you got here,' Preston said.

'Come back and have a proper look around,' Dyer told him.

'I'll do that.' Then Preston turned and went out,

leaving Alex and Dyer facing each other across the desk.

'They've already stamped the file "Guilty",' Alex said. 'They're serious about this one.'

'And we're doing what for them?'

'If you're asking me to assign someone else to the job after all this . . .' Dyer said.

Alex shook his head, picked up his files and went to the door. 'What about the others waiting to see me?'

Men would have been woken hours earlier, escorted from their cells to where Alex worked and forced to wait there until he was ready to start his questioning. Few of them would have been given anything to eat or drink, and none of them would have been told in advance what was happening. Each prisoner would have been accompanied by two guards. Some would have been shackled, and all would have been handcuffed while they were in transit.

'I'll have them sent back,' Dyer said dismissively. 'Perhaps they'll think they've been reprieved.' He laughed coldly, put on his spectacles and looked closely at the paperwork on his desk.

Alex left the office and descended the staircase.

Outside, on the driveway, he saw Preston standing with several other Americans beside a jeep. After a few minutes, these others dispersed and Preston climbed in beside his driver, who then drove in a complete circle around the disused fountain before continuing along the driveway. Everyone standing nearby and in the entrance hall turned to watch, and afterwards to comment on the noisy display.

At the bottom of the stairs, Alex looked again for Eva Remer, and again he was disappointed not to see her.

5

He saw her soon afterwards, however – as he rounded the corner of the hotel and made his way to where Johannes Walther awaited him. She was coming towards him, in the company of two other women, and all three of them were talking loudly and laughing.

Upon seeing Alex, they fell silent, and then the women on either side of Eva Remer linked arms with her, and one of them whispered to her, raising her hand to cover her mouth and thereby emphasizing the gesture. Whatever she said was funny, and all three of them laughed again.

As they approached Alex, Eva pulled herself free of her companions and came to him alone. The two women followed her and waited several paces behind, watching the pair of them closely. They fell silent for a moment, and Alex knew he was being assessed.

'I'm pleased to have met you again,' Eva said to him. She glanced sideways. 'Ignore them. They are my friends. Nina and Sonja. We have been sent to collect records.'

Like her own name, these two others sounded exotic to him.

'I just spoke to Dyer,' he said.

'Oh?'

'About the bodies.'

'Are you still concerned with their identification?'

Following the drama of the discovery, the cursoriness of the remark surprised him.

'He wanted me to keep an eye on things, that's all. To report a satisfactory conclusion to events.' He mimicked Dyer.

She smiled at this. She brushed her fringe from her eyes and watched him closely. 'I spoke to my father. It is unlikely that the bodies have not been already identified and claimed.' She was talking about the corpses of the locals laid out in their neat and respectful row.

A few yards away, the two women resumed their whispered speculations, calling to Eva to ask her if she was going to introduce them to her 'young man'.

Alex was about to say something to them when she put her hand on his arm to stop him. She winked at him and then called to the women that he was a poor, lost Englishman a long way from home.

They laughed again at this and asked her questions

about him, clearly convinced that he understood little or nothing of what they said.

Although caught unawares by the gesture, and unsure of Eva's reasons for making it, he felt reassured and encouraged by what she'd done, almost as though the two of them had shared a confidence. He regretted that he could not spend more time with her. She, too, was in a hurry, and she, too, or so it seemed to Alex, regretted this. The woman she had introduced as Nina called to her and held up her watch.

'I have to go,' she told him. 'They'll pester me with questions about you for the rest of the day.'

'Do they think—?'

'They think whatever they choose. You are all fair targets – game – for us poor, desperate German girls.'

'Even Dyer?'

She laughed. 'Ah. The exception that is proof of the rule?'

'He's the exception to every rule,' Alex said.

Nina called to Eva and asked if she was going to kiss her boyfriend – she used the word *Mann* – goodbye, and Eva said that she might, but that this was unlikely.

'Kiss him,' Nina insisted.

'You see my predicament,' Eva said to him.

'I'd appreciate being able to see you again,' he said, surprised by his own forthrightness.

'You'd "appreciate" it?' she said, as though she hadn't properly understood him.

'To discuss the corpses. The unidentified ones. What happens next. Perhaps we could go for a drink. After work. Later.' It was the faltering end of his bravery.

Nina called to ask Eva what he was saying.

'He's inviting me to dinner at the Hotel Rehstadt,' she said, her eyes fixed on Alex, smiling again.

The hotel was the largest in the town.

The two women were suitably impressed and resumed their own conversation.

'If you like—' Alex said.

'What? The Hotel Rehstadt? The place is overrated and overpriced.' Now there was an unexpected coldness in her voice, and only as she spoke did Alex remember that the place was owned by the man who had usurped her father as mayor.

'You choose,' he said quickly, before his invitation could be refused, and when she hesitated he said, 'Six o'clock. I'll come to your office.' And before she could answer him, he waved to the other women and walked quickly away from them. He expected Eva to call after him, but nothing came, and he felt further encouraged by this.

Turning the corner, he began to whistle.

6

Johannes Walther was waiting for him in the corridor outside his room. He sat on a bench with a guard on either side of him. Usually, the prisoners were made to stand while only their guards sat, but Walther, Alex saw, remained handcuffed to both men. It was rare for this to be done once they'd arrived; rare, too, these days, for there to be more than one guard for each prisoner.

Walther was the first to see him, turning his head slightly and watching as Alex came towards them, doing nothing to alert the guards to his arrival.

Eventually, the closest of the two men saw Alex and rose slowly to his feet. He dropped the cigarette he'd been smoking and ground it out with his boot, leaving a stain on the tiled floor. He waved the smoke from his head. Thus alerted, the second guard did the same, and between them the two men pulled Walther to his feet.

'Mister Foster,' the first guard said. 'We've been here an hour.'

'Captain,' Alex said.

The two men exchanged a glance.

'And you know smoking is prohibited in the corridor.'

The two men looked surprised and offended at the remark.

'You should have been here an hour ago. Dyer told us nine o'clock.'

'He didn't tell *me* until after that,' Alex said, wishing he hadn't spoken. He nodded to Walther, who returned the gesture.

'We're to bring him in and stay,' the first guard said.

'You'll bring him in and do whatever I tell you to do,' Alex said, unlocking the door to his room.

He went in first, laid the files on his desk and then opened the shutters at the high window directly behind it.

The guards and Walther came sideways into the room. The guards pulled and pushed the man, showing no concern for his fixed position between them.

'Unfasten him,' Alex said. He sat at his desk and pretended to be preoccupied with the files.

'We was told to keep—'

'Either release him and then wait outside, or take him back to his cell now and then report to Dyer and tell *him* what's holding things up.' He avoided looking at them as he said this.

'This is an urgent one,' the second guard said. 'Priority. They want this one doing soonest.'

Walther stood between the two men without speaking, only grimacing slightly at the pain each of their sudden gestures caused his wrists.

The guards conferred behind his back, as though by this they might exclude both Walther and Alex from what they said. Neither man knew what to do.

Alex looked at his watch and closed the files. Eventually, the first guard said they would release Walther, but that at least one of them would remain in the room with him.

Alex shook his head. 'Tell it to Dyer.' He rose, crossed the room and walked out into the corridor.

The first guard called him back. He swore at Alex and told him they would release Walther, but that both of them would then remain immediately outside and that the door to the room must be kept unlocked. Alex agreed to this, and the two men took out their anger on Walther as they unfastened him from their wrists. Their own halves of the handcuffs were padded with leather and were loosely fastened. Those around Walther's wrists were uncovered and locked tight.

Once released, Alex noticed, Walther resisted the urge to rub the red marks left by the cuffs.

'Are you bleeding?' Alex asked him in German.

Walther held up his hands, splaying and closing his fingers. 'I've survived much worse.'

'What's he saying?' the first guard said. 'Whatever it is, it's not our fault. Regulation cuffs. Procedure. He wants to pull against them, he suffers the results, simple as that.' The two men shared a smile.

'Outside,' Alex told them. He held the door open.

'We're going to wait there.' The man pointed to the bench. 'Any trouble, and you shout. They told us to watch this one close.' He looked hard at Walther as he said this. 'He's an evil bastard. They already know who he is and what he done. Don't you go making the mistake of giving him chances and listening to his excuses now.'

'Shut up,' Alex shouted at the man, angry at how much he might just have revealed to Walther. He looked at the German, trying to assess how much of this he had understood.

Walther stood where he had been released, looking across the desk and through the window.

The two guards finally went, murmuring to themselves as they brushed past Alex. The second man paused in the doorway, his face only inches from Alex's.

'They picked you personally for this one, mate. Shout at me and him all you want, because you're an officer and that's what officers do, but don't make no mistake about your part in whatever's going to happen to him.' He grinned as he spoke. Turning to Walther, he said, 'See you later, pal. Knowing your luck, me and him will probably pull the detail taking you to the scaffold.' Both men laughed again at the remark, and again Walther gave no indication of having understood them.

Alex closed the door, waiting by it for a few minutes as he prepared to begin.

Returning to his desk, he pulled a chair from the wall and stood it beside Walther.

'If your wrists need attention, then you should ask the medical staff.'

Walther finally rubbed his wrists, wiping the faint bloody smears on his trousers. He wore an Army shirt, pale patches on the collar and chest where insignia and ribbons had been torn off, and a pair of shapeless trousers. His boots, too, were another man's. They were laceless, loose on his feet. He wore no socks.

Alex poured him a glass of water and Walther took this and thanked him.

'Colonel Dyer has asked me to question you,' Alex said.

Walther nodded. He drank the water quickly and Alex refilled the glass.

'I speak English,' Walther said. 'But you probably already knew or guessed that. Not perfectly, but I speak it. If I am unclear about anything then, please, speak German.'

'You heard what they said?'

'About the kind of man I'm supposed to be? I imagine they say the same of everyone they now have the opportunity to threaten and abuse. Am I really so urgent a case for questioning after all this time?' He seemed genuinely unconcerned about why he might be there. His head was shaved close to his scalp. Cuts showed through the bristles. 'They gave me a haircut and a shave yesterday evening,' he said. He turned his head to show Alex the smaller cuts on his cheeks and neck. 'A very blunt razor. I imagine they wanted me looking my best for you. Or perhaps my worst. And after my haircut, they gave me an "Institute shower"'.

'A what?'

'A bucket of cold water.'

Alex had heard of the treatment.

'I stand in the doorway of my cell and they throw it in over me – over me, over all my few possessions and over my bedding. It's what they call it.'

'Make a complaint,' Alex said.

Walther smiled. 'Of course.'

Alex re-read the sparse details of the file Preston had given him.

'You were arrested at Diepholz, not far from here, only six weeks ago. How do you think you managed to stay at liberty for so long?'

' "At liberty"? You think I was in hiding? I first surrendered myself, along with the remainder of my men, in April of last year, when I finally understood how hopeless everything had become. Everything was lost. I had no desire to lose my life, nor for any of them to die. Some of them I'd known for years, but most were new to me, acquaintances of weeks, possibly a few months at most. I surrendered in April, was put in a compound, questioned by the Americans, and then released three months later, in July, the summer. I told them where I was going – to my parents' farm in Diepholz – and I went there. It was where I stayed until six weeks ago, when I was again arrested.'

'And since then?'

'I was taken to Frankfurt. Left there without anyone paying me the slightest attention, then taken to Bielefeld, where the same thing happened. And then the Americans came and took me to somewhere near Kassel, where I was questioned day and night for a week. After that I was told I'd been wasting their time and I was brought here. So, as you can see – I've "done the rounds". I came here with a dozen others, most of whom have a similar story to tell.'

'And so why *do* you think you're here, in Rehstadt, now?' Alex wondered why none of these simple and easily verifiable details had been included in Walther's file. He wondered, too, how much Preston had told Dyer before his own summons to see them.

Walther paused before answering him. 'Here, in Rehstadt specifically?' he said. He looked slowly around the room, and then let his gaze rest again on the window and the distant view over the town. 'I certainly know I haven't been brought here because the Americans wanted to get rid of me,' he said.

'So you think you're here for us – for me – to continue their dirty work for them?'

Walther shrugged. 'I know, for instance, that no one here has so far mentioned Malmédy to me. At Bielefeld it was all I heard. I imagine that is why I am still of some interest – some consequence, even – to your allies.'

'They believe you were there, that you had some involvement, some responsibility for what happened.'

Walther smiled at the remark. 'So they insisted on telling me. Yes, I was there. Yes, I heard what happened a few days after it was supposed to have taken place. And no, I had no involvement in it whatsoever.'

'"Supposed"?' Alex said. 'Those men had surrendered and they were killed in cold blood.' He regretted the phrase.

Walther lowered his head and pinched the bridge of his nose. 'Yes, I know,' he said. 'I was not trying to suggest otherwise.'

Alex lit a cigarette and offered one to Walther, who took it and then quickly smoked half of it in a succession of long draws, closing his eyes as he did this.

Neither man spoke for several minutes. Alex again read the sheets in the file. They told him nothing Preston hadn't already been at pains to impress upon him, and he wondered again at his own precise role in these proceedings.

'Did you live in Diepholz – the farm?' Alex asked him.

'No. My parents were always elderly, already in their

forties when I was born. I left home at seventeen to attend university in Hamburg. My younger brother took over the farm.'

'Was he later a soldier?'

'Alas, no. Although it was always his ambition, especially when we all understood that the war was coming. He enrolled in the local training corps in Diepholz, waiting to be called up. He was eager, he would have made a good soldier. But, as I said, it never happened.'

'Why not?'

'Because in 1939 – of all years – possibly only weeks before his enlistment would have gone ahead, he had an accident with the baler. His arm was badly injured, mangled. There was little the doctors could do to save it, and it was amputated below his elbow. He became very bitter, resentful.'

'He resented your own position, your promotions?' Alex tapped the file, hoping to suggest that it contained more than it did.

'Of course he did. The irony is, I would happily have traded places with him and spent my time on the farm. He started to drink heavily – more heavily. No one ever made their concerns public, but I believe my parents lived in fear of him.'

'Oh?'

'He became violent. He worked in the local Party, made some very questionable friends. He took delight in reporting people – acquaintances, neighbours – for the slightest infringement of regulations.'

'And worse?'

'Denouncing people, you mean?' Walther took a deep breath, drawing the remaining inch of his cigarette down to his fingers. 'I imagine so. We grew apart once I was living in Hamburg. He did not confide everything in me.'

'What happened to him?'

'He was arrested last summer. Arrested, questioned and released. I don't know if there are proceedings against him. I doubt it. My parents went to see him, as did I, and he refused to see us. He told us nothing. He's back at the farm now. He married a local girl fifteen months ago.'

'Did *he* ever ask you about Malmédy?'

Walther ran a hand over his face. 'Once or twice. I was wounded, sent home on leave. He told me he was proud of me, of what he thought I'd done. When I denied it, he just winked at me and said "of course". He said he understood. He wanted to introduce me to his friends. My parents warned me not to listen to him, not to be taken in by all his hopes and dreams for the future. By then they were powerless to resist him, to deny him anything where the running of the farm was concerned. To hear him talk, you'd think he'd lost his arm in Normandy.' He paused. 'If I'm being entirely honest, I suppose there was a time, after the war, when

I just appreciated – enjoyed, even – being his brother again. I was someone he looked up to.'

'But you still went on denying all knowledge or involvement of what had happened at Malmédy?'

'Involvement, yes. To him and to all my other questioners. I quickly came to realize that people believed what they wanted to believe. Just as I imagine you and your masters may do now.'

'Tell me about why you were home on medical leave,' Alex said.

'I was in a field hospital. I was wounded.'

'I know all that.' Alex tapped the closed file again.

Walther unbuttoned his shirt from the collar down. 'May I?'

Alex motioned for him to continue.

Walther unfastened several more buttons until he was able to pull the shirt off his shoulder and down his left arm. The whole of his shoulder and upper arm was a mass of discoloured scar tissue. Darker lines showed where wounds had healed and where the flesh had been cut and stitched back together. He raised his arm to show that the injuries covered its entire upper surface. The motion caused him pain and he flinched.

'What happened?' Alex asked him.

'Does your file not tell you? My tank was struck. We started to roast. I burned. One man died, I was burned like this, another man lost his sight, and yet another escaped without a single mark on him. We were caught on an open road by a flight of Typhoons. They came down to almost tree-top level to make sure of us. In one minute, less, after a week of fog and snow, we lost seven tanks and sixteen men. I don't know what happened to the other wounded. I was taken to a field station a few miles away. My gunner did his best for me until I got there. He poured cold oil over my burns to keep the air from them. It was what we did. Crude, but effective under the circumstances. At the field hospital I imagine they just waited for me to die. Lots of morphine from captured American stores. I scarcely remember anything that happened to me for a week after that.'

The field station was mentioned in the file. It was part of the evidence connecting Walther to the massacre.

'You went from the hospital to another, in Daun.'

'And from there to Hagen, over the Rhine. They operated on me in Daun to drain off the fluid and contain the infection. They told me then that because everything was in such disarray, because we were being "overtaken by events elsewhere", that the best they would be able to do for me was to try and save my arm. There would be nothing cosmetic. Like I said, I didn't really understand or pay much attention to what they were telling me. I think I was supposed to be grateful that I was able to keep my arm.'

Seeing the healed flesh now, Alex could only guess at the severity of Walther's injuries eighteen months earlier.

'Me and my brother, what a coincidence. My left arm,

his right. If I'd lost it, we would have made a single man between us.'

Alex listened closely to all that Walther was telling him. He knew that the same had already been recounted to countless others. He knew, too, that they were being drawn away from the events at Malmédy.

'There are no specific dates, only approximates,' Alex said. 'Your hospital records.'

'Really? I always imagined it to be the one thing the German Army excelled at – keeping good and concise records.'

'Does it matter to you?' Alex asked him. He tried to make the remark sound offhand.

'I was wounded two days before the events at Malmédy took place,' Walther said firmly, looking directly at Alex as he spoke.

'Nothing here proves or confirms that,' Alex said, equally firmly.

'Nevertheless . . .' Walther leaned back in his chair. He inspected his arm and shoulder for a moment before carefully pulling up and buttoning his shirt.

Alex was about to suggest again that Walther might seek medical help for any pain he was still suffering, when there was a single loud rap on the door and one of the guards reappeared. He looked at the two men for a moment before speaking.

'We've had a call to take him back,' he said.

'I'm the one who says when we're finished,' Alex said.

The man smiled. 'Apparently not. The order came directly from Dyer.'

Alex repeated all this in German to Walther, who answered him likewise. He wasn't certain why he'd done this, but he was grateful that Walther hadn't answered him in English and exposed the deceit.

'Find out anything useful?' the guard asked him.

Alex ignored the remark and told the man to go back outside.

'We need to take him now.'

'He'll be out in a minute.'

The man looked at Walther, who turned away from him and finished buttoning his shirt. 'He better be. No new cuts or bruises, I take it? Self-inflicted, of course.' He left the room.

Alex took the cigarettes from his pocket and a box of matches from his desk and gave them to Walther.

Walther held them for a moment and then gave him them back. 'They'll search me when they handcuff me.'

'You're allowed to have cigarettes,' Alex said.

'I know. They'll still take them. Thank you.'

'Then smoke another now,' Alex said, and he lit a cigarette and gave it to Walther.

Walther smoked it as quickly as the first, and only as he finished it did Alex finally call to the guards.

Both men stood and watched as Walther rubbed the last of the burning tobacco between his thumb and finger.

'You shouldn't have given him that,' the second guard said to Alex.

'And *you* should salute me and call me Sir,' Alex said to him. He waited where he stood as the two sets of handcuffs were fastened around Walther's wrists.

'Tight enough?' each guard asked him.

Alex knew to remain silent, that the responsibility for the man had now passed to them. He also knew that any further goading from him would only be taken out on Walther as he was returned to his cell.

As the three men left, Alex told Walther in German that he would see him again soon, and Walther told him that he looked forward to this.

7

It was almost half past six before he reached the office behind the reception desk. Few of the staff remained. A male supervisor – an obese German – sat at his desk, his stomach divided by its edge, and in the adjoining office several typists still worked at their machines, whose amplified clatter filled the high room.

The supervisor rose panting at Alex's appearance and asked him brusquely what he wanted there.

Alex was about to answer the man when Nina, one of the two women he had encountered with Eva earlier in the day, appeared in the doorway and called to him in German. She told him mock-seriously that he was late for his date with his girlfriend.

He repeated 'Spät?', maintaining the earlier charade of not being able to understand her.

Nina told the supervisor to go back to his desk, and

the man shook his head and obeyed her, asking her how late she was working that evening and what she was doing afterwards. He licked his lips as he spoke.

'Whatever I'm doing afterwards,' Nina said slowly, 'I'm doing with someone else. And whatever *you're* doing afterwards – or, more likely, *not* doing afterwards – you'll be doing with your fat, old, ugly wife.'

Alex smiled at the exchange and all it revealed.

The supervisor swore at Nina and returned to his desk.

'Late,' Nina said to Alex. 'She wait. You late. She go home. She cry. She never want to see you again.' But even as she said this in her deliberately clumsy English, and as Alex felt the sharp jab of disappointment, he saw that she was lying to him and doing her best not to burst into laughter at his response.

'Where is she?' he asked her in German.

She repeated the words '*Wo is sie?*', feigning surprise at them. She was about to say more when Alex began a lengthy explanation, also in German, and more lies than truth, about why he was late. He told her he knew Eva would have waited for him.

'You seem very sure of that,' she said. She came to him and gently slapped his chest.

The supervisor laughed at her and she gestured at the man without turning.

'Very clever,' she said to Alex. 'I begin to see what our Eva sees in you.'

What she sees in me? Alex thought. Did this mean he'd been the topic of conversation through the day? Or had Eva said nothing, denied everything while her two excitable friends had done all the guessing?

'Where is she?' he said again.

'She'll be here in a minute,' Nina said. She indicated a door at the far side of the room. 'I hope you've got enough money for the Rehstadt.'

'We won't be going there.'

'What a surprise. Perhaps you'd be happy just to entice her up to your room here and get away with spending nothing.' She waited for his answer to this, her eyes following his as he looked away.

'She knows I wouldn't do that,' he said. 'We have work to do, things to discuss.'

She laughed at the awkward remark. 'Of course you do. Things to discuss. At least some good came of all the corpses, eh?'

Before either of them could say any more, the far door opened and Eva Remer appeared.

'My apologies,' Alex said to her.

The remark surprised Eva, who looked at the clock on the wall and said that these days any appointment kept within an hour was an appointment kept on time. 'I wasn't even sure you'd come,' she added dismissively.

'I've been—'

'I meant if you'd be *able* to come,' she said, perhaps sensing his disappointment at her last remark.

'No. Right.'

She put on the same coat she'd worn two days earlier and pulled the same headscarf from her sleeve.

'I offered to lend her my new dress and gloves,' Nina said to Alex. 'I told her she should make something of herself. All she did was accuse me of being a tart and told me that if she wore my clothes, then that's what you might think *she* was, too.' She laughed at the implausibility of both suggestions.

'It's true,' Eva said. She put her arm around Nina's shoulders and kissed her cheek.

As the two women parted, Alex raised his elbow slightly, and Eva, almost as though she was unsure of what was expected of her, slid her hand beneath his arm.

'Careful,' Nina told her loudly. 'The pig's watching you.' She called to the supervisor to ask him if he wasn't going to tell Eva to take her hand from Alex's arm. 'She's fraternizing with the enemy,' she said, revealing even more about the man to Alex.

At the doorway into the lobby, Eva pulled her arm free and walked out ahead of Alex. They crossed the open space a few feet apart.

'Please,' she said to him once they were outside. 'We are warned weekly about the nature of our relationships with the military and medical staff here. Usually by him.' She gestured over her shoulder with her thumb. 'It happens, of course.'

'Nina?'

'Nina. Practically everyone else. But it's still wise not to be too obvious. We get lectures on appropriate and inappropriate behaviour.'

'And is it "fraternizing" – you putting your arm through mine?'

She smiled. 'Of course it is. Who knows where it might lead.' She held his arm again.

They walked to the vehicle compound, in which stood a row of jeeps. These were for the use of senior and authorized staff, and when the occasion demanded it, a driver might also be found.

Leaving the Institute, they drove the short distance into Rehstadt.

Alex had visited some of the town's bars and smaller restaurants, each as poorly provisioned as the next, in the company of Whittaker and others, but he had never felt entirely comfortable in any of them, surrounded by the drunkenly silent or lugubriously inquisitive locals.

He asked Eva where she wanted to go. She considered this and directed him to a bar at the northern edge of the town, beyond the centre and close to the railway.

'It's used more by travellers than by the townspeople,' she told him, suggesting to him that this might be why she had chosen it for their first public outing together.

The bar was dimly lit and largely unoccupied. It contained only half a dozen small tables, with benches along two of its walls. Six other people already sat there, a group of four, and two men sitting alone, their luggage standing beside them.

The barman clearly knew Eva and he called to her as they entered. She went to him and he leaned across the bar to kiss her. She asked him about business and he answered her with a shrug and a fluttered hand. Only the two single men sat with drinks in front of them. The group of four – a man, two women and a child – sat and ate sandwiches wrapped in newspaper.

'You should insist they buy a drink,' Eva told the barman.

'So everyone tells me,' he said. He held out his hand to Alex as he came to stand beside Eva.

Alex introduced himself and the man said he was pleased to meet him. Without being asked, he poured them both a drink – a kind of fruit brandy, Alex thought – and put these on the bar. Alex took out his wallet, but the man said he hadn't seen Eva for some time and that the drinks were on the house. He turned back to his work, and Alex and Eva crossed the room to a corner table, watched by everyone else there.

'He's a friend of my father's,' Eva said as they sat down, and she took off her scarf, again running her fingers through her hair to loosen it. It was not cold in the room, but nor was it warm enough for them to sit comfortably without their coats.

'Does your father know you'll be late?' Alex asked her.

'It won't worry him. He calls me "resourceful".'

'Does he depend on you?'

'Only my wages. And we survived for long enough without them. He has his own work.'

'In the town?' He tried to remember what she'd told him two days ago.

'At our home. In Ameldorf. He's a stonemason. He specializes in decorative carving. Monument work, churches, public buildings, that kind of thing.'

'I imagine he'll be kept busy, then,' Alex said, only realizing as he said it how callous the remark might sound.

She saw this. 'Don't apologize. If nothing else, my father is a realist. My mother – his wife – died two years ago, my elder brother a year before that.'

'Were they killed?'

'My brother in Russia. His body was never recovered. All we received from the authorities was a letter of notification and condolence, and a campaign ribbon. My mother we are equally uncertain about. Her sister was injured in a raid. In Hamburg. My mother went to see her and we never heard from her or saw her again. We believe she may have been on a train, in the station, or in sidings outside the city, also during a raid.' She drained her glass. 'I say we believe this, but so far it's little more than a story, something with which to console ourselves. It sometimes helps to pretend to know something rather than for there just to be nothing.' She shook her head. 'I'm not making much sense. And especially to a man such as you.'

'Such as me?'

'I meant your work, not you personally. When they told us Wilhelm was dead we could not begin to imagine where he might have been in so vast a country. It was before Stalingrad. At least if he'd survived that long, we'd have had somewhere to start looking. What chance is there now of us ever truly knowing?'

'There are organizations,' Alex began uselessly.

'Please.' She held up a hand to stop him. 'The world is full of organizations. My father and I spent two months in Hamburg after the war. If you knew how many of those organizations we visited, how little we achieved, each of them raising and then destroying our hopes, pretending to be of some comfort to us, pretending to share our loss, promising us things, even if it was only a better way of coming to terms with what might or might not have happened.'

'And none of it helped?'

'My father said afterwards that we should never have gone, that we should have stayed at home and grieved for the two of them there, alone, in our own way. He came to resent the involvement – the lies and platitudes – of all these others.' She raised her empty glass to the barman and the man nodded once to let her know he was coming.

Waiting until they were again alone, Alex said, 'Is it

because of what happened to your mother that you're prepared to help with identifying the bodies now?'

She laughed at the suggestion. Having finished her first drink in a few seconds, she sat with the second glass cupped in her palm without raising it. 'I didn't even know what I was volunteering for. And in all likelihood they will all already have been identified. The mayor will have seen to that.'

'You mean the ones that are deemed worthy of being identified?'

She paused before answering him. 'Precisely,' she said. 'They're already talking about raising a monument to the dead – to the Jedentot, the heroic dead – of the place.'

'To include people like your brother?'

'Perhaps. Perhaps not. Perhaps only to the people whose bodies were found. Or perhaps only to those soldiers who died bravely, doing their duty.' She raised her glass in a toast, but still did not drink from it.

Alex wasn't sure he understood her, and the remark made him uneasy.

'Ignore me,' she told him. 'Russia, the East, we heard such tales.'

'But you must have known – known in your heart – what kind of man your brother was, what he was and wasn't capable of.'

'Yes, I did. In my heart. He was my brother – my older brother – and I loved him with all of that heart.' She finally sipped from her glass. 'Now I'm becoming melo-dramatic. Maudlin?'

In truth, the spirit was raw and sour and it burned Alex's mouth. Countless other bottles stood along the rear of the bar.

'You don't like it?' she asked him.

'I – it's—'

'It's disgusting,' she said. 'A local speciality, probably made from rotten leaves and soil. But it's what he gives me and what I take. Ask for anything better and you'd probably insult him.'

A further hour passed. Several others came into the room, workmen mostly, who stayed for one or two drinks and then left. The group of four departed and the barman gathered up the paper from their table and screwed it into a ball. The bar grew slowly warmer and a layer of smoke rose and settled against its low ceiling, making patterns in the dim yellow light.

'I'll tell Dyer that the business with the bodies is under control, nothing to worry about,' Alex said. 'We can leave everything to the mayor. If that's what you'd prefer.'

'Who can continue to petition for his blessed monu-ment and then use this as the basis for his re-election when the time comes.'

'I'd like to meet your father,' Alex said, hoping to divert her from this unhappy speculation. He was uncertain by then of how much he'd drunk, but guessed from his experiences of Whittaker's whisky that the drink was not so potent as either Eva or the barman might believe.

Eva stopped talking, saying nothing in reply to his suggestion.

They sat and talked for a further hour. He felt comfortable with her, relaxed. She laughed when he said something amusing. Occasionally, she put her hand on his arm, and once she took his hand in both her own and held it tightly. They spoke further about their families, about their pasts, and he was careful not to mention the mayor again, or the monument, or those bodies in the cellar which were never likely to be either identified or claimed.

At nine, Eva told him it was time for her to leave.

Alex offered to drive her to Ameldorf and she accepted. He held out his hand to show her how little affected by the drink he was.

'Who cares?' she said.

The barman called to them as they rose to leave, and then he came to them and again embraced Eva.

Outside, it had grown much cooler, and the road ahead of them, beyond the station, ran unlit into an expanse of near-complete darkness. The journey through the trees took longer than before, and fewer lights than previously showed away from the road.

Arriving at the crossroads, Eva again insisted on walking the remaining distance to her home. She climbed quickly out from beside him, and just as Alex believed she was about to walk equally quickly away from him and disappear into the darkness, she came back to where he sat, laid her hand on his own, thanked him for their evening together and then kissed him, first on both of his cheeks and then briefly on his lips.

8

He was woken early the following morning by
Whittaker, who knocked repeatedly on his door and
called in to him. It was not yet six. He'd sought
Whittaker out upon his return the previous night, but
had been unable to find him. A nurse had told him
that she thought a group of the doctors had gone
into the town and that perhaps Whittaker had been
among them.

Letting Whittaker into his room, Alex fell back on to
his bed.

'An emergency at the camp,' Whittaker said. He
gathered up Alex's clothes and threw them at him.

'What camp? What are you talking about?'

'DP. On the Ameldorf Road.' He waved for Alex
to hurry.

'Don't they have their own hospital, clinic, something?'

97

'Of course they don't. It's a relative of someone on our staff.'

'I'm due to start work mid-morning,' Alex said, fastening his belt.

Whittaker held out his watch. 'It's only half past five. We'll be back before either of us is missed.'

'Missed?' Alex hesitated. 'Meaning we – you – aren't supposed to be doing this?'

Whittaker shrugged. 'I know the woman on our staff. Clerical. It's her sister who's in trouble. I couldn't refuse to help her. I don't know if anyone there will speak English and understand me. Hence you. If it helps, you can say I forced you to go with me at gunpoint.' He formed his hand into a gun and pointed it at Alex. Neither man possessed a weapon or had even fired one. 'I have everything I need downstairs. Try not to make too much noise.'

They descended the staircase and walked silently past the sleeping sentry. The man was laid full length along a bench, his rifle and boots beneath him.

Once outside, the two men started running.

Climbing into a jeep, Alex said, 'Is it Eva?'

Whittaker laughed. 'I wondered how long that would take you. No, it's not her; one of her friends. Has she even got a sister?' He asked Alex about the previous evening, and Alex told him about the bar and their journey afterwards.

Whittaker listened with growing amusement and

feigned disbelief. 'You sound as though you'd have had a better evening sitting on your bed and thinking of home,' he said.

'It wasn't like that,' Alex insisted. 'I enjoyed myself. Being alone with her, I enjoyed myself.'

'Whatever you say,' Whittaker said.

But Alex was grateful all the same for Whittaker's curiosity and attention, and for his inquisitive and suggestive remarks.

'You and her . . . ?' Whittaker finally asked him as they left the town and followed the same road Alex had driven the previous night.

When Alex refused to answer him, Whittaker said, 'Still, plenty of time. Footloose and fancy-free and all that.' But suddenly there was no enthusiasm in his voice, only a sense of tired resignation, and Alex knew he was thinking of his own wife and daughters.

'That's me,' Alex said. 'Footloose and fancy-free.'

Approaching the crossroads, they continued across the open heathland beyond. After this, and following a glimpse of the rising sun through the encircling forest, they were again beneath the trees.

The forest was thicker here than before the turning to Ameldorf, the trees coming to the edge of the road on both sides, where they ended at a shallow drain, filled in places with dirty, stagnant water, but mostly blocked with piles of fallen branches, and with earth where the road had been damaged at its edge. It was much cooler in these denser plantations, and on both sides the trunks and lower limbs grew together to create an impenetrable screen only ten or twenty yards from the road. The forest floor was deep in needles, level and with little undergrowth. The trunks of the trees close to the road were mottled yellow, grey and white with lichen.

'How far is it?' Alex asked as they slowed to walking pace on the rutted surface.

'Less than a mile.' It was more than a guess.

'You've been here before?'

'A few times.'

'Does Dyer know?'

'None of his business. I'm a doctor. What am I supposed to do – refuse to help? Mostly it's just a question of sending out a few ridiculously simple medicines or bandages. I doubt if they even have clean drinking water most days, let alone anywhere even remotely sterile to do whatever it is they need to do.'

'You send them via the woman on our staff?'

Whittaker turned to him. 'It's Nina. Eva's friend. You've probably met her.'

The revelation silenced Alex. 'I know her,' he said eventually, signalling his apology to Whittaker, and guessing that if Nina was involved, then Eva probably was too.

Ahead of them, at a fork in the forest road, someone stepped out from the darkness of the trees and waved a white cloth at them.

'That's her now,' Whittaker said, suggesting to Alex that this was perhaps how they'd arranged their meetings in the past. He slowed the jeep as they arrived beside the woman.

'Why did you bring him?' she immediately asked Whittaker.

'Because you only half-understand half of what I say, and vice-versa,' Whittaker said.

Following her remarks and behaviour the previous evening, her hostility towards him now surprised Alex.

Whittaker tried to say more to her in his poor German, and then looked to Alex, who explained to her why he was there.

As they resumed their journey, Alex restricted himself to listening to what Nina said and then translating for Whittaker. Eventually, she accepted his presence and apologized to him.

'It's my sister,' she told him. 'She's pregnant. We thought another six or eight weeks. Last night, she went into labour. But now nothing's happening. Except she's in pain, screaming with it. And there's some bleeding.'

Alex repeated all this to Whittaker and watched closely for his reaction.

'She ought to be in the town hospital,' Whittaker said simply.

'No,' Nina shouted at him. 'She won't come. She can't.'

The two men considered in silence all this might suggest.

After a further five minutes, during which they were still unable to drive at little more than walking pace along the narrowing track, they arrived at the clearing in which the displaced-persons camp had been constructed.

A large central square, now mostly mud and small pools, was surrounded on three sides by lines of raised huts. Alex counted ten in each row. Several more substantial buildings – some of them brick- and block-built – stood beside the entrance. Smoke rose from a few chimneys, and several fires burned in the open.

Despite the time, there were already people moving around the camp. Duckboards and stepping-stones had been laid between the huts. Most of these early-risers stopped whatever they were doing and watched the arrival of the jeep.

Whittaker pulled up on to a piece of firmer ground outside the entrance. He sat with his hands on the wheel for a moment and looked at everything ahead of him. Alex guessed immediately what he was seeing.

Nina was the first to leave the vehicle. She pulled on Whittaker's arm, urging him to hurry. She took one of his bags and led the way along the huts. Several women called to her and she shouted back that she was too busy to stop. They shouted things about her sister. One woman stood directly in front of her, and as Nina pushed past her she spat heavily on to the ground at her feet. Nina ignored the gesture and continued walking.

She stopped at the door to one of the huts and called for Whittaker and Alex to move faster.

Inside the hut was little warmer than outside. The long room was partitioned along each side, and bunks were pushed against its walls. Cases and other possessions stood piled inside each partition. Two metal stoves stood at the centre of the space, but gave out little warmth. Logs lay stacked against these.

Halfway along the room stood a small group of men and women, and Nina pushed through them. Alex and Whittaker followed her, and people withdrew at their approach.

At the centre of the crowd stood a bed, upon which lay a young woman, a girl, a solitary brown blanket rising in a mound over her stomach. A wet cloth lay over the girl's face. She had been silent as the three of them had entered, but now, suddenly, at their approach, she started screaming, gasping for air, her cries convulsive and strained.

Whittaker knelt beside her and told those nearby to give him more room. He took the cloth from the girl's face. Her dark hair was plastered to her forehead and cheeks, and he wiped this back. Her eyes were closed, her neck arched.

Whittaker spoke to her. He drew the blanket from her, looked quickly at what lay beneath and then called for Alex to join him. He told him what to say to the girl. This amounted to little more than reassurance that she was going to be all right and that her suffering would soon be over. Then Whittaker told him what to tell those still gathered around them. He wanted clean hot water and clean cloths, towels, sheets, anything. He held his hand to the girl's forehead and then measured the pulse at her wrist. Alex looked down at her as she continued screaming.

Several in the small crowd moved away. Nina repeated everything Alex relayed to them, one moment imploring them to help her sister, and the next cursing them for their uselessness.

'That's all you people ever do,' she shouted at them. 'Stand and watch. Stand and watch while everybody else does everything for you. What are you waiting for? What do you want to see?' She pushed away several old men who were slow to leave the bed. None of them resisted her in any way, or even protested at the violence of her actions.

Alex called for her to calm down while Whittaker continued his examination of the screaming girl. Whittaker held a stethoscope to her chest and then to several points on the mound of her stomach. He covered her with the top half of her blanket and then lifted its lower edge. The girl's legs were folded, her knees up. He pushed these apart, looked between her thighs for a moment and then drew back the blanket.

He motioned for Alex to go back to him.

'She's bleeding heavily,' he said simply.

Alex saw the stained sheet and thin mattress. A small pool of blood lay on the floor beneath the bed.

'The baby's in trouble,' Whittaker said. 'I'm not sure what, exactly. Obstetrics was never my strong point. It might be a breech.'

'Can you do anything?' Alex asked him.

'Not here. She's probably going to need surgery. She doesn't have anything going in her favour stuck out here. Including her age and her size.' He put his hand back to the girl's forehead as her screaming finally subsided.

Nina brought him the water and the few cloths she had managed to collect.

'The baby won't come of its own accord,' Whittaker told her. 'How old is she?'

'Eighteen.'

Whittaker sighed.

Nina closed her eyes. 'Fifteen,' she said.

'And the father?'

'Guess. A soldier. The first and last time she saw him he did this to her.'

'British?'

'She *thinks* he was an American. She'd got it all worked out, the stupid little tart.' She wiped her sister's face and neck.

'Whoever it was, what matters now is that she gets to a proper hospital,' Whittaker said firmly. He pulled Nina's arm until she looked at him.

'And then everyone in the town will know,' she said.

'Meaning they don't already?' He shook his head. 'Look, if she doesn't get proper help, she may die. At the very least, the baby will either strangle or suffocate or its heart will beat itself to death in its distress.'

It seemed to Alex that he spoke as though he believed this was now inevitable.

'And you think that would be a *bad* thing?' Nina shouted at him.

'After which, she will probably contract an infection, septicaemia at the very least, and die herself.'

'She's fifteen,' Nina said disbelievingly, as though this alone might protect her sister.

'There's a radio in the jeep,' Whittaker said to Alex.

'You want me to contact the hospital?'

'You won't be able to do it directly. You'll have to call someone at the Institute, tell them where we are, what's happening, and get them to contact the hospital from there.'

'Dyer will get to hear of it,' Alex said.

'I know. And perhaps another hour of this and the baby will die and then she'll die and the problem will go away of its own accord. Just do it. You came here under duress, remember?' Whittaker stopped talking to prevent himself from shouting.

Alex left the hut and ran back to the jeep. He called the Institute, and though both transmission and reception were poor amid the trees, he managed to make himself understood. He told whoever had answered him that both he and Whittaker were already at the camp. The two names, he hoped, might lend some authority and urgency to whatever happened next.

Convinced he had been understood, and that the hospital would now be contacted, he ran back across the compound to the hut.

There were now more of the camp-dwellers out in the open, woken and alerted perhaps by the commotion surrounding the screaming girl.

At the hut door, he met Nina, coming out with a bowl of water held to her chest. She threw this across the ground in front of Alex, causing him to stop running.

'I thought Whittaker would be able to help,' she said, and he heard both the conviction and the affection in her voice.

'His name's James,' he said.

She smiled. 'James Jonathan William,' she said.

It was more than he had known.

'I'm sure he'll do everything he can for her,' he said. The words sounded too much like an excuse, and she repeated them to herself.

Then she shook her head and apologized to him. 'It's just that you sound so . . . so English,' she said.

'I'll try to do something about it.'

'No, don't,' she told him. 'Either of you.'

'Hopefully, the hospital will send an ambulance,' he said.

'They only have one.' She held up a finger.

'Then it's on its way.' He tried to sound more hopeful than he felt.

Smoke from a nearby fire drifted through the cold air, thinning and spreading as it came towards them.

'At least she's stopped screaming,' Nina said.

'She's so young,' Alex said absently.

'What, and you think things like this don't happen to girls of her age? You think there aren't a million others just like her, all over Germany, wherever, going through exactly what she's going through now?'

He hoped it was a deliberate exaggeration, but he said nothing to contradict her. He offered her a cigarette, which she took.

'How old do you think *I* am?' she asked him.

He guessed at twenty-three.

'Eighteen,' she said. 'A year younger than Eva.'

'She—' he said, unable to stop himself.

'She what? Is *she* twenty-three also?'

He tried to remember if she had ever told him her age. 'She never told me,' he admitted.

'Why, because an English gentleman never asks?'

'Something like that. Do your parents know about your sister?'

'Her name's Maria,' she said.

'Maria. Perhaps we could contact them when we get back to town.'

'They're both dead. My mother eight years ago, my father five years later.'

'During the war?'

She shook her head. 'He died of a tumour. Let's just say that the priorities of the hospital lay elsewhere.' She looked away from him as she spoke.

'Is it another reason why you don't want Maria taking there?'

'It might be. Or it might be because everyone in the town will then see her and judge her for what she is.'

'She's a girl, that's all,' Alex said.

Nina was about to deny this, then stopped herself and instead agreed with him.

'I know,' she said. 'A girl. Tell me about your evening with Eva. It sounds like a musical-hall play – *My Evening with Eva.*'

Alex told her about the bar.

'What?' she said. 'That dump? There are a dozen better places.'

'Places *you* might have been?' Alex said.

'Exactly. Except not *last* night.'

They both stopped speaking as the screaming from inside the hut suddenly resumed. Few people paid it much attention other than to divert their glances or to interrupt their own conversations for a few seconds.

'Look at them,' Nina said. 'They're pathetic. They could all have gone home by now and yet they choose to carry on living here, like this. Pathetic.' She spoke loudly enough for everyone to hear her.

'You think they're cowards – that there's something they can't face up to?' Alex asked her.

'Of course they're cowards. Otherwise why would they still be drifting around in all this slop and eating with their fingers?'

It was a remark born of something other than her fear and anger, and he didn't pursue it.

'It could just as easily have been me in there,' she said a moment later. 'Me, not her.'

'But not any longer?'

'Not any longer. A few months ago, perhaps. But not now. If anyone else had—' She stopped abruptly, and at first Alex imagined it was because she had been about to reveal something to him – something about herself, or about Eva, perhaps – but as he waited for her to go on he saw that she had stopped talking because her attention had been attracted by something at the camp entrance.

He followed her gaze. At the gateway, close to where the jeep now stood, a group of men had congregated.

'Who are they?' he asked her, his voice low. It was clear by the look on her face that she knew the men.

'From the other camp,' she said. 'Not far. Further along the same track.'

'*Another* camp?' Alex said. 'I didn't even know this one existed until today.'

'It's not much of a place. Just a few old run-down barracks. It's where the Volksturm were stationed and trained at the end of the war.'

'What, and some of them are still there?'

'They act as though they still own the place,' she said, putting Alex on his guard.

'And they come here occasionally?'

'They go wherever they want in the town. They're as pathetic as this lot, really. I suppose this is the one last place they can still play at being soldiers.'

Alex looked more closely at the men, several of whom now stood with their hands on the jeep, inspecting it.

He called for them to get away from it, and most of them did this.

'Give them an order,' Nina said, smiling. 'Pretend you're an officer. The ridiculous bastards will probably line up and salute you.' She stiffened her arm and raised it to the men. 'That sort of salute. Look at them. They're desperate enough to do it.'

But it seemed to Alex that the men knew exactly who he was and what he was doing there, and several of them left the jeep and came into the waterlogged compound.

He counted eight. Four men and four boys. Most of them wore forage caps; some had scarves over their mouths and noses. Three of the men still had their army-issue boots, and all wore military overcoats.

At their arrival, the others in the camp had drawn away from the entrance.

'Will they come here?' Alex asked Nina.

'Clap your hands and they'll scatter like crows,' she

said dismissively. 'They might play at being little soldiers, but they avoid the authorities like the plague. They've seen the jeep, they know who you are, that's all. Ah, now that one—' She started to raise her arm, but then lowered it again.

'What?' he asked her, searching for whoever she might have been about to point out to him.

'Nothing. They steal from the local farms. They turn up and make demands. They want the locals to see them as the men who never surrendered. True Germans. I know for a fact that there's a list at the Institute containing every single one of their names.'

'Do they still have homes locally?'

'Some of them.'

As they watched the men, several of them turned to look back along the forest track. Then they called to each other, and just as quickly and quietly as they had appeared, so they gathered back together and left, crossing the track and moving back beneath the trees, where they were quickly lost to sight.

'Good riddance,' Nina said.

'It's the ambulance,' Alex told her, pointing to the lights coming towards them through the gloom of the trees.

'You go to it,' she told him. 'I'll tell Whittaker.' She left him and went back inside the hut.

The ambulance came more fully into view and stopped short of the camp entrance. The driver climbed down from his cab and walked cautiously forward. He looked in at the fires and at the figures moving between them. A nurse in a blue and white uniform climbed from the passenger seat and waited a few paces behind him. Both of them looked into the camp as though they could not believe what they were seeing there.

Alex called to them, and at the sound of his voice, the woman moved quickly to stand beside the driver, stepping into a deep puddle in her alarm.

9

They followed the ambulance through the forest to the road and then back into Rehstadt. The vehicle was old, with a rigid suspension, and it lurched and skidded over the rough surface, sending up sheens of spray and occasionally slipping sideways where the road was poorly edged.

Whittaker grimaced at each of the more violent lurches. He had insisted that Nina travel with her sister. The nurse had at first refused him this, but Whittaker had argued with her until she had acceded to the simple demand.

'Do you think she'll make it?' Alex asked him as they emerged from the uneven track on to the better road.

'The pregnancy, or to the hospital?' Whittaker said.

'You think she's going to lose the baby?'

'You saw her,' Whittaker said. He concentrated on his own driving as he spoke.

'Would arriving at the camp sooner have helped?'

Whittaker shrugged, his eyes still on the ambulance, which showed little sign of speeding up on the better road.

Entering the town, they passed both the station bar and the mounds of rubble still surrounding the excavated cellar.

It was not yet eight in the morning, but there were already men working amid the piles of brick and timber. Generators filled the air with their noise and smoke. Queues had started to form along the road leading into the town square.

At the hospital, there was no one waiting for them. The ambulance drew up at a side entrance and the driver climbed down, stretched his arms and walked slowly inside. It occurred to Alex that the man already knew that there was no longer any urgency involved.

Whittaker sounded his horn. The rear door opened and both Nina and the nurse appeared. Nina came to them.

'How is she?' Whittaker asked her.

'Still alive, if that's what you're asking. The so-called nurse hasn't got the faintest idea what to do.' She watched the woman as she spoke. 'All she's concerned about is the mud on her skirt and shoes.' She paused. 'Maria's bleeding more heavily.'

'It might be because of the journey,' Whittaker said unconvincingly. 'I'll go and find someone.'

As he left the jeep, the ambulance driver reappeared, accompanied by a doctor.

Nina recognized the man. 'Him,' she said. 'Can you go with her?' She held Whittaker's arm as she asked him this.

'Do you know him?' Alex asked her.

'He's the director of the hospital. He gave himself the title. He's been here for ever. And he's as useless now as the day he arrived – worse.'

'Wait here,' Whittaker told her.

They watched as the director went into the ambulance and then as he reappeared and called into the hospital for assistance. Then he came to where the three of them waited.

'Your concern in all this?' he said dismissively to Alex.

Whittaker explained who they were and what had happened at the camp.

The man looked hard at Nina. 'I remember you,' he said slowly. He began to recall details of her family, of her father's fatal illness. He took cold pleasure in this act of remembering. 'At least your parents are not here to witness this,' he said. 'A small blessing, but a blessing all the same.' He smiled at Alex and Whittaker, clearly expecting them to share his opinion.

'Why don't you just do your job and go and take care of her?' Nina said.

He turned to look at her, but neither answered nor obeyed her.

116

'Apologize,' Whittaker told her.

'What?'

'Do it. Maria is our concern here, nothing else.'

The director smiled at her, waiting.

'I apologize,' she said.

'And?' the man said.

'I was forgetting myself. Please, help her.'

'Your apology is accepted,' he said. He turned to the nurse and told her to see that Maria was taken inside and found a bed. He told her to call for orderlies to help her.

They all watched as Maria was finally taken from the ambulance, laid on a trolley and wheeled into the building.

Whittaker started to follow her, but the director held up his hand to stop him.

'Herr Doktor,' he said. 'Many thanks for your concern and attention. I believe my own staff are now better placed and able to care for the –' he paused deliberately '– child.' It was clear to them all that this was a reference to Maria and not her unborn baby.

'I'm sure,' Whittaker said. 'But perhaps I might help in some way?'

The director held his palm an inch from Whittaker's chest. 'You called for *my* ambulance, you brought her to *my* hospital, using *my* staff. I'm sure, Doctor Whittaker, that you are fully aware of the true nature and extent of your authority in this matter.'

'Of course,' Whittaker said, relieved now that Maria

had at least been taken indoors and that others might already be caring for her.

'Now, if you'll excuse me,' the director said, and he turned and left them, pausing to examine the ambulance, inside and out, wiping a finger through the liquid mud on its sides.

'Bastard,' Nina said beneath her breath. 'He's behaved like this from the moment he arrived.'

'I'm sure they'll do all they can for her,' Alex said, hoping he sounded more convincing than he felt.

'So what now?' Whittaker said.

'I want to wait here, with her,' Nina told him.

He warned her against intruding and antagonizing the director and his staff any further.

She drew a cross over her heart and said, 'Promise.'

'I mean it,' Whittaker told her. 'Your sister needs rest and constant care, whatever that might now amount to. I can still guess at a dozen complications connected to the birth, but no one will know for certain until the labour progresses.'

'And if it doesn't progress?' Nina asked him.

'It's something you have to prepare yourself for,' he told her.

'I'm sure she'll be fine,' Alex said, again regretting the words.

Whittaker looked at him. 'The eternal and ignorant optimist,' he said, immediately signalling his apology for the remark.

Alex translated what he'd said for Nina, who agreed with Whittaker, then kissed both men on their cheeks, thanked them for all they'd done for her sister, and followed her into the hospital.

Alex and Whittaker returned to the jeep.

'Will Dyer have heard about this?' Alex said.

Whittaker looked over Alex's shoulder. 'He's already here,' he said.

Alex turned and looked behind them.

Dyer and two others had just then arrived at the far side of the hospital entrance and were making their way towards them.

'He might not see us,' Alex said. But even as he spoke, Dyer stopped walking, pointed to the two of them and beckoned them to him. He started shouting at them – demanding to know what they were doing – before they reached him, the same few questions over and over.

'It was an emergency,' Whittaker said, interrupting this tirade.

'But not *our* emergency,' Dyer shouted at him. '*Theirs*. Not ours. Not ours.'

The two men accompanying Dyer nodded nervously to Alex and Whittaker. Alex recognized them both as junior members of Dyer's staff, both clerks.

'And the camp?' Dyer said. 'Of all places, you had to go to the camp.'

'It's where she was,' Whittaker said. 'We had no choice.'

119

Dyer turned to him. 'Don't talk to me about choice. I know it's where she was.'

Alex felt a fine spray on his face. He waited for a moment until Dyer had stepped back from him and then he wiped a hand over his mouth.

'I know it's where she was,' Dyer repeated. 'But what I *don't* know is what in God's name possessed the two of you to jump and run just because some stupid little tart clicked her fingers at you. Or am I missing something here? Is it precisely *because* of what she is that you jumped and ran? Is that it? Is that what this is all about? I'm waiting.'

Whittaker shook his head at the suggestion.

'Shake your head all you like, Whittaker,' Dyer said. 'But make no mistake – I'm going to get to the bottom of this, and you two are going to be made to understand the error of your ways. What in God's name does any of this have to do with us?'

'She was the sister of a member of our staff,' Alex said. 'Her name's Nina.'

'Nina? Nina what?'

But Alex did not know Nina's surname. And if Whittaker knew it – which Alex suspected he did – then he didn't say. Both of them now understood that whatever they said to try and calm or reassure Dyer, the outcome of the morning's events would be the same.

Dyer took advantage of his small victory. He asked them a dozen further questions, but none of their answers satisfied him. He repeated these in disbelief, calling to the two clerks to ask if they believed any of what he was being told.

'No, Sir,' each man answered him, and then both of them signalled their helplessness to Alex behind Dyer's back. Alex let them know that he understood, realizing that any further involvement on their part would only buttress Dyer's anger and prolong his pointless accusations.

After several minutes of this, Dyer fell silent and caught his breath.

Noise from the square around them attracted his attention. A klaxon sounded, and as this died, several nearby walls, already free-standing and precarious, were toppled to the ground. Clouds of dust rose around them. A few bricks fell and rolled across the surrounding open space.

'A word, Captain Foster,' Dyer said eventually. He took Alex by the arm and walked with him out of earshot of Whittaker and the clerks. When he was certain they could not be overheard, he said, 'Colonel Preston wants you to talk to our Mister Walther again. And sooner rather than later.'

'I thought—'

'I don't care what you think. I'm just passing on the message.'

One of the clerks called to Dyer and he turned sharply and told the man to wait. A lorry now sat close behind the jeep in which Dyer had arrived, and the driver sounded his horn.

'Move it,' Dyer called to the man, and both the clerk and Whittaker rode the jeep a short distance from the hospital entrance.

'Walther will know we're doing their bidding if I see him again so soon,' Alex said. It was customary to leave at least five days between interviews. 'And he'll know that we're after something to—'

' "After something"? Of course he'll know we're "after something". That's because we are.'

Prisoners were usually questioned intensively only before having final assessments made of them, or immediately prior to being sent elsewhere.

'Preston's pushing me,' Dyer said. 'He's keen – they all are. As far as I can tell, they don't actually need Walther for their case to stand up against all the others, but he's still a big piece of icing on the cake.'

Alex almost laughed at the words.

'They've got dozens more men in the frame.' Dyer paused, lowering his voice. 'According to Preston, they're going to call for the death penalty for at least thirty of them.' He spoke now as though he was sharing a confidence with Alex.

'Including Walther?' Alex said.

'He's a big name. I don't know. Perhaps. Probably. That part of things is none of our concern. What *is* our concern – *my* concern – is that Walther is one of the last of the men they're after. And he's ours. However he came to us, he's ours.'

But only because they deliberately brought him to us, Alex thought.

'They've had their hands on the rest of them for some time. They took their eye off the ball and Walther slipped through the net. That's all. Now he's ours. Am I making myself clear? Do you see what I'm saying?'

Perfectly, Alex thought. 'You want me to tell them what they want to hear,' he said.

Dyer clenched his fists in exasperation. 'What are you talking about? Of course we're going to tell them what they want to hear. Dress it up, if you like, throw in any doubts or concerns you might have, but when all's said and done—'

'They're going to take him back and do exactly what they please, only this time they'll have our blessing.'

The remark stopped Dyer for a moment. 'Of course they're going to do what they want with him. What are you, Walther's defence lawyer? What's important now is what we all get in return from them – you, me, everyone.'

'He's—'

'He's a guilty man, that's what he is. In all likelihood. Whatever story he tries to spin you. As guilty as the rest of them. One falls, they all fall.'

'So why not just hand him back now, let Preston and his own interrogators get everything they need from him?' The question needed no answer.

Dyer smiled. 'Protocol, that's why. Another one of those nice new words we're all going to have to start getting used to. And perhaps because Preston and his men messed up with Walther when they had their chance. And because Preston knows that better than I do, and because we're going to make good on that mistake and save Preston's neck where his prosecutors are concerned.' Dyer smiled. 'And, yes, because we're who and what we are. It's all a question of doing things properly – honourably, you might say – following the rules.' He was again pleased with his vague answer and continued smiling.

And because all this makes you *look good, gives you some real power and credit for the first time in your life*, Alex thought.

'Anyhow, I've given Preston my word on all this,' Dyer said, as though in unassailable confirmation of all he'd just said.

'I'm sure you have,' Alex said.

'What's that supposed to mean? I think you're forgetting a few important details here, Captain Foster.'

Alex said nothing.

'After meeting you, Preston told me he thought you were the man for the job.' The remark was meant to appease and encourage him, and Alex knew that.

'You saw him again after yesterday morning?' he said.

'What does it matter when I saw him?'

'Did he say anything about handing over any of that

other evidence – on Walther, the others – for us to have a look at? All *I've* got to go on is what little he deigned to keep in the file. Nothing there is going to convict Walther.'

'He knows what he's doing. All this is just a means to an end.'

'And the end – in this instance, Walther and the others up on the scaffold – will always justify the means?'

Dyer sighed and shook his head. 'Look, just do what I tell you to do and get things moving. You tell me, I tell Preston, it's as simple as that.'

'It's a man's life,' Alex said.

'*They* were men, kneeling in the snow and waiting to be taken into captivity. Imagine if they'd been British. Remember the Royal Warwicks at Dunkirk.'

Alex ignored the remark, and guessing that Dyer was about to leave, he seized his own small advantage and said, 'It looks as though I might get tied up in all of this – the girl.' He gestured towards the hospital. 'Both of us will, Whittaker and me. Especially if there's any sort of investigation into what's just happened, what rules we broke.'

Dyer understood him perfectly and grinned again. 'Finally, you're actually listening to what I'm telling you. You get on with your work and there'll *be* no investigation. The girl can take her chances without any further help from you or Whittaker. It's not as though you're being asked to do anything other than what you're here for, what you're being paid to do.'

'No,' Alex said, disappointed with how swiftly he had acceded to Dyer's demands. And angry, too, at the realization that, as far as Dyer was concerned, there could have been no other outcome to their encounter.

'At least think of Doctor Whittaker,' Dyer said.

'He did what he had to do,' Alex told him.

'Of course he did. Of course he did. That's what I'm talking about – about doing things properly. About us – you, me and him – being what we are. At last, we understand each other. Besides, none of us wants to see Whittaker get a black mark against him, not now, after all this time, after all he's done for all these years.'

It was a cruel and unnecessary remark and Alex could not resist responding to it. 'You think he'd care? You think he wouldn't fight you all the way if you pushed him on it? The girl in there would have died if he hadn't intervened. She still might. At the very least, it looks as though she'll lose the baby. She's fifteen.'

Dyer, angry and surprised by this sudden turn in the argument, said, 'So? Whose side of the argument does either of those two little scenarios come down in favour of?' Even he looked momentarily confused at the convoluted question. 'His? Yours? I doubt whether she – whether either of them, her or the baby, living or dying – is going to cast any of this in a better light. Think what you like, Foster, but that black mark on an otherwise unblemished record is always going to be there. You're not going to wipe it away. No one is.' He took several paces away from Alex, standing with his back to him to watch the workers on the far side of the road. 'Think about what I've said, Captain Foster, think about it hard. I'm sure you'll come to the right decision, the right way ahead.'

After that, neither man spoke for a moment.

'When is Preston coming back?' Alex said eventually.

'Later today,' Dyer said. 'But not in connection with Walther. He's got other business with us. He wants you to see Walther again tomorrow at the latest and to give him some kind of preliminary report. He said verbal would be fine.'

'Tomorrow?'

'I've looked at your schedules.' Meaning he'd already rearranged them again to include Walther and to satisfy Preston.

Dyer started walking to where his clerks and Whittaker still waited for him.

At his approach, Whittaker left the jeep and returned to his own. Dyer passed close by him, but said nothing. Whittaker began to speak, but Dyer held up a hand to stop him.

Whittaker came back to Alex. 'Is he going to pursue it?'

Alex shook his head. 'He just wanted to jump up and down and shout at us.'

'And that's the end of it?' Whittaker said disbelievingly.

'What else can he do?'

Whittaker remained unconvinced by these answers, and he let Alex know this. But he also understood something of what might just have passed between Alex and Dyer, and of the greater and closer power Dyer exercised over Alex than himself, and so he said nothing.

'Any news from in there?' Alex asked him.

'Nothing so far. I doubt they'll do more than find her a bed, try to clean her up, and wait.'

'Will it be enough?' Alex said.

Whittaker shrugged. 'What would *I* have been able to do for her? My guess is that the director will approach Dyer for some kind of payment for his services, his facilities and his inconvenience in wasting his time on some little tart who should have known better and who got all she deserved. And following that, of course, our own little führer will make sure that you and I are once again made only too aware of our stupidity and irresponsibility in the matter.'

Dyer passed close by them in his jeep, gesturing in the direction of the Institute.

Whittaker drew himself sharply to attention, saluted, and then laughed at the look of surprise on Dyer's face as he was driven away before being able to return the gesture.

10

Arriving back at the Institute, Alex and Whittaker parted. Whittaker promised to let him know if there was any news from the hospital.

Alex sat on the terrace overlooking the empty pool. People came and went along the driveway beneath him, mostly the civilian administrative staff arriving to start work. He looked for Eva, but didn't see her. An hour remained before he was due to start his own work.

On an average day he would see eighteen or twenty men. Two dozen would be brought from their cells to await him. If he was prompt, if he suspected nothing beneath the surface of any of the prisoners, he would question them all. But if any lied too forcibly to him, or too cleverly, then he might see only a handful of the men. Those he didn't see would waste a day waiting and then be rescheduled, perhaps for the next day, perhaps for a week later.

As he watched, a jeep raced through the entrance gates, increased speed along the driveway and drew to a halt immediately below where he sat, leaving dark lines in the raked gravel. Men and women who had been forced off the driveway shouted their complaints to the driver, who pushed himself up to sit high on the back of his seat, enjoying and encouraging their complaints, and who then swore back at them.

There were white stars on the bonnet and doors of the jeep. American. Alex recognized the driver as the man who had driven Preston the previous day, the one who had made an equally loud and disruptive display of his departure.

Several men and women – both military and civilian staff – went to the jeep and gathered there.

After a few minutes, the driver, a slight, dark-skinned man, leaped down from his perch and went to the rear of the vehicle, where he drew back a tarpaulin to reveal several cases. He took packages from these and began passing them to the small but growing crowd.

Intrigued, Alex left the terrace, skirted the empty pool and went down to the man. At his approach, several of those standing close to the jeep drew away from it.

The driver called them back to him, angry at Alex's intervention.

'Help you?' he shouted to Alex. He wore his

shirt-sleeves rolled to his shoulders, and his arms were muscular and smooth. He spoke with an accent that sounded Spanish. The rim of the cap he wore shielded his eyes. He chewed emphatically as he watched Alex's approach.

'You're Colonel Preston's driver?' Alex said. He guessed the man to be little older than twenty.

'I'm *a* driver. Yesterday it was God Almighty Preston, here to see God Almighty Dyer; today it's just me. Here on my own business. Like I already asked, something I can do for you?' He looked at the others around him. 'No offence, pal, but you're hardly good for business.'

'What are you selling?' Alex asked him.

'What do you need?'

Alex drew aside the tarpaulin which the man had pulled back over the rear of the jeep. Cigarettes, drink, cosmetics and tins of food stood loosely packed in half a dozen crates.

'Where do you get all this from?'

'You accusing me of stealing it?'

Alex searched briefly through the cases.

'I got receipts for everything that's there. It's called private enterprise. I buy it cost and then sell it to the people only too happy to buy it at a small mark-up. You here to make something of that?'

'Does Preston know?'

The man laughed. 'That would be Colonel Preston to you, pal. What do you think? You think I didn't come loaded with exactly the same merchandise yesterday? You think that stuff doesn't rattle around on these roads? You think Preston's deaf?' He grinned at the weight of his rebuttal.

'And he sanctions this?'

'Never heard the word. You talking English?' He stopped grinning. 'Look, tell you what, see something you like, take it. Make me an offer, anything, just take what you want and let my other all-too-willing paying customers here get back up to the counter.' He gestured around them and Alex caught the averted and resentful looks from the people clearly anxious to approach the jeep.

'If any of this *is* stolen . . .' Alex began, uncertain of what he might add.

'What? If any of this is stolen, what?' The man came closer to him. He was six inches shorter than Alex. He clenched his fists and raised his elbows to his sides, looking suddenly and alarmingly like the boxer he might have been. He smiled at the look of concern on Alex's face.

'What? What you thinking now? You thinking, "Jesus Christ, the guy's a boxer"? Bantam-weight, perhaps? Light-featherweight?' He jabbed and then quickly withdrew his fists. 'You thinking that? Because you'd be right. Boy champion of all Puerto Rico, early contender for the All-New York championships.' He raised his fists to his chin and held them there, shuffling back and forth on the balls of his feet.

Alex calculated the man's reach and hoped he was beyond it.

'Footwork,' the man said, and he skipped from side to side, bending slightly at the waist, but keeping his fists in position close to his face.

'I believe you,' Alex told him.

The man dropped his hands and stood upright. He shook his arms loosely for a moment, releasing their tension.

'You believe me and what? You believe me and know that the second I lay a finger on you I'll be hauled out of here faster than a rat out of a hole and that I'll never be back? Never get back to these happy hunting grounds and all my desperate and grateful customers here?' Now there was amusement in his voice.

'Something like that,' Alex said, still convinced that the man would never have actually struck him. 'And you honestly do all this with Preston's sanction?'

The driver lit a cigar and shrugged. He offered one to Alex, who declined it. 'Suit yourself.'

'Preston,' Alex prompted.

'Preston turns a blind eye. We have a kind of arrangement, me and Colonel Preston.'

'I'm sure you do,' Alex said.

The remark made the man angry again. 'You're beginning to annoy me,' he said, his words little more than a snarl. 'Like I said – like I said *politely* before – why don't you just walk away and mind your own fucking business? Just turn around and walk away, Mister stiff-upper-lip?'

Alex resisted the urge to respond to the remark. His rank counted for nothing with the man, especially if he did operate with the approval or complicity of Preston.

'Go somewhere else, somewhere less obvious to do your dirty work,' Alex told him.

'I'm looking all around me, and so far there's only you who thinks that's what all this is.' The man held up his arms. Then something occurred to him and he went to one of the cases and took out a bottle of whisky. It was an unfamiliar brand. 'Recognize it?' he said to Alex.

Alex did recognize it, and was unable to disguise the fact.

'Hey, that's right,' the man said loudly. 'Your good pal Doctor Whittaker. Good old Doc. Whittaker. Good old honest, dependable Doc. Whittaker. Now, where do you imagine *he* gets his own private stash of this stuff? You think he finds it in the town? You think he—'

'Shut up,' Alex told him.

'No – *you* shut your mouth,' the man said immediately. 'I don't answer to you. I don't answer to any of you. I was two full years in combat. Italy, France, Germany. I was a month in the Hurtgen Forest. Twelfth Infantry, Fourth Division. Three hundred per cent casualties. I was there. Where were you? Four separate wounds. Look at your thumbnail.'

'What?' Alex said, wondering if he'd heard correctly.

'Your thumbnail. Look at it.'

Alex looked.

'See how thick it is? Look hard. That's how close I was to being killed. And I heard that from the surgeon who took the pieces out of my back. As close to dying as your thumbnail is thick. His very words. He couldn't even measure it.'

Alex lowered his hand. 'And you think that gives you the right to do all this now?'

'Do what? I earned the right to do *something*. You think anybody ever got rich off looted souvenirs? I got iron crosses by the caseload. They must have handed those things out with the rations.' He dropped the bottle of whisky back into its case. 'This is what matters now, *this* – food, drink, nice things to wear, a few medicines, life's little pleasures.'

'You disgust me,' Alex said, wishing he'd kept the thought to himself, knowing it was an exaggeration of his true feelings, which remained uncertain.

'Hey, guess what?' the man said. 'I don't give a flying fuck for what I do to you. And you want to know something else? I don't even—' He stopped abruptly, looked over Alex's shoulder and grinned.

Alex heard footsteps behind him and turned to see Eva approaching him.

'Leave him,' she said to Alex. She reached out and held his arm.

'Aah, she wants you all to herself,' the man said. To

Eva, he said, 'You come for your usual? I'm having such good fun with your friend here, I might even let you have what you want at a discount. One day only. Until he really starts to hack me off.' He looked behind her. 'And where's your other little friend? She want *her* special discount today?' He licked his lips and winked at Eva, wanting Alex to be clear about what he was suggesting.

'She's at the hospital,' Eva said, glancing at Alex and silencing him.

'Shame,' the driver said.

'Just go, Jesus,' Eva said. She pulled Alex away from the man.

The driver looked back and forth between the two of them. 'That's me,' he said to Alex.

'What is?'

'Jesus. That's my name. Jesus Hernandez. Except it's pronounced "Hay-sus". None of these German dames ever say it right. "Hay-sus". Not even the grateful ones. Not even the ones like Eva's little friend.'

'Jesus?' Alex said, and then 'Hay-sus.' He smiled at the ridiculous name.

'You find it funny?' Hernandez said.

'Not funny,' Alex said. 'Ironic, perhaps.'

'Yeah, ironic, whatever you say.'

Alex followed Eva away from the man, repeating the name over and over.

'Hey, I'm proud of it,' Hernandez called to him. 'Jesus Hernandez. Proud of them both.'

'I'm sure you are.' Alex paused. 'Hay-sus.'

Hernandez spat the cigar from his mouth, took several paces towards Alex and Eva, and then stopped and walked back.

'Come away from him,' Eva said again. 'He enjoys antagonizing people.'

'What he said about Nina . . . ?' Alex said.

'You've met her,' she told him. 'Whatever I tell you, you'll make your own mind up about her. Nina does what she has to do.'

'She's – her—'

'I know,' Eva said. She lowered her voice. 'Not in front of him. Someone came to tell me. Is there any further news – of Maria or the baby?'

Alex shook his head. She'd known about the girl all along.

They were again interrupted by Hernandez, who shouted, 'Very cosy,' playing now to the rest of his increasingly impatient audience. 'I wish I could open up shop and get on with things, but Captain Foster here thinks that what I'm doing is wrong.'

It surprised Alex to hear the man use his name. Perhaps Preston had mentioned it.

'Pity I can't say the same for his girlfriend,' Hernandez went on. 'The beautiful Eva.'

Eva's grip on Alex's arm tightened. 'Leave him. You're not going to stop him. Don't get involved.'

He knew from her tone, and by the way she avoided

137

looking at the man, that what Hernandez had suggested had been true, and that she herself was one of his customers.

'Here,' Hernandez called to her. He took another bottle from the case and threw it to where the two of them stood. Alex caught it.

'Brandy,' he said to her.

'I know what it is,' she said angrily.

'Do you want it?'

She hesitated a moment and then she shook her head.

Without giving any warning to Hernandez, Alex threw the bottle back to him. Hernandez was unprepared for this, fumbled the catch, and dropped the bottle at his feet, where it lay unbroken on the gravel.

'Lucky for you,' Hernandez shouted to him, retrieving the brandy.

'I sometimes buy it for my father,' Eva said to Alex, immediately causing him to regret having thrown the bottle back.

'Were you coming to see him?' he asked her.

'No – you.'

At first he imagined this was a lie, an excuse for having been seen by him as she came to the jeep.

'The mayor wants to see you,' she said. 'I told him I'd arrange a meeting. About the bodies. He's been to see Dyer again, who told him to see you. Afterwards, he came to Ameldorf. My father refused to see him.'

'And so you've been left to do the dirty work for all three of them?'

She smiled at the remark. 'Two of them. Besides, I thought that was *your* part in all this – other people's dirty work.' She smiled at him and squeezed his arm again. '*Can* you see him? Tonight? When you've finished here?'

'If he comes to the Institute,' Alex said.

She nodded once.

'And only if you're present,' he added.

'You don't need me,' she said.

'I might,' he said. 'At least by being there you can keep your father up to date on everything that's happening.'

'He knew two of the men in the cellar,' she said, lowering her head.

Angry at being excluded from this conversation, Hernandez called to Eva. 'Tell her I got more of what she likes. Your friend. The friendly one. Tell her I got plenty more of what she likes.' He rubbed a hand over his crotch as he said this. 'Tell her she knows where I am. Hay-sus Christ. And tell her the day of reckoning is almost here. She owes me and she knows she owes me.'

'Stuff she's been taking to Maria,' Eva whispered to Alex. 'What time shall I tell the mayor?'

Alex felt suddenly tired and she saw this. She put her arm against his back and rubbed it.

'You look exhausted,' she said. 'And now I've just made your day longer.'

'Perhaps you and her ought to go somewhere more private,' Hernandez shouted, and several of those still standing around him laughed at this.

'You're blushing,' Eva said to Alex.

And you're shaking. 'I know I am,' he said.

'Let's do as he suggests,' she said.

'Go somewhere private?'

She laughed and slapped his chest. 'No – I just meant we should leave him to get on with things.'

'Oh,' Alex said.

She looked at him. 'You're as transparent as he says you are,' she told him, and again there was both reassurance and affection in her voice.

'When did he say that?'

'As he suggests, then.'

'It's not much of a vote of confidence,' he said.

'You don't need it.' She paused. 'At least not from me. I know who you are and what you are, and I trust you.' She held his gaze as she said this, ensuring he believed her, and the force and honesty of the remark made him catch his breath.

When he spoke again, his throat was dry. '*Will* you come? With the mayor?'

'Of course,' she said. 'If you'll come away from here now.'

He wondered if she was afraid of what Hernandez might reveal next.

'Please,' she said, and he knew by the calm firmness

140

of her voice that it would be the last of her urging.

'Hey,' Hernandez called to his crowd, some of whom were by then standing alongside him at the jeep with money in their hands. 'Looks like they took my advice.'

Alex and Eva walked together along the raised terrace.

'Hey, I just thought,' Hernandez called to them.

Alex paused and Eva stopped beside him.

'He thinks he's won,' she said. 'That's all. You walked away from him and so he thinks he's won. That's the kind of man he is.'

'Catch,' Hernandez shouted at them.

He threw something else, smaller, a packet, aiming high so that whatever it was went over their heads and landed ahead of them.

'Keep walking,' Eva said.

At first, Alex thought the man had thrown a packet of cigarettes. They walked to where this lay and, ignoring Eva's advice, Alex reached down to retrieve it, regretting that she withdrew her hand from his arm as he did this.

He picked up the small package without looking closely at it, and he had already turned to Eva when he realized that what Hernandez had thrown, and what he now held towards her, was not cigarettes, but a packet of condoms. The word was written across the front, and along each side of the small box.

Eva laughed at seeing them. 'He's hardly bankrupted himself,' she said. She took the packet from him and pushed it into her pocket.

'The—' Alex said.

'Call him all the names you want,' she told him. 'He'll still be the same man.'

He nodded at this. 'I don't even know where Puerto Rico is,' he said.

'Birthplace of Hay-sus,' she said. 'The son of God-knows-who,' and they both laughed.

He could see the outline of the packet through the material of her skirt as she walked.

11

He questioned fewer than half the men sent to see him that day.

When he'd started this work, first in England, and then afterwards in Paris and Brussels until the war's end, he had imagined that the men interrogated by him might want to slough off their guilt or anger, or whatever other confused and shifting feelings they might have been harbouring, in a single dirty skin, and that they had truly believed they might achieve this in front of him. And then that they might leave him, unencumbered by all their doubts, regrets and secrets.

But it had never been like that. Where he had once imagined that such grandiose and misleading notions such as redemption or atonement were involved, he now understood that the transactions between himself and all these men were founded on a variety of other baser, lesser, and all too human emotions, needs and desires. No one sloughed off that dirty, bloodstained skin in the face of his questioning; instead they picked at it in small pieces, dry and flaking scabs, bit by bit, good flesh and bad, leaving themselves bleeding and raw, and often in more pain and uncertainty than when they had started.

No one that day appeared on any of his priority lists. In Paris and Brussels it had been part of his work to search captured files and the testimonies of others and to compile those lists of men and women the occupying forces needed to find. Here in Rehstadt, he was sent other men's lists, forced to respond to other men's priorities and urgencies.

He preferred to work alone, as did most of his fellow interrogators. With category D prisoners – the men he was seeing today – it was the only practical way to reduce the numbers, to keep the sluices open. Where those men on the priority lists were concerned, there were usually two questioners, though one of them might remain silent throughout the interviews. After a year, the prisoners had learned all of the tricks, and behaved accordingly.

Shortly after six, as Alex was questioning a fifty-nine-year-old quartermaster about his work in Normandy, one of Dyer's clerks opened his door without knocking and told him that the mayor had arrived and was waiting to see him.

Angry at this interruption, and knowing that Dyer himself wanted nothing to do with the man, Alex told the clerk to tell the mayor that he would be another hour. 'Let him wait,' he said.

'Whatever you say,' the clerk said. 'He's with the skirt. Just thought you might like to know.' He withdrew and closed the door loudly behind him.

He meant Eva.

Alex regretted that he was now about to meet her in the company of the mayor, in whose presence she would most likely remain reserved, hostile and silent. He'd seen and heard enough of the man since his arrival in Rehstadt to know how self-regarding he was, and how influential he considered himself to be in the matters of the town. He was protective of the prestige and protocol of his office, and happy to collude with Dyer in doing all he could to keep those local concerns beyond the reach of the occupying forces.

If Alex had thought about the appointment at all during his work, then it was to imagine it spent alone with Eva, the two of them achieving in a fraction of the time what they would achieve with the mayor.

' "Skirt"?' the quartermaster said, then understood. 'Oh, a woman?' He drew a quick outline with his hands.

The man had spent three years requisitioning milk, meat, eggs and butter from local farmers, stockpiling these and then controlling the military and domestic markets. He'd been taken prisoner a month after the

Invasion and had spent most of his time in captivity complaining to everyone who would still listen to him how much more efficient and productive he had made those farms and markets. He told Alex that he had only ever fired a rifle once, and that had been at a fox.

Alex might have finished with the man after a few minutes, but instead he spent an hour with him, indulging the man's reminiscences and amused by his stories, knowing even as he listened to these that they were diversions, serving the man's purpose. The quartermaster, too, appreciated the attention he was finally receiving, and was in little hurry for the questioning to end.

'Am I finished?' he asked Alex eventually.

'Yes,' Alex said. 'You're finished.' He wondered why the man had been held for so long without already being released or sent elsewhere.

The old German rose from his seat and held out his hand. 'You're a civilized man,' he told Alex. Throughout their time together, he had spoken with an accent Alex had had difficulty in understanding, a different language almost.

'I know,' Alex said. 'Civilized.' He closed the man's file and stamped its cover, noting the relief on the man's face as he did this.

'Thank you,' the quartermaster said. 'Perhaps now I can see my grandchildren again.' They all spoke of their children, or grandchildren, or wives, or nephews and nieces.

'How many?' Alex asked him.

The quartermaster hesitated before answering. 'Three. Three daughters. Three grandchildren.'

A lie?

'There were once five children. Two were killed. I still think of them as being five.'

'I'm sorry,' Alex said. He moved the file from one side of his desk to the other and called for the guard waiting at the door.

'What now?' the quartermaster asked him.

'Perhaps you'll go home,' Alex said, knowing nothing of what lay ahead of the man, knowing the file might yet be slid to the bottom of someone else's pile.

As the man left, Alex told the guard to arrange for all those others still waiting to be seen by him to be taken back to their cells. Those sitting nearby who understood him complained at this. Several rose to their feet and gesticulated at him before being pushed back down. Alex ignored them.

Waiting until the corridor was empty, he left the wing in which he worked and walked to the administrative building, stretching the ache from his shoulders and neck as he went.

Entering the lobby, Alex immediately saw the mayor standing at the centre of the open space. The man had positioned himself at the middle of the tiled and patterned floor and stood as though its design now radiated from him.

Alex was disappointed at not seeing Eva waiting with him, but as he approached the man he saw her in the room beyond. She looked up at his arrival, nodded once to the mayor and then turned back to her work. Alex wanted to bypass the man, to go directly to her and ask her to join them. He watched her. She was standing with another woman, reading together from a single sheet they held between them.

'Captain Foster,' the mayor said loudly as Alex approached him.

'Wait,' Alex said. 'I— ' he indicated the adjoining room.

'Wait?' the man said, momentarily confused by the command, then becoming briefly angry before regaining his composure. 'I've already *been* waiting an hour.' He held out his watch.

'I've been busy,' Alex told him. He waited in the doorway until Eva again looked at him.

'I'll be there in a moment,' she said, holding her finger on the sheet of paper. 'Bring him in here. Dyer's cleared one of the side offices.' She indicated the empty supervisor's office beside Alex.

The supervisor himself, angry at this temporary expulsion, sat at a nearby desk and watched closely everything that happened.

Alex offered the mayor the supervisor's seat behind the desk, and the man was pleased to accept the position and whatever authority he believed this now conferred upon him.

Eva arrived and laid a pad and a pencil on the desk, further adding to both the farce and the formality of the occasion.

'Before we begin,' the mayor said, 'am I to understand that you, Captain Foster, are here as Colonel Dyer's representative, and that you will report the details and the outcome of our meeting to him?'

Outcome? Alex thought. *What outcome?* As far as he was concerned, this was just another way of keeping everything to do with the corpses in the cellar as far away from Dyer as possible. He hoped Eva understood this, too.

'Or,' the mayor went on, pausing and glancing at both Alex and Eva to ensure they understood that this was a considerably less acceptable option, 'or are you acting in your own right? Are you appointed, so to speak, by Colonel Dyer, to act on your own initiative in the matter?'

Alex glanced at Eva, who signalled to him with a raised eyebrow that she, too, did not fully understand what the mayor was asking, or what he might be about to suggest.

'I act independently,' Alex said. 'But, naturally, everything will be reported to Colonel Dyer.' It was a non-committal half-answer, and it didn't satisfy the mayor.

'I see,' the man said. 'You are aware, of course, that a committee has already been formed by other councillors with myself at its head?' Meaning *he*'d formed it prior to coming there.

'What sort of committee?'

The mayor nodded at Eva. 'Perhaps she might start taking notes on the matter.'

'Perhaps I might,' Eva said.

The man ignored the remark.

'What sort of committee?' Alex repeated.

Eva sat back from the desk and picked up the pad.

The mayor took a breath. 'We here in Rehstadt have for some time been considering raising a monument to our War Dead.' He clearly intended both Alex and Eva to be impressed by the revelation, and when they showed no sign of this, or even any genuine interest in the prospect, he stopped speaking, reluctant to continue in the face of such indifference.

Sensing the man's anger, and unwilling to prolong the encounter any longer than was necessary, Alex apologized and feigned interest.

Eva smiled at his discomfort.

'It's just a surprise, that's all,' he said.

'It certainly is,' Eva said.

Again the mayor ignored her. He went on to list the other members of the committee, and then its aims. The names meant nothing to Alex, but Eva, he saw, knew most of the men. She either smiled coldly or shook her head at each name.

When the mayor had finished speaking, she said, 'The same old faces, eh?'

Finally provoked by this, the mayor turned and

jabbed a finger at her. 'They are all good and decent people. All of them have very good reasons for wanting the memorial, the monument. The war may not have truly come to Rehstadt as it did to so many other places, but there has been suffering here – suffering, loss and grieving – all the same.'

'Including your own?' Alex asked him, drawing the man back to him.

'Including my own,' the mayor said, dropping his head and lowering his voice in a practised gesture. Later Alex learned that the man's ninety-year-old uncle had been killed during a raid on Berlin.

'And including my brother?' Eva asked him.

'Of course including your brother. Your brother was a brave soldier. He died fighting for what he believed in, protecting his country, his family, you.'

Eva shook her head at the words.

Alex wondered if the man even knew her brother's name. And then he struggled to remember if she had ever told *him* the name.

'Tell her,' the mayor said to Alex. 'There will be such monuments in every city, town and village in every country in Europe. Why should we here in Rehstadt be denied our own?'

'No one's denying you anything,' Alex told him. He knew how many more years might pass before the monument was unveiled. He knew what bureaucratic entanglements were yet to be unravelled. 'What concerns me now, here, are the as-yet-unidentified bodies in the cellar. Are you also telling me you wish to include *their* names on your monument?'

The mayor avoided his eyes. 'There are problems,' he said. 'Disagreements, arguments. There are those on the committee who want the names of everyone killed to be remembered; and there are those who want only the men who died in the service of their country to be remembered. There are many other distinctions to be considered.'

I bet, Alex thought.

Eva was smiling again.

The mayor went on. There were those people who had died in the town and those who had died elsewhere. There were those whose bodies had been retrieved and accorded a proper burial, and there were those who had never returned. Those who had served their country in ways other than fighting and those . . .

Alex stopped listening. Everything the man said took them further from the corpses. He had watched Eva closely at the mayor's mention of those men whose bodies had never been retrieved and returned to Rehstadt. She had briefly closed her eyes, but had otherwise made no other protest.

The mayor continued talking.

Eventually, Alex stopped him by raising his palms.

'What?' the man said. 'They are all distinctions that need to be considered.'

'And it's all a matter for you and your committee,' Alex said. 'Not for me or Colonel Dyer.'

'But until I am afforded some authority in the matter, until I am given the go-ahead –' something about the phrase amused him and he smiled '– until I am given these things then there will continue to be countless other delays. The Graves Registration people are already involved, the Red Cross. So far, I have been contacted by four separate repatriation authorities, all of whom claim to be interested in the names of the men who might have been – who might . . .' He faltered and fell silent.

'Who might have been prisoners or forced labourers?' Alex said.

'*Ostarbeiter*, yes,' the mayor said.

'I take it there'll be no place for *them* on your monument.'

The mayor was ready with his answer. 'They will one day have their *own* monument. I am certain all those other worthy bodies will see to that. *My* concern is Rehstadt.' He spoke now with something approaching a sneer, and it was all Alex could do to restrain himself from rising to his feet and telling the man that their meeting was over. But if he did that, he knew, then the mayor would only find his way back to Dyer with his demands and complaints doubled.

'I'm sure,' Alex said. And again he hoped Eva understood his true feelings on the matter.

She continued writing in her pad. She asked the mayor to speak more slowly, telling him that she was having trouble keeping up with him and all the important and wonderful things he was suggesting.

'Perhaps next time you could find someone more experienced in note-taking,' he said to Alex. 'Perhaps a qualified stenographer. You do have them?'

'I'll look into it,' Alex said, and saw another of Eva's quick smiles. 'She does her best,' he added, prolonging her amusement. 'But I agree – it's not very good. You deserve better.'

The mayor nodded at this. 'Hardly surprising,' he said. 'This is what happens when such riff-raff are employed.' He used the word *Gesindel*.

'You knew her father,' Alex said quickly, before Eva could speak.

The mayor fluttered his hand. 'I inherited a great many mistakes and a great deal of confusion from the man when I succeeded him as mayor.' He showed no embarrassment at saying this in front of Eva.

'I'm sure,' Alex said. He sat back in his seat, rubbed his face and yawned.

'If I'm tiring you . . .' the mayor said.

Alex said nothing.

The meeting lasted a further hour, and at the end of that time little had been achieved or guaranteed or confirmed. The mayor's tirade against all the other concerned bodies – he called them *Die Leute die sich einmischen*, meddlers – moved in a circle, quickening and repetitive, and then slowing and failing.

The names of all the corpses in their neat row were already known, he announced, as though he himself had discovered these. It was a start. Every single name. Men, women and children. All inhabitants of Rehstadt. All known and now properly mourned after only three days.

Just go, Alex thought. *Just go*. Over and over until he arrived at the point where he wondered if he would be able to resist actually saying the words out loud, if he might not be carried by some unstoppable momentum into forming them and then shouting them in the mayor's face.

It was almost nine before the man finally stopped speaking, looked at his watch and told them he was expected elsewhere, at a dinner, in half an hour. In one of the town's better restaurants, he added, naming it, and expecting them both to be impressed by this. Like the supervisor, the man was overweight, but Alex saw by the way his waistcoat hung loosely over the globe of his stomach that he had once been much fatter. It had been part of his training to look for these signs of change and suffering in the men he questioned, and then to somehow use this understanding in his assessment of what they might be telling him.

Whittaker had already told him how simple it had been at the Belsen camp to distinguish the disguised former guards from even the more recent of the arrivals there. 'An ounce of flesh on the cheeks,' he had said, squeezing Alex's face. 'An ounce. Less.' 'And the smell of fear?' Alex had suggested. They both knew it existed. 'And that,' Whittaker had agreed.

'Then I won't detain you,' Alex said, rising from his seat. 'You must be hungry.'

The mayor ignored the remark and instead asked him to confirm that everything he'd raised would be passed on to Dyer.

'Every single thing,' Alex assured him. 'I'll check the notes myself.'

'The minutes,' the mayor corrected him.

'I'll type them up now,' Eva said. 'I'll work late.'

'For some of us,' the mayor said, again ignoring her and looking directly at Alex, 'there is no early or late, merely work to be done on behalf of others.'

'I'm sure you're selfless in your devotion to duty,' Alex said, this time causing the man to become suspicious, uncertain of what he was being told.

'Yes, well . . .' he said. He walked into the outer room and paused at its centre. Alex and Eva remained in the office. 'Am I to be offered a lift back into town?' the mayor shouted.

'No – walk,' Eva said, her voice low.

'Excuse me?' the mayor said.

'Walk to the motor compound,' Alex called to him. 'Tell one of the drivers I sent you.'

'Perhaps I should say Colonel Dyer sent me,' the mayor said. He turned and then paused. 'I shall inform you when it is necessary for us to meet again.' It was important to him now that the few people still at work in the outer room listened to what he had to say.

'Just keep walking, you fat pig,' Eva said. But this time the man was beyond hearing.

'Did you get everything written down?' Alex asked her.

She turned her pad to him to reveal the drawing she had made of the man, giving him a snout and the spear-shaped ears of a pig.

'Ah,' Alex said.

'It's what he is,' she told him. She grunted, almost choked, and then laughed.

They waited several minutes before following the mayor into the outer office.

As they left the building, he passed ahead of them, already in a jeep, sitting behind the driver, his arms folded across his chest.

They walked to where Alex had sat earlier overlooking the empty pool.

He took off his jacket and put it over Eva's shoulders, and in response to this she pulled his arm around her neck and held it to her chest.

'Are you cold?' he asked her.

'Something like that,' she said.

'What if he'd asked to see what you were supposed to be writing?'

'He probably knew,' she said.

'And that's why he didn't ask?'

'Something like that.' She laughed again and pushed her fingers through his own.

12

They sat on the cold stone of the terrace, mostly in silence, for a further ten minutes. On one occasion, as they were approached by someone passing behind them, Alex had tried to take his hand from where Eva held it, but she had responded to this by clutching him more tightly. He could feel her heart beating beneath his palm. The tip of his forefinger rested against the flesh in the hollow of her throat. He moved it in small, barely perceptible circles and she sighed at this. When he stopped, she told him to go on.

Eventually she said, 'I ought to go. Find Nina. See how Maria is.' She made no effort to rise from beside him, and as she spoke she lowered her chin and pressed it hard on his finger.

'I'll come with you,' he suggested.

She shook her head. 'And if Dyer finds out you went

back to the hospital after everything that happened this morning?'

'I can deal with him.'

'No, you can't,' she said. 'And besides, it might only create more problems for Maria. Or Whittaker.'

He acknowledged this. 'I'm sure everything will be fine,' he said.

She finally drew away from him at the words. 'You're confusing where you came from with where you are now,' she said.

He didn't understand her.

'You come from a place where everybody has the luxury of waiting and seeing and hoping for the best,' she said. 'Because that's usually what happens. Because things usually do "work out fine". But that's there, England, not here. This is the other side of the looking glass. How is everything going to be fine here, for Maria, for Nina? How? How is it going to be fine for any of us? Tell me.'

The vehemence of this sudden outburst surprised him.

'All I meant was that I *hoped*—' he began.

'Another luxury. All you ever—' She stopped herself by clasping a hand over her mouth. 'Ignore me,' she said.

Beneath them a group of passing soldiers turned to look at them, attracted by her raised voice. One of the men whistled at her.

'All I ever what?' he asked her.

She sighed heavily. Then she took back his hand and held it in both her own. 'All *you* ever did was try to help. It isn't you I should be shouting at.' She rubbed her arm at a sudden chill. 'I need to wash,' she said.

'There's a sink in my room.'

Both of them stopped at the suggestion.

' "No Unauthorized Visitors",' she said. The sign hung at the hotel reception.

'Visitors, authorized and otherwise, in the rooms most of the time,' he said. 'Along with hot, running water, clean towels and real soap.'

She considered his offer.

'Plus,' he added, 'Whittaker will probably already be back there. You can ask him about Maria and the baby.' Despite this contrivance, she needed little convincing, and he saw this.

'You invite people back to your room all the time, then?' She was making fun of him now to disguise whatever embarrassment or uncertainty they shared.

'Parties most nights,' he said. He had been there almost five months, and the only person who had been in his room apart from the cleaning staff and Dyer's clerks, seeking him out with orders or boxes of documents, had been Whittaker.

They walked to the Institute entrance and then followed the path to the old hotel. Overgrown rhododendrons hung across the stone flags, joined above them in places.

161

Arriving at the hotel, Eva hesitated. Alex imagined she was about to change her mind, but before he could say anything to her, they were joined in the lobby by Whittaker, who put his arm around both their shoulders and kissed Eva on the cheek. He looked exhausted.

'I saw you arrive,' he said. 'I was sitting in the last of the sun. You finally persuaded him to bring you,' he said to Eva, winking.

'She needed to wash,' Alex said.

'He's pulling your leg,' Eva told him.

Whittaker pressed his face into her neck and breathed deeply. 'Wash?' he said.

They climbed the stairs together, and until they had entered Alex's room none of them spoke about Maria or the baby.

Whittaker left them to fetch a bottle of drink, telling them he'd be gone long enough for Eva to have her wash.

When they were again alone, Alex gave her a towel and the remains of a small bar of soap. He ran the water in his sink until it steamed and condensed on the mirror.

Eva took off her cardigan.

'I promise not to look,' Alex said.

She stood facing him. 'It's a small room,' she said. She came to him, held him and kissed him on the lips. He moved his hands across her back, over and beneath the thin material of her slip. They stood like this for a full minute, until she clasped his shoulders and stood back from him.

'Whittaker,' she said. She kissed his cheek and then his chin.

It occurred to Alex only then that Whittaker might not be coming back.

'I know what you're thinking,' she told him. She held her hand against his face. And then she turned away from him and washed herself. She dried herself on the towel and then washed herself again.

She was putting her cardigan back on when Whittaker knocked, waited a few seconds and then came back in with a bottle and three glasses. 'I brought the finest crystal,' he said, tapping the hotel glassware together. Alex recognized the bottle from Hernandez's case.

Eva watched the two of them closely.

'I kissed him,' she said bluntly to Whittaker.

'I heard his screams as he tried to fight you off,' he said. 'It's why I brought a full bottle.'

'Then he kissed me back,' she said.

'He's a fast learner.' He unscrewed the cap from the bottle.

'And then I had my wash. Two washes.' She took the glasses from him and held them out for him to fill.

'So – twice as clean,' he said. 'Cleaner than clean.'

Alex pulled the room's two chairs to the window. Eva sat on the edge of the bed.

'Maria?' she said.

Alex had known from the instant Whittaker had joined them that the news from the hospital wasn't good, and he saw now that Eva understood this too.

'About Maria,' Whittaker began. He looked at the glass in his hand.

'Did the baby die?' Eva asked him. She sat with the rim of her own glass touching her lips, waiting for his answer before tipping the whisky into her mouth.

'There wasn't much anyone could do,' Whittaker said. 'They lost it. Noon.'

'*She* lost it,' Eva said. 'Maria.' She swallowed the drink and Whittaker refilled her glass.

'What happened?' Alex asked him.

'Does it matter?' Whittaker said. 'The delivery was complicated from the start. The baby never presented properly. I don't know. We might even have been fooling ourselves out at the camp. Someone called me from the hospital to let me know what had happened. I tried to talk to Nina, but never managed to.'

'Is she still there?' Alex asked him.

'Nina? I imagine so. There were other complications. For Maria. They performed a caesarean. There's probably some infection to deal with. It can't have been the easiest of operations for someone so young and so—'

'So stupid?' Eva said, causing them both to turn to her. There were tears on her cheeks.

'I was going to say someone so malnourished and underweight,' Whittaker said.

164

'I know you were,' she told him.

'So you think her losing the baby isn't entirely—' Alex began to say.

And again, Eva interrupted him. 'Isn't entirely what? A disaster? A tragedy? Something not as upsetting or as distressing as it might otherwise have been? Under different circumstances?'

Whittaker put his arm around her. 'There aren't any other circumstances,' he said.

'I know.' She looked at Alex. 'I'm sorry.'

'I think we both understand what you're telling us,' Whittaker said.

She began to cry uncontrollably. 'And once again I am berating the last two people in the world I ought to be berating,' she said.

'I shall consider myself berated,' Whittaker said, touching her glass with his own.

'Is that not the correct word?' she said.

Whittaker took a photo from his wallet. 'This is my wife, Ruth, and my two daughters, Janet and Sarah – Janet after her mother, Sarah after my own. The eldest, Janet, is three years younger than Maria.'

She took the photo from him and looked at it closely, treating it like the precious possession it was.

'I haven't seen any of them since before Christmas,' he said. 'In my world – in that other world, at least – *that* counts as unbearable suffering.'

'I understand,' she said.

'But you still know which kind of so-called unbearable suffering is the worst?' he said. 'Of course you do. And so you should.'

She gave him back the photo and he slid it carefully into his wallet without looking at it. He refilled all their glasses.

Alex told him about their encounter with Jesus Hernandez.

Whittaker pointed the bottle at him. 'I know him as well as I need to know him,' he said. 'My advice to you is to stay away from him. He came to the infirmary one day offering to sell me whatever I needed. When I asked him to be more specific, he told me to make him a list. Apparently, he could get his hands on stuff I hadn't seen for months.'

'What happened?' Alex said.

'I told him in no uncertain terms that I never wanted to see him again. At least not for that kind of thing. My own personal weaknesses, however . . .' He shook the bottle again.

'He sells all sorts of stuff in the camp,' Eva said. She looked at Alex. 'I didn't say anything earlier because it didn't seem to have anything to do with what happened then. Nina told me about him.'

'Oh, he'll know Nina all right,' Whittaker said, stopping abruptly. He closed his eyes. 'Me and my big mouth. Sorry.'

'She is what she is,' Eva said. 'It's hardly a secret.'

They sat in silence for several minutes.

Then Eva said to Whittaker, 'Will your daughters become doctors, do you think?'

'I just want them to grow up healthy and happy,' he said. 'I once swore I would never resort to homilies like that, but after all that's happened . . .'

'The war?' Eva said.

'The war, everything.'

'The war's over,' she said, feigning surprise that he might not have known this. 'Did nobody tell you?'

Whittaker shook his head. 'Not a word,' he said. 'Otherwise I would have gone straight home.'

'When will that happen?' she asked him.

He shrugged. 'I'm counting on another month. At the latest.'

The remark surprised Alex, who had no idea that his friend was so close to leaving.

'Seriously?' he said.

'Insofar as any of this can be taken seriously,' Whittaker said. He was reluctant to say more on the subject, and so Alex told him about the mayor's visit and the monument.

'He came to the hospital earlier,' Whittaker said. 'The unidentified corpses are still in the morgue there. He and the director had a big row. I missed most of it. When I asked the director what it had been about, he told me it was nothing. None of my business. The morgue is probably full to overflowing while the corpses remain unidentified.'

'Then they'll both be glad to see the back of them,' Alex said.

'I wonder where Maria's baby's name will come on their blessed memorial,' Eva said. She raised her glass again and whispered, 'Maria's baby,' before drinking from it. This time she only sipped at the whisky, pulling a face as though she were tasting it for the first time.

Whittaker rose from beside the window. 'I'm going to bed,' he said. It was not yet ten o'clock. 'I'm back on duty at midnight.' He leaned down to kiss Eva where she sat on the bed. 'The soap,' he whispered loudly to her. 'Take it with you when you go. The soap-supply-and-delivery man – and I'm certain there is one somewhere – will bring a new bar tomorrow.'

'Cake,' she said. 'A new cake.'

'I sign for them in triplicate,' Alex said. He was still considering Whittaker's near-imminent departure from the place.

Whittaker picked up his bottle, put it down, then picked it up again, filled his own glass and handed the rest to Alex.

He left them, and for a few minutes afterwards they could hear him singing in the adjoining room. A door opened and closed, water ran through pipes, and the springs of his bed creaked, a radio played, muted piano and violins.

'He's been through a lot,' Alex said, conscious of how useless the words sounded, knowing and regretting how much they concealed and made forgettable.

'I doubt she even had a name for it,' Eva said.

'The baby?' They had never asked Whittaker if he had known if it had been a girl or a boy. They would know everything in the smallest detail soon enough.

He looked at her where she sat on the bed. He wanted her to stay with him. He wanted to suggest this to her, but dare not, afraid of the spell the words might break, afraid that she would become aware of the time and of her need to return home to her father and young brother. Or perhaps she would want only to find Nina and to sit and console her friend.

By then he'd drunk three large glasses of whisky. He hadn't eaten since lunchtime and he felt drunk, unable to drive her wherever she might now want to go.

And almost as though reading these thoughts, she looked at him and said, 'Do you want me to leave?'

He shook his head. 'It's the last thing I want. I want you to stay.'

'All night?'

'All night.' He was grateful for the way she guided him.

'It's what I want, too,' she said. 'Do I sound drunk to you?'

'Very,' he said, making her smile.

'My father will have heard about what happened at the camp and afterwards. He'll think I'm with Maria. Or Nina.'

He understood the excuses she was offering him.

'Of course he will,' he said, his own complicity clear. 'And I can take you home as early as you like in the morning. Or to the hospital, or to Nina.'

She let herself fall backwards on to the bed, her empty glass upright on her stomach. Her breasts rose flattened to the neck of her cardigan and Alex looked at them.

'I didn't mean what I said about Maria,' she said, her eyes closed. 'It's not the end of the world for her.'

'She's young. Perhaps now she can get on with her life, make a new start.' More regrettable but hard-to-avoid reassurances.

'It's what we're all meant to be doing,' Eva said, her eyes still closed. She raised her arm slightly and then let her hand fall back to the bed, casually beckoning him to lie beside her.

13

'May I ask, did you yourself ever kill anyone?' Johannes Walther stood beside his chair.

Alex looked up at him. 'Me, personally? Kill someone directly, you mean?' He regretted having responded to the question. He should have remained silent. Having killed or not having killed divided men, created distinctions, and they all used this in one way or another. At the very least, he should have immediately asked Walther why he was asking the question, what point he believed he was making. A hundred other interrogators might simply have told him to shut up and then left him standing in silence for a few minutes longer.

'My apologies. I shouldn't have asked,' Walther said.

'If you're asking me if I ever knelt a man down in front of me and stuck a pistol into the back of his head and pulled the trigger, then the answer is no,' Alex said.

Walther nodded. It was the end of any pretence between them.

'Sit down,' Alex said.

Walther removed his cap and sat with his hands on his knees.

'And you?' Alex asked him.

Walther nodded. 'I fired my cannon into groups of men and into the buildings in which they were hiding. And at other tanks. Of course I killed many men. I saw my enemy, I saw my shells explode, I heard their screams, I saw their corpses afterwards. I don't hide from any of that, from the consequences of my actions.'

Meaning I do? 'And do you distinguish clearly between the nature of *that* killing and what happened at Malmédy?' It was a clumsy question, but now that there was no pretence between them Alex wanted the events at Malmédy to remain to the fore. He was due to see Dyer again later in the day, perhaps in the company of Preston, and the two men would want to know how far he had progressed.

'Of course I do,' Walther said. He, too, seemed disappointed by the question. 'I once directed my machine-gunner to a line of men, Russians, running from the cover of one ruined building to another. He killed them like shooting tin ducks at a fairground. The men, stupidly, ran in a straight line, one after the other, perhaps following their leader. My gunner found the range and the trajectory fast enough, killed the man at the head of the line and then just waited for the others to run into his sights. Most obliged him. And by the time those at the rear of the line had worked out what was happening and tried to turn back, it was too late. They all died. Or were left there badly wounded.'

'But it still wasn't *your* finger on the trigger,' Alex said.

'Yes it was,' Walther said. 'Without my call, the gunner might have missed seeing them completely.'

'I understand what you're saying,' Alex said. 'But at Malmédy, the men had already surrendered and—'

'And if I'd been present instead of lying in a field hospital five miles away wondering if I was about to follow the family tradition and lose my arm, then perhaps I might have participated in what happened. Yes, I don't deny that. Sometimes, and as I'm sure countless others have already made clear to you, Captain Foster, choice in these matters is an unattainable luxury.'

'Or the excuse you make it sound?' Alex said.

'Yes, or that.'

During the first week of his work at Rehstadt, a delegation of Russians had arrived, a hundred men, with a list of almost four times that number of German prisoners they were searching for. At first, Dyer had protested at the Russians' demands, and then, less than an hour later – and following a succession of telephone calls during which all responsibility was cast elsewhere

– he had acceded to them. He read aloud the Russians' authorization to his assembled staff, and though he still did not fully understand why they had been granted the right to remove his prisoners, he did nothing to prevent them searching for the men. Eventually, both to speed up the work and to impose the last of his own lost authority on the proceedings, he had instructed his own guards and interrogators to assist the Russians in their work.

The Russians gathered up only seventy of the men they were looking for. The lists they waved around were written in a language unintelligible to everyone on the British staff. Dyer had been refused an interpreter from elsewhere. The prisoners were taken first to a separate compound and were then driven away from Rehstadt in two of the Russian lorries.

Alex had watched all this. The Russians drank as they worked. They gave bottles of drink to the men they took away. And some of those men even seemed pleased to be leaving Rehstadt in this way. A crate of drink was delivered to Dyer's office, and several of the Russian commanders stayed with him while the search was carried out around them.

Dyer said afterwards that they hadn't seemed genuinely concerned about who they found and who they missed, just that they should have something to show for their visit.

A fortnight later, word reached the Institute that all

the men who had been handed over had been summarily tried en masse for their alleged war crimes, and then executed.

But at that time, and especially in places like Rehstadt, rumours like this one circulated endlessly, and Alex, only then recently arrived and still uncertain of his own place or role in the hierarchy of the Institute, had not taken it seriously.

He had accompanied one of the junior Russian officers, a German-speaker, into the cell blocks and had helped him find a dozen of the men he was searching for. Alex believed him when the man pointed to the indecipherable names on his list. He asked him what was going to happen to the prisoners and the man jerked an imaginary rope round his neck and laughed. Then, upon seeing Alex's concern, and being even more amused by this, he reassured him that they would not be hanged. Hanging was for civilians, he said, still laughing. The prisoners would be shot. He took the pistol from his holster and jabbed it at the men being taken from their cells.

'I see my file remains considerably depleted,' Walther said, interrupting these thoughts.

'Depleted how?'

'It was once much thicker.' Walther held his thumb and forefinger half an inch apart.

'You're mistaken,' Alex said, wondering again how much more Preston had already shown to Dyer. 'You probably saw administrative files, registrations, application notices. They'll have followed you around for a while and then been taken out and filed elsewhere.' The remark sounded exactly like the excuse it was.

'I see,' Walther said.

'You think I'm lying to you?'

Walther shrugged. 'I think that perhaps you have only been given what the Americans saw fit to reveal to you.'

'Why the Americans?'

Walther laughed. 'You would insult my intelligence if you told me they weren't behind my questioning now. It was Malmédy. Of course all this is happening now at their urging.'

'Everything is happening now through the proper channels and in the proper way,' Alex said.

'I don't doubt that,' Walther said. 'I'm sure everything will be done with absolute certainty, authority and conviction. No one would deny them their own show trial. I hear the French are calling for another regarding Oradour. Perhaps even the Czechs will want to get in on the act.'

'Your name is still everywhere one looks in the testimony of others,' Alex said. 'The testimony of others who have already confessed to their part in what happened.'

'That, too, I do not doubt. But is there one piece of that recorded testimony that places me – *me* – at the actual scene of the crime, let alone participating in it?

Perhaps *that's* why my file has grown so thin. Perhaps it's just a very expedient way of removing all that untidy and irritating doubt.'

Alex rose from his desk and went to the window. A woman crossed the driveway beneath him, and at first he thought it was Eva. But then she turned and he recognized another of the secretaries. He felt a sudden lurch of disappointment.

'I don't know what more the Americans expect of you,' Walther said behind him. 'Unless it's simply to tie everything up neatly with a ribbon, stamp my file and hand it back to them with your concurrence and blessing.' He paused. 'Did you know that I have my supporters in the town, here in Rehstadt?' There was now something approaching amusement in his voice.

'Oh?'

'Several councillors.'

'Including the mayor, no doubt.'

Walther laughed. 'He runs a tight ship. They do nothing without his say-so. A delegation of them – or is that too grand a word? – tried to see Dyer to protest my innocence to him.'

'And Dyer, no doubt, refused to listen to them.'

'Of course he refused.'

'In what way protest your innocence? Did they know something?'

Walther shrugged. 'They cannot have known me from Adam, or what I had or hadn't done at Malmédy, or elsewhere. I think they just wanted to let Dyer know that they believed he was prosecuting men – others, men like me – unjustly. I believe the crux of their argument was that the war had been over for long enough and that all the necessary prosecuting was now being done elsewhere, and by men far more capable than Dyer of determining responsibility and guilt.'

'At Nuremberg, you mean?'

'And whatever secret trials the Russians are currently holding.'

'There aren't any secret—'

'Oh no? So tell me – why have the Russian judges accepted such minor roles at Nuremberg? It makes no sense. Unless, of course, they're satisfying themselves elsewhere. The mayor himself said he saw no end to it all. You know he was a Party member? It's probably why he's doing his best now to ingratiate himself to his unhappy electorate.'

'How do you know all this?' Alex asked him, returning to his desk.

'What, the Russians or the mayor?'

'The mayor.'

'You think there's anything happens in this place or in the town that we *don't* get to hear about? It's the nature of prisons and prisoners. A lot of men with a lot of time on their hands and nothing to do except listen and talk, listen and talk. You'd be surprised at what we get to hear about.' He looked directly at Alex as he said all this, and

Alex returned his gaze.

'Very good,' Alex said.

'Good? I'm sorry . . .'

'All these diversions,' Alex said.

'Ah,' Walther smiled. 'Meaning we should return to Malmédy, and that I should stop wasting your time and tell you what you will later need to repeat to others.'

'It's why you're here,' Alex said bluntly. 'And to allay any doubts you may have – yes, of course the Americans are interested in you and your part in it all. And if—'

'They still chose you to do their dirty work for them.' It was an uncharacteristically unguarded and hostile remark for Walther to make, and Alex noted this. It was also an easy and obvious accusation to make; and an even easier one to avoid making. Walther himself would already regret having spoken.

Neither man spoke for a moment.

Alex opened a packet of cigarettes and gave one to Walther.

'When I finally returned to my brother's farm, he wept at seeing me,' Walther said eventually. 'He held me with his one arm and he wept. I'd never seen him cry before. Even when he had his accident, he didn't cry. I showed him my wound, my burned flesh. And then he laughed through his tears. His new wife stood beside us, her arms out to me, but never breaking our bond. He said it joined us, his loss, my own injury, joined us together. He insisted that I stayed with them. I told him

179

I'd been captured and released, but that in all likelihood they'd come looking for me again.'

'Because of Malmédy?'

'Because of Malmédy. And like the mayor, he too tried to convince me that too much time had already passed for that to happen. I was a free man. He was convinced of it. The world had been crazy for a few years but now it was sane again. Why prolong things? He finally released me and his wife came forward to hold me. She'd been a girl when I'd last seen her, and now she had grown solid and older. Two years. He asked me about Malmédy, said he'd seen stories in the papers. That's what he called them – stories. He didn't believe a word of them, of course. That's what they were to him – stories.' He tailed off, remembering.

'But you remained convinced that someone some-where would still be looking for you?'

'Someone somewhere, yes.'

'When *did* you first hear of what had happened?'

'The shootings?' He paused for a second to assess all that the question implied, the path it might now direct them along. 'Three or four days afterwards. I can't be any more precise. When the same men with whom I'd been driving towards Antwerp started passing back through our lines in disarray and retreat. Some of them were brought to the same field hospital. They told me what they'd seen and heard. I knew from their voices that it was something important. They were already trying to make it a secret. They whispered the name of the place – Baugnez; it was only ever referred to as Malmédy afterwards. They said prisoners had been killed. No one was able to say for certain by whom.'

'Or *willing* to say,' Alex said. He made notes as Walther spoke, something to take to Dyer. 'Did anyone confess direct involvement to you, to you directly?'

'Names for you to cross-check, you mean? I won't tell you. Besides, do you imagine any of them ever spoke about being directly involved? They heard things, second-hand tales, rumours, gunshots, warnings from higher up, accusations from other prisoners. I wonder if any of them ever truly understood how far beyond their reach this so-called secret already was. You know how these things work. If you think war is a disorganized affair at the best of times, then those December days in Belgium were unbelievable.'

'Someone somewhere must have believed in its success,' Alex said.

'Ah, this "someone somewhere" again. Of course *someone* must have believed in our success. Do you think so many men and so many tanks would have been thrown away for no good military reason? They were my friends, my colleagues.'

'You ran out of steam, that's all,' Alex said.

'No – we ran out of petrol. They told us to depend on captured supplies. What captured supplies? The Americans destroyed almost everything we came near.

We were reduced to siphoning it out of abandoned trucks. We only succeeded in getting as far as we did because the troops we encountered were so inexperienced. We were probably the first Germans they'd seen. And Eisenhower had made the mistake of letting them believe that the war was almost over, that there would be no fighting beyond the Ardennes, and certainly not over the Rhine, on German soil. They surrendered in their thousands. We weren't prepared for it. It's why—'

'It's why Malmédy happened.'

Walther shook his head. 'It's why there was so much confusion, nobody ever knowing where the enemy was, where whatever existed of a front-line lay.'

'It's why Malmédy happened,' Alex repeated.

Walther fell silent for a moment. 'Malmédy happened somewhere every month of the war for five years,' he said eventually.

'Oh?' Alex stopped writing.

'You were never in the East, Captain Foster. Whatever happened at Malmédy, it was nothing compared to what took place throughout Poland, the Baltic, Russia.'

'You seem very convinced of that.'

Walther wiped his face and stubbed out his cigarette, gesturing to the packet and taking another. 'Or perhaps it's just another of my diversions, my feints,' he said.

The pages of the file that had already been removed might have contained the names of all those others already implicated in what had happened at Malmédy.

With those names, Alex might have started moving through Walther's story. Without them, he was entirely dependent on what Walther himself chose to reveal to him. It was both a strength and a weakness. What he was told would gain a greater value for having been acquired like that, but validation would only come later, with all the necessary cross-checking Walther had suggested.

'Any name I give you might condemn an innocent man,' Walther said. 'You hear the same name a dozen times from a dozen others, and how can that man *not* be guilty, or at the very least involved in some way?'

'It's why you're here now,' Alex told him.

Walther nodded. 'I'm not playing games with you,' he said. 'There are plenty of your own superiors, as well as the Americans, who will be only too happy to see justice done for what happened at Malmédy.'

'The same men who never saw or cared about what happened in the East?'

'Perhaps,' Walther said. 'We spoke earlier about the luxury of being only indirectly involved, of not pulling the trigger ourselves. Well, however harsh or uncaring it might sound, Malmédy is a luxury to the Americans now. It's a place, an event that they can scrutinize, whose every tiny detail they can now collect and make secure. They can find out everything – *everything* – that took place there. Everything that happened and every-thing that didn't happen. They can list the names, perpetrators, victims and suspects. Thousands of hours of testimony. All those little interconnecting lines and events, whispers and assurances. All those same repeated details. One after another after another. Everything. They can *know*, know with absolute conviction. And once they know, once they possess that conviction, then they can act; they can act with certainty and be completely justified in everything they do. There will be no doubt, it cannot be allowed to exist, not even a solitary distant cloud in that blindingly clear blue sky.'

'And *you're* that doubt?' Alex said.

'Me, others like me. People who might have seen, might have heard, might have participated, might have tried to stop those others, might have encouraged them and then applauded them.'

'In which case, it would be just as easy and as necessary to eliminate you,' Alex said, regretting his choice of word.

Walther looked up at him and smiled. 'Perhaps *you* could suggest that to Colonel Preston,' he said.

14

It was early evening before he was finished for the day and able to go in search of Eva. He had seen a dozen other men after Walther and had learned nothing new or of any real value from any of them.

There were few people in the room where Eva worked. A woman told him that she'd left an hour earlier.

'Looking for Remer?' someone called to him, and he turned to see the supervisor.

The man held a cup and saucer in one hand and a wrapped package of food in the other.

Alex waited.

'You missed her,' the supervisor said.

Alex wondered if he was about to make a joke at his own or Eva's expense. Usually when the man spoke that loudly, it was a signal for everyone else in the room to pay attention to him.

'She went an hour ago,' the man said, his eyes fixed on the cup, filled to its brim, which shook in the saucer as he continued towards his desk. 'You want my advice?'

Alex still waited.

'Well?' the man said.

'Go on.'

'You'll find yourself somebody else.'

Another of the women in the room laughed at the remark.

The older woman to whom Alex had already spoken mouthed, 'Ignore him,' to him.

Alex acknowledged her and then told the man that he was too busy to play his petty games.

The supervisor pretended to be offended by the remark. 'Too busy? Or too desperate to get back into her bed?' He laughed, and this time several others laughed with him.

Whatever the reason for all this, Alex knew that Eva herself would have said nothing about what had happened the previous night, and especially not to him.

'You seem to know a great deal more than—' Alex began.

'Oh, I do, I do,' the man said. He finally reached his desk and was able to put down the cup and his food. He brushed non-existent crumbs from his hands. 'Anything you want to know about Remer, feel free to ask.'

It occurred to Alex to wonder why the man was provoking him in this way, and he became cautious.

Perhaps he *did* know something of what had happened between Eva and himself. And perhaps he might now be about to broadcast what he knew to the others in the room. He wondered, too, what the man might already have said to Eva. It was not difficult to imagine his taunts and insults.

'And what *I* know,' Alex called to him, 'is that *you* ought to be a little more discreet, more professional.'

The man hesitated at hearing this, and then laughed. 'Is that a threat? Are you threatening me?'

'Just a piece of advice,' Alex said.

'Then, once again, *my* advice to *you* is to stay away from Remer. And while you're staying away from her, you can also stay away from that whore of a friend of hers, Lehman.'

The name meant nothing to Alex.

'Nina,' the older woman told him.

'Oh?' Alex said. 'And why is that?'

'You're interested now, are you?' the supervisor said. 'That got your interest, did it? Thinking that if you get nowhere with Remer, you might try your luck with Lehman?' He invested the word 'luck' with a cold, lascivious edge. None of the women who had shared his laughter earlier shared it now.

It surprised Alex to see how quickly the two of them had come to this confrontation, and he was still uncertain of the man's purpose in provoking it. But he guessed from his remarks about Nina that he knew less than he was suggesting about Eva and himself.

Alex took several paces towards him, and the man retreated to stand behind his desk.

'You think that'll save you?' Alex said.

The man rested both his hands on the clear surface, spreading his fingers. He was relieved that Alex had stopped moving towards him.

'Does anyone know where Eva Remer might be?' Alex asked the others. He felt brave, asking them openly like that, and knowing what it would suggest to them.

None of them answered him, most of them glancing at the supervisor before returning to their work.

The older woman touched Alex's arm. She alone seemed not to be cowed by the man. 'She went to the hospital,' she told him. 'To see Maria Lehman. Nina's been there since her sister was taken in from the camp. She lost her baby.'

'I know,' Alex said, acknowledging the woman's kindness and concern. 'Are there regular visiting hours. Am I too late?'

She looked at her watch. 'The director changes the rules all the time.'

'I can imagine,' Alex said.

Overhearing this exchange, the supervisor shouted, 'And he doesn't think much of pregnant children, either. Children made pregnant by foreigners who should have known better.'

'Ignore him,' the woman said to Alex. 'He treats this

188

place like his own pathetic little harem. Or he would do if any of them would have the slightest thing to do with him. He promises them work and then promotion. None of which ever comes, of course. You'd think they would have learned by now.'

'You listen to me, not her,' the supervisor called to Alex. 'She's no use to you, no use to anyone. Look at her.' Again, he laughed alone.

'He enjoys being cruel,' Alex said to the woman, and she smiled her concurrence at the remark. 'I'll go, and then at least you can all endure it without someone – me – looking on.'

'We don't *all* endure it,' she told him.

He held out his hand to her and she took it, surprised and gratified by the gesture.

'You can shake mine, too, if you like,' the supervisor called, making his meaning clear to the women closest to him.

As Alex finally turned to leave, the man said, 'Tell Lehman that if she isn't back at her desk tomorrow morning, then she can look for work elsewhere. You can tell her, like I'm telling you now, that my recommendations count for a lot here. You think Dyer is going to concern himself over something like this? No – he listens to me. Tell her to say goodbye to that other little whore in the family, and then to get herself back here.' He paused, pretending to think. 'In fact, you can tell the same to your beloved Eva. She should have been working late tonight, but instead she ran off to the hospital and her so-called friend at the first opportunity.'

'I told her she could go,' the older woman said. 'She was here late last night with the mayor.'

'So what?' the supervisor said. 'Perhaps all three of you ought to hike up your skirts and get back on the streets.'

This time, several of the others laughed.

Alex finally left the room, unwilling to prolong the woman's humiliation any longer. And unwilling, too, to listen to whatever further allegations the man might have been about to make concerning Eva.

He crossed the reception hall and left the building.

The transport compound was empty, and so he walked into Rehstadt, arriving at the hospital twenty minutes later.

It was a cool evening and few of the townspeople were out. He passed several bars, all as dimly lit as the station bar had been, and with as few customers. As he crossed the town square, the air was filled with the smell of roasting meat and he paused to breathe this in.

At the hospital entrance, he was surprised to see Nina Lehman sitting alone on the low wall there, her elbows on her knees, her head in her hands. She wore the same clothes she'd worn on their visit to the camp.

He went to her and sat beside her. She looked up at him, her face wet with tears.

'I'm sorry about the baby,' he told her.

She resumed crying at hearing the words, gasping for air. 'You're probably the only one,' she said.

'You don't believe that.'

She shook her head.

He put his arm around her and she immediately pulled herself free of him.

As he considered what to say next, Eva came to them from the hospital. She carried a steaming cloth, which she wrung out as she walked.

Alex rose and stood as though she was about to embrace him. But instead she held out the dripping cloth to prevent him from touching her.

'It's warm,' she said, giving it to Nina.

'I went to the office,' he said.

'I left.' She smiled at him. And then she held him briefly and pressed her cheek against his. Beside them, Nina held the wet cloth to her face.

'How's Maria?' he asked Eva.

'Not well. It's like Whittaker predicted. She has an infection. Her blood.' She motioned to Nina. 'She accused them of killing the baby and then of doing nothing to help her sister. I've spent the last two hours trying to persuade her she's wrong.'

'Don't forget the bit about me being ridiculous,' Nina said, finally composing herself. She sounded to Alex as though she might be drunk.

He looked at Eva, who nodded once and then sat beside her friend.

'They did all they could for the baby,' she said. 'And now they're doing all they can for Maria.'

Alex heard the forced conviction in her voice.

'She's my little sister,' Nina said.

'Of course she is,' Eva said. 'And soon she'll be well enough to leave. She can come back to live with you, and you can take care of her.'

'With me?' Nina said, as though the thought had not occurred to her.

'Of course. Where else?'

'She'll want to go back to the camp. She says it's where she feels most at home. With all those other gypsies and scroungers.' Saliva ran from the corner of her mouth as she spoke, and she wiped it away with the cloth. Steam still rose from its warmth.

'No, she won't,' Eva said. 'Besides, there are plans for the place to be emptied and then destroyed.'

'Are there?' Alex asked her, wondering if what she'd said had been invented for Nina's sake.

'Apparently. No one in the town likes it still being there. I imagine they think it's time everyone just went home, that they stopped being a problem here and became one somewhere else.'

'Even the ones who have no home to go to?' Alex said.

'Of course they've got homes to go to,' Nina shouted at him. 'They just don't want to go back to them, that's all. They'd rather hang around out there, playing the victim for ever and ever. Pretending it's all still happening, that they're all still a part of something big and important.'

'Ignore her,' Eva said to him. 'If the camp was closed, then Maria would have no choice but to live with her.'

Nina conceded this, but said nothing.

'A woman in your office told me where you were,' Alex said. He described the woman to Eva, hoping she might reveal something of why she had spoken out for her.

'She used to run the hotel,' Eva said. 'During the good years of the war, when it was a place for officers. She was in charge. Everything – housekeeping, the accounts, the staff, grounds, meals, everything. She's a good woman. She was good at what she did. Until the new supervisor arrived – another of the mayor's cronies – she was also in charge of the secretarial staff. I've known her since I was a small girl. She sometimes visits my father.'

'I'd like to meet him, too,' Alex said.

'I think she was a friend of my mother's,' Eva continued, as though he hadn't spoken. And then she fell silent and looked away from him.

'I said—'

'I heard what you said,' she told him. 'And I heard you last time, in the bar.'

'If he doesn't like visitors . . .' he said.

'It's not that.'

'Foreign visitors . . .'

'It's not that, either. It's just that he's an old man – or

193

that's how he seems. He's been through a lot the past few years.'

'His wife and son . . .'

'Stop trying to make it all sound so bloody simple and straightforward,' she said angrily, then checked herself. She held his arm and put her cheek back to his. 'I'll tell him you want to come and see us,' she said. 'All he needs is advance notice. He'll be pleased to see you. Leave it to me.'

He knew not to persist. He was happy to feel her so close to him. He could smell the soap he had given her. He wanted to raise his hand from her arm to her face, to kiss her properly.

Beside them, Nina said, 'Oh, God,' and started to retch.

Eva left Alex, knelt beside her friend and then held her so that she was leaning over the low wall.

Nina continued to retch, and then she vomited.

Eva spoke to her, stroking her hair away from her face. She rubbed her other hand in circles over Nina's back.

'Leave me alone,' Nina said. 'Both of you. Just go. Why are you even here?' She vomited again, but this time only a string of viscous saliva fell from her lips. 'That's the lot,' she said, half laughing and half coughing.

Eva sat her upright and wiped her face with the cloth.

'I'm sorry,' Nina said. 'I didn't mean any of that. Do you really think Maria will come to live with me? Honestly?'

'Of course she will,' Eva said. She helped Nina to her feet, motioning for Alex to hold her while she wiped her chest and hands. There was vomit on Nina's thin coat and on her shoes, and Eva wiped these clean too.

'Am I presentable?' Nina said. 'Is that what you're doing – making me presentable? A first time for everything, I suppose.' She let her head fall on to Alex's shoulder, and he smelled her sour breath. She tried to kiss him, which made Eva laugh. Then Nina clasped her hands around his neck, pulling him forward until Eva pushed herself between the two of them.

'Where now?' Nina said. 'Let's go for a drink.'

'Great idea,' Alex said, his meaning clear to Eva.

'She lives near by,' Eva told him. 'A few minutes.' She asked Nina if she could walk. Nina told them that of course she could walk, everybody could walk, why shouldn't she be able to, what did they think was wrong with her, it was her stupid fucking sister who had lost the stupid fucking baby, not her, so why shouldn't she be able to fucking walk? She faltered, close to tears again. 'Walk where?' she said.

'Wherever you like,' Eva told her. To Alex, she said, 'It was a girl. A baby girl.'

195

15

He next saw James Whittaker the following morning, sitting alone in the empty lobby, as he went down to prepare for the day ahead.

Whittaker sat on a low, ornate couch, rubbing his eyes. A blanket lay crumpled on the floor beside him.

Alex went to him. 'Did I wake you?'

Whittaker looked at his watch. 'I was working most of the night. I came back an hour ago and sat down for a moment. Someone must have put the blanket over me.'

Only then did Alex see the blood which stained the front of Whittaker's white coat, one arm of which was dotted red almost to the elbow. 'What happened?'

Whittaker rubbed his arm and a smear of red showed on his palm. 'An attempted suicide. New arrival.'

The instant he said this, for no obvious reason, Alex

thought of Johannes Walther. 'Anyone I might know?' he said, feigning a lack of concern.

Whittaker shrugged. It was rare that the two of them ever discussed their work or each day's routine in anything but the most general or dismissive of terms.

'Man called Menschler,' Whittaker said. 'One of the Einsatz lot. He's been in every camp this side of Moscow, just getting passed around to see who throws the most mud at him, I suppose.'

It was someone Alex had neither heard of nor seen.

'Arrived a week ago,' Whittaker went on. 'He's been left to stew in solitary for all that time. He's a nasty piece of work, our Mister Menschler. The Russians and Poles have started shouting loudly to get him back. One of your lot was due to start on him tomorrow, or the day after, or the day after.'

'But not now?'

'Unlikely. He managed to get hold of a piece of glass. Both wrists and then, superficially, his throat. Imagine that, doing one wrist then changing hands with the glass to do the other. The blood must have been pouring out before he was even halfway through.'

'Did he lose much?'

'Enough. It ran under his cell door, alerted the guard. He was in one of the tiled cubicles. By my reckoning, he lost half of what was in him.' He paused and smiled. 'Luckily, cross-matching it from our supplies was simple enough.' He raised his arm and tapped beneath his armpit.

'Is he still here?' Alex asked him.

Whittaker retrieved the blanket and roughly folded it. 'I wanted him taken to the town hospital. But others insisted otherwise. I stopped the bleeding and stitched and bandaged him up. Another one saved for the gallows.' He rose and stretched, rubbed his eyes and then the stubble on his neck. 'Menschler,' he said. 'He's called "The Murderer". Quite a distinction, that, apparently. A world full of murderers in a time full of murderers and he gets the epithet all to himself. I imagine it's something he might once even have been proud of. "Butcher" always seems so . . . melodramatic. "The Butcher of Riga", "The Butcher of Minsk".' He paused. 'Have you had any dealings with him?'

Alex shook his head.

A group of doctors and orderlies entered the hotel, acknowledged Whittaker where he sat, told him when he asked that Menschler was still alive, and then climbed the broad staircase together.

'I went to the hospital,' Alex said. 'I saw Nina.'

'Her sister would have lost the baby with or without the hospital,' Whittaker said. 'She was malnourished. She had the body of a ten-year-old child herself.'

'I imagined as much. Nina blames everyone involved.'

'She's no different from the rest of them – blaming everybody else for everything that's still wrong with the world. And if that's the case, then she's going to be angry for a long time to come. Perhaps for the rest of her life.'

Alex described for Whittaker the room to which he and Eva had helped Nina return. It had been bare apart from a bed, a dresser and a solitary chair. No curtains, no carpets. Nina's few clothes had hung on hangers behind the door. The blankets on the bed were American Army issue. Candles on saucers were her only illumination. There was no heating, and the closest running water came from a tap on the floor beneath. Alex had filled a bowl and an enamel jug and carried these back up to Eva, who had half undressed her friend and then tried to coax her into her cold bed. Nina had been sick again, first on the stairs, and then on the landing outside her room.

'What did you expect?' Whittaker asked him. 'This kind of four-star luxury?' He waved his arm at the room around them, at its grand proportions, its faded splendour.

Alex looked at the skulls and antlers high above the empty fireplace.

'Whatever it was, it was better than her sister was used to at the camp,' Whittaker went on. He took a deep breath, and just as it seemed to Alex that he was about to leave, he gave an involuntary gasp, put out his arm and fell backwards, landing hard against the sofa. He regained his composure almost immediately, looking at Alex in surprise at what had just happened.

'Are you all right?' Alex picked up the blanket Whittaker had dropped.

Whittaker blinked and slowly shook his head from side to side. 'Just exhausted. I felt faint for a second, that's all.' He then sat with his head down, breathing deeply. 'I shan't be unhappy at seeing the back of this place,' he said eventually.

'I never realized you were so close to the end of your posting,' Alex said.

'It ended officially two months ago. My successor got dropped into the machinery at one end and never re-appeared at the other. The last I heard, he was still in Berlin, part of somebody else's little regime. I was asked, cajoled, told, persuaded to stay here until a replacement replacement could be found.'

'By Dyer?'

'Who else?'

'You're an important man,' Alex said. 'How would the place run without you?'

Whittaker laughed. 'How indeed?' He lit a cigarette. 'Of course I'm an important man. And you're right – the whole shoddy edifice will come crumbling down the moment I walk through the gates with my bags.' His disillusionment became clearer to Alex with everything he said.

'With a spring in your step and a song in your heart?' Alex said.

'Naturally.'

'You'll be missed,' Alex said.

'Perhaps. But I can't pretend that this is what I ever

imagined I'd be doing a year after the war's end.'

'You think your skills are being wasted here?'

'Taping up suicides so they can walk to the noose? What do you think? I spent four months in proper military hospitals before I came here. In Bremen, Dortmund and Essen. At least there I was part of something useful, something moving forward, something which dragged itself up out of the mire every now and again.'

'And here you're not?'

'Here I'm the highly qualified stitcher-upper who puts his stamp of competence and authority, of even-handedness and respectability on everything Dyer and his minions tell me to do. I look at the wounds, cuts and bruises, and I bandage them over.'

'"Minions" including me? It was "lackey" before.'

Whittaker smiled. 'You're minion number, oh, a hundred and fifty. No, not you. Others. You'd be surprised how many cuts and bruises some civilized conversations can result in.' He turned to look at Alex. 'Now I've said too much and offended you. Ignore me. Like I said – I'm just exhausted. I just want to go home. I want there to be something else, something more. I want to be able to walk away from things. I want to be able to walk from one room into another and have things change.'

'You miss your wife and daughters,' Alex said.

Whittaker considered the remark. 'And I miss my wife and daughters,' he said. He intoned their names to himself. 'To hear Dyer respond each time I ask him if he's heard anything about my replacement, you'd think he wanted to try me for treason. Is it too much to ask, just to want to go home? For the world to stand still, even if it's only for a few days, and for us all to get back to where we started? Don't you ever feel the same?'

Alex considered this.

'Oh, I forgot – perhaps not now that you and Eva have found each other.'

Both men laughed at the remark.

'Ignore me,' Whittaker said again. 'I'm jealous. Not of her; of your happiness, or whatever it is. Look, I'm going to try and stand again. Give me your arm.'

This time Whittaker rose and was able to stand unaided for a few seconds. 'There – cured,' he said. Alex held his arm as he retrieved his blanket.

Alex was about to suggest meeting him again at the end of the day, when a young soldier entered the hotel, came to them, stood to attention and saluted.

Neither Alex nor Whittaker responded to this, and the soldier repeated the gesture.

This time, Alex saluted back.

'Let me guess,' Whittaker said to the youth. 'You're new here.'

He looked no more than sixteen or seventeen, like many of them those days. Conscripts to a war gone by.

'Arrived here yesterday, Sir.' He held his hand to his

temple for longer than was necessary. 'Only my first week overseas. Active Service, Sir.'

'Is that what they call it?' Whittaker said.

The remark confused the boy, and then made him wary of them.

'I'm looking for Captain Foster, Sir.'

Whittaker pointed at Alex and the boy turned to face him.

'Colonel Dyer's compliments, Sir.'

'His what?' Whittaker said.

'His compliments, Sir. He wondered if you could join him right away.'

'That's a "jump" and a "now",' Whittaker said to Alex. To the boy, he said, 'Tell Colonel Dyer that Captain Foster sends his best wishes and that he will be along presently. Perhaps morning tea on the terrace might be nice.'

'That's all I was told to say,' the boy said.

'Tell Dyer I'll be right behind you,' Alex said.

'Sir.' He made no attempt to leave them. 'Colonel Dyer said I should wait and accompany you, Sir.'

'So, "jump", "now" and "absolutely no diverting left or right",' Whittaker said.

Alex had been due to meet with Dyer, and possibly Preston, later in the day, and this early summons caught him unawares.

'I'd better go,' he said to Whittaker.

'Of course you had,' Whittaker said. 'Me, too.' He

pulled back his shoulders and finally saluted the boy, who eagerly returned the gesture.

Whittaker left them.

'He looks done in,' the boy said, watching as Whittaker climbed the stairs, his hand on the rail, pausing after every few steps.

'He is,' Alex told him.

A few minutes later, the two of them arrived at Dyer's office. The soldier announced Alex's name to the sergeant sitting at the door.

'Urgent delivery, is it?' the sergeant said, as amused as Whittaker had been by the boy's eagerness. He knocked once on the door, pushed it open and called Alex's name in to Dyer.

Alex went in.

Amos Preston stood at the window, looking down at the garden, his briefcase at his feet.

Dyer rose from his desk. 'You already know Colonel Preston,' he said to Alex, almost in warning.

Preston turned to greet him.

'I understood our meeting was arranged for later,' Alex said.

Preston smiled at the remark. 'Sometimes these arrangements get . . .'

'Rearranged?' Dyer suggested.

'Precisely,' Preston said. He indicated a seat beside his own. 'I take it you've had the opportunity to talk to our Captain Walther,' he said to Alex.

'I've seen him twice,' Alex said. 'But it's still early days.'

Preston repeated the phrase, understood what Alex was telling him and held up his hands. 'My apologies. I didn't mean to question your capabilities. I merely . . .' He let the sentence trail off, its work done.

'This isn't about Walther,' Dyer said, surprising Alex, and suggesting to him that Dyer, as at their previous meeting with Preston, was again unhappy at not being more directly involved in what was happening, that he was not, as everywhere else in his small domain, directing and controlling the encounter.

'Oh?' Alex said, his attention still on Preston.

'Of course we're still more than interested in Walther,' Preston said. 'Colonel Dyer here is wrong – I would have gotten round to Walther. But, as you might have already deduced from this ridiculously early hour, I do have a somewhat more pressing concern.'

Alex heard the evasion in his voice.

'Someone else we want you to see,' Dyer said.

'Man called Ochmann-Schur. Joachim Ochmann-Schur. *Von* Ochmann-Schur. Oberstgruppenführer der Waffen SS. He's turned up here. Christ knows how, but here he is. He's been here for a few days.'

'Six,' Dyer said.

'I haven't seen him,' Alex said, looking from one man to the other.

'That's the point,' Preston said, smiling. 'No one has. He's been a "mid-priority" for all this time. And now, all of a sudden, our Russian friends are screaming in my ear that *they* want him and that they want him now.'

'In connection with what?' Alex said.

'In connection with things they are not currently letting me – us – in on. Except to let me know that Ochmann-Schur is very definitely the man they want, and that he has very definitely committed the crimes they want him for.'

'Meaning you've already looked through his files and uncovered what those crimes are?' Alex said. It was only half a question. *Another bargaining tool*, he thought. Another polite and protocol-filled little drama with either the shadow of the noose on the wall or the sound of a firing squad in a distant high-walled yard somewhere towards the end of the third act. Far enough away to seem avoidable, and yet always close enough to be within earshot and inescapable.

'I know what you're thinking, Captain Foster,' Preston said. 'More back-scratching. And you're right. But, believe me – it's how these things work. I was hoping you might have understood that better by now.'

'Then why not just take him and hand him over to them?' Alex said.

Preston smiled again. 'Because that's exactly how these things *don't* work. Procedure needs to be observed. He's your detainee, he was arrested by you in the first instance in your zone. Until he's been seen by you and either released or recommended for further action, then nothing's going to happen. Besides, Ochmann-Schur probably knows this – and his rights – better than any of us. He's that sort.'

'And once those recommendations *are* made?'

'Then he becomes someone else's responsibility,' Preston said. 'Ours.'

'After which, it's up to you what happens to him?'

'It's all a lot more straightforward than you're making it sound. We're handing him over to the Russians. It's as simple as that.'

'Except by then you'll once again be doing it with our blessing; we'll be complicit in whatever it is you've already decided to do.'

Dyer watched Alex closely as he said all this, not entirely certain whether he was confirming what Preston had just suggested, or if he was objecting to it.

Preston looked coldly at Alex. 'Tell me, how else do you imagine it works, Captain Foster?'

'And is that how it's working for Walther?'

'That all depends on you, I would imagine,' Preston said, unconcerned.

'But either way, Walther will come to you in the end and you'll get exactly what you want out of him.'

Preston considered the remark before speaking. 'You'll have guessed by now that the bulk of Walther's file remains elsewhere, yes?'

Alex nodded.

'Then suppose I was able to show you a frame of film

207

in which Walther is clearly identifiable as a man with his pistol held to the back of a kneeling man's head. Suppose I was able to show you a photograph – more, a dozen photographs, a hundred – of Walther with his buddies posing over a field of executed corpses.'

'Then show me them,' Alex said.

'I said "suppose", Captain Foster. "Suppose".'

'So they *don't* exist?'

Exasperated, Preston raised his voice. 'That's not the point I'm trying to make here. The point I'm trying to make is that you – you, personally, your whole outfit and operation here – you can rest easy that nothing will be done to Walther – to anyone – once they leave here that someone else doesn't already have a damn good reason for doing.'

It was the first time Preston had lost his composure, and Dyer clearly appreciated seeing this.

'You can have my word on that,' Preston said. 'And if *my* word isn't good enough—'

'What? You'll show me the photos?' Alex said. 'The photos that might or might not exist? But which you still couldn't resist mentioning to me, sowing the seeds of doubt? All we're doing for you is going through the motions so that—'

Dyer slapped both his palms on his desk and shouted at Alex to shut up.

Alex stopped talking.

'Gentlemen . . .' Dyer said. But that was the limit of his powers of intervention.

No one spoke for several minutes.

'I could ask the Russians to let you see what they've got on Ochmann-Schur,' Preston said eventually, his tone conciliatory.

Alex shook his head.

Preston took a file from his case. It was as thin as the one he had handed over on Walther. 'Just a few details to get you started. He served in Russia until the spring of forty-three. There's no question about that. I've underlined a few of the places and dates you might want to mention to him.' He handed the file to Alex, and as he did so he turned to Dyer and said, 'We heard about Menschler, by the way. He survive?'

Dyer clearly knew nothing of what had happened in the cells during the night. 'I, er – I can—'

'He's still alive,' Alex said.

'Good,' Preston said. 'By all accounts he was a real butcher.'

'He's known as The Murderer,' Alex said. 'Apparently, there's still a distinction to be made.'

'I'm sure there is,' Preston said. 'And I'm sure it's one Menschler is keen to maintain.'

Even after trying to kill himself? Alex thought. He rose from his seat, surprising Dyer. 'I'd better get started,' he said.

'Thank you,' Preston said, interrupting Dyer, who was

about to speak, and he held out his hand to Alex. 'And my sincere apologies for my outburst earlier. I truly do appreciate all you're doing for us. It might perhaps seem corrupt or misguided to you for us to be doing things this way, but we're looking for a few favours from Ivan ourselves, and something like this Ochmann-Schur business will put us in *his* good books for once.'

'Still looking for your rocket men, then?' Alex said.

The remark caught Preston off guard and his laughter was a second too late.

'And here's me thinking it was all a big secret,' he said. 'Something like that. We've got most of the ones we want. But, who knows, there might still be one or two out there that no one has yet bagged for themselves.'

'Meaning there's definitely someone, that the Russians have got him without the faintest idea of who he is, and that they'll trade him for Ochmann-Schur.'

'We'll fly to the moon one day,' Preston told him. 'And believe me when I tell you – I'm as convinced of *that* as I am of the guilt of Walther, Menschler and Ochmann-Schur.'

'Or any combination?'

Preston considered the remark. 'Take your pick,' he said.

Alex left them and went to where Ochmann-Schur would now be waiting for him.

Outside, on the terrace, parked precisely where he

had been two days earlier, he saw Jesus Hernandez and his small crowd of eager customers.

Hernandez noticed him and came to him.

'Won't they ransack your wares?' Alex said.

'Wares? Yeah, sure. They know better. Steal from Jesus and they get their fingers broken.'

'Charming.'

'No, it's not charming. It's a fact. A dirty, fucking, painful fact. And here's me trying to be friendly. I only came over to see if there was anything I could do for you. Who knows, I might even have another free little gift for you.'

'As opposed to one that would cost me the earth?' Alex said. He turned away from the man and continued walking.

Hernandez laughed at the remark. 'You know where to find me.' He returned to the crowd at his jeep and shouted for them to back off, to give him room, to give him their money and to go.

16

The narrow corridor was more crowded with men than usual. All the doors were closed. Shouting could be heard through one of these, and those sitting close to it strained to hear what was being said. The prisoners sat mostly in silence; the guards laughed in an exaggerated manner at everything they heard.

Alex negotiated his way through the waiting men. Some drew in their feet for him, some did not. The few men he recognized, guards and prisoners alike, acknowledged him as he passed them.

At the end of the corridor, opposite his own closed door, sat a man in full uniform, a guard on either side of him. The man sat upright, looking directly ahead. And even when he could not have been unaware of Alex's approach, he still refused to look at him.

In turn, Alex ignored him as he unlocked his door.

'Ochmann-Schur?' he said to the guards.

'*Von* Ochmann-Schur,' the man between them said.

Ignoring the remark, Alex repeated the name.

'This is him,' one of the guards said. 'It's just "Ochmann" on the docket.'

'Ochmann it is, then,' Alex said.

Ochmann-Schur began to rise to his feet, but was pulled back down by both men.

'You stay sitting until you're told to stand,' Alex said to him, his back to the man. 'And wait.'

He went into the room alone.

Like Walther's, the file he had been given contained very little. A succession of places and dates, few more specific than signifying months. The initials CPA were repeated in several margins. Counter-Partisan Activity. It signified a great deal in general and a few things specifically. To Alex, it was little more than a starting point, something with which to prod Ochmann-Schur.

He waited a further ten minutes before calling for the man, during which time he was rewarded with the sight of Eva and Nina crossing the grass beneath him. He opened his window and called down to them.

Both waved back to him. He asked Eva if he would see her later, and she said she'd wait for him. He was reassured by the enthusiasm he heard in her voice, and by her lack of inhibition in responding to him so publicly. It was a clear, bright day and there were others on the grass, and most had turned to look up at his call.

He shouted to Nina that he was pleased to see her back at work.

'Happier than me,' Nina called to him.

Eva indicated the files they were both carrying and the two women continued on their way.

Opening his door, he said, 'Ochmann,' again, and taking their cue from Alex, the guards jerked the man roughly to his feet, coordinating their actions so that their every movement caused the man pain.

Ochmann-Schur rose without speaking, bending his head to replace his cap. One of the guards immediately took this from his head and pushed it back into his hands.

'No headwear,' he said. 'Manners. Where was you brought up?' The two men and other guards along the corridor laughed at this. Alex saw that none of the waiting prisoners shared in this small indignity, and that those sitting closest to Ochmann-Schur avoided looking at him completely.

'Bring him in,' Alex said.

Inside, he directed Ochmann-Schur to a seat, motioning for the guards to release him.

'You sure?' one asked him.

'What's he going to do?' Alex asked him, the question more for Ochmann-Schur's benefit than the guard's.

'He's top priority,' the other guard said.

Alex wondered if this were true. Or if the guard himself had promoted the man. Or if Preston had again been lying to him. The file was still stamped on every page with the designation M-P – mid-priority.

Ochmann-Schur, Alex saw, took a small pleasure in this exchange and the confusion it caused. He waited with his arms held out from his waist for the two men to release him.

In the first few months of Alex's work at the Institute, when there had been considerably more high-priority prisoners there, it had not been uncommon for these men to be delivered for questioning wearing both hand-cuffs and shackles, the latter never being unlocked, and frequently being used to fasten the prisoners to the chairs upon which they sat.

'Thank you, Captain,' Ochmann-Schur said.

'Speak when you're spoken to,' Alex told him.

Ochmann-Schur's uniform, Alex saw, had been stripped of none of its insignia of rank or status, and bore a full complement of campaign ribbons and medals. All it lacked were the higher medals he would undoubtedly have been awarded over the past six years. It was a rare sight. Few of the others possessed more than a badly fitting shirt or pair of trousers by the time they arrived in Rehstadt.

'Sit down,' Alex told him.

'Thank you.'

The guards waited, uncertain of whether to leave or stay.

'You can wait outside,' Alex told them, noting their reluctance to do this.

Ochmann-Schur smiled.

Alex saw this and said immediately, 'But cuff him to the chair first.'

Ochmann-Schur started to protest, but stopped himself.

'Common practice,' Alex told him, his face expressionless.

'Oh, really?' Ochmann-Schur said.

'Either the guards stay and you remain cuffed to them, or they go and you get the chair. Either way, it's my choice, not yours.'

The guards fastened the man to the chair as roughly as they had pulled him into the room.

'What about his feet?' one of them asked Alex.

Alex considered this. 'Attach one of them,' he said.

The man knelt and secured one of Ochmann-Schur's ankles to the chair.

'Is all this entirely necessary?' Ochmann-Schur asked Alex in German.

'Is he complaining again?' one of the guards said. 'What did I tell you – no manners.'

Alex told them to leave and they went, pulling the door firmly shut behind them.

Ochmann-Schur waited without speaking. He looked slowly around the room, as they all did, along the lines of the ceiling, into each of its high corners, around the skirting and the window frames.

'I imagine everything I say is being recorded and overheard elsewhere,' he said.

'Imagine what you like,' Alex told him. He read again the few details of the file.

'May I ask,' Ochmann-Schur asked him, as Alex was about to start. 'How is poor Menschler?'

'You know him?'

Ochmann-Schur smiled at the small trap. '*Of* him. I know *of* him. By reputation.'

'Then I imagine he knows of you in the same way,' Alex said.

Ochmann-Schur seemed genuinely surprised and offended by the suggestion. 'I fear you may be confusing me with someone else, Captain Foster.'

'Or perhaps not just "someone" else. Perhaps thousands of others. Why "poor" Menschler?'

'I thought that much would be obvious. Especially to you.'

This last remark made Alex curious. 'Tell me anyway,' he said.

'All those years of devotion and conviction, and then this? Put poor Menschler up against a wall and blindfold him and he'll probably thank you.'

'And if I had the power to ensure *you* ended up against that same wall?'

Ochmann-Schur considered the remark. 'Is that what you think? Unlikely, wouldn't you say? However, I shall convey your veiled threat to my lawyer.'

'Who is?' Alex said. He opened the file again.

'If I may observe, your records seem woefully inadequate for the task at hand, Captain Foster.'

'Who is?'

'Doctor Seidl.'

Alex shook his head at the name.

'Seidl. Sauter's second. Hans Frank's counsel. At Nuremberg. Seidl is working with Sauter.'

'What, and when they've finished with Frank they come here to save *your* neck?'

'Here, wherever,' Ochmann-Schur said.

'No one's coming to save you, Ochmann.'

'Whatever you say.'

Alex read out the places and dates listed in the inadequate file.

'So?' Ochmann-Schur said. 'I served in the East. I did my duty. I did what was asked of me. The same as you are doing now. Some places I recognize, some I do not. Names change. I'm a soldier. It was a long war. Not for you, perhaps, but for many of us.'

'Did what was asked of you? You were an Obergruppenführer. You acted on your own initiative,' Alex said.

Ochmann-Schur laughed. 'You must surely have learned a few things about the German Army after all this time, Captain Foster.'

'You acted on your own initiative,' Alex insisted. 'And there are plenty of people – Germans and others – now ready and willing to testify to that effect against you.'

218

'What, the same people queuing up to condemn Menschler? I doubt it. I was a soldier, I *am* a soldier. I carried out my orders. That is not an excuse or an evasion, incidentally, simply a statement of fact.'

'You persecuted civilians and took excessive action against non-combatants.'

'Partisans, Captain Foster. My work was fighting soldier-partisans.'

Alex smiled at the term. He knew how unsatisfactory his own provocation had been.

Neither man spoke for a minute.

Then Ochmann-Schur said, 'What did you hope I was going to tell you? Did you think I would confess to everything you call a crime, and be pleased to do so? "War Crime" – what a tangle of unhappy contradictions that ridiculous phrase contains. Or did you perhaps think I might have hatched myself the perfect excuse, like your good friend Captain Walther?'

Alex looked up at the mention of Walther's name.

'Ah, I see I finally have your interest,' Ochmann-Schur said.

'You know nothing about Walther,' Alex said. He tried to remember exactly what, if anything, Preston might have told him regarding Ochmann-Schur's recent history prior to arriving in Rehstadt.

'Oh? You seem very certain of that. Perhaps I knew him while the war was still being fought. Perhaps he and I obeyed the same orders, undertook the same actions.'

'Actions?' Alex said. It was a slip on Ochmann-Schur's part, and he wanted the man to know that he understood what he was saying.

'The same campaigns, battles.'

'You said actions,' Alex said.

Ochmann-Schur shook his head slowly. 'So? You think everything was so clear-cut or so noble as to be called a battle? Go ahead – ask me your questions, Captain.' He paused. 'May I ask again, *is* a full record being kept of everything that passes between us?'

Alex ignored the remark. 'And you executed civilians as part of these actions,' he said.

'I participated in the suppression of partisan activity. They killed us, we killed them. Sometimes they executed us and sometimes we executed them. It really was that simple, and they understood the rules of these engagements as well as we did. Whatever else they were, they were no longer civilians, I can assure you of that. It was war, and that is how wars are fought. Again, these are not excuses I am making. And certainly not excuses for myself, for my own behaviour. Yes, I was at Kovno, Dvinsk and Ostrov. You say Polotsk. I think you certainly have me confused with someone else where Polotsk is concerned.'

The remark was enough to create doubt; it was why Ochmann-Schur had made it, and Alex understood this. There was an asterisk beside the place in the file, signifying that someone elsewhere had already considered that it might be central to Ochmann-Schur's questioning.

Alex listed more places, and the man agreed to having served in or close to all of them.

'There are eye-witness accounts of everything that happened,' Alex told him. It was another regrettable signal of uncertainty to Ochmann-Schur.

'I'm sure there are,' Ochmann-Schur said, reassured. 'And perhaps I could produce my own eye-witnesses to refute everything that these others have said. Where are they, these witnesses? Are they here? Are they the ones gloating at the sight of the blood running out of poor old Menschler's slit wrists? No, I thought not. Peasants, mostly. Peasants and cowards. Give them to Seidl, let him deal with them.'

'Frank will hang,' Alex said.

Ochmann-Schur shook his head. 'No, he won't. They already know who they are going to hang. And the ones they need to be seen to punish. And the few to whom they are now going to show their magnanimity. A game, Captain Foster. Just like this one here. You know it as well as I do, and if you deny what I'm saying, then I can only conclude that you understand this particular game – shall we call it a "charade" – better than most.' He laughed. 'Eye-witnesses? What do you take me for?'

Alex sensed that a balance had been tipped between them, and he knew, too, how little his questioning would now achieve because of this. Ochmann-Schur clearly considered himself impregnable. It was why he still wore his full dress-uniform complete with its insignia and ribbons.

Alex left his desk and went back to the window. The lawn below was now empty. A line of prisoners walked slowly across the terrace, back and forth, exercising. Their guards sat on the stone wall and shouted at them.

He turned back to Ochmann-Schur, who looked directly at him.

'Having spoken to Johannes Walther, I imagined you might show me a little more consideration,' Ochmann-Schur said. 'A little more civility. That you might have considered a little more closely what I might have had to reveal to you. But in truth, I see that you are no different from any of the others. Perhaps you should indulge yourself a little. Perhaps you, too, want to slap me across my face. Or perhaps if that is beyond you – and what, after all, can we expect from non-combatants? – then you might want to suggest to the two cavemen waiting outside to help me fall down the stairs or walk into my cell door. How clumsy so many of us appear to be these days.' He closed his eyes briefly.

'They're handing you over to the Russians,' Alex said.

Ochmann-Schur opened his eyes. 'What? What did you say?'

Alex sighed. 'I said they're-handing-you-over-to-the-Russians.'

'Impossible. I am a prisoner of—'

'All those non-existent eye-witnesses. Most of them – the ones who don't grunt like pigs, that is – only speak Russian.'

'The Geneva Convention stipulates—'

Alex laughed at hearing the words. 'Go on – tell me.'

But Ochmann-Schur refused to continue. For the first time, he pulled at his tethered hands.

'Perhaps you could tell the Russians what you've told me. I'm sure they'll understand better – them being combatants, so to speak – what you're trying to convince *me* of. Perhaps they'll even agree with you about war being war and all that. Perhaps by then you'll even have remembered everything about your time at Polotsk.'

Alex returned to his desk.

'I wish Seidl to be informed immediately,' Ochmann-Schur shouted at him.

'All in due time. You know how slowly we non-combatants work.'

'You must tell him to inform the Russian authorities that under no circumstances are they to—'

'Tell them yourself,' Alex said. 'I daresay they'll be here far sooner than Seidl is able to let go of Frank's hand and come to hold your own.' He closed the file and tapped its edge on his desk. 'I think that concludes our business today. I want to thank you for your honesty and your courtesy. It was a pleasure meeting you.' He pretended to yawn. And then he called for the guards, who came immediately.

The two men unfastened Ochmann-Schur from the chair and then secured his wrists to their own. Ochmann-Schur said nothing as they did this, his eyes fixed on Alex.

'Looks like you've upset him, Captain Foster,' one of the guards said.

'Oh, I doubt that,' Alex said, looking directly at Ochmann-Schur as he spoke.

17

Eva was waiting for him outside the hotel. She stood with a group of other women and girls, and she signalled to him the instant she saw him. An outer circle of soldiers and clerks surrounded the group. Alex searched to see if Nina Lehman was among the women, but he couldn't see her.

When he was close, Eva held his arm and kissed him quickly on the cheek. Several of the men who knew Alex called to him, and the women close to Eva laughed good-naturedly at their remarks.

'Ignore them,' she told him, and he saw that she, too, was enjoying this attention.

'It's good to see you,' he said.

'Of course it is. I thought I'd surprise you.'

'Does that mean you're free for the evening?'

She fluttered her hand.

'Meaning?' His first thought was that she'd already arranged to return to see Nina and her sister.

'Meaning I told my father – the old man of the woods – that we might be having a guest for dinner.' She drew back from him and watched him closely.

'Me?' he said.

'Whittaker said you had a fondness for stating the obvious.'

'I have a fondness for you,' he said, and she lowered her eyes briefly in acknowledgement of this.

When she looked up at him, she said, 'Well?'

He told her he would take the satchel he was carrying to his room and change his shirt.

'You don't have to,' she said. 'I doubt he'll be polishing the best cutlery or getting the Meissen dinner service out.'

'Still . . .'

'I'll wait for you here,' she said.

For a moment, Alex considered taking her hand and telling her to come up to his room with him. But he saw that the gesture would have been misjudged in front of all these others.

As though sensing his intentions, she pushed him and said, 'Go. I'm not the kind of woman to be kept waiting.'

He left her, and as he entered the hotel, she crossed to join the other women, many of whom abandoned their circle of admirers and went to talk to her.

When Alex emerged a few minutes later, she came to him accompanied by three others.

'I said we'd give them a lift into town,' she said, raising her eyebrows to let him know that she had been given no choice in the matter.

'They probably want to check me over,' Alex said in German, prompting a chorus of amused denials from the women, one of whom held his arm and smoothed her hand across his clean shirt. She told Eva to pass him on to her when she'd finished with him. Another of the women held Alex's other arm and asked him where they would live in England when they were married.

At first he misunderstood her, believing her to be talking about Eva and himself. He looked at Eva and said he hadn't given the matter any thought.

'Not *her*,' the woman said, slapping him. '*Me*. Where will you and *I* live in England when we're married?'

Realizing his mistake, Alex started to make several guesses.

The woman told him she would live anywhere except in a city.

'Why not?' Alex asked her, and then understood. 'In the country, then. We'll live in the country.' He tried to catch Eva's eye, but she avoided him.

The woman said she accepted his proposal.

Then the third woman pulled her from Alex's arm and took her place. 'Ignore her,' she told him. 'This time

227

last week she was all ready to leave for New York. New York's a city.'

'Oh?' Alex said. 'What happened?'

'What happened,' the second woman said, 'was that my ticket left without me.' She burst into laughter, and Eva and the two others joined her.

He walked at their centre to the jeeps, and after a journey of only a few minutes they arrived in the town square, where the three women climbed out. They embraced and kissed Eva and then walked together arm in arm towards the closest bar.

'You have a lot of friends,' he said when they were again alone.

'Not as many as they have,' she said, watching as the women, now calling out to those around them, diverted from their path towards another group of soldiers standing at the rear of an open lorry.

Leaving the town, they drove through the trees to the crossroads.

The track leading to Ameldorf was heavily rutted, with a central strip of high grass. In places, the ruts were filled with water; elsewhere, stones had been set into the soft surface like cobbles.

'It's a back road,' Eva told him. 'The true road enters the village from the other direction, off the Minden road. We live at the edge of the place. This way's quicker.'

They drove for a further half mile, crossing a patch of open land and then diverting towards a slight rise topped with a crown of high trees, silhouetted now against the evening light.

A scatter of buildings stood beneath this, a house and several outbuildings, flanked with a long shed roofed with corrugated iron. Pale smoke rose from the chimneys at either end of the house.

Alex drove across a flagged yard to where Eva indicated.

The door to the house was open and he followed her inside.

The room was empty. One of the two windows was also covered with corrugated iron.

'Smashed,' she said, meaning the window. 'Something else on my father's list of things to never actually quite get around to doing.' She called for her father, but received no reply.

The room was low-ceilinged and crowded with old, heavy furniture. A fire burned at one end, a mound of ash and embers spilling on to its broad stone hearth. At the opposite end stood a cast-iron stove, its doors open, and the fire inside burning fiercely. A stack of logs stood against the walls beside each blaze.

'One thing we have plenty of – wood,' Eva said.

'You own some of the forest?'

'Ten acres, down to the river from the hill.' She spoke as though he was already familiar with the features.

She opened a door and called up a narrow staircase, but there was still no reply.

A long table filled the centre of the room, cluttered with the crockery and remains of previous meals. Eva shook her head at seeing this. Tools lay on the surface between the plates, and here and there lay small mounds of wood shavings.

'You might say my father's priorities lie elsewhere,' she said, clearly disappointed by the state of the room and the preparation which might have been planned in advance of Alex's arrival, but which had clearly not taken place.

She went to the doorway and called out over the yard, stopping at the sound of distant humming. She came back in to him.

'He's in the stone-yard,' she said. 'Working.' She sat at the table. 'He promised that either he or Kurt would do something before we returned.'

Alex sat beside her and put his arm around her. 'It doesn't matter,' he said. 'It'll still be a pleasure to meet him.'

'Why will it? Because he's my father?'

He considered the question. 'Yes – because he's your father.' And he held her gaze to convince her of this.

The distant machine continued humming, and after a few minutes this changed to a much louder, harsher, grating sound.

Eva rose from the table and told him to follow her.

They crossed the yard and entered a gate in a high wall. This hung loosely from its hinges and she held it clear of him as he stooped to negotiate it.

'Something else he never got around to,' she said.

Ahead of them lay a much larger yard, a workplace, surrounded on two sides by low, open sheds. Timber lay on exposed shelves, and the floors were coated in shavings and dust. Blocks of stone stood out in the open, some already cut into cubes, others with only a single dressed edge. Further blocks had been carved into rectangles and curves, and these stood stacked on pallets as though awaiting collection.

The noise was much louder in this second yard, amplified by the roof of the shed in which the cutting machine stood.

Eva indicated this to him, and then the man who came briefly into view through the cloud of dust the machine created.

She led Alex to the centre of the yard, stopping him at the edge of the dispersing cloud. She cupped her hands to her mouth and called to her father, but he now stood with his back to them and still couldn't hear her above the noise. He wore a cap with flaps fastened over his ears. On the machine in front of him a circular saw cut a clean plane along a piece of raw stone. It was close to completing its slow work. Water fell on to the blade from a slender spout.

They waited. A minute later the blade was through the stone and its pitch changed again before the man reached across the stone and silenced it.

Still unaware of his daughter's presence, he then came

out of the shed brushing the dust from his arms and chest, keeping his head down and spitting heavily to clear his throat.

He was a few paces from them, stamping the dust from his boots, when he finally became aware of them watching him. He took off his cap, pushed it into his pocket and approached them.

Eva embraced him, coming away from her father coated in the same pale dust. He tried to keep her away from him, but she insisted. She introduced him to Alex.

Alex held out his hand and the man took it. The dust and grains of stone were everywhere. The man apologized for this and offered Alex his handkerchief.

'Don't touch it; it's disgusting,' Eva said, her voice loud in the suddenly silent space.

Her father studied the filthy cloth he held. Alex took it from him, wiped his hand and gave it back.

'You'd forgotten we were coming,' Eva said to her father.

'You said seven,' he said.

She held up her watch to him. It was half past.

'Ah,' he said. Turning to Alex, he said, 'Captain Foster, my apologies. I was busy. I lose track of time. And some days, believe me, that's a blessing.'

Alex assured him that it didn't matter. He asked if he could look more closely at the block he'd been working on, and the two of them went back to the machine, leaving Eva alone in the yard.

'My name is Peter,' the man said as he and Alex stood at the cutting table. He wore a thick leather apron with a broad belt, into which several chisels and other, unfamiliar tools were pushed. He reached into a pocket beneath the apron and took out a small silver flask, which he offered to Alex. 'For the dust,' he said, smiling at the excuse.

Alex took the flask, drank from it and handed it back. Peter Remer drained its remaining contents in a single swallow.

'Is she still watching us?' he asked Alex.

Eva was watching them closely and had seen everything.

'I think so,' Alex told him.

The man shook his head slowly. 'She sees everything,' he said. He turned and held up the flask to his daughter, tipping and shaking it to show her it was empty. 'She disapproves,' he said. 'I'm not a drinker, not like some.'

Alex asked him about the piece of stone on which he'd been working.

'Church work,' Peter Remer said, a mixed note of pride and achievement in his voice. 'I have several commissions – from the elders in the town and from other towns near by. I doubt I shall grow as rich as the masons in the cities, but it's work. I specialize in ornamental masonry. Finials, arches, decorative windows.' He indicated a mound of blank slabs. 'And gravestones, of course. Lots of gravestones.'

'Eva told me you used to be mayor of Rehstadt,' Alex said.

'*Used* to be,' Peter Remer said, making it clear that it was all he wanted to say on the matter. He looked again to where his daughter stood. 'I was supposed to have prepared something for us to eat, wasn't I?'

'Yes, you were,' Eva called to him. There was no anger in her voice, only a sense of accustomed frustration. 'I'll do it now.' She turned and walked out of the yard, leaving the two men alone, each as awkward as the other in her absence.

'I'm sorry for the loss of your wife and your son,' Alex said.

'Thank you.' Peter Remer looked around him, spitting again and wiping the dust from his eyes. 'Eva says I work too hard, and that I only work at all to keep my thoughts occupied and away from their otherwise morbid course.'

It seemed a strangely formal revelation to make.

'Goethe,' Peter Remer said. '*Young Werther*. He's a great favourite of mine. Eva can't stand him. She looks ahead, you see, not back. And I, as you can see, I am more of a grandfather than a father to her. And even more so to Kurt.'

'Your youngest son,' Alex said.

It was true: he did look much older than Alex had expected. He was short and squat in build, with thick arms and a heavy chest. He was almost bald, with a beard of close-cropped grey bristles, and with a head which sat directly on his shoulders, folds of skin bunching at his chin and at the base of his skull. Alex tried to remember what else Eva might have told him about the man.

'I made a stone for my wife,' Peter Remer said. 'And another for Wilhelm, of course. None of the churches will find a place for Wilhelm until someone – "the authorities" – tells them what they can and can't do.'

'I imagine it's a common problem throughout Germany,' Alex said, immediately wondering if the remark sounded insensitive.

Peter Remer nodded. 'And a long way beyond.' He paused, and then said, 'That's all you'll see in the house.'

Alex didn't understand him and said so.

'Absence, Captain Foster. Absence, loss, emptiness. Empty spaces. Something that should be there, but isn't.' He drew a tarpaulin over the cutting-table and the newly sliced stone and indicated that the two of them ought to return to the house.

'So you live here now with just Eva and Kurt,' Alex said.

'Ha. When he deigns to honour us with his presence. He spends as much time away, living with his stupid friends, as he does here. I sometimes hardly see him from one week to the next. Until he wants something, of course. I see enough of him then. I daresay Eva's already told you all about him.'

'No, not really,' Alex said, realizing only then that she had told him very little about any of them.

The remark made the older man guarded, and he changed the subject, commenting on the hanging gate and the number of years it had been waiting for his attention.

Inside, Eva had cleared and then re-laid the table. Hot food – potatoes and other vegetables – stood in dishes on the open range. It seemed impossible to Alex that she could have done so much in so short a time, and then he saw the mound of dirty dishes and other detritus that she had simply stacked on the dresser in the corner of the room.

Her father made no comment on the transformation, and went to the fire and threw on several logs. These were dry and they caught and burned immediately, warming and brightening the room. He lit a kerosene lamp, pumped it for a moment and then hung it from the rafters above the table. Then he went to the over-crowded dresser and pulled out a framed photograph to show to Alex.

'Wilhelm,' he said. 'He was nineteen when that was taken. A year before he was killed. It was taken here in the town, professionally.'

A black ribbon had been fastened across a corner of the frame.

'It was his mother's proudest possession.'

'I can understand why,' Alex said.

236

Peter Remer gave no answer; instead he exchanged a glance with Eva and said, 'I was telling Captain Foster about Wilhelm.'

She smiled at the remark and said nothing to break her father's brief reverie. Then she asked him if Kurt was joining them to eat. Her father laughed at the question.

'Here, in this fine wining and dining establishment?' he said. 'No, I don't believe he's made a reservation for this evening. Perhaps, once again, we fail to come up to your brother's exacting standards.'

Eva silenced him with a glance, and Peter Remer immediately apologized to Alex.

'He's only sixteen – sixteen – and already there has been a parting of the ways. My son knows everything and I know nothing. We—'

'He's still just a kid,' Eva said. 'Forget him. Even if he had been here, he would just have picked the same old pointless arguments with the two – three – of us.' She laid plates in front of them and then took a dish of sliced meat from the oven. Its aroma filled the room. The slices lay in bubbling juice and fat. Peter Remer took a piece of bread from a bowl and dipped this into the warm liquid, noisily sucking the bread and then dipping it again.

'Next she'll accuse me of having no table manners,' he said to Alex. He motioned to the bread. And because he could not do otherwise, Alex took a piece and copied him. The juice was rich and salty, and the liquid fat coated his lips and tongue.

'Philistines,' Eva said, before joining them at the table and doing the same.

They drank what Alex took to be a kind of homemade cider, which Eva warned him against.

The meal lasted an hour, during which time the photograph of the dead son and brother remained at the centre of the table.

When they had finished eating, Eva took it back to the dresser. Peter Remer started to say something about this, but then acceded in silence to her. He showed Alex a photo of his wife, of the two of them together, and then of the two of them a decade later with their three small children.

He then brought out a bottle of brandy and offered it to Alex. Eva insisted on his taking a glass, and Alex saw by the way she sought out and then washed the two glasses that the brandy was a rare luxury for her father.

Peter Remer sat by the fire and invited Alex to pull a chair closer to the blaze. Eva came and sat between them, her hand on Alex's arm.

Later, after further talk of the town, of Peter Remer's work and the prospects for the future, Eva told her father that it was time for Alex to return to the Institute. It was almost ten, and though there was no urgency for Alex to leave, he agreed with what she'd suggested.

He thanked Peter Remer for his hospitality and said

he hoped to see him again soon. Next time, he said, he'd be better prepared for the visit.

'You and me alike,' Peter Remer told him.

Eva and Alex walked outside. It was much cooler than earlier.

She put her arm through his and steered him away from the jeep towards the open land at the rear of the house, indicating a path between stacked stone and overgrown bushes towards the nearby mound of trees. They walked to this and then followed a track of footprints half way to its low summit. The night air was filled with the scent of lilac.

They sat there together. In the distance they could see the glow from the town lights. Other, vaguer and more scattered lights revealed the surrounding dwellings to him.

'I came up here the night the bombs fell on Rehstadt,' she said, holding his arm around her. 'We could see they were bombing Hanover, see the clouds lit up with the searchlights there. We had no idea they'd come to Rehstadt, though, and bomb here, too.'

'Like you said before, it might have been an accident, or a secondary target,' he said. 'Just somewhere to lose their bombs before flying home.'

'It scared us – me and Kurt – to see them so close. There were never any anti-aircraft batteries in Rehstadt, only in Hanover. We saw them on the move all the time, but they were never brought here to help defend us. I doubt if anyone in that cellar had the faintest notion that they might actually be beneath the bombs. Every time the siren went, the townspeople went to their cellars, to the few public shelters, and they just sat there talking and reading and then sleeping until the all-clear sounded. Most never stayed for more than an hour or two. It was always someone else's problem, someone else's nightmare, somewhere else.'

'But not on that night?' Alex said. He looked down on the lights of nearby buildings and she identified these for him.

'They sent us a leaflet,' she said, smiling at the memory. 'The authorities. Telling us what to do in the unlikely event of a raid. We were supposed to fold ourselves in half and then take only shallow breaths. That was to avoid our lungs bursting in the bomb blasts.'

'I suppose it makes sense,' Alex said.

'Sitting directly beneath a bomb weighing a ton and falling towards you at a hundred miles an hour?' She laughed. 'There was lots of that kind of advice. Towards the end, when the Russians were supposed to be sweeping over us like a sea, they said that for women to avoid the attentions – avoid the *attentions*? – of the soldiers, all we had to do was to go as high up in a building as we could get.'

'Oh?'

'Because the Russian infantry were all supposed to be

conscripted from the peasantry – that was the word they used – and they were all supposed to live in crude, single-storey hovels, and were mistrustful of stairs and unhappy at having to fight upwards.'

'Where would you have gone?'

She shrugged. 'Nina used to say that "upwards" was where the beds were, and that perhaps all the advice *really* suggested was that we were to make things as easy and as comfortable for ourselves as possible.'

'Still, it never came to that,' Alex said.

'No,' she said. 'It never came to that.'

Afterwards, she rose abruptly and said he ought to set off back to town. The night was moonless and dark, and the track from Ameldorf to the forest road was unlit. He would be unable to drive at little more than walking pace until he reached the road. She told him her father would already be asleep in his chair in front of the fire. It was where he slept most nights during the cooler weather. He would be awake at five, she told him, and back at work by half past. He heard the affection in everything she said.

They walked together back to the house, and just before they emerged from between the stone, he pulled her close to him and kissed her. She responded to this, and afterwards whispered to him that she wished she were going back with him.

'Then come,' he suggested.

'I'll see you tomorrow,' she said, and kissed him again.

He knew by her tone and by her glance at the house that there was no possible argument and he accepted this.

Then he left her and drove slowly along the rutted path.

The dark night became darker still when he entered the impenetrable trees. At one point he saw lights in the forest, and smelled the drifting smoke of a fire. He wondered if it was from the DP camp, but was unable to estimate how far he had come or where the camp might be amid the trees.

After twenty minutes, he saw the whitewashed oil drums of the marker ahead of him. As he drew nearer, relieved that he was finally back on a familiar road, a figure – a short, slight man – stepped on to the track from beneath the trees and stood ahead of him, clearly outlined in the jeep's headlights.

As Alex approached, the man withdrew and stood to one side. He carried a length of timber, a branch, and held this across his chest in both hands. Alex waved to him, but the silhouetted figure gave no response, merely standing at the side of the track.

Alex considered stopping and asking if he wanted a lift into town, but as he approached, the man left the side of the track and went back to wait beneath the trees. Alex reduced his speed even further, and as he did this the man raised the branch and pointed it at him as though he were holding a rifle.

Alex continued driving. The noise of the engine drowned anything the man might have shouted at him. Alex imagined him aiming the branch and shouting 'Bang.'

Pulling on to the road, he finally stopped the jeep and turned around. But by then the figure had retreated even further beneath the trees and was invisible to him.

Part Two

18

'When did you realize that the war was lost?' Alex said. He cleared the contents of his desk into a drawer and opened Johannes Walther's file. He had retrieved it only an hour earlier from Records. It was thicker than previously, and Alex had immediately noticed this. It was still not a complete history of Walther's military service, but it now contained a copy of a document – presumably inserted there by Preston with Dyer's compliance – listing the names and ranks and the testimony references of others who had already been interviewed in connection with what had happened at Malmédy.

It occurred to Alex to wonder why this had been withheld from him until now. And why it had been so surreptitiously revealed to him. There were no charge-sheets as such, no transcribed confessions implicating Walther, just the names of the men whom Walther would have known. Men who might or might not have been involved in the shootings. Men for whom he might still feel some responsibility. Perhaps even men to whom some notion of unfulfilled duty might still exist.

'For me personally, or for Germany as a whole?' Walther said.

His guards had released him at the door and sent him in alone.

Alex looked up from the file.

'New information?' Walther asked him, seemingly unconcerned.

'From Preston.'

'I see. I don't know how to answer your question.' He crossed his legs and sat to one side, his face in profile to Alex.

'You think I'm asking you to say it ended when you held a gun to a kneeling man's head?' Alex said. 'I'm not. I'm not trying to trick you into anything.'

Walther considered the remark. 'Is our time together, here, coming to an end?'

The names in the file were intended to provoke *something*. Or perhaps they were there now to finally convince Alex of Walther's guilt. To make it easy and expedient for him to draw his own line under these proceedings, to pass his own judgement and then to hand Walther over to Preston.

Alex shrugged. 'The American prosecutors will be

becoming impatient. If they need you, they'll just reach in here and take you.'

'And there's nothing you will be able to do about that?'

Alex left the question unanswered.

'I see,' Walther said. 'Whatever happens, I still appreciate having met you, Captain Foster. My only true regret now is that I was not the man you expected or were looking for.' He finally turned to face Alex, and Alex saw for the first time that one of his eyes was badly bruised and swollen. There was another bruise on his cheek, and a cut on his chin. His lip had been split and a scab of dried blood still stuck to it.

'What happened?' Alex asked him.

Walther shrugged. 'Perhaps I fell on the stairs.'

'Was it the guards?'

'They would never do this. Not to me, at least.' He smiled. 'The two who brought me here wanted to take me first to the Infirmary to try and clean me up a little. They act uncaring, but that's all it is – an act. They told me you'd insist on doing something similar. Please, don't.'

'Why not?'

'Perhaps I deserved it. Perhaps I *am* the traitor I was accused of being. Who knows?' He took the cigarette Alex offered him and slid it carefully between his lips. Alex lit this and studied the bruises more closely.

'Is your vision clear?'

Walther flinched as Alex touched the skin above his injured eye.

'Who was it?'

'Forget it,' Walther said. 'The man who did this was not acting on his own account.'

'Then whose?'

Walther shook his head.

'Does someone here think you're informing on the others involved at Malmédy?'

Walther pursed his lips and flinched again.

Alex picked up one of the new sheets and recited the first few names to Walther.

Walther considered them and said, 'Dead, dead, whereabouts unknown – probably a prisoner in the East – dead, living at home with his family, dead, never knew him, living at home. You see what a lottery it all is? Of course I knew these men. How long is your list? I'll have known most of them. Look for a man called Mauke, Konrad. Is he on there? He was the man who saved me. Dead. Stiegler? In the field hospital with me. Killed a fortnight later. Ritter? I rode with him when the hospital was evacuated. I last saw him in a farmyard outside Schleiden. He jumped off a cart to take a piss and then just stood and watched us as we left him behind. I was probably the only one who saw what he'd done. Go on, read them all out to me. Every one of them. Read the list of the men being prosecuted, the ones you expect to find guilty, to execute or to imprison.

I'll know most of them, too. Read it. Perhaps I'll be able to tell you whether they *are* guilty or not.' Aware that he was now shouting, Walther fell silent.

'There's no prosecutors' list,' Alex said.

'At least not one they feel able to reveal to you? Perhaps that's because my name's at the top of it. Perhaps it's even a list compiled by the German authorities and not the Americans. God knows, we made lists of everyone and everything else.'

'Whatever your own involvement, you'll still be called to testify,' Alex said.

'Against my comrades, you mean? Against my friends?' Walther paused, his eyes closed. 'You asked me a moment ago when I finally understood that the war was over, that it was lost.'

Alex waited.

'I saw the Volga, Captain Foster,' Walther said.

'At Stalingrad?'

'At Stalingrad. We were there to put a little backbone into the Yugoslavians and Hungarians. That was the exact wording of our orders. I was there from September to November. We were pulled out before the calamity. I was back in France by the time Von Paulus was made to walk along that road lined with carefully arranged frozen German corpses to sign the surrender. And nor was I at Kursk. I believe that was my greater escape. We used to say that the Russians hit us with a hammer at Stalingrad, that the city itself was an anvil and the Red

251

Army a hammer. At Kursk we tank men said that the entire forge and all its anvils and braziers had been dropped directly on top of us. Most of the men I know who lost their lives in the East lost them at Kursk.'

'A battle fought in retreat,' Alex said.

'No one ever told *them* that. So, I looked down on the Volga. And then beyond it to the thousands of miles and millions of men, shells, tanks and planes waiting for us there. Russia, Captain Foster, that's where the war was lost. How in God's name were we ever going to conquer and then control so vast a country?'

'I imagine many believed it possible.'

'The same men who told us we would simply reach through the Americans and grasp Antwerp? I, for one, never made the mistake of believing that what happened in Russia was in the slightest way comparable to that last, long winter in Belgium. The Americans might have been there, along with everything they ever needed, but they were never happy to fight in situations where the outcome was not already heavily weighted in their favour. The Russians, on the other hand . . . Please, read some more of the names.'

Alex did this, reciting the next half dozen, and Walther remembered those men he had known without remarking on them.

Alex read a further five names, to the bottom of the sheet.

'All dead,' Walther said. 'On the road to Bastogne.

Another so-called fighting withdrawal. Bombed and strafed. That's one problem with a tank. Nothing fires upwards and we're easy to spot from the air. We leave marks. Easy to spot by all those planes flying so low. All those planes with all the fuel and all the ammunition they could carry. They were the days we prayed for the low cloud to continue. It was the only protection we had. A day after Mauke was killed, we came back into Germany. For us it was like the promised land. There was talk that neither the British nor the Americans would follow us, that a surrender would be negotiated now that Germany itself was the battleground.'

'That was never likely,' Alex said.

'I think deep in our hearts we all knew that. But after what had just happened in the Ardennes, I suppose there were some of us beginning to understand how close the end was.' He paused. 'But I wonder if any of us truly understood then how forcibly that ending would be brought to us.'

Alex read out more of the names, and Walther listened in silence, occasionally smiling or nodding at a memory. He no longer listed the dead and the living and the lost.

When Alex had finished, neither of them spoke for several minutes.

'I interviewed a man called Ochmann-Schur,' Alex said eventually.

Walther smiled at the name. 'I know him.' He touched

253

a finger to the scab on his lip. 'Or at least I do now.'

'He did this?'

'Not him personally. Ochmann's an aristocrat. They don't get their own hands dirty in matters like this.'

'Report him to someone,' Alex said, uncertain of what procedures governed the cell blocks.

'You've seen him,' Walther said. 'He'll feign surprise and then pretend to be insulted. Then he'll flick a speck of dust from his perfectly polished boots and accept your apology with all the magnanimity his thousand years of breeding have given him.'

'He accused you of betraying the men responsible for Malmédy?' Alex said.

'Or perhaps of refusing to admit to my own part in it all? Of betraying *them*, my country, my leader, my blood. Take your pick. The man Ochmann sent to see me – presumably having bribed the cell guards – told me it might be best for all concerned if I could take a leaf out of Menschler's book. A matter of "honour", I think he said. Or was it "duty"? I forget.'

'Ochmann has a few dirty secrets of his own,' Alex said, immediately wondering if he'd said too much.

Walther understood this. 'Don't worry. I won't tell him you told me that. Besides, everyone seems to have their own dirty little secrets these days.'

'I could try and have you moved out of Ochmann's way. You're obviously important to Preston. The last thing he wants is to lose you.' The remark sounded too harsh. 'Even if it's only as a witness,' he added.

Walther saw this, too. 'And even if it's only as a witness who saw nothing?'

'Does Ochmann-Schur talk to anyone?' Alex asked him.

Walther shook his head at the question. 'You must ask him about his social diary. Did you know that he intends one day – one day soon – to become part of the new German government?'

'I didn't know one was imminent.'

Walther tapped the side of his nose. 'Then perhaps he knows more than you do.'

'Not if others have anything to do with it,' Alex said.

'Meaning Ochmann, or the government?'

'Ochmann,' Alex said.

Walther leaned back in his seat.

'So, the Russians *are* after him.'

'I don't know who's after him.' But the lie was unconvincing.

There was a further silence. A succession of vehicles arrived at the Institute entrance and men started unloading cases there. Alex went to the window and watched them.

'For me,' Walther said unexpectedly behind him, 'I knew the war was lost the day we entered a small town called Usch, near Vianden, in Luxembourg. I'd been out of hospital a fortnight.'

'Were you attacked there?'

255

Walther shook his head. 'Nothing like that. By then we were playing at hare and hounds with the Americans. We retreated twenty kilometres daily, and they advanced either twenty-two or eighteen. It was that close. We went and slowed and searched for fuel, and they came on faster and tried to catch us before we could again move out of reach. The next road, the next river, bridge, railway. Always the next strongpoint. Reach the next strongpoint and then we would be able to re-arm, re-fuel and turn and fight. And then they'd see what they were up against. *Then* they'd understand what fighting on German soil was going to mean for them.'

'What happened at Usch?'

'We were unprepared, in disarray all along the front, such as it was. Everyone believed we would be saved by the Rhine. They came sooner than we anticipated. The first breaks in the weather, and they started pushing at us. Push push push. We never truly knew from one day to the next how close behind us they were, or if they were alongside us or over the next hill. Or if they were already ahead of us and waiting for us around the next bend. They started using open radio frequencies to try and contact us as we ran ahead of them, telling us how close behind us they were. Telling us who they had finally overtaken, who they had taken prisoner, calling on us to stop running, to stop prolonging the war and our own chances of getting killed, and to surrender.'

'Did you answer them?'

'Sometimes. And sometimes we lied and said we were waiting for them. We thought it might delay them, give them pause for thought. They were cautious men, and we knew that.'

'And at Usch?'

'In addition to talking on our radios, they even had the wonderful idea of telephoning the next town or village along their path. They cleared one place, found the number of the next police station or town hall, whatever, and then made a call to let the place know they were coming. Usually, civilians answered. They were told who was calling and then asked if there were any German military units still in the place. If there were, the caller warned, then the town or village – or often just a hamlet of a few farms – would be heavily shelled unless it surrendered. If there was no military presence, if we'd already arrived and then gone on our way, then the people were told to hang white sheets and towels from their upper windows. If the Americans saw this, they would arrive without shelling.'

'Did it work?' Alex said.

'Of course it worked. After all those years of the war being somewhere else?'

'Is that what happened at Usch?'

'At Usch I led my twenty-seven tanks – we'd been thirty-six the day before – along the road from Diekirch. The Americans were close behind us – my guess was three or four kilometres, and with nothing between us to slow them down. I arrived in Usch to find hundreds of those clean white sheets and towels hanging from every window. They looked like snow from a distance, there were so many of them. The Americans had called ahead before we'd even arrived there. The street was lined with people waving handkerchiefs and cloths. They saw us coming and came out in their hundreds to welcome us.'

'Because they thought you were the Americans?'

'Some of them had even hung American and English flags from their windows. Where do you suppose they got those from, eh?'

'What happened?'

'I drove into the place. I couldn't do otherwise. That three or four kilometres might just as easily have been one or two.'

'And the people there?'

'Ah, the good townspeople of sleepy little picture-postcard Usch. They all went on waving and cheering until we came close enough to be identified by them. And then they fell silent. And I mean silent. One moment the air was full of cheering like at a football match, and the next they were standing and looking up at us as though we were a giant funeral procession. There was even a small delegation, a welcoming committee. I remember a man standing with a tray of drinks, another with an unopened bottle in each hand. There were young women, girls, all of them dressed in their Sunday best, flowers in their hands.' He shook his head at the memory.

'What did you do?'

'I just kept moving. Peiper was on a parallel course. He called me to ask if we'd found any fuel and I told him what had happened. He told me to fire a few shells into prominent buildings. He said the whole place was committing an act of treason. He wanted me to arrest and execute the mayor or head councillor or chief of police.' He tailed off, remembering.

'And?'

'And I told him the Americans were close behind us, that there wasn't time.'

'You could have fired your shells and still kept moving.'

Walther shrugged at the suggestion. 'Yes, I could have fired my shells and still kept moving. Is that what *you'd* have done – obeyed orders? Instead, I told my commanders to open their turrets, to get up into the fresh air and to take a good look at what was happening all around them. I wanted them to see those people, those women and girls and dignitaries in the streets of Usch with their flags and their drink and their flowers. And, above all, I wanted *them* to see *us*. I wanted them to see who was doing all the dirty work on their behalf, who was dying and bleeding and burning for them. I wanted them to see the men who were more animal than man in those days, and all so they could hide their best wine and save their Sunday suits and bouquets for the Americans. No, Captain Foster, I fired no shells or machine guns; I just kept on moving. In fact, as I passed the small delegation with the wine, I pulled myself upright and I saluted them. And do you know what – half of them saluted me back. Some military salutes, some Party salutes, but half of them saluted me back. I told my other commanders to do the same. Some did, some didn't. It was beyond me to insist. We just kept on moving until we were through the place and they were all left standing there behind us, probably wondering what had just happened to them, wondering what was about to happen to them next.'

'The Americans, presumably.'

'Presumably. Perhaps the wine and pretty girls even slowed them down. Perhaps those people of Usch helped us to stretch our lead by a few more kilometres. Who knows?'

The cut on Walther's mouth had reopened and resumed bleeding. He touched it and then wiped the blood from his finger on his chest.

19

'You saw Kurt,' Eva said to him as he returned to sit beside her with their drinks.

'Where?'

'On the track from the house.'

'He was the one beneath the trees with a stick for a rifle?'

She smiled at the remark. 'It might have been a *panzerfaust* – a bazooka,' she said. She sipped her drink.

'I thought it was a man from the camp,' he said, trying to remember the fleeting encounter.

'No, just a stupid boy,' she said.

They were in the railway bar, the same landlord, who had again greeted her warmly upon their arrival, and the same few anonymous people waiting for late trains, their cases and packages at their feet.

'He arrived home twenty minutes after you'd gone,' she said.

'Did he know I'd been there earlier?'

She nodded. 'He was watching the house. He left halfway through the evening and went to wait with the others.'

'What others?'

'He heard your jeep and ran to watch you drive past. He didn't mean you any harm. Anything he might have had to say concerning your visit, he'd already said to me and my father.'

'Such as?'

'You can imagine. He accused me of being a whore and my father of collaborating with you.'

Alex laughed at the word.

Eva held up her hand. 'I know, but that's how he sees it.'

'You said "others",' he said, and she paused before answering him.

'His other "comrades". Men from the old Volksturm. When they were disbanded, some of them stayed on at the old barracks. It's beyond the DP camp. It's nothing: a few old huts and an overgrown parade ground, most of it waterlogged. They were originally housed in the DP camp itself, before that was taken away from them by the refugees.'

'Are there many of them?'

'Twenty or thirty. It varies. Some arrived from else-where and stayed. Some of them live there permanently, and some drift back and forth from their homes. Most of them – those like Kurt – have no idea *what* they want.'

'Only what they don't want?' Alex said.

She nodded. 'Kurt spends half his time there. He sleeps at home two or three nights a week, often without speaking to my father. He says he feels betrayed, that only the men in the camp truly understand him. He says *they*'re his family now.'

Alex remembered the men who had gathered at the gate of the DP camp on the morning he had gone with Whittaker to attend to Maria Lehman.

'Most of them laboured on a few local farms when the war was over, but the work ended in the winter. Now they just forage and scavenge and live on charity. Kurt takes his food and drink from the house. My father used to try and stand up to him, but there was one occasion when Kurt hit him and knocked him to the ground. Kurt regretted it, of course, but it changed things between them. It created a line from which neither of them was afterwards able to step back.'

'And you?'

'You mean has he attacked me? Once or twice. I know him. He's angry and he's confused. He's a boy. Sixteen. He spent his life as a child in my father's workshop and yards. All he ever wanted to be was a stonemason. Everywhere you looked in Germany, monuments and grand buildings were being erected. They were good times for masons and builders. They needed thousands of them. Even the war wasn't going to stop that. And after the war, well . . . My father always believed Kurt would take things further – that he might even qualify as an architect, perhaps.'

They were interrupted by the barman, who, seeing their empty glasses, had brought them more drink.

Eva held his arm as he put this on the table. 'We were talking about Kurt, the barracks,' she said to him.

The barman glanced behind him at his few other customers and sat down beside her.

'Paul was Kurt's officer in the Volksturm,' Eva said.

The man again held out his hand to Alex. 'Paul Weiss,' he said. 'Is he in trouble?' he asked Eva.

'Just the usual.'

Alex told him what he'd seen on the forest track.

'A stick?' The man smiled. 'Nothing much has changed there, then.'

Alex understood then why Eva had insisted on coming to the bar on both occasions they had been alone together in the town. He understood, too, Nina Lehman's knowing look and dismissive remarks when he'd told her where he and Eva had spent their first evening together.

'He listens to Paul,' Eva said, meaning her brother.

'Do you see him regularly?' Alex asked the man.

'They come here sometimes, at the times when there are no trains. I give them drink, sometimes food. What little there is to spare.'

'Including Kurt? You give him drink?'

The man looked to Eva in answer. 'It was all a joke,' he said. 'Geriatrics and boys with sticks and stones against trained soldiers with artillery and aircraft. If I taught those men anything useful, then it was to keep their heads down and their mouths shut, to look out for themselves and their families instead of trying to fight anyone.'

'Tell him about Altmann,' Eva said.

'My predecessor. He felt the same as I did, but made the mistake of making his views a little too public.'

'What happened to him?' Alex asked.

Paul shrugged. 'He was arrested, taken away.'

'He never returned,' Eva added. 'And, yes, before you accuse us of avoiding the truth, we do know what that means.'

'His arrest was intended as a lesson to the rest of us,' Paul said. He briefly held Eva's arm again. 'And believe me, it was a lesson we all learned. Some of the men – boys – under my command – I rose to the giddy heights of Master Sergeant – were only too eager to do what they could, only too happy to sing the songs and march up and down for hours on end. Others, myself included, were a little less convinced that we would truly achieve anything with our sticks and stones.'

'And Kurt was one of the enthusiastic ones?' Alex said.

'He thought he was going to protect the town single-handedly.'

'My father tried to reason with him,' Eva said. 'The war

265

was over. The last thing anyone needed then, and especially here, was boys performing heroics.'

'Some of them took things into their own hands,' Paul said. 'Eventually, they looked to our illustrious leader rather than to me.'

'Hitler?'

Both Paul and Eva laughed.

'He means the officer in overall command of the region,' Eva said. 'Guess.'

'The mayor?' Alex said.

'Mister fight-to-the-last-man mayor.'

'What happened?'

'When he heard the British had arrived in Lauenau, only eight kilometres away, he was driven there to negotiate the surrender of Rehstadt. I doubt they took much notice of him. He came back, told the Town Council what had happened and what to do, what wonderful terms he had negotiated on our behalf. Most people – most sensible people – were happy to comply. Everybody was just relieved that it was all finally over and done with. Less than a week earlier, they'd hanged two officers from a bridge less than a kilometre from the town centre.'

'Who did?' Alex said.

Paul shrugged. 'They, them. I don't know. We just found them there. Cards round their necks denouncing them as cowards and deserters.'

Alex looked at Eva, who watched Paul closely as he

related all this. 'Do you think it might have been some of your own fanatics?' he asked him.

'I don't know. I honestly don't know. I confronted them with it, but they only laughed in my face and said that if the men *had* been cowards or deserters, then they got everything they deserved.' He shook his head at the memory. It was a terrible half-secret which bound him even tighter to Eva.

'Did *you* ever confront Kurt with the incident?' he asked her.

She bowed her head. 'What good would it have done? I try hard to believe that he would not have been capable of such a thing.'

'There were two of my boys in the bombed cellar,' Paul said, seeing how much the question had upset Eva, and diverting them from the subject of her brother. 'When they were identified, the mayor said they shouldn't have been there. I told him they would have been directing people to the cellar and then gone in themselves when everyone else was safe inside. What else did he expect them to do – throw stones at the bombers?'

'You can imagine how far underground *he* will have been when the bombs started falling,' Eva said.

Paul raised the bottle he still held and both Eva and Alex touched it with their glasses.

'You can tell Kurt I had no idea who he was,' Alex said to Paul.

'It'll make no difference,' Eva said. 'He listens to no one now except the others out there.'

'Do you know them all?' Alex asked Paul.

'Most of them. There aren't too many locals still among them – Kurt, a handful of others. They're mostly men who came back to this part of the world at the end of the war and found nothing waiting for them. The old barracks was just the first place they were able to stop themselves from running in circles and so they stayed there.' He stopped talking and looked at Eva. 'You know there's talk of demolishing it, don't you?'

Eva looked alarmed at the suggestion. 'I thought that was just the DP camp.'

'The camp and the barracks both. They want to bulldoze the two of them. Get rid of everyone there. There's talk of re-planting the forest, of timber companies taking it over.'

'Is all this imminent?' she asked him.

'As imminent as these things ever are these days. Nothing for months and then everything all at once and without any real notice. Don't look so worried. It might be for the best. Perhaps Kurt will decide to come home and take up where he left off. You never know.' He was distracted by one of his other customers, who had gone to the small bar and who now stood there tapping it with his glass to attract Paul's attention.

'Good to have met you,' he said to Alex, rising from beside them.

He paused on his way to the impatient customer, returned to Eva and Alex and refilled their glasses. The man at the bar shouted to him that he was still waiting.

Paul winked at Eva. 'And he'll be waiting for twelve hours yet. They've cancelled his train.'

'All these "theys" and "thems",' Eva said to Alex when they were again alone.

'Does it concern you – that the barracks might be demolished?' he asked her.

She considered the question. 'Of course they'll be demolished. And perhaps Paul's right – perhaps Kurt will finally see sense and return home.'

He heard her lack of conviction.

They had driven to the bar from the Institute, and on the way there Eva had told him to stop at one of the two low bridges over the river. She had held his hand and had then sat on the parapet, in full view of the passing people and traffic. She had shown him the broad rock beneath one of the stone supports where she had sunbathed as a girl. She had pointed out the concrete foundations where she and her friends had congregated. When the river was deep they had dived into it from these platforms. She had told him all this and then she had kissed him. He had told her they should return there together in the summer, but the suggestion had unexpectedly upset her and she had dropped from her seat on the bridge and returned to the jeep. Alex understood that he had disappointed her in some way, but did not grasp the true source or nature of that disappointment.

From the bridge they had driven to the bar.

'Will Kurt know we're here now?' he asked her as the customer at the counter finally fell silent.

The question surprised her. 'I don't know. Is that why you think I come here – in the hope of seeing him? He knows about you and me, if that's what you're asking me. And he knows about Maria Lehman and the baby. He called her what all the others are calling her. He said that the baby was lucky to have died. Then he said it would be the best thing for Maria herself. He said that the two of them – Nina and Maria – ought to leave Rehstadt and go somewhere where nobody knows them.'

'He's a boy,' Alex said, repeating what she'd said earlier, but knowing what an inadequate excuse this was.

'I know he is,' she said. 'And I know he's only repeating the words of others who should know better. I'm just afraid that he'll say or do something stupid that will get him into real trouble with the authorities before everything has had chance to settle down.'

'Before he starts to study to become an architect?' he said, and he saw that she took comfort from the unlikely suggestion.

They sat and talked for a further hour, and because she had told him all there was for him to know about her brother, her mood grew lighter.

He told her about his own life in England, his

expectations and prospects for the future. She laughed at a great deal of what he said. He wanted to talk about *their* future together, but knew not to broach the subject, that it was too soon, that she might tell him not to; and he knew, too, that even this small and understandable rejection would be too much for him to bear.

Shortly afterwards, as they were considering leaving, the door to the bar was pushed open and Jesus Hernandez arrived, carrying two cases in front of him. He didn't see Alex and Eva where they sat in their dimly lit corner, and went directly to where Paul Weiss stood. He dropped the cases noisily on to the counter and then turned to look around him at the bar's few occupants. Hernandez saw them and came to them. He pulled up the seat Paul had vacated and then called for a drink.

'Well, well, well,' he said. He grabbed Eva's hand and kissed it before she knew what he was doing. She pulled it away from him.

'You saw the jeep,' Alex told him.

'So what? I was on my delivery round. You think I came into this dump just to make trouble for *you*?' He turned and shouted again to Paul, who brought him a drink. 'On the house?' Hernandez said, and drained it in a single swallow. 'I'll take that as a yes. Got my money?'

Paul Weiss gave him a wad of folded notes, embarrassed to be made to do this in front of Eva and Alex.

Hernandez spread the money on the table and slowly counted it, embarrassing Paul further. Alex signalled to Paul that both he and Eva understood what was happening.

'All there,' Hernandez said eventually. He feigned hurt surprise at Paul Weiss's reaction to all this. 'What?' he said. 'They thought you had a legit wholesaler who sold you the stuff cheap?' He looked at the empty glasses on the table.

'I daresay *you*'re the only one making any real profit,' Alex said.

'Think what you like,' Hernandez told him. 'You got a problem with any of this, you can always report me to look-the-other-way Dyer. And while you're there, crying to papa, you can ask him where he gets *his* four-star brandy and Havana cigars from. We all need a few of life's little luxuries every now and again. Especially in places like this shit-hole. Speaking of which—' He took a small tissue-wrapped package from his pocket.

At first, Alex thought the man was about to produce more condoms and he raised his hand, ready to sweep them from the table. But instead, Hernandez unwrapped the tissue to reveal a bottle of perfume still in its sealed box.

'The real McCoy,' he said. He slid the perfume towards Eva, who picked it up, looked at it for a moment and then stood it back on the table.

'Perhaps lover-boy might want to buy it for you,' Hernandez suggested.

'I don't want it,' Eva told him.

'You don't want it? Or you don't want it because it's me who's selling it?' He smiled broadly at her.

'Both,' she said. 'Either,' momentarily confused by what she was being asked.

'Shame,' Hernandez said, looking from her to Alex. 'Don't get this quality of merchandise too often. And never in its proper packaging.' He turned the box as he spoke. 'See, Paris. Gay Paree. The word alone is worth an extra five bucks on the price. Why don't you ask me how much it costs, Mister Captain Foster?'

'Because I already told you – I don't want it,' Eva said. She rose from her seat and pulled on her scarf and gloves.

'You can see she's lying,' Hernandez said to Alex. 'Or at least you would if you had even half an idea of what it was women really wanted in this world. Look at her, you can see she's tempted. Looks like it's up to you to make the decision for her. Scent like that isn't going to hang around for long. If you don't want to buy it for her, then buy it for one of her friends. Get you a long way, a bottle of scent like that.' He flicked the box until it fell over and then stood it upright again.

'We ought to go,' Eva said to Alex.

'If you wanted it . . .' he suggested.

She looked at him hard for a moment. And then

273

she pushed her chair to one side and walked away from them.

'Looks like you've missed your big chance, lover-boy,' Hernandez said. 'Looks like I'm going to sell it to good old Paul here. And then *he* can hand it out a drop at a time to all *his* lady-friends.'

Paul Weiss shook his head at the remark.

Eva went to him and embraced him, looking angrily over his shoulder at Alex, who finally rose from beside Hernandez.

'Don't all go on my account,' Hernandez said to them, laughing. 'I'm a busy man myself, people to see, money to collect.'

Alex and Eva went to the door, and Hernandez followed them, pushing ahead of them to bar their way.

'The scent's still on the table,' he said to Alex in a mock-whisper. 'I hear what she's saying as loud and clear as you do, but perhaps what we're hearing still isn't what she's telling us.'

Eva went back to the table, picked up the perfume and pushed the small box into Hernandez's stomach. He took it from her.

'You're pathetic,' she said to him.

Hernandez looked slowly around the room, at everyone else now silently watching what was happening. He shouted to ask them what they were looking at, and those who understood him turned back to their drinks. The others followed a few seconds later.

'See – *they* understand what's good for them,' he said.

'You're being ridiculous,' Alex told him. 'You just antagonize people for the pleasure of it. Everything you say and do is a challenge to someone else. Why?' He knew that everything he accused Hernandez of was already well understood by everyone who knew the man, and that he was making himself sound ridiculous by putting this understanding into words, a sharp tool made blunt by reduction.

The remark surprised Hernandez and he hesitated for a moment.

'Leave him,' Eva said, and she pulled Alex's arm.

'No – he's right,' Hernandez told her. 'I *am* ridiculous.' Turning to Alex, he said, 'It's a short list – ridiculous. Want to add to it while you're on a roll?'

Seeing that Alex was again about to respond to this provocation, Eva finally turned and left him and he went after her.

Hernandez followed them outside. His jeep was parked alongside Alex's, its back seat again covered with a tarpaulin.

'Just leave,' Eva said, sitting beside Alex and waiting as he started the reluctant engine.

Neither of them responded to Hernandez's continued taunting, and eventually, after revving his own engine loudly for a minute, he left them and drove back into the town centre, a cloud of exhaust fumes hanging in the air long after he'd gone.

'I wouldn't have bought the scent – the perfume – not if you didn't want it. I mean, not if it wasn't what you wanted me to do,' Alex said, faltering with every word.

And she turned and looked at him as though he hadn't understood the first thing about what had just happened in the bar.

20

He tried to see her the following day, but she was not at her desk, and the woman who had taken her place there told him Eva hadn't appeared that morning. He asked her if there was a telephone number he could call, and she told him there wasn't. She laughed at the suggestion, and then asked him if he knew how many telephones there were in the whole of Ameldorf.

The supervisor appeared and asked Alex what he wanted. They were all very busy, he insisted.

'He was looking for Eva Remer,' the woman told him.

'Oh, and where is she?'

'She hasn't turned up,' the woman said.

The supervisor smiled at the news. 'Never knows when she's well off, that one,' he said, shaking his head. 'The number of warnings I've given her about her time-keeping, about her poor work here. I think I shall have to have further words with our Miss Remer.' He turned to Alex. 'If that's all right with you, Captain Foster.'

All this was for Alex's benefit, and he regretted having alerted the man to Eva's absence.

'Perhaps you wish to leave a message?' the supervisor said.

'No message. I just wanted—'

'Unless this was another *social* visit, of course.' He and the woman shared a smile.

'She may be ill,' Alex suggested, immediately wishing he'd said nothing.

'Of course,' the supervisor said. 'Ill.'

Unwilling to prolong this charade any longer, Alex turned and left the room.

'I'll tell her you were looking for her, shall I?' the man called after him. 'If she deigns to honour us with her presence, that is.'

Arriving at the side-entrance to his own block, Alex met James Whittaker there, standing with several orderlies and with a small group of Germans near by.

'Who are they?' Alex asked him.

'Patients. The fresh air will do them good. At least that's the idea.'

The men looked pale and thin. Several of them sat on a stone bench; the remainder stood in the sun with their backs to the wall. Some held up their faces, their eyes closed.

'Are they allowed out like this?' Alex asked him.

'You mean is that why we're skulking round here instead of out in the open? What Dyer doesn't see . . . They give me their word not to try and run for it – three of them can barely shuffle, let alone walk – and I promise not to shoot them in the back if they decide to break their word and try. See the tall one?' He motioned to a man standing apart from the others. He wore a long overcoat with a scarf wrapped around his shaved head. 'That's the Professor. Ernst Pfitzner, some distant relation to the composer. He came here from Kassel. He was a Professor of Literature at Berlin University. Spent most of the war in Paris, a so-called Educational Administrator. The French have had him for the past six months. Now he's ours. TB.'

'Are you treating him?'

'For what it's worth. First he was imprisoned by the Germans, then he was freed and arrested by the French. Apparently, he tried to help some of his colleagues at the Sorbonne.'

'Jews, you mean? Communists?'

'Jews, communists, all those men who once perhaps thought that their titles might protect them from the storm of horrors blowing outside. He did a good job, by all accounts.'

'Meaning he saved—'

Whittaker shook his head. 'Meaning he probably delayed the inevitable for a month or two.'

'Long enough for people to escape?'

279

'Unlikely. Chances are, they refused to believe what he was telling them, what he was trying to convince them of, while it was happening to thousands of others all around them. Come and meet him.'

Alex looked at his watch.

'You've got time,' Whittaker said. 'I want you to hear something. Something he told me.'

Alex's first appointment of the day was not for another hour. He followed Whittaker to the man at the wall.

'Ernst,' Whittaker said, alerting the man to their presence. He introduced Alex to him. The man bowed and held out his hand. Alex took this and felt how thin and enervated it was in his own. Even the effort of shaking seemed too much for him.

'Ernst was telling me about the Kingdom of Ashes,' Whittaker said, prompting the man.

Pfitzner withdrew his hand and tucked it back beneath his arm.

'The Kingdom of Ashes?' Alex said.

'A German folk tale,' Ernst Pfitzner said in perfect English.

'Tell him,' Whittaker said. 'Please.'

'It's Bavarian,' Pfitzner said to Alex. 'Variant sources, original author unknown. It was a largely oral tradition. Late sixteenth, possibly early seventeenth century.' He spoke by rote, as though addressing one of his student classes for the fiftieth time. 'It concerns a king who owned a vast kingdom composed of disparate parts and many different peoples. The king was a very mistrustful man, and one who insisted on the absolute and unwavering loyalty of his subjects. He feared constantly that the more distant and potentially more hostile of these subjects were plotting against him.'

He paused to gain his breath. A fly landed on his cheek for a few seconds and he seemed not to notice it there.

'And so, at the end of the first year of his reign, he ordered the destruction of the outer, scarcely known reaches of his vast kingdom. Lands, towns and villages were razed and burned and all their inhabitants either killed or dispersed.

'The year after that, the king grew suspicious again of all those people living immediately inside this outer circle of destruction, and so he ordered the same thing to be done to them. All of this, you must realize, was still a long, long way from where the king himself lived in his fortress at the centre of his domain.'

Alex nodded, already guessing the rest of the tale and how it had acquired its title.

'And then the year after that, he grew suspicious of the people inside *that* circle and so he pointed his finger at them. But by now, you see, he was pointing at his own horizons. No matter. Everything was razed and burned, and again everyone was either killed or scattered to the wind.'

By now, the man had attracted the attention of some of the other patients, and though few of them could have understood him, they still came close to hear the story he was telling.

'*Das Königsreich Von Aschen,*' Pfitzner said to them, and the men nodded in understanding.

Turning back to Alex, he went on. 'For over twenty years of this constant suspicion and fear the king sent his soldiers and wreckers to ever-closer parts of his kingdom, until eventually he was razing and burning and killing in the lands immediately beyond his own fortress walls. And all the time this was happening, he grew neither happier nor more secure. And nor did he grow any less suspicious of his subjects. Until eventually, after decades of this futile destruction, the king turned on the men and women who lived alongside him inside his fortress, and finally on his own family, his own sons and daughters and hitherto trusted retainers.

'And so, after fifty years, he was finally free of all those imaginary plotters and enemies and the places that had harboured them. But by then, of course, his entire kingdom was devoid of all life, burned to the ground and useless.'

'And he still didn't feel secure,' Alex said.

Pfitzner closed his eyes. 'Of course not.'

'And you see the same thing here, now, in Germany?'

'Perhaps,' Pfitzner said. 'Though it wasn't why I told

Captain Whittaker the tale. A hundred others might draw equally forceful comparisons. After all, we were promised a thousand years by our own little king. By anyone's standards, we fell a long way short.'

'And others did most of the burning and scattering for you,' Whittaker said.

Pfitzner started to cough, and then stood for a moment regaining his breath. 'A thousand years,' he said. 'Perhaps that, too, might one day become a folk tale to be told to our own great-great-grandchildren.'

'Do you have any?' Alex asked him.

Pfitzner nodded. 'Children. Three sons. All of whom served, and all of whom are still alive, thank God.'

'Two of them are prisoners,' Whittaker said. 'One in Russia.'

'Nevertheless,' Pfitzner said, 'I have heard from him there, so I might continue to hope for his release one day. He was a clerk. Eventually, they gave him a rifle. In the German Army, "for every soldier, two clerks". Perhaps it was true.' He repeated the phrase to the nearby men and they concurred with it. Then he held up the watch he still possessed to show Whittaker the time. 'He lets us out into the sun to warm ourselves like lizards on a rock,' he told Alex. 'He tries to convince us that it's part of our cure.'

Whittaker called to the orderlies and told them to take the patients back to the infirmary.

Alex expected the men to complain at this, but

instead they all offered their thanks to Whittaker for the small measure of freedom they'd been allowed.

Pfitzner held out his hand again to Alex. 'It was a pleasure to meet you, Captain Foster. Perhaps we will meet again.'

'I hope so,' Alex said.

He and Whittaker waited together as the men walked slowly away from them. Several needed to be helped by the orderlies.

'Why did the French send him here?' Alex asked.

Whittaker shrugged. 'The same reason most of them are pushed from pillar to post, I imagine. Perhaps the TB helped them decide. Or perhaps everybody's just waiting for the time when somebody finally shouts, "Enough's enough" and we can just open the gates and let them all go home and get on with their lives, the good, the bad, the innocent and the guilty alike.'

Neither man spoke for a moment. Then Alex told Whittaker what had happened the previous evening in the bar.

'And you think it has something to do with why she hasn't shown up today?' Whittaker said, unwilling to share Alex's concern. 'You're worrying about nothing.' He continued watching the departing patients. 'The medical report from the French gave Pfitzner a month to live. Someone even recommended a sanatorium. Switzerland, perhaps, all that clean, uncontaminated mountain air.' He laughed at the impossibility of the suggestion. 'I knew another man like him, another Professor of Literature.'

'Back home?' Alex said. He heard the sudden shift of tone in Whittaker's voice.

'No, not there – here, in Belsen. A Belgian Jew from Leuven University.' He paused, remembering. 'Albert Huy. I was treating him there. He seemed to be recovering. All *he* ever wanted to do was to talk. About books, literature, writers, drama, poetry, that sort of thing. Talk about all the things that had been important to him before – well, before everything that had happened to him. It was air and blood to him, all that, all the book stuff. And all he really wanted to do was to talk about it with someone who'd listen to him, someone who might know about some tiny part of it all, who might share or dispute his opinions.'

Alex began to wonder where the anecdote was leading.

'He died,' Whittaker said. 'I was with him, outside, talking – or, rather, listening to him talk – as close to him as I am to you now, and he thanked me for listening, said he appreciated everything I'd done for him, and then he just collapsed, dead.'

'Do you know what killed him?'

Whittaker laughed. 'A post-mortem, you mean, an autopsy? No. The world – their world – had seen enough of all that kind of thing. Besides, I didn't want – didn't *need* – to know what had killed him. There were already those on the medical staff who believed it had been a waste of time and resources to have started treating him in the first place.'

'And you disagreed with them?'

'And by doing so I might have denied someone else – someone who might have survived – the treatment they needed.'

'Not if—'

'Talk, you see. That's all he wanted, Albert Huy. To have one last civilized conversation with someone about the one solid, decent thing he knew about and loved best.'

'Then the others were wrong to have tried to persuade you otherwise,' Alex said.

Whittaker shook his head. 'No, they weren't. They were being practical, responsible. Huy was close to dying when we got to him, and they all saw that. Perhaps I did deny some other poor soul the chance of survival.'

Again, neither man spoke for a moment.

'And what about Pfitzner?' Alex said eventually. 'Is he close to dying, too?'

'By my reckoning, he's already two months past it.'

'So he'll die here?' Alex said. 'Sorry, I . . .'

'Every possibility. And whether it takes him days or weeks, he'll still spend all that time more concerned about his son in Russia than about himself.' He looked around them, at the neglected lawns and drives and flowerbeds.

Still hoping to find Eva, and anxious now about her likely encounter with the supervisor, Alex told him he had to go.

'Of course,' Whittaker said, still locked in his own thoughts. 'Me, too. Wherever I am these days, it always seems I should be somewhere else.'

21

The following day was Saturday, and the civilian staff at the Institute finished work at noon.

Alex sat with Whittaker in the canteen. The clerks and other staff walked past the window on their way home. Few of the senior interrogators worked on Saturday, and most followed the workers into the bars and few other establishments of the town rather than sit and bemoan the emptiness of the weekend in the cavernous hall of the near-empty canteen.

Whittaker sat with his head in his arms.

Alex spoke to him, but the most Whittaker gave in reply was a muffled 'yes' or 'no' or the flick of a raised finger.

Their meals lay untouched in front of them. The dozen or so other men in the room kept their voices low; the noise of their cutlery and crockery was amplified in the high space.

A whistle caused Alex to stop talking and turn to the entrance.

Eva beckoned to him from the doorway.

A group of men close to the door invited her to join them and she went to them briefly, standing beside them and declining their offer of a seat among them. The men had bottles of beer on the table – one of Dyer's few other weekend concessions – and one of these was ceremoniously opened and presented to her. She took it and then drew back at the sudden eruption of foam, causing laughter at the table. She gave the bottle back to the man who had offered it to her, and he in turn gave her his handkerchief to wipe her hand.

She left the men and came to Alex.

'Is he asleep?' she said, indicating Whittaker.

'Yes, he is,' Whittaker said, his face still in his arms.

She looked at the plates of uneaten food and pushed them further along the table. 'Don't eat it,' she said to Alex. She watched him closely, and he avoided her eyes. 'Look at me,' she told him, and he did. 'I owe you an apology for the other night.' She held his gaze. 'I mean it. I'm sorry.' She took his hand and spread his fingers on the table.

Beside her, Whittaker raised his head. 'Sounds interesting. You two not made up after your argument yet, then?'

'Go back to sleep,' Eva said affectionately. 'Is an argument better or worse than a row?'

'An argument is something unmarried people have; a row is for married couples.'

'Is he serious; is that a proper distinction?' she asked Alex.

He shook his head. 'Ignore him.'

She stroked Whittaker's hair and he moaned into his folded arms. 'He misses his own wife,' she said. 'That's all.'

'Don't stop,' Whittaker told her as she took her hand away. She ran a finger beneath his collar and then pressed his ear.

'Is that what *she* does?' she asked him.

'I could imagine it happening,' Whittaker mumbled. 'Sometimes.'

Turning to Alex, Eva said, 'So, you forgive me, then?' And before he could speak, added, 'Of course you do. And to prove to you how sorry I am, I have a treat for you.'

'I thought you were treating *me*,' Whittaker said.

'You can share in it, too,' she said.

'A treat?' Alex said.

She indicated the doorway. 'Food and wine. A picnic.'

'You'll be boating on the river next,' Whittaker said.

It was a much warmer day than usual, and the sky was clear, a day of early summer rather than late spring.

'Where?' Alex asked her. It was unlikely that there would be any jeeps left in the compound.

'A surprise,' she told him.

'A treat *and* a surprise,' Whittaker said. 'It would be too much for me. I'm going to bed.'

'Are you coming?' Eva asked Alex.

'He'll probably tell you he's got too much work to do,' Whittaker said, denying Alex his excuse, even if it was what he'd wanted. If he hadn't seen her during the remainder of the day, he had planned to return to Ameldorf the following morning.

'I have a basket. At the door.' Eva rose from beside Whittaker and he tried to hold her and to gently pull her back down. She prised his hand from her own and held a palm to his brow.

'Just go,' he said, more to Alex than to her.

They left the table and walked to the door. She paused beside the men sitting there. She thanked them again for the beer and told them to enjoy their thirty-six hours of freedom. The men laughed at the remark and then told her that they were all working over the weekend. One of them explained to her that five tons – he said he used the figure literally – of unsorted documents had recently arrived and that they were spending the next few days building shelving and sorting through all the paperwork at Dyer's insistence.

Alex remembered the arrival of the lorries two days earlier during his questioning of Johannes Walther.

'A pity,' Eva said to them. 'I was going to invite you to our picnic.'

The men laughed again.

It was the most flirtatious Alex had seen her.

'Just have to be the two of you, then,' one of the men said to him.

Eva feigned disappointment, then slid her arm through Alex's and led him outside.

On the driveway stood a wicker basket.

'Wine, bread, meat, cheese, wine, fruit, wine,' she said. She opened the top of the basket to reveal the two bottles and the wrapped food inside.

He told her there would be no transport.

'Good,' she said. 'Then we can walk. Besides, this way I will feel less . . .' She looked at him.

'Conspicuous?'

'Exactly. Conspicuous. This way I will feel less conspicuous.'

She hadn't been inconspicuous sitting on the parapet of the bridge with him, remembering her childhood, and Alex wondered if it was what she'd wanted to say, if he hadn't put the wrong word into her mouth.

They walked towards the town, and as they approached the same bridge, she indicated a cobbled lane leading uphill to the left.

'It's steep,' she warned him, and he took the basket from her.

After ten minutes, they were both out of breath. The lane climbed the hillside in a zig-zag, cobbled to the point where it became too steep for buildings, and then continuing in near-level terraces into the surrounding trees.

In places, the high sun shone directly on to their path and caused them to sweat.

At one point, after they had been walking for half an hour, Eva ran ahead of him and climbed on to an outcrop of rock. She beckoned him to her. He climbed and stood beside her, and she swung her arm to show him the sweep of the valley below.

'I used to come up here with Wilhelm,' she said.

Alex saw that they had come up the steepest part of the hill, gaining height quickly.

'We're almost at the top,' she said. 'Except you'd never know it because of the trees.'

He looked at the town and the river, at the roads and lines of buildings which followed it. He tried to orientate himself. Only the hospital and the town hall rose above the cluster of otherwise undistinguished structures.

She pointed out the road leading to Ameldorf, lost mostly beneath the forest canopy.

'You see how unlucky the people were who died in the bombing,' she said. 'It's such a small and pointless target.'

Except that a plane following the line of the river and then releasing its bombs at the first substantial bridge, at the first black line drawn across the waving, moonlit course, could hardly fail to miss something in the narrow and closely built streets. He agreed with her, revealing nothing of these thoughts.

She left their vantage point and continued climbing. Beyond, the trees came to the side of the path and shut off their wider view. It was instantly cooler out of the sun and she assured him that in only a few minutes they would reach open ground and be warm again.

The dead and rotting limbs which littered the path indicated that few others visited the forest so high up. Occasionally, a branch lay directly across their path, forcing them either to climb it or to make a detour beneath the trunks.

Eva continued ahead of him, until eventually she ran out into an open space. She stopped there, held out her arms and turned her face to the sun.

'See,' she called to him. 'It's warm.'

He joined her and felt the sudden rise in temperature, holding up his own face and feeling the sweat running down his neck and between his shoulder blades.

She took the basket from him and walked to a low grassy mound.

'It's the exact spot,' she said, grinning broadly.

'Where you came with Wilhelm?'

'We roamed and played all over this hillside.' She sat on the mound and took a blanket from the basket. She closed her eyes and breathed deeply.

Alex sat beside her. Small flowers bloomed in the grass, vividly blue and white and yellow. She told him their names and then pointed out another dozen species scattered all around them.

He drew the cork from one of the bottles and they both drank from this. It was sweeter and colder than he'd expected, tasting more like chilled cordial than wine.

They ate the bread and cheese and cured meat, cutting it crudely and then brushing the crumbs from around them.

'Kurt came to the house the night we encountered Hernandez in the bar,' she said.

'What happened? Is that why you've not been to work?'

She lay flat beside him, her arms by her side, her eyes closed in the glare of the sun.

Alex saw how her breasts rose to the neck of her blouse, how they swung slightly as she settled herself on the warm ground.

'Was there another fight?' he asked her. 'Between Kurt and your father?'

'My father accused him of having been offensive towards you.'

'Me?'

'He said Kurt should have made the effort to come home that evening. You can imagine Kurt's response to that. He didn't stay long. Just long enough for my father to decide to get drunk in his son's absence. I stayed at home yesterday to make sure he was all right. Kurt, of course, never showed his face again. Not yesterday, not last night, not this morning.'

Alex pushed aside the remains of the food and lay close beside her, edging towards her on the blanket until their faces were almost touching.

'They used to talk about chopping down all the trees,' she said. 'They were going to clear the entire hillside. A big company was going to come to the town, build a power plant, factories. The place was going to double in size, and then double again five years later. Now look at it. All that's happening here now is that they might knock down a few lousy huts.' She stopped abruptly, wiping her fingers across her lips, and then across Alex's.

'You're worried about what might happen at the barracks?' he said.

'They fought about that, too,' she said.

'The rest of the place doesn't appear to be rushing headlong into the future,' he said, hoping the obvious remark might reassure her.

'No, I know.' She crushed a seed-head in her hand.

Alex propped himself on his elbow and looked down at her.

'Are you looking at me?' she asked him, her eyes still closed.

He waited without answering her until she opened them.

She pushed her face into his chest, held him, and a moment later she started crying. He held her, rocking her gently and then stroking back her hair as she had earlier stroked back Whittaker's. She made no attempt to pull away from him, and so he held her tighter. She clasped her hand over his fingers on her shoulder.

After a few minutes of sitting like this, she stopped crying, wiped her eyes and pulled away from him. She drew her knees to her chin and wrapped her arms around them.

Alex opened the second bottle and she took this from him and drank from it.

'Where's it from?' he asked her.

'Everybody in the town has a cellar full of the stuff.'

'Including your father?'

'What's left of it. Kurt and his friends took most of it a few months ago. It's probably one of the reasons he's stopped coming back so often. They call the Americans "cowboys". He calls you "Tommy". I won't tell you what he calls the Russians.'

'I can imagine,' Alex said.

'He thought your army, the Americans, the French and the Germans would all turn against them, that the war would go back to the East, and that Rehstadt and everyone in it would all be once again left a long way behind the lines. I don't know where the bombers fitted into his plan.'

He took the bottle from her. 'I told a German officer I was questioning that he was soon to be handed over to the Russians, and that in all likelihood he would be tried and executed by them,' he said.

'And will he?'

'I don't know. I think so.'

'You sound as though you regret telling him,' she said. 'Perhaps he *deserves* to be handed over to them.'

'He made me angry,' he said. 'That's all. He thought he was above everything, that everything was going to be forgotten, hidden away, forgiven, wiped clean.'

'The Russians won't be doing any forgetting or wiping clean for at least another hundred years,' she said, seemingly unaware of the enormity of what she was suggesting.

Alex pointed to a bird circling high above them and she shielded her eyes in an effort to identify it for him.

'A large hawk,' was the best she could do.

'Not a vulture, then?'

'Could be.'

She told him that there used to be storks in the town, before the war, migrating birds which nested and reared their young there. People complained of blocked chimneys, of the birds' mess in the streets. A nest was brushed from the town hall clock-tower, falling into the square with its clutch of unhatched eggs. The parent birds flew away and nested elsewhere. She told him the birds had once been considered to be symbols of good fortune and that the first sighting of them each year had been front-page news in the local newspaper. She and Wilhelm had vied with each other to be the first to spot them flying over Ameldorf. The birds had returned to Rehstadt throughout the war.

'I had a plan for this afternoon,' she said when both the story of the birds and the second bottle of wine were finished.

'What was it?' he asked her, and then almost apologized for the stupidity of the question as she rested both her hands on his chest and pushed him firmly down on to the warm blanket.

22

They parted an hour later, at the bridge, and Alex sat and watched her go until she was out of sight. Occasionally, she would turn and wave him away, as though she were shooing off a dog that persisted in following her, and he would wave back at her vigorously, pretending to have misunderstood her and prolonging his pleasure in watching her go. Eventually, she was lost to him, and he left the bridge and returned to the Institute.

As he let himself into his room, Whittaker appeared and followed him inside.

'Waiting to hear all the details?' Alex asked him.

'Nina Lehman's here,' Whittaker said. 'She arrived an hour ago. She was looking for Eva. She thought she was here, with you.'

Alex followed him to his room.

Nina sat on the bed with a drink in her hand. The

bottle stood at her feet. She'd been crying, and her hair hung over her face. Whittaker's glass stood half-empty on the bedside cabinet. She looked up at the appearance of Alex.

'I was looking for Eva,' she said absently. She wiped her face on the corner of a sheet.

Whittaker sat beside her and put his arm around her.

Alex pulled a chair to face her. He sat in this, held her hand and asked her why she was looking for Eva.

'The hospital director's discharging her sister,' Whittaker said.

'Is she well enough?' Alex asked him.

'Of course she isn't,' Nina shouted at him. He felt flecks of her saliva on his face. Her hands were wet with her tears.

Behind her, Whittaker shook his head.

'Then why?' Alex said.

'Because he's a bastard, and because he thinks his precious fucking hospital has a reputation to protect, that's why.' She lifted her glass to her mouth, but then seemed unexpectedly repulsed by the smell of the drink and turned away from it.

'He says he needs the bed,' Whittaker said. 'In his opinion, Maria can recuperate at home just as easily as in hospital. He's wrong. I've seen her every day since she's been in there. She still has an infection, a temperature.' He mouthed the word 'blood' to Alex.

'Can't he be persuaded?' Alex asked.

'By whom?' Whittaker said. 'Us? I doubt it.'

'When does he want her out?'

'He told Nina some time today. Saturday. He wasn't even prepared to wait until Monday.'

Nina finally drank from her glass. 'I ought to be with her,' she said. 'I should have stayed there instead of coming here. I made a mistake in thinking you could help me.'

'There must be *something* we can do,' Alex said to Whittaker.

'Such as?'

Nina rose unsteadily between them, pushed Whittaker away from her, and told them she was leaving. She asked Alex where Eva was, and he told her she'd returned home. Then she asked him how the two of them had spent the afternoon together and he recounted how they had climbed the hill to the sunlit meadow. What had happened only hours ago now seemed to him to be days past.

'A high, sunlit meadow above the world,' Whittaker said. 'It sounds like something out of one of Pfitzner's tales.'

'Just a hill and the path and the trees,' Alex said, unwilling to share any more. He had felt drunk during their slow descent, but he was sober now.

'I'm going,' Nina repeated. She looked around the room. 'Did I have a coat?'

'No coat,' Whittaker said. He went to the wardrobe

and took out one of his jackets, putting it over her shoulders and feeling her sag beneath its unaccustomed weight. Only the tips of her fingers showed beneath the cuffs.

There were still no vehicles in the compound, and Alex told them this.

'I don't need one,' Nina said angrily. 'How do you think we all managed before you lot arrived? I'll walk. I spend my entire life walking. I'd better go to Maria.'

'We'll come with you,' Alex suggested.

She considered this and then shook her head. 'You'll only make things worse. The director will think I came running to you with my sob story because I was too pathetic to do anything about it myself.'

'We'll still—' Alex began.

'I said *No*.' She turned to him. 'One day, soon perhaps, who knows, you'll all be gone – you, him, all of you – and then who am I going to run to, eh? He's a powerful man, the director. I can't think *he*'ll be going anywhere for a long time, can you? No, I thought not. They're already saying he's going to be the new mayor. Perhaps the old mayor will take over the hospital. Who'd notice? The point is, none of you lot will be here to see it. Then it'll just be me and my stupid little whore of a sister walking round the town while all and sundry point their fingers at us and call us names. Who am I going to run to then, eh?' She fastened the buttons on Whittaker's jacket and turned up the collar.

Let her go, Whittaker mouthed to Alex.

Nina picked up her empty glass and tipped it to her mouth. She went to the door, paused to tell Whittaker that she'd return his jacket, and then she left them.

'We should still have gone with her,' Alex said, wondering if he was suggesting this for the sake of Nina and her sister, or because he could already imagine Eva's disappointment in him when Nina recounted her story of the afternoon. And perhaps by then Nina would be even drunker and her accusations and condemnations would have multiplied and grown more damning.

'Let her go there first,' Whittaker told him. 'We'll go later.' He looked at his watch.

'Is her sister seriously ill?'

'She certainly wouldn't be leaving my hospital in her current condition. And where's *home*, exactly? The camp? I can't think of anywhere that would do her *more* harm.'

'There's talk of the place being dismantled,' Alex said.

'Demolished. I know.' Whittaker rinsed Nina's glass and gave it to him, pouring an inch of whisky and then refilling his own.

'I didn't know you'd visited her sister,' Alex said.

'I often have some business or other at the hospital. I bribed a nurse with a few rolls of toilet paper to let me see her each time I went. The nurse told me she'd let me in without the paper, but you know what an honourable man I am . . . ' He slurred these last few

304

words, pretending to be drunk. 'The director found out what she'd done and shouted at her in front of everyone. I don't know . . .' He became distracted and turned to look out of the window.

Alex told him in greater detail about his afternoon with Eva, omitting only their love-making, but knowing that Whittaker had already guessed this.

Whittaker continued to gaze out of the window as he listened to all this, and Alex knew that little of what he was saying was actually registering with him. After a few minutes, Alex stopped talking, and several more seconds passed before Whittaker realized what had happened and turned to him.

'What is it?' Alex asked him.

Whittaker opened the drawer in his bedside cabinet and took an envelope from it. He handed it to Alex, and immediately Alex imagined the worst it might contain – bad news from home, news of his wife or daughters, an accident, sickness, another man. He took out the single sheet of paper and read it.

'I'm going home,' Whittaker said simply.

The sheet was the official notification of Whittaker's release from military service.

'And I'll probably get there in time to see the first of the roses come into bloom above the door.'

'Congratulations,' Alex said. He read the form closely.

'If there were any roses, that is,' Whittaker said.

The form was dated almost a month previously, and

just as Alex was about to remark on this, Whittaker said, 'I know. Dyer assured me that *he*'d only just received it from Hamburg.'

'And you believe him?'

'Not really. But it hardly matters now.'

Except that he might have been back at home for the past four weeks, already reattaching all those severed links and pieces and living his life to the full again, the abyss bridged.

'He thinks another eight to ten days to sort things out,' Whittaker said. 'My replacement should be here by then.'

'You think Dyer held on to this until he was certain of that?'

But whatever Whittaker believed, he remained unconcerned. 'Should I throw a party, do you think? I told Nina. I don't know how much of it she took in. She was drunk when she arrived. It was probably the cause of her outburst about us all leaving.'

'Probably,' Alex said, knowing his own recall or re-posting notice might arrive just as unexpectedly. 'Have you called your wife?'

Whittaker shook his head. 'I wanted to make sure it was real first. I spoke to Dyer. I wanted his confirmation.'

'And to let him know that you knew *he* was the cause of the delay?'

'Perhaps. Or perhaps I was just too pathetically –

there's that word again – grateful to say anything that might upset him or make him reconsider. No, I just went along with everything he told me. Like I always do, like we all always do. I accepted his congratulations and his cigar.' He took this from his drawer and showed it to Alex. 'I thought I'd save it until my bags were packed and the taxi was pulling up at the door. I've worked it all out. Here to there in only twelve hours, and that includes a lot of waiting around.'

He put the cigar back in the drawer and closed it. Then he went to his small sink and splashed water on to his face. Drying himself on his sleeve, he said, 'Let's go to the hospital. I feel brave.'

They left the Institute and walked into town.

Arriving at the hospital, Whittaker led Alex to the room at the rear of the building where Maria Lehman lay.

The girl was now dressed and sitting on her bed. She wore Whittaker's jacket, her legs pale and bare, and on her feet she wore an oversize pair of shoes. Nina sat beside her.

At the arrival of Alex and Whittaker, Nina came to them. The bed behind her was stripped to its metal frame and thin mattress.

'She was like this when I got here,' she said. 'They burned her clothes. They expected me to bring some others. How many do they think she's got? They were all she had. And anything she might have left behind at the camp will be long gone by now. The bastards had taken her out of the bed and then stripped it.'

Maria Lehman sat with her arms folded across her stomach. She looked up at Alex and Whittaker, but then lowered her head again as Nina went to them. Even in the jacket, they could see that she was shivering.

'I told her she can come to my apartment,' Nina said.

Alex remembered this from the night he and Eva had taken Nina home. He remembered its emptiness, the single bed, narrower than the one upon which the girl now sat.

'Is it far?' Whittaker asked her.

'Usselstrasse,' Nina said.

'A ten-minute walk,' Alex told him.

Whittaker went to the girl and spoke to her in his halting German. She recognized him from his previous visits. He measured her pulse at her wrist and then held his fingers to her neck. He asked her when she had last eaten and been medicated, and she told him she couldn't remember.

'Yesterday,' Nina said. 'She threw it all straight back up. Swill.'

Alex was about to ask him how he intended moving the girl, when the door was pushed open and the hospital director entered. He looked closely at each of the four people in the room and then beckoned to someone outside. The mayor entered.

'I told her sister it was time for her to go,' the director

said to Whittaker. 'I don't expect my words to go unheard or unheeded. And now I receive a telephone call at my home – at my home – to tell me that a military delegation has arrived here to further contest and confuse the matter.'

'We're here as friends,' Whittaker said, leaving the girl and coming to him. 'Show some compassion. You can see how she is. A few more days and she—'

'Absolutely out of the question. You think I made my decision to discharge her lightly?'

'I think you made it on grounds other—'

'And what's *he* doing here?' Nina shouted, pointing at the mayor, who remained in the doorway, and who seemed uncertain of why he had been summoned there.

'He's a family friend,' the director said. 'A close friend. I asked him to come just in case there was any confusion.' He turned to Alex. 'Confusion concerning our various responsibilities, Captain Foster, and where their boundaries might lie. Now, I insist again that the girl be removed from this hospital.'

'Or what?' Nina shouted at him.

'See?' the director said to the mayor. 'I told you what we were dealing with here, the depths to which we had sunk in this matter. One a hopeless alcoholic, the other – well, I doubt there's any need for me to spell it out.' He smiled, and because he smiled, the mayor smiled too. But unlike the director's smile, which was no more than a cruel, insistent prod, the mayor's smile was nervous and apologetic and short-lived.

Confused by her own drunkenness and by the director's convoluted and evasive language, Nina said, 'What? What's he talking about?' and she returned to sit beside her sister.

'Of course, my other possible course of action,' the director went on, 'is to contact Colonel Dyer directly and to ask him under whose authority you two are here to countermand my instructions.' He looked at his watch. 'Seven o'clock on a Saturday evening. I hope he has nothing planned, nothing he now has to leave behind to come here in person, again, to tell me that you two are here with his authority and blessing, and that he supports you in the – the – what? In the rescue of this wretched child?'

The mayor looked even more uncomfortable at the words. 'If I might make a suggestion,' he said.

The director turned to him as though the man had just pushed a stick into his back. 'What?' he said sharply.

'Perhaps an ambulance back to the camp?' the mayor said.

'She's not going back there,' Whittaker said immediately. 'It's freezing, uncomfortable and unsanitary, and there are no facilities whatsoever for her to be treated properly or taken care of.'

'Perhaps she should have thought of all that before she—' The director stopped abruptly, knowing better than to finish the sentence in front of Nina, but knowing, too, that its work was done.

Alex wondered who the man feared most, him and Whittaker together, or Nina alone. Or perhaps there had been some truth in the rumour about him becoming the town's next mayor, and something about this coming glory made him careful in front of the present incumbent.

'We'll carry her,' Whittaker said to Alex. 'We have no choice.' His remark was intended to defuse the situation, and Alex understood this.

'At last,' the director said, seizing this opportunity. 'Someone is talking sense.' And he turned and left the room, leaving the mayor standing alone in the doorway.

'I wish the girl a good recovery,' the mayor said, and then he too left them.

'*Will* he call Dyer?' Alex asked Whittaker.

'Unlikely. All he's concerned about now is getting rid of the girl and protecting the reputation of his hospital. He can already feel that gold chain sitting on his stomach.'

Nina laughed at hearing this. 'They took all the chains and other stuff away. Now all he's got is a fucking ribbon. Look close enough and you'll probably even be able to see the outline of the swastika his fat wife spent a day carefully stitching on and then unpicking again.'

The nurse Whittaker knew came into the room. She had clothes for Maria, and several blankets. She told

Whittaker she'd retrieved these from the furnace room, where they had been awaiting incineration. She had clearly been waiting for the director to leave, and she glanced nervously at the door as she handed them over to him.

Sitting on the bed, and as though suddenly overwhelmed by all that was happening to her, Maria Lehman started to cry.

'*Now* she cries,' Nina said, holding out her hand to her young sister, but making no real effort either to calm or to comfort her.

23

Two days later, just as he was about to start work, Alex was called by Dyer and told to go to the Institute gate, where there was a 'commotion'.

'What sort of commotion?' Alex asked him.

'If I knew that, I wouldn't be sending *you* to find out,' Dyer told him. 'I've already sent some guards. Someone said there was a fight. Germans. I don't know. All I *do* know is that everything will get sorted out faster if someone who speaks the bloody language deals with it.' He hung up before Alex could say anything else.

He left his room and the building and walked towards the main entrance. As he went, he heard raised voices ahead of him, and turning the final corner on the driveway, he saw the small crowd gathered at the closed gates.

People called to him as he approached. Most of the

crowd stood in a semi-circle away from the entrance, leaving a space at their centre. Several guards stood inside, looking out. One of these saw Alex approaching and went to him.

'It's the Yank,' he said. 'He's selling stuff at the gate again. Things got a bit nasty for him. Leave 'em to it, that's what I say. Dyer wants us on the outside, dispersing them.'

The man walked with Alex back to the gate.

On the far side stood Jesus Hernandez's jeep, with Hernandez standing beside it. In front of him was a youth, Hernandez's arm held firmly around his neck. The boy was struggling to free himself, but with no success. Hernandez held him firmly and easily. In his free hand he held a baseball bat, jabbing this at the crowd and occasionally threatening the youth with it.

The boy stood with his head down, both his hands on Hernandez's arm, cursing him, his voice choked and barely audible above the shouting of the crowd.

Alex told the guards to unlock the gate. They were reluctant to do this, but complied. He went out alone and the gate was immediately closed behind him. He regretted this display of unwillingness and unease in front of the locals. He recognized some of the townspeople. It was not a mob, not particularly united or violent in its protest, merely an angry gathering.

Hernandez turned at his approach and smiled

broadly. 'See,' he called to those around him. 'Now you're going to *have* to listen to reason.'

'Let him go,' Alex said. He repeated the words in German, and hearing this, many of those also calling for the boy's release fell silent.

'Why should I?' Hernandez said. 'He was robbing me.' He swung the baseball bat at the packages scattered around the jeep. 'Him and his thieving bastard friends.'

'I said let him go.'

The youth in Hernandez's grip looked up at him for the first time, and Alex recognized him as Kurt Remer, Eva's brother, the boy he had mistaken for a man on the forest track.

'Give me one good reason,' Hernandez said.

'I know him. His name's Kurt Remer.'

'So? Just knowing his name doesn't mean he *isn't* a thieving little bastard. I let him go, first thing he's going to do is make a run for it.'

It was clear to Alex that Hernandez hadn't made the connection with Eva, and he was grateful for this.

'Where to?' Alex said. He waited. Ever since hearing Alex say his name, Kurt Remer had held his gaze.

Hernandez relaxed his grip on the boy and he gasped for air and then started to cough as he cleared his throat.

'What happened?' Alex asked Hernandez.

'What happened was I was waiting for one of your bone-idle guards here to open the gates when *he* appeared with his mates.' He pointed again with the bat, this time to a group of men standing apart from the crowd. 'And as soon as my back was turned – as soon as I started setting up my stall – he jumped on to the jeep and started throwing stuff. His thieving bastard pals there were just waiting to pick it all up and run.'

'Then why didn't they?' Alex said. 'Why are they still here?'

The question puzzled Hernandez. 'What are you talking about? Because I managed to grab the little bastard and hold on to him, that's why. Because they knew I would have chased them and grabbed hold of them, too. Because they know not a single fucking one of them would have gotten away from me. Because in addition to being thieves, they're also cowards. Take your pick.'

'Are you OK?' Alex said to Kurt Remer.

The boy glanced at him without speaking, anger and resentment in his eyes.

'Hey, cat got his tongue?' Hernandez said. 'Another minute and I'd have clubbed his fucking brains out. Saved us all a lot of trouble.'

Others in the crowd came forward and stood closer to Alex.

'Looks like we got a delegation,' Hernandez said.

Alex indicated for one of these, a woman, to speak. She told him that what Hernandez had just said was true, but that she didn't believe Kurt Remer intended stealing what he'd thrown from the jeep, just that he

316

was angry at what Hernandez was doing, and that his actions were more a protest than outright theft.

Alex repeated what she said to Hernandez, who turned to the woman, waved the bat at her and then spat on the ground close to where she stood. A man standing beside her raised his fist to Hernandez and said in German that everyone in the crowd agreed with his wife, and that what Hernandez was doing was wrong, that by his actions he was prolonging the suffering of others.

Alex regretted this formal and melodramatic turn of phrase, but he translated the man's words for Hernandez.

Hernandez laughed at hearing them. ' "The suffering of others"? Tell him to look around him. What suffering? Where? Who? Tell him *I've* seen suffering, me, Jesus Hernandez, tell him that. Tell him I've seen suffering in this miserable fucking ant's nest of a country like he wouldn't believe. Suffering caused by him and all the other smug, self-satisfied, face-stuffing bastards just like him. Don't talk to me about suffering, not me. Tell him that. Tell him.'

Alex complied.

The man looked suddenly contrite and pulled at his wife's arm. Others in the crowd fell silent at hearing what Alex said.

'Ask him *how* I was pro–long–ing that suffering, ask him that.'

Alex asked the man.

'People here deserve better than to be denied all the things he was selling so freely,' the man said. And again the remark disappointed Alex.

' "Deserve better"?' Hernandez said. 'The people who *deserve* what I'm selling are those who can afford to *pay* for it. What doesn't he understand about that simple fucking little equation?' He studied the crowd for a moment. 'Does he want me to point out my customers among his friends? Is that what he's waiting for? Does he want to ask *them* why they do or don't deserve what I sell to them, and what they're only too fucking happy to buy from me?'

Sensing that the argument might be moving beyond his control, Alex told Hernandez to release the boy completely. 'I'll vouch for him,' he said. 'You can gather up what he threw down, see what's damaged or broken.'

'And then what – *you*'ll pay for it?'

'Just let him go.'

Hernandez released his grip on Kurt Remer, who leaned forward and rested his hands on his knees.

It occurred to Alex that the boy might straighten up and make a run for it, into the crowd and beyond. Or that he might even attempt something more drastic, such as seizing the baseball bat from Hernandez and then attacking him – attacking them both, perhaps – before making his escape.

Men in the separate group called to the boy, telling

318

him to forget about trying anything and to go to them. One of the older men even told Kurt Remer to thank Alex for his intervention.

It seemed to Alex that the boy's rash and unpredictable behaviour had made them all uneasy amid the townspeople. He saw, too, that while the locals were now prepared to support and tolerate these men – perhaps because they still acted as some kind of moral conscience in the town – there were limits to that tolerance, especially when this was tested so publicly, as now.

'What are they saying?' Hernandez asked him.

'They're telling the boy to stay calm, to go back to them.'

'No way. Not until I find out what this has cost me.'

Kurt Remer, Alex saw, showed no sign of running.

The woman who had spoken to Hernandez earlier came to Kurt and held him briefly. She spoke to him, but he refused to answer her. Then the woman looked up, saw something over Alex's shoulder and turned the boy's face to look.

Alex glanced at the gate and saw Eva arriving there.

She came through it, telling the guards to leave it open, and went to where her brother and the woman stood. The woman released her hold on Kurt at her approach. Eva held her brother close, pulling his face into her shoulder. Knowing what he did of the boy, Alex expected him to resist the gesture, but instead Kurt stood limply in his sister's embrace and allowed her to caress him.

When Eva eventually looked to Alex, he told her briefly what had happened, starting with Dyer's call. He wanted her to understand that it had not been his decision to get involved.

'He's not a thief,' she said.

This was probably untrue, and both he and she knew this. But he also understood the deeper truth of what she was telling him, and he agreed with her.

'People *are* getting sick of him monopolizing things and keeping prices high,' she said in German, indicating Hernandez.

'Now what's she babbling on about?' Hernandez asked him.

'They're voting on your popularity rating,' Alex told him.

'Whatever way she wants to dress this up, the little bastard was thieving from me. And now that I see who he is, *your* part in it all suddenly becomes clear. For crying out loud, why can't him and his stupid thieving friends get it through their thick German skulls? *They lost.* It's *me* who gets to decide what happens next, me. *I'm* the one who decides what I do and don't sell to them, and what the price is. They lost. How simple can it be to understand? They get no say.'

Alex refused to translate the words, and he hoped Eva would also say nothing.

'What, all of a sudden you're on their side?' Hernandez shouted at him, angry at his sudden impotence. 'Oh, I get it.' He looked at Eva and grinned. 'You do her a big favour where little brother's concerned, and she does you an even bigger one later. That it? Tit for tat?' He laughed at the remark. 'Tell *them* to pick everything up.' He jabbed the bat at the men still waiting for Kurt Remer to go back to them.

Alex called to the group, and several of them came forward, older men in their fifties or sixties. The others remained where they stood. These were all younger men, most of them older than the sixteen-year-old Kurt, but still young.

'What's wrong with the others?' Hernandez said. 'They deaf?'

The old men began retrieving the packages and putting them back on the jeep. People in the crowd came forward with others.

After a few minutes, the collecting was finished.

'That the lot?' Alex asked Hernandez. He motioned for Eva to hold on to her brother until Hernandez was satisfied with what had been returned to him.

One of the older men approached Kurt and spoke to him, asking him why he'd done what he'd done. 'None of us knew what he was planning to do,' he said to Eva.

Then something in the crowd distracted the man, and

Alex saw that Paul Weiss had arrived. He stood for a moment out of breath, presumably having run all the way from his bar. Someone told him what had happened at the gates, and he went to where Eva stood with Kurt.

Turning to Jesus Hernandez, he said, 'One day, and sooner rather than later with any luck, you'll get what you deserve. He's a boy. Look at him.'

'What's he saying?' Hernandez asked Alex, who told him.

'So what he's a boy?' Hernandez shouted back at Paul. 'And what *do* I deserve? Seems to me like I already get everything I deserve.' He rubbed his thumb and fingers together. 'And as far as I can see, the real pity of all this – the real *problem* here – is that none of *you* – you, them, the boy and all his rag-tag fucking soldier friends – ever got what *they* deserved.' He turned to Alex and pointed at him. 'How many of *them* you ever had up there to slap around? How many of *them* ever put their hands up to anything? At least what *I* do, I do out in the open. I don't fuck around playing at soldiers – either up there behind closed doors or out in the woods pretending none of this ever fucking happened. Go on – ask him, ask any of them what one solitary thing any of them ever did that had the slightest bearing on how all of this turned out. Go on – ask them. Ask them loud and clear. Because from where I'm standing, they're the ones who are prolonging all this, not me.' He paused to draw breath. 'Or perhaps I'm wrong. Perhaps there *are* one or two among them who did get their own hands dirty in something or other. Perhaps they rigged up a booby-trapped bottle of wine someplace; perhaps they got their hands on a few deserters and did whatever dirty work was asked of them; perhaps they helped a few old men, women and kids to pack their suitcases; perhaps they even took them to the railway station and waved them off. Go on, ask them, ask them, because I want to hear it, me, Jesus Hernandez.'

A few in the crowd understood what he had just said and they whispered to those around them.

'Shame on you,' the same woman shouted at Hernandez. 'You accuse *us* of all those things? Shame on you.' She held a hand to her throat and looked genuinely aggrieved as she rebutted the remarks. Most of the others remained silent.

Paul Weiss took Kurt from Eva, and she finally released her grip on her brother.

'I'll take him back to the camp,' he said. 'It won't be for much longer.'

The boy pulled free of the man and raised his arm, as though about to strike him. But then he thought better of the gesture and walked ahead of Paul into the crowd. He paused beside his older companions. Several men spoke to him, but he ignored them. The crowd parted as he passed through it. Some of the younger men cheered

323

as Kurt finally reached them. In their company, he turned and looked back to where his sister, Alex and Paul Weiss still stood. And from them, he looked to Jesus Hernandez, who had climbed on to his jeep to continue checking his goods.

'Yeah, you're a brave man *now*,' Hernandez called to him. 'Big man now. You think this is finished? Think again.' He looked down to Alex. 'Same goes for you, Mister means-to-an-end Foster.'

'What?' Alex said, surprised by the remark.

'Never heard that one before? It's what Preston calls you. It's what he calls this whole fucking set-up. "Means to an end." He's just treating you nice until he gets what he wants.'

'Is he here now?' Alex asked him.

'He didn't come with me, if that's what you're asking.' He took pleasure in Alex's concern and uncertainty. 'Nah, him and a few friends were up late. Preston's sitting today out. It's why I thought I might get a bit of business done. And then all this happens.' He picked up a can without a label, shook it, pulled a face at the dent in its side, and then he called to Kurt and the others and threw the can at them. It struck one of the older men on the shoulder and Hernandez laughed at this. 'Bull's-eye,' he shouted. 'Take it. A free sample.' He picked up another can and pretended to throw it into the crowd, laughing again as people raised their arms to protect themselves.

'You're being ridiculous,' Alex told him.

'You already told me that. Besides, coming from you, that's probably a compliment.'

'I'll go with them,' Paul Weiss said. He embraced and kissed Eva and shook Alex's hand.

'You seem very friendly with the natives all of a sudden,' Hernandez called down, making sure this time that the guards at the gate heard him. He threw cigarettes at them and they scrambled to retrieve these where they fell. There were six men and he threw six packs.

'See – I'm a businessman,' he said to Alex. 'Got to keep my customers sweet. Now, can you, them and fucking Gretel here all disappear so that these other good, suffering, deprived people can tell me what it is they desperately want to buy from me without you looking on and passing judgement.'

Others in the small crowd had started to leave, but most, Alex saw, remained, waiting for precisely what Hernandez had just suggested.

Eva came to him, held his arm briefly and then walked back into the Institute.

'Hey, she kissed the other guy,' Hernandez shouted to Alex. 'Twice. Kissed him *and* held him. Double rations. What are *you* getting?'

The guards at the gate all laughed at the remark.

Alex followed Eva back into the Institute and the men fell silent as he passed them. He kept his pace slow and made no effort to catch up with her. One of the guards blew smoke at him, and another said something beneath his breath as Alex continued walking. The rest of them waited for him to move further away before laughing again.

24

He went later with Eva and James Whittaker to visit Maria Lehman.

Nina opened the door to them, and they filled the small room.

Maria Lehman was now barely conscious. She was sweating heavily, and Nina sat beside her on the narrow bed, continually wiping her sister's face and neck.

Whittaker had visited the girl earlier in the day, and had sought Alex out to express his concern at her deteriorating condition since leaving the hospital. But following the events of that morning, Alex's own thoughts and concerns had been largely elsewhere.

Whittaker took Nina's place at the bedside and listened to Maria's breathing and her heart. He took her temperature and examined her eyes.

'She was awake earlier,' Nina insisted. 'She drank some milk.'

The room contained the faint but unmistakable aroma of vomit.

'She needs to be back in the hospital,' Whittaker told Nina. 'And if not the one here, then another.'

'Where? Hanover? It's ten kilometres away. No – she's better off here, with me, where I can take care of her. She hasn't coped all that time through the war, losing our parents, and then in the camp and with everything that's happened to her since, to give in now to some stupid infection. She's a survivor. That's it – she's a survivor.'

None of them responded to this misplaced pleading, all three knowing that just as Nina considered all these things to be her sister's strengths, so they were now also working against her.

On their journey there, Eva had told them that, according to Nina, Maria now believed that her baby was alive and that it was being kept from her. She had surfaced briefly from her delirium, calling for it to be given back to her. She had even given it a name – Nina.

'She has a serious infection,' Whittaker said. 'Septicaemia.'

But this only caused Nina to push herself even closer to the bed and to grip her sister's hand harder.

'I know she has,' she said. 'And she's fighting it. Look at her. That's why she cries out; that's why she's sweating so much.'

'And her shivering?'

'That, too,' Nina said.

'It needs to be properly identified and treated,' Whittaker said.

'Then *you* do it. Do it here. She can't go to Hanover. *That's* what would kill her. She needs to stay here. I'm all she's got now. I need to stay with her. You work out what's wrong with her. All she needs is rest. And time to heal. A few more days and she'll start to recover. Every time I went to the camp, there were people suffering like this, worse. And most of *them* recovered. So if you can't help her, then tell *me* what to do.'

She avoided looking at them as she said all this.

Eva sat beside her and put an arm around her shoulders.

Whittaker motioned Alex to the door and the two of them went outside on to the landing.

'That's right,' Nina shouted at them as they went. 'Go outside and whisper about us. Just like everybody else does.'

'*Would* she recover if she went to Hanover?' Alex asked Whittaker when they were alone.

'I don't know. I don't even know how she'd get there or if she'd survive the journey. But I'd be a lot happier if she at least made the attempt. All I can do for her here is to give her a sedative to keep her calm, and perhaps penicillin in the hope that it's effective against whatever strain of infection she's suffering from. When I saw her this morning, she'd been bleeding again. The sheets are still stained.'

'And since?' Alex asked him.

Whittaker shook his head.

'Where will you get the drugs for her?' Alex said.

Whittaker said nothing for a moment. 'I'm sure there are pharmacies here in the town, or somewhere near by. I'm sure these things are available at a price.' It was his way of telling Alex not to ask, and Alex understood this.

'You could try the hospital again,' Alex suggested.

'I did. No luck. The director was adamant. Does he look to you like a man who changes his mind?'

'You also have to consider yourself in all of this,' Alex said. 'I'm serious. Especially now with your own departure imminent.'

'I know. And I appreciate your concern. Stop worrying. There isn't anything I haven't already considered.'

Including stealing drugs from the Institute for the girl? Alex thought. *Including buying them on the black market, knowing they will probably have been stolen? Including buying them from Jesus Hernandez?*

'Who knows,' Whittaker said. 'Perhaps Nina's right – perhaps Maria *is* a survivor. Perhaps she'll ride everything out and recover of her own accord. It happens.'

'You don't believe that any more than she does,' Alex said.

'Oh? So what do *you* suggest I do? Stand back and

330

watch it happen? Again. Stand back like the rest of them, wring my hands, say "What a pity, what a shame," and then later suggest to someone that perhaps it was all for the best?'

'If Dyer finds out that you're even—'

'Save your breath,' Whittaker said angrily. 'We all know what Dyer will do. I'm sick and tired of being at his beck and call, sick and tired of jumping just because he says so.'

Like me, you mean, Alex thought. *Like I do.*

Whittaker looked at him, guessed what he was thinking, and said, 'Like we *all* do. Like *I* spend the rest of my time doing.'

They were distracted by the noise of something metallic falling or being dropped inside the room, and they went back inside.

A jug of water had been spilled, soaking into the blankets and pooling on the floorboards. Eva stood beside the bed brushing it from her coat.

'I tried to give her a drink,' Nina said. 'I thought she needed one. I knocked the jug over. My fault.'

Maria lay on the bed as they had left her.

'She said "water",' Nina said. 'My face was close to hers. She asked me for a drink. That's when I knocked over the jug.'

Eva shook her head once.

'Ask Eva,' Nina went on. 'She heard it, too.' She turned to her friend. 'You heard her, didn't you?'

'She asked for a drink,' Eva said.

'See?' Nina said to Whittaker, and then laughed with relief.

It had been Alex's intention upon leaving the Institute to drive Eva home. Kurt had promised her earlier that he would remain with either Paul Weiss or their father until she returned.

'You two go,' Whittaker told him now. 'I'll stay a little longer. Nina and I can work out what to do for the best here.'

Nina nodded eagerly at the suggestion. 'Half the nurses in the hospital aren't even properly qualified,' she said. 'Anything they can do, I can do. She's *my* sister.'

Whittaker motioned for Alex and Eva to leave, and they said their farewells.

On the road out of Rehstadt, she asked him what Whittaker had said on the landing and he told her.

'Does he think she might die?' she asked him.

'She was bleeding earlier.'

'I know. I saw.' She sensed his reluctance to repeat everything Whittaker had suggested to him, and so she said nothing more on the subject.

Arriving at her home, the door opened and Peter Remer came out to greet them. He walked around the jeep, examining and admiring it. He asked Alex about its manoeuvrability and fuel consumption and was amused by Alex's ignorance in these matters. He declined Alex's offer of getting behind the wheel himself and driving around the yard. He whispered something to his daughter.

'He thinks you might be wiser parking it in one of the sheds, out of sight,' Eva said.

The remark surprised him.

'Kurt's home,' she said.

'What, and you think he might try to steal it?' He was only half serious in suggesting this.

She shrugged. 'After this morning, I don't know what he's capable of any longer.'

'He wouldn't,' Peter Remer told him. 'But if he's here, then there's every chance one or two of his friends will be hanging around in the woods.'

Alex drove the jeep into the closest of the open sheds, parking it there amid the blocks of uncut stone awaiting Peter Remer's attention.

In the house, Kurt sat at the long table, an empty plate in front of him.

'You're late,' he said to Eva. 'We started without you. Steak and champagne again.'

Her father's plate sat on the table filled with cold potatoes.

'We've already eaten,' Eva lied to her father.

' "We've already eaten",' Kurt said, mimicking her. '*Where* have you already eaten? *What* have you already eaten? With him? In a restaurant? In the restaurant at the Institute?'

'It's a canteen,' Eva said. 'You eat as well here as anyone does there.'

'See,' Kurt said to his father. 'Everything she says is an excuse for him, for herself, for what she does.'

Unconcerned by this, Eva took off her coat and went to stand by the fire to dry the dampness.

'They've been to visit the Lehman tart,' Kurt said.

'We went to see Maria Lehman,' Alex told Peter Remer. 'She's ill.'

'I heard,' Peter Remer said. 'She lost her child. It would have been something, at least.'

Kurt rose at hearing his father say this. '*What* would it have been?'

Peter Remer pushed his son back down in his seat and then stood behind him with his hands on the boy's shoulders, making him look suddenly much smaller and younger than he was. 'Just shut up,' he told him. 'You're not with your friends now. And the way things are going, none of *them* are going to be around here for much longer. And then what are you going to do? So just shut up while you're in my house. I knew the Lehmans, we all did. Just stay where you are and keep your big mouth closed.' He slid his own plate in front of Kurt. 'Go on, eat it. You heard her – it's the best you're going to get round here. Just eat it and be grateful. At least give me the satisfaction of knowing that you're not starving to death.'

He looked at the photograph of his older son as he said all this. And then he left the table and went to the cupboard, from which he took the bottle of brandy and three glasses.

He poured Alex and himself a drink. 'To youth,' he said, and they touched glasses.

'Except not this one,' Eva said. She left the fire, came to her brother and ran her hand through his hair. Kurt pulled away at her touch and then struck the air behind him. But Eva was too quick for him. She avoided the blow and continued rubbing his head until her brother started laughing at what she was doing.

When she finally stopped, she poured herself a drink and sat beside him. She picked up a potato from her father's plate.

'Have them all,' Kurt told her.

She looked at the food and shook her head. 'Have you heard anything – anything more specific – about the barracks finally being cleared?' she asked him.

'It's why they were in the town earlier,' her father said. 'He says a group of soldiers turned up there. British. Said they'd come to look the place over. Engineers.'

'They had plans with them,' Kurt said. He looked at the glass his sister held. 'They just walked in and told us all to get out. They'd been told the place was deserted.'

'Why were they there?'

'Why do you think?'

'To demolish it?'

'Better than that. The man with the plans and charts said they were going to use the place to park their equipment and transport, bulldozers and stuff. They were there to demolish the DP camp, not the barracks. They wanted the barracks for themselves while they worked on the camp. He said they were there on a reconnaissance. Their transport and equipment was arriving later, and they wanted somewhere to store it all, a base. He even said they'd need one or two of the huts for the men who were going to stay out there and keep guard on it all.'

'You can imagine how they responded to finding Kurt and the others still living there,' Peter Remer said to Alex.

'At least they gave us all a lift into town,' Kurt said. 'Said they wanted us away from the place while they made their plans.'

'And in the long term?' Eva asked him.

'Said we'd got five days to be gone for good. After that, they'd be back with men to evict us forcibly. And when that was done, he said they'd flatten all the huts they didn't need themselves. He wanted to clear a way along one of the forest tracks between the barracks and the camp. They were going there after we'd gone.' He laughed. 'They seemed to think that that place was empty, too.'

'Someone must have warned them otherwise,' Alex said.

'Who?' Kurt said. 'You? Your bosses? Guess who told them it was empty, that at most there were only a few stragglers there, and all of them now trespassing on private land?'

No one answered him.

'The mayor, that's who. They'd already been to see him and he'd guaranteed them the cooperation of everyone involved. As though *he*'d be able to do anything. He told them that arrangements had already been made for everyone to leave the camp, even the ones who were refusing to move on.'

'There must have been hundreds living there when we went for Maria Lehman,' Alex said.

'There still are,' Kurt told him. 'Some might have gone in the past few days, but not many. Lorries keep being sent to take them, and then drive away empty.' He looked again at the drink in his sister's hand. 'Can I have a drink?' he asked his father.

Peter Remer refused him.

'A small one,' Eva said. She took the bottle and poured half an inch into a cup for her brother.

'He told me what happened at the Institute,' Peter Remer said to Alex. 'He owes you an apology and I owe you my thanks.'

'Jesus Hernandez is probably not the best man in the world to have as your enemy,' Alex said.

'And is that really his name, Jesus?'

'Perhaps it was an immaculate conception,' Eva suggested.

'I've told Kurt to stay away from him. When the barracks are destroyed, he comes back here.'

'Will you come home?' Eva asked her brother.

Kurt shrugged. 'I don't suppose I'll have much choice.'

'He still thinks his so-called friends will look out for him,' Peter Remer said.

'I didn't see any of them looking out for you this morning,' Eva said. She put her hand back on her brother's shoulder. 'And if Captain Foster hadn't been sent to deal with things, then the town police might have been called for. And how long do you think *they* would have negotiated with Hernandez for your release? How long would he have talked to *them*?'

Kurt laughed at the remark. '"Sent"? Sent by Dyer, you mean? Don't be so stupid. Dyer knows who Hernandez is, knows why he's there every morning. Your boyfriend here was sent precisely because the town police were the *last* people Dyer would have wanted there.' He turned to Alex. 'Face it – he sent you because he sends you to do *all* his dirty work for him.'

The same accusation made twice in one evening, Alex thought, amused. 'It still worked in your favour,' he said.

Kurt drained his glass and rapped it on the table.

'You're not in a bar now,' Peter Remer told his son. 'Apologize to Captain Foster.'

'No need,' Alex said, defusing the situation. 'Besides, he's right – Dyer probably did know more about what was happening at the gate than he let on to me. Perhaps he also believed I already knew Kurt.'

'Because of me?' Eva said.

'Or the supervisor,' Alex said. 'Either that, or he put two and two together when he came to the hospital the morning Whittaker and I took Maria Lehman there. I don't know.'

Kurt Remer watched his sister closely. 'What's wrong?' he said. 'Your exciting little secret not quite so exciting now that everybody knows about it? Now that everybody knows about it and can start to use it to their own advantage?'

Peter Remer again told his son to shut up, and the boy fell silent. 'The simple fact is that Kurt was lucky to get away from the situation without the authorities becoming involved. And the others were wise just to keep their heads down and not to reveal their true colours.' He looked at each of them as he spoke.

He clasped his hands together until the small glass he held was lost to sight, enclosed in the ball of his palms and fingers. His hands were coated with fine, pale powder from his saw, and in that light they looked to Alex more like stone than flesh, more like the carved and rigid hands of a statue than the bone, skin and sinew of an old man. Seeing this, and seeing the fingers tighten further, it seemed impossible to Alex that the glass they still held might remain hidden within them without shattering.

25

Alex spent an uneventful morning seeing most of the men sent to him, four of whom, recently arrived in Rehstadt, had been garrisoned on the Channel Islands and had been marooned there following the Invasion. They all spoke with a measure of guarded fondness of their time on the Islands, of the people and their work there, and each man complained of the deterioration in his health since the war's end.

Two of the men had visited England a decade earlier, one of whom had worked for three years as a waiter in London. Those two spoke perfect English, and Alex allowed them to act as translators for their companions. At every opportunity during his own questioning, the waiter described for Alex the meals he had helped to prepare and serve. It was his intention, he said, to return to London and to work there again. He was sick of living amid ruins, and sick of living among the savages who inhabited those ruins. Alex noted the remark – just as he had noted the tenor of the man's translations – and told him he'd visit him in London if he ever made it back there. They both knew how unlikely this was. The man gave him the address of the restaurant where he'd once worked, convinced that it would still be standing and open. He wrote it down for Alex and made a small ceremony of handing the note over to him, watching closely as Alex slid it into his tunic pocket and tapped it.

Shortly afterwards, around midday, Alex was distracted by a low humming sound, and then by the faint vibrations which trembled through his office like a draught. He heard voices on the driveway beneath him and looked out at the men and women gathering below. Seeing Eva among these, he returned the four men to their guards and went down to join the growing crowd. Everyone stood with their eyes shielded, looking up into the sky.

High above them, a continuous stream of planes flew overhead, silver outlines, flashing where they caught the sun and clearly visible at the head of their vapour trails, long and straight in the cold, still air at that altitude.

There was excited speculation among the crowd as to where the planes had come from and where they might now be going.

He went to Eva, who stood with a group of other women.

She smiled at seeing him, and then turned back to the planes.

He'd hoped to be able to ask her what had happened following his departure the previous evening, but he understood immediately that this was not what she wanted amid these others. And even if they spoke in English, the women would insist on a translation from her.

'Where are they going, do you think?' she asked him.

'Home, perhaps,' he guessed. 'Back to breakers' yards in England or America.'

The surrounding women were disappointed by this answer.

'No – to Russia, to the east,' one of them suggested, and the others agreed with her.

'They're flying west,' Eva pointed out, disappointing them again.

'To bomb France, then?' one of them said.

'That's probably it,' Eva said. 'The Americans have finally turned on the French.' She and Alex shared a smile.

'Seriously?' the woman said, repeating to the others what Eva had just suggested.

Eva held Alex's arm and drew him gently away.

'Everything's fine,' she said, before he could ask her. 'Last night, and stealing from Hernandez, that's just how he is. Don't worry – it wasn't you. Whoever I'd taken home, Kurt would have been the same.' She continued staring up into the sky as she spoke. 'Where *are* they going, do you think?'

Alex made several guesses, none of which either surprised her or satisfied her curiosity.

'It's how we knew the war was lost,' she said. 'Two years before its end – three.'

'The bombing?'

She shook her head. 'The British – you – always came at night, under cover of darkness and in planes painted black. The Americans came in broad daylight, in the sun, in planes painted silver. We might never have seen you, but we saw *them* clearly enough.'

'It was what they intended,' he said. He rested his hand on her shoulder and she held it briefly before moving away from him.

'My father said it would be enough for them just to fly back and forth over us – that they didn't need to drop their bombs to do their job. Then he said they should stick to visiting Berlin, that everything they needed to do, they could do there and there alone.'

'And not in places like Rehstadt?'

'Of course not here.'

'They suffered terrible losses coming in the daylight,' he said.

'I know. There was once a report in the local paper about captured airmen being paraded through the streets of Hanover. People stoned them.'

Alex had seen the same reports.

'We were told that by bombing us, civilians, they were fighting a dirty war, and that they got everything they

343

deserved. My father also pointed out to me that most of them seemed little older than Kurt.'

'And Kurt?'

'You can imagine what *he* thought of them, what he said *he*'d do if he got his hands on them. Look.' She pointed to the start of a second formation of planes following in the trails of the first.

'I never imagined there would still be this many over here,' Alex said.

Someone slapped him on the back and he turned to see Whittaker. Eva, too, turned to acknowledge him. He took her hand and kissed it.

'Apparently, they're on their way to bomb Paris,' Whittaker said. 'And then they're going to turn round and push the Russians back into Poland. Failing that, the Luftwaffe have regrouped and stolen the planes and are now on their way to Washington.'

Eva watched him closely as he spoke, waiting for news of Maria Lehman.

Whittaker saw this and shook his head. 'No change,' he said, his voice low.

She turned away from him.

The noise of the approaching planes grew louder. This second formation was flying lower than the first, and their trails, instead of streaming out in unbroken lines, quickly lost definition in the warmer air and were scribbled together.

'Busy morning?' Whittaker asked Alex.

'Holiday reminiscences,' Alex said. He explained about the men from the Channel Islands.

'I suppose it beats being sent to invade the Crimea,' Whittaker said.

'That's what they said.' He wondered how much Whittaker wasn't telling them about Maria Lehman.

Beside them, Eva put her hands over her ears at the rising drone of the planes.

'It's not that loud, is it?' Alex shouted at her.

She lowered her hands. 'I just don't want to hear them,' she told him.

He looked around them. Others in the crowd stood with their ears covered. Some waved and shouted at the planes, and others stood and watched them in a kind of awed silence, their eyes fixed on the high formation, craning their necks as the planes passed directly overhead. He imagined Rehstadt would be full of people doing exactly the same.

'My money's on France,' Whittaker said. He looked at his watch. To Eva, he said, 'If there's any change, I'll let you know.' And then he left them, calling for others among his own staff to follow him.

Eventually, the last of the planes passed over the horizon. It had taken no more than fifteen minutes, but it seemed to Alex to have been much longer.

The women Eva had arrived with called to her, beckoning her back to them.

'I have to go,' she told him.

'I was hoping we might have had some lunch together,' he said, the idea only then occurring to him.

'That *was* my lunch break,' she said. 'Now I have to return to work.'

'Later, then?'

'I promised my father I'd return straight home,' she said. 'After last night, and all that might be about to happen at the barracks . . .'

He knew immediately not to suggest accompanying her to Ameldorf, or even to offer her a lift there. He wanted her to tell him how much she regretted this dutiful obedience, how much she wished that she and he might spend the evening alone together again, but she said nothing.

The women continued calling to her, and then moved away in a group. Eva ran to join them.

Alex continued looking above him, to where the tangle of trails continued to merge and drift, and then beyond, to those trails higher still, where the lines of vapour remained unbroken and expanded, and looked to him now like nothing more than drawn-out balls of thick white woollen yarn.

26

The next day, early in the afternoon, Alex encountered Johannes Walther and a single guard sitting on the terrace and looking out over the garden below. The guard rose at Alex's arrival, pulling Walther up by his arm, and saluted. He was another boy, someone else Alex hadn't seen before. Walther spoke to him as Alex approached them.

Holding his salute, the boy said, 'Captain Foster, Sir, on our way to see you, Sir. Went to your room but you weren't there and it was locked. Sir.'

Beside him, Walther smiled at the boy's enthusiasm.

Alex returned the salute and the guard lowered his hand, immediately retrieving the rifle which stood propped against the bench.

'We were taking the sun,' Walther told Alex.

It was another warm and cloudless day, another promise of the approaching summer.

'Might as well make the most of it,' Alex said. He heard his father speaking.

'Before I'm locked in a deep, dark dungeon and let out only into the gloom of a high-walled prison yard for a few minutes each day?' Walther said in English, deliberately confronting Alex's fears for him now that Walther fully understood the true nature of his value to both Dyer and Preston.

Alex pretended to dismiss the remark and all it implied.

'What's he talking about?' the guard said, but with no real concern in his voice. 'I thought you was one of the good ones, Walther.' He pronounced it 'Walter'.

'I am,' Walther said, his eyes fixed on Alex.

The boy's boots shone with polish. The coarse material of his tunic and trousers was stiff and perfectly creased, and his beret sat at the exact prescribed angle on his shaved head. 'What's he saying, then?' he asked Alex.

'He's speculating pointlessly on his future,' Alex said.

'Prison? Is that a future? What, is he a bad 'un, then? You been lying to me, Walther?'

'I wasn't expecting to see him today,' Alex told the boy.

The guard took a clipboard from the bench. 'New schedule, Sir. Colonel Dyer said he'd talk to you about it later. He said it was a final "A and R", a stamp job.'

'Assessment and Recommendations?' Walther said.

The guard turned to him. 'Spot on. So, if I was you,

I'd keep that –' he pointed his rifle at Walther's mouth '– buttoned.'

'He's right,' Alex said, the remark intended as a warning to Walther.

'Thank you, Sir,' Walther said to the boy.

Alex had been anticipating a few hours of freedom, time to catch up with all the other reports and evaluations Dyer still expected of him.

'Shall I take him back up, Sir?' the boy said.

Before the encounter, Alex had also considered walking into Rehstadt to see for himself how well Maria Lehman was recuperating at her sister's.

Nina had been to work only intermittently since her sister had been admitted to the hospital. The supervisor had already complained to Dyer about this, and Dyer, wanting rid of the man and his endless and petty complaints, had told him to do whatever he saw fit. Meaning Nina would now probably be harangued and humiliated before being fired.

'Sorry?' Alex said.

'I said, shall I take him back up? Sir.'

Alex nodded. The guard saluted again and then pushed Walther ahead of him.

Alex remained where he stood. 'I'll be there in two minutes.'

He waited until the two men were out of sight, then sat on the bench and lit a cigarette. He was tired, having slept only fitfully. He'd spent the evening alone:

Whittaker had gone into Rehstadt to tend to Maria Lehman, sitting long into the night with Nina as the two of them waited for the first signs of the girl's recovery.

Whittaker had confided in Alex about where he was going, and when Alex had asked him what he believed he was able to do for Maria that rest and time alone would not now achieve, Whittaker had said, 'Nothing,' and had then told Alex that he was probably right in all his other assumptions. It was a necessary evasion, and both men had understood that. 'I only hope you know what you're doing,' Alex had said, meaning Whittaker's contravention of Dyer's orders, regretting the glib remark in the silence which followed. 'You know where I am,' Whittaker had said, and had then left him. Afterwards, Alex had waited for Whittaker's return, intending to apologize to him. But Whittaker was not back at the Institute by two in the morning, and when he'd returned after that, Alex had been asleep.

After a few minutes more, he left the warmth of the terrace and went to his room.

The corridor was crowded, and noisier than usual, the cacophony of voices rising as he climbed the stairs. Some fell silent at his appearance, but most resumed their conversations upon identifying him. Normally, the prisoners were content to sit without talking – perhaps for fear of either giving something away or being overheard by someone – but today they had few inhibitions.

350

Alex called for silence. The door beside him opened and another of the interrogators came out.

'Why all the noise?' Alex asked him.

'You not heard?' The man went back into his room and reappeared a moment later with a newspaper. 'Three days old. *The Times.* Apparently, *questions* –' he endowed the word with a cold and disbelieving emphasis '– have been asked in Parliament about the purpose of this place, about what we're doing here, and why. Can you believe it? In Parliament. Bastards. And not just here, either.'

Alex scanned the short article. Dyer was mentioned twice. 'It doesn't say much,' he said.

'I know it doesn't *say* much. But this lot still got wind of it. Just think about where those *questions* leave us, you and me. This lot probably think we're going to apologize for everything and then let them all just go home.'

'Not very likely,' Alex said, his lack of concern or even interest making the man angry. Alex knew him only slightly. He had a reputation for violence against the prisoners and was one of Dyer's favourites.

'I know,' the man said. 'But it doesn't help for us to be stabbed in the back by our own bloody lot. Bloody politicians. Sticking their noses into things they know absolutely nothing about. Bastards, every bloody one of 'em.' He looked around him and lowered his voice. 'It's this new fucking government. Churchill would never have stood for this kind of thing.'

Alex looked along the corridor to where Walther and the young guard awaited him. 'Can I borrow this?' he asked the man.

'Of course.' He was already searching the corridor for the next prisoner on his own list. Whoever it was, Alex pitied him. He considered telling the man to calm down before he started work, but he said nothing. He left him and went to his own room.

Walther and the guard rose at his approach. Alex told the boy to wait outside.

'Is that procedure?'

Several other guards laughed at hearing this and told the boy to stop making life hard for himself and to join them at their game of cards. Waiting for a nod of confirmation from Alex, he unlocked the handcuffs attaching him to Walther and went to them.

Inside, Walther carried a chair from the wall and placed it in front of the desk.

'Our final meeting, perhaps?' he said.

'Perhaps.' Alex looked at the healed cuts and fading bruises on his face. 'No more encounters with Ochmann-Schur, then?'

'None. He's a changed man. Haven't you heard?'

'In what way?'

'It's just more rumours. Apparently, he's started being very helpful. He knows a lot of people. He even knows those men who—'

'What he knows is that he's being handed over to the

Russians,' Alex said. 'He's doing everything he can to save his neck, to make himself invaluable to someone else in the hope of avoiding what's coming to him.'

The remark surprised Walther and he stopped talking. 'On whose orders?' he asked after a moment's thought. 'The Americans?'

Alex shrugged.

'Not yours, surely?' Walther said. 'Oh, I understand. They're handing him over in return for someone else. Another of their rocket men? I thought *they*'d all been rounded up by now. Are the Americans still pretending they want them to help them fly to the moon? After Japan? In that case, tell Dyer *I*'m a rocket man. I know as much as most of them. So, the Russians get Ochmann-Schur, and the Americans get me. Does everyone really owe them so much?'

'*They* seem to think so,' Alex said.

Walther shook his head. 'It's not them you owe; it's the Russians. They're the ones who fed themselves into the grinder, and us along with them. Not the Americans.'

'The Russians have a good claim on Ochmann-Schur,' Alex said.

'And presumably they don't know how important the man is who the Americans want in exchange for him.'

'Presumably.'

'Are *you* happy with handing him over just because the Americans have told Dyer to do it?'

'Not my decision to make or to contest,' Alex said.

'No, of course not. And if the Russians came back tomorrow and asked for me, for me specifically?'

'They won't,' Alex said.

'Why? Because the Americans want me more for their own perfect little trial?'

'And you'd rather be tried by the Russians than the Americans? I doubt that.'

Walther considered this. 'Are guilt and innocence so easily negotiable, then?'

'You'll get a fair trial,' Alex said, angry at the divergent course their meeting had once again so swiftly taken.

Walther, too, regretted this, and said, 'Of course I will. No – you're right: give me Uncle Sam over Uncle Joe any day. I bet the Russian prosecutors are already licking their lips at the prospect of getting their hands on Ochmann-Schur.'

Alex opened Walther's file. It contained no more than it had done at their previous meeting. If, as the guard had suggested, this encounter was intended as their final one, then he would need to be more alert than usual to the consequences of his own remarks and revelations. He was in no doubt now of Preston's power, or that Walther would be taken from Rehstadt to stand trial alongside all the others already collected together for the massacre at Malmédy. Whatever he wrote concerning his own belief in Walther's innocence or guilt would count for little once that other machinery had started to turn. And any overt suggestion now of Walther's innocence might later be seized on by his defence counsel and perhaps be used to embarrass the Americans.

'What will you say?' Walther asked him, interrupting these thoughts. 'In your report.'

'About what?'

Walther shook his head at the evasion.

'It's not me you need,' Alex said. 'It's the accounts of all your comrades, of the field hospital staff, of the men who were with you when the shootings took place, of the survivors, civilian witnesses. Find *them*, let *them* speak up for you. In all likelihood, the Americans will already have seen them. You know how thorough they are. Talk to *them*.'

'Unless, of course, everything I've told you so far was a pack of lies and I was there with the rest of them, holding my pistol to all those skulls,' Walther said.

Alex refused to respond to this. Perhaps Walther knew as well as he did that only a solitary way forward remained open to him.

'Do you want me to go over it all again?' Walther asked him. Then something occurred to him and he smiled. 'Or shall I tell you what the Russians want Ochmann-Schur for?'

'Another story?'

Walther shrugged.

'Is it the truth?' Alex asked him.

'What's—' Walther stopped. 'I was going to say, "What's the truth?" But knowing what you and I now know about all this behind-the-scenes dealing, what does it matter what's true and what's a lie?'

Alex offered him a cigarette, which Walther took.

'According to one of those tales I've heard from others here – and, yes, unfortunately, it is that sort of tale – Ochmann-Schur did a terrible thing at Polotsk.'

It was the one place Ochmann-Schur had denied all knowledge of to Alex.

'He was in command of counter-partisan operations there,' Alex said.

'Plenty of scope, then. "You're a partisan – bang. You're the mother of a partisan – bang. You knew a partisan – bang. You were the neighbour of a brother of an uncle of a partisan – bang."'

'I imagine so,' Alex said. 'And at Polotsk?'

'Apparently, one of Ochmann-Schur's companies lost some men – the figure varies – in an ambush there. Could have been ten men, could have been fifty. All of them either killed outright or executed after being wounded in the ambush and abandoned there. Retribution was called for, and a thousand notices warning that this was on its way were posted in Polotsk and the surrounding forest. An investigation of sorts was made, but nothing of any real value was discovered. I daresay a few of those neighbours of brothers got a bullet for their trouble, but there was nothing that

356

placed the actual perpetrators in Ochmann-Schur's hands.

'And then he had two strokes of luck. An informer. According to whom, the partisans who had carried out the ambush came from a camp on the River Dvina. A camp in the forest. And the forest, of course, deep, dark and impenetrable, was not somewhere most of Ochmann-Schur's troops enjoyed working.'

'Just like in a fairy tale,' Alex said.

'Perhaps. Plus, of course, the forest was where a lot of Ochmann-Schur's men had already died.'

'And Ochmann's second stroke of luck?'

'That same informer told him that when the partisans, men and women, had formed their group and gone to live in the forest, some of them – and again the numbers vary; I heard ten from one man, twenty from another – some of them had young children whom they didn't want to take with them. Most aged under twelve, some babies. There was an orphanage near Polotsk, and these people put their children there. New identities were created and documents forged. All links between these allegedly parentless and homeless children and their partisan parents were severed.'

'Except that Ochmann's informer knew who these children were?'

'According to one of the men who told me this, he was something to do with the orphanage. A janitor, cook, something.'

'Someone who thought he deserved better?'

'It's often the case.'

'And he gave the names of the children to Ochmann?'

'I think "gave" might not be the right word.'

'Do the Russians have this man?'

Walther shrugged. 'I doubt he survived for too long having sold his story to Ochmann-Schur. What the Russians probably have are plenty of other eager witnesses to what happened next.'

Alex waited.

'Ochmann-Schur went to the orphanage, found the children whose names were on his list and had them all brought to him to listen to their stories.'

'And what did the babies tell him?'

'That they were hungry? Who knows? Perhaps they just lay in their cradles at his feet and cried for their mothers. He listened to the older ones and they told him nothing. Because they knew nothing. Just that they had been brought there and left there by their parents, who had gone away to fight in the war.'

'Did any of them tell him—'

'What does it matter what they did or didn't tell him? None of that mattered to Ochmann-Schur. He had *them*, the children. What more did he need?'

'What did he do?'

'A thousand new proclamations were posted saying that anyone who had abandoned their children at the orphanage to become partisans might be interested to go back there on such and such a date at such and such a time.'

'Otherwise?'

'Otherwise the children would be hanged. He built a gallows directly in front of the place.'

'And on the date specified?'

'He hanged them. No one showed up to save them, no one intervened. The few who tried to reason with Ochmann-Schur . . .'

'And the babies?'

'Apparently, he hanged three children who were not yet able to walk or to stand unaided. Someone held them, their heads in their own tiny nooses, and then simply dropped them. The others were stood on benches that were kicked away. There are photographs, lots of photographs. I can't imagine the Russian prosecutors haven't already seen them. You think that kind of hanging is a quick thing? Some of them were said to have hung there alive for almost an hour. The man who told me all this said that eventually staff from the orphanage were told to go and add their own weight to the smaller ones and to the babies. Three who refused – the first three who were told to do this – were shot.'

Neither man spoke for several minutes.

Then Walther said, 'But, as you say, and as you may still want to believe, it is all a story, another tale among a million others just like it. Perhaps only the photographs tell the truth, perhaps only they can be relied on. Or perhaps witnesses have been found. Perhaps Ochmann-Schur himself has started blaming someone else. Perhaps they've even found one of those men who wrapped his arms around one of the screaming babies and jumped up and down with him until he died, until his small neck broke. I don't know. The last I heard was that the Russians were executing men in their tens of thousands simply for having fought against them. There are camps in Siberia where a thousand men a day are worked and starved to death, Russians as well as Germans.'

'More tales,' Alex said.

'I know. A never-ending whirlwind of tales. And perhaps every one of them is either true or a lie and there is nothing in between. Tell me, how much "truth" do you imagine the Russians will seek to uncover once they get their hands on Ochmann-Schur? *I* may be on my way to a very public, widely reported and scrupulously documented show trial, but I doubt if Ochmann-Schur will ever see the light of day again.'

Alex was scheduled to see Ochmann-Schur in three days' time. Another final assessment. Another pointless engagement, more protocol observed. Another instance of Preston's carefully timed patience finally running out.

'Do you think the Americans know any of this?' Alex asked him.

'They usually look at all the cards in their hand before

playing the first one,' Walther said. 'I wanted you to know just in case you were once again thinking of standing up to either Dyer or Preston. Preston might already know everything there is to know about Ochmann-Schur. Perhaps it's because he's so important to the Russians that Preston knows they'll hand over the rocket man without too many questions of their own. You think the Russians wouldn't fly up to the moon if they could?'

'Perhaps they'll have a race,' Alex said.

'Of course they will. Like I said, Uncle Joe lost far too much over the past five years to start playing second fiddle now.'

'And everybody else will want their pound of flesh, whatever the outcome?'

'Including you,' Walther said.

'Me?'

'I meant Dyer, the British.'

Alex concurred with this.

'Perhaps you should go and talk to your colleagues,' Walther suggested. 'See if the story I told you is also being told to them. A thing like that won't stay a secret for long. And especially not in this place. Perhaps the orphanage is still there. Or perhaps only its ruins. I imagine Ochmann-Schur was a very thorough man.'

'We'll see,' Alex said. He closed the file and let his hands rest on it.

'My brother contacted me,' Walther said unexpectedly.

'Here?'

'There are ways. He sent a message to tell me that his wife is expecting their first child. And how much hay he gathered at the end of last summer, how well his tractor is running and what price his cattle are fetching at the local market.'

'If you give me his address . . .' Alex suggested.

'Thank you. I'd appreciate that very much.'

Alex passed him a pen and a sheet of paper, and then the file of all his details for Walther to lay across his knees as he started to write.

27

Later, upon returning to his room, he found a note beneath his door telling him to contact Dyer as soon as possible. The word URGENT was written across the top of the message. He screwed the sheet of paper into a ball and threw it into a corner of his room.

He lay fully clothed on his bed, intending to rest for a short while before going in search of Eva. But he fell asleep, and when he woke several hours had passed, and he knew by the failing light that he was too late.

Something had woken him from his sleep, and as he lay on his bed he heard raised voices coming from Whittaker's room. He tried to hear what was being said, but this was difficult. At first he imagined Nina might have returned. But then he heard the voices again and recognized that of Jesus Hernandez.

He left the bed, went to Whittaker's room, knocked and went in without waiting for an answer.

Whittaker sat on his bed, and Hernandez paced back and forth across the small room.

'Hey, come right in, why don't you? Pleased to see you,' Hernandez said to him.

'You were the one shouting loud enough to wake the dead,' Alex told him.

'Oh, not them,' Hernandez said, smiling. 'Nothing's ever going to wake them, believe me. I've seen them, lots of them, and they're *never* coming back.'

Alex looked to Whittaker, who signalled to him not to continue antagonizing the man.

'We were having a heated discussion,' Whittaker said. He tapped the small package on the bed beside him.

'Let me guess,' Alex said. 'He told you a price and then he doubled it.'

On the cabinet beside Whittaker stood three unopened bottles of whisky.

'Hey, fair's fair,' Hernandez said. 'I threw in the drink for free, gratis.'

'What is it?' Alex asked Whittaker.

'Something that will help Maria Lehman.'

'Exactly,' Hernandez said. 'Something that'll help – and I think we might be pitching things a little low here, gentlemen – help as in save-the-life-of. Something that'll help the sister of the friend of the sister of the thieving little bastard who tried to rob me. You two might not want to see that particular connection, but I do – oh yes, I see it clear enough.' He went to the cabinet and unscrewed the cap on one of the bottles, looked briefly for a glass and then drank from the bottle. 'That little bastard still owes me.'

'And this is how he's decided to recoup what he thinks he's owed,' Whittaker said to Alex.

'How much damage did the boy do?' Alex asked Hernandez, and saw by Hernandez's averted glance that whatever it was, he was now exaggerating it.

'Hey,' Hernandez said. 'You either want the drugs or you don't. This isn't a bottle of scent, cigarettes or a pair of nylons we're talking about here. I'm out on a limb here. And if you don't believe me, ask the guy I bought them from. You think *he* didn't need a big sweetener?'

'*He*'s the one taking the risk,' Alex said, indicating Whittaker, who sat on the bed and remained silent.

'What risk?' Hernandez drank again from the bottle. 'He's a doctor, right? They got an oath. It's their duty to help the sick and the suffering.' Something about the remark amused him and he laughed. 'And it's three good bottles of booze.'

'It's a girl's life,' Whittaker said firmly to Alex. 'Can we just stop arguing over it. She needs the drugs, and he's the only place I'm going to find them without everybody asking awkward questions, all right?' He turned to Hernandez. 'I'll pay you. I just don't have it all on me right now. You'll get it. I'll give you what we agreed now, the rest later.'

Hernandez remained unconvinced.

'Then take half of them back with you,' Whittaker said, sliding the package towards him.

'No way,' Hernandez said, taking a step away from the bed.

There were no markings on the package, nothing to say what it contained or where it was from. Alex heard the faint rattle of glass as Whittaker moved it.

'I handed it over, as requested,' Hernandez said. 'From here on, it's your responsibility. I never saw the stuff. I never even *came* here. This heated discussion never took place.'

'That's why you were shouting, is it?' Alex said. 'That's why everybody for three or four rooms in both directions knows you're here?'

Hernandez smiled again. 'And that's going to help him, is it, if all this gets blown wide open?' He nodded to Whittaker, who held out his hand for the whisky. 'Besides, all I came for was to deliver the Doc his booze here. That right, Doc?'

'That's right,' Whittaker said.

'Some for Whittaker, some for Dyer, some for a dozen others. So, yeah, I was shouting. So what? Perhaps Whittaker tried to cheat *me*.'

'Both of you, shut up,' Whittaker said. 'Hernandez, just go. You'll get your money. You're not going to take

366

the risk of carrying the drugs around with you. Even you know the line you're crossing with this one. So just go, keep your mouth shut, and wait for the rest of your money.'

Hernandez knew there was no other option open to him. 'Yeah, well, perhaps you'll get the girl fit and well again and she can start earning back some of what she'll owe you for saving her life. Or, if she doesn't make it, then perhaps that sister of hers will oblige. You be sure to let the pair of them know where you got the stuff from, won't you? Perhaps you could even tell them what a big favour they owe me.' He picked up another of the unopened bottles. 'Plus, I'm making that a two-bottle bonus now. Again, on account of all this heated discussion you saw fit to have.' He jabbed the bottle at Alex. 'And one more word from the fucking professor here and I'm picking another of them up.' He took the money Whittaker held out to him and went to the door.

Waiting until he'd gone, Alex said, 'He could get you into a lot of trouble.'

'Not without seriously implicating himself, he couldn't.'

'And if he denied everything to save his own neck?'

Whittaker shrugged. 'Whatever happens, he's right about me having some kind of obligation towards Maria Lehman.'

'No, he's not,' Alex said. 'The hospital had that. Not

you. And whatever you might feel you have to do for her, you have no obligation under these circumstances, at so much risk to yourself.'

'If there is any risk, then it's going to be short-lived,' Whittaker said. He took a sheet of paper from his bedside cabinet and gave it to Alex. It was the final authorization and the travel details of his return home. 'Eight more days,' he said. 'It all looks very efficient and organized. Jeep, train, train, boat, train, followed by a quarter of a mile of overgrown and scented country lane under a clear blue sky.'

'It's England,' Alex said, smiling at his friend's coming good fortune.

'So? Under a clear blue sky and with the air full of birdsong and with the voices of playing children coming from beyond a stone wall and a white gate.'

'Too cold; they'd be inside,' Alex said, prolonging this reverie.

'No, they wouldn't. Not once they knew who was coming up the lane.'

'You've changed. They might not even recognize you.'

And for an instant, a look of uncertainty crossed Whittaker's face. A second, less, a blink of his eyes.

'I didn't—' Alex started to say.

'I know,' Whittaker said. 'But I *have* changed.'

'Not to them, you won't have. All they'll see is their father. They won't know anything of all this.'

'No,' Whittaker said. He drank again from the bottle

he held. 'There was a children's camp at Belsen. Did I tell you that?'

Alex nodded.

'Everything. Typhus, diphtheria, influenza, hepatitis, anaemia, pyorrhoea – that's good old-fashioned scurvy to you and me – and with a healthy dose of malnutrition thrown in for good measure. I think we saved half of them. Perhaps more. Some of them looked as fit and as healthy as—' He stopped abruptly. He had been about to say the names of his own daughters, but they had dried in his throat.

'I know,' Alex said. It was Whittaker's way of explaining to him why he was doing what he was doing for Maria Lehman now, and Alex regretted more than ever his own unthinking remarks. 'You did what you could then, and you're doing the same now,' he said.

'Is that an explanation or an excuse?' Whittaker asked him.

Alex smiled and shook his head. 'Neither. Just one of those conversations you and I usually manage to avoid having.'

'I saw *The Times* article,' Whittaker said.

'So? Whatever happens here, it'll soon be nothing whatsoever to do with you.'

'Because I'll be walking up that country lane?'

'Under that clear blue sky.'

'You forgot the birdsong,' Whittaker said. He closed

his eyes and pinched the bridge of his nose between his thumb and forefinger.

Alex left him shortly afterwards, accepting Whittaker's offer of one of the bottles as he went.

'Oh,' Whittaker said, remembering. 'Eva was here earlier, looking for you. I saw her in the office. I think she went home.'

'I'll see her tomorrow,' Alex said, turning away to conceal his disappointment.

He returned to his own room, and because he could not settle, he drank some of the whisky and then went downstairs.

The night air was cool. He passed the windows of a communal room – one of the hotel's old sitting rooms – and saw the men inside. There was a poorly stocked bar and a billiard table. Some of the men played at cards and others sat alone and read. A wireless set glowed on a high shelf.

Turning the corner of the building, he encountered Jesus Hernandez, who was sitting in his jeep, smoking a cigar. Alex went to him, and at his approach Hernandez shone a torch in his face.

'Still here?' Alex said.

'I'm waiting for three-star Preston. He's with Dyer.' He turned the torch off.

Alex sat beside him. 'I think I was meant to join them.'

'So? Tell Whittaker I meant what—'

'Tell him yourself,' Alex said, tired of the man's threats.

'He didn't send you to see me – to try and talk some sense into me about the money?'

'No one sent me. Besides, we all know you've got just as much to lose as he has, more probably.'

Hernandez remained unconvinced and unconcerned by this. 'Like I said, I'm only here because Preston wanted a driver.'

'Watching your own back,' Alex said.

'It's good advice. Besides . . .'

Alex waited.

'This time next month I'll be Stateside. No more sitting around with my feet in this cesspool.'

'Home to a hero's welcome?' Alex said.

'What, after all this time? Nah. A year ago, perhaps, but not now. All this is old news. *I'm* old news.' There was genuine regret in Hernandez's voice.

'It'll mean an end to all your money-making,' Alex said.

'Which is why I'm stepping up business before the big silver bird flies me away.' He flew his hand between them. 'I've been sending money home for three years now. I got receipts for everything I sent. My mother has everything safely stashed away for me. Don't you worry about PFC Jesus Hernandez. He'll make out. I got plans.'

'That's why you got Whittaker the drugs, and why you then got greedy,' Alex said. He was struck by the sudden parallels of the two lives – Whittaker's and Hernandez's – but he said nothing to the man beside him that might give him even more of a hold over Whittaker.

'I'm a wealthy man,' Hernandez said. 'Wealthiest man in my family. I'll *be* somebody when I get home. People will look up to me, respect me. I might even get in touch with a few old Army friends, let them see how good I turned out.'

'Do you have someone waiting for you?' Alex asked him.

'I already told you – my mother. Oh, you mean a girl. I got fifty girls waiting for me. Make that a hundred when they see all the dough I'm carrying.'

His bragging seemed even more pointless now that the two of them were alone.

Hernandez offered Alex a cigar, which he took and lit, choking on the acrid smoke.

'Like this.' Hernandez showed him how to inhale and blow out the smoke.

'*Did* Kurt Remer do any damage?'

'The kid? Not much. A few bottles cracked, a few tins dented. Don't worry – I'll be calling in all my debts before I leave.'

'I'll pay you whatever it is,' Alex said.

'And what if I don't want it from you? What if I want it from him, in person? I suppose I better keep closer tabs on him now that the camps are going to be flattened.'

'You know about that?'

'It's the reason Preston's here. You Brits got a bulldozer that couldn't knock a plant pot over. One. This big.' He held his thumb and forefinger an inch apart.

'Whereas you—'

'Whereas we got fifty, a hundred, a thousand even. And all of them big enough to flatten one of those dumps in an hour. Preston, Dyer and the mayor are cooperating on the thing.'

'The mayor?'

Hernandez laughed. 'They're using him, letting him stand up at the front of everything. Any problems, anything goes wrong, and it's down to him to get it sorted out. Besides, times change. Apparently, they now need to have the civilian authorities involved in all of this. You need the bulldozers, we need your men, and the mayor needs the approval and applause of all the townspeople here. It's a regular fucking back-slapping daisy-chain.'

'Because the locals want to see an end to the camps and all those people still living out in the forest?' Alex said.

'Added to which, the fat bastard's got his election chances to consider. Is that where the boy's still living – out in the woods?'

'At the old barracks. He'll probably go back to his father's in Ameldorf.'

'Thanks for the information.'

'I meant what I said about paying anything he owes you.'

'I'll think about it. Top of my list right now, though, is turning all those demolition workers into customers. "Come to Jesus" – that's what I tell them. "Come to Jesus and see what he has to offer you."' He laughed loudly at this.

'How long will it take them – the demolition?' Alex asked him.

'Both camps? A few days, no more. They'll move in, flatten everything, and then just burn what they're left with. The mayor's already talking about planting the trees back. The sooner everything's gone, the sooner that happens.'

'Everything wiped clean and ready for whatever comes next.'

'The guy's even pushing for help from Preston with his fucking monument. That's the clincher, that's what he thinks will get him re-elected and back on top of the pile with his snout back in the trough. Good times coming to this country.' He rubbed his thumb and fingers together. 'Dough. Lots of it. Investment.' He laughed again.

'You sound as though you'd like to come back and share in it all,' Alex said.

'Me? I'm never leaving home again. I've been out in the real world too long. You can keep it. I'm going back to live with civilized people. You don't know what I'm talking about. Ask Whittaker – he knows.'

Alex understood what he was saying. 'I know he does. It's why he's trying to help Maria Lehman now.'

'Is that an appeal to my better nature? We friends all of a sudden?'

Alex climbed down from the jeep.

'How long are you waiting?'

'For Preston? As long as it takes. You think I'm going to go in and knock on Dyer's door and tell him I'm getting cold and that I want to go to bed? Last time it was two o'clock. Don't worry about me – I'm good with my own company. It's the best way to be.'

Alex left him, retracing his steps to the entrance, pausing above the Institute garden to look at the town below. Few lights showed, mostly irregular streetlights radiating from the centre. Little else was visible in the all-encompassing darkness. He heard owls somewhere in the surrounding forest, and the vague and distant barking of a dog. The pale quarter-moon showed briefly through the moving cloud.

28

'I see by your manner – your caution – that the tales have reached your ears, too, Captain Foster.' Ochmann-Schur sat upright, his hands on his knees, his neck straight, chin out. He looked to Alex like someone about to give a recital. Or someone upon whom sentence was about to be passed.

'And are they tales? Is none of it true?' Alex said.

Ochmann-Schur remained silent for a moment. 'Do you honestly still believe that Seidl will allow me to be handed over to the Russians after all this time as easily as that?'

His calmness and conviction were an act, a taut and necessary surface over what lay beneath, and Alex understood this.

'They were Russian children.'

Ochmann-Schur raised and then lowered his hands.

'So? I've seen Russian children crawling on their hands and knees to cut the buttons from the tunics and trousers of dead German soldiers, Captain Foster. I've seen those same children, with their mothers and grandmothers, pulling the boots from men not yet dead.'

'Save it for your trial,' Alex told him.

It was another bright day, and the sunlight fell into the room in a block, crossing the floor beside Ochmann-Schur's chair, running over the square of threadbare carpet and starting to climb the wall behind him. It touched his left leg and side, and he ran his hand down to feel the warmth.

'I imagine Doctor Seidl, this man in whom you place so much faith, might have got enough on his plate at present,' Alex said.

For a moment, Ochmann-Schur did not understand the colloquialism. 'Oh, I see – with the trembling, singing Frank, you mean. Perhaps, perhaps not. I understand from Seidl that Old Hans is likely to be considered a "good German" by the judges – possibly excepting the Russian judge, of course, who will now keep his mouth shut on the matter in return for concessions elsewhere – or if not "good" exactly, then at least not one of the murderous mob sitting alongside him. Goering with his ridiculous nail varnish and all that flirting with the court clerks. Besides, even if Seidl *is* too busy to come here in person . . .'

'What?'

'I was going to suggest that I might still call on the intervention and influence of my brother. A new German government must, sooner or later, one day be formed. Surely even you – you yourself, Captain Foster – can see that?'

'And you believe that your brother will be a part of that government?'

'Of course he will. And, who knows, perhaps it will one day be more important to be owed favours by a grateful member of that government, than to be so responsive – no, so subservient – to the Russians now. It's just a thought, Captain Foster.'

And one you're convinced both Dyer and Preston will already have considered, thought Alex. 'You're wrong,' he said firmly. 'I suspect the Russians want *you* even more than Preston wants *his* man.'

'And Preston still deceives himself into believing that the Russians have no idea who that man is? Or that they are unaware of his precise value to Preston? Face it, they've already had him for a year. What do you think remains for him to reveal to the Americans that he hasn't already long ago revealed to them?'

It was something Alex hadn't considered, and Ochmann-Schur saw this.

'And has Seidl visited you here yet?' Alex asked him.

Ochmann-Schur was disappointed that he had changed the course of their conversation, and he let

378

Alex know this by refusing to answer him, merely shaking his head once.

'And what about you?' Alex said. 'Will you be in that new government?'

'One day, perhaps.'

'Even with all this on your record?'

Ochmann-Schur shrugged. 'You still make more of it than it warrants, Captain Foster.' Then he leaned forward and pointed directly at Alex. 'And do you know *why* you make too much of it?'

'Tell me,' Alex said.

Ochmann-Schur lowered his arm. 'Because you have had no war. Because all *this* – a comfortable office, a hotel room, three meals a day – because *this* is your war. This isn't war, Captain Foster. This is what follows war, something completely different. This is the silent, empty crater. This isn't even the fabled birdsong of the morning after. That particular dawn has yet to rise on this blessed country. Yes, even after a year, that particular sun has yet to show itself. And because *this* is your war, you want it – and your own part in it – to be more than it warrants. You possess power and respect and authority, Captain Foster, but you haven't *earned* any of those things.'

'And you earned yours by hanging Russian children?'

Ochmann-Schur considered the remark and smiled. 'What do you want me to say? That they breed like animals, like penned swine, like rats in a full sewer?

That two minutes in any so-called stinking maternity ward will replace a day's losses? Well, perhaps that's true. Except perhaps now some of those new litters might have good German blood in them. So perhaps at least some of them might grow up straight and tall and strong.'

'A long time since any German anywhere in Russia has had the time or the appetite for any of that,' Alex said.

Ochmann-Schur laughed at this. 'Touché. Perhaps, but I'm sure you understand me.'

'Oh, I do,' Alex said. 'I understand you as well as the Russian prosecutors will understand you when you repeat it all to them.'

'They and I will never—'

'You're going to them,' Alex said. 'Indulge yourself as much as you like with me, here and now, think what you like of me and the war I've had, but you're going to them and that's where all of this is going to end. Not here, not in this room, not with me, not with all those letters and summonses Seidl has yet to answer. And the first thing the Russians will do is to take away your smart, clean uniform and boots, your cap, belt, medals, ribbons. Everything. And after that, you'll live barefoot, with a shirt and trousers made out of sacking if you're lucky. This might be my war, but after this, you're going back to the men who know exactly what that other war – that real war you're so fond of telling me about – was

380

really like. There are photographs, Ochmann, witnesses. Lots of witnesses. Russian *and* German.' By now Alex was shouting, and realizing this, he lowered his voice.

'Men like Menschler?' Ochmann-Schur said after a pause. 'I doubt it's a journey he'd survive. He's been on his knees for months, begging to be kept here among all you camp-followers. What does he think – that he's going to be found innocent of all his own crimes and then be released and allowed to go on living here, to marry and to settle down and, what, become the town gardener or a cobbler or a bar-keeper?' He shook his head. 'You know as well as I do that that isn't going to happen. Just as you sit there and tell me you know what's going to happen to me. Perhaps Ivan had the right idea after all – thousands and thousands of firing-squads even before the war ended. You've never been to Russia, Captain Foster. I can tell that just by listening to you. I can tell by your ridiculous notions of justice and retribution, of atonement and forgiveness that you haven't been there. If you'd been there even for a single day – Russia, Poland, anywhere across that civilized divide – at the height of *our* time there, then you wouldn't be here now, conducting all this like a ridiculous schoolmaster talking to a wayward pupil.' He smiled to himself. 'What do you want to know, Captain Foster? Tell me. What about Polotsk do you truly want to know? Tell me and I'll relate everything in the smallest, most terrible detail for you. Do you want to know what clothes those children were wearing? What food was smeared around their small mouths? When the babies had last been fed? Whether or not they stank of their own piss and shit, and whether or not the men holding them at the gallows complained to me of the fact? What? Ask me.' He folded his arms briefly, clasping his biceps, and then he relaxed and rested his hands back on his knees.

There was a rap at the door and a guard appeared. It was the same youth Alex had encountered with Walther the previous day. He looked in at the two men.

'I heard shouting,' he said. 'One of the others told me to look in.'

'Everything's fine,' Alex told him, angry at this intrusion, at the joke that had been played on the boy.

'I just thought—'

'Please, go,' Alex said.

'Oh, and Colonel Dyer said to tell you to go and see him as soon as possible. Said to make sure I told you to your face, that you got the message.'

'Get out,' Alex said. 'And tell Dyer I'm busy.'

'*I'm* not going to him,' the boy said. 'I'm just here to deliver the message.'

Ochmann-Schur turned to him. 'Then consider it delivered, child. Now obey the order of your superior officer and go away.'

The boy looked at him. Anger flushed his face, and

instead of leaving, he came further into the room, leaving the door open behind him.

'Who do you think you're talking to?' He spat the words at Ochmann-Schur, who now sat with his back to him and looked directly at Alex, smiling at the conflict he had so swiftly and easily created.

Alex rose from his seat. 'I said get out,' he said, conscious now of the men outside who would be straining to hear the outcome of their joke.

'He wants to watch his mouth,' the boy said. 'I'm just doing my duty.'

'As a messenger boy,' Ochmann-Schur said, provoking him further, and gaining some additional pleasure from Alex's growing unease.

Alex went to where the guard stood. 'Tell Dyer, whoever, one of his clerks, that I'll come as soon as I can.' He stepped sideways until he stood between Ochmann-Schur and the boy.

'You ask me, he needs teaching a lesson,' the boy said.

'No one did,' Ochmann-Schur said, and then, 'All right, please accept my apology. I apologize for any offence I may have given. I apologize unreservedly.'

The boy grinned at hearing this. 'See?' he said to Alex.

Ochmann-Schur turned to them. 'Is my apology accepted?' He pursed his lips.

'This time,' the boy said. 'Just watch yourself in future.' He returned to the door, closing it firmly behind him. Both Alex and Ochmann-Schur heard the eruption of laughter as he returned to sit with the others.

'*Diese Kettenhunde*,' Ochmann-Schur said. It meant 'chained dogs' and was German slang for the military police. 'Would he have clubbed me with his rifle, do you think?'

'Perhaps I should have let him,' Alex said. 'Perhaps then Dyer might think I was doing my job properly.'

'Some of your colleagues would have had no hesitation in letting it happen.'

'Then perhaps they're the ones who've been beyond that divide,' Alex said. 'I think that concludes our business here.'

'So what now? You write your report and make your recommendations? I'm sure you will make a note of how cooperative I have been, of how valuable and productive our short time together has been.' He paused, thinking. 'Perhaps I might even give your name to Seidl as a character witness. I'm sure he would appreciate a little help.'

Alex shook his head.

'Oh, I see. Perhaps you have already promised the same to others. Captain Walther, for instance?'

Alex resisted the temptation to respond to this, but Ochmann-Schur saw by his momentary hesitation at hearing Walther's name that it had caught his attention.

'Are you finished with him, too? Is he also to be handed over to others in the name of expediency? Did

384

you wash your hands of him, too? Perhaps it is something you actually do, being English – wash your hands, I mean.'

Despite himself, Alex said, 'Walther denies nothing of his own part in what happened at Malmédy.'

Ochmann-Schur laughed in exaggerated disbelief. 'Of course he doesn't. He wasn't there. What is there to confess? However, he still told you a pack of lies, Captain Foster. Lies from beginning to end. You say you have photographs of me, witnesses, well what if Preston had those same photos of Walther? What if he's had them tucked up his sleeve all along? Walther simply fed you his lies and you believed him, swallowed them one after another. Do you think men like Walther and I don't understand each other completely? And do you truly believe that men like *you* will ever have even the smallest idea or share of that understanding? Lies, Captain Foster, lies. Persuasive lies, believable lies, lies supported by other lies and by altered documentation, perhaps, but lies all the same.'

Unwilling to listen to any more of this, Alex called for the guard.

A different man appeared, followed by another.

'Take him,' Alex told them.

The two men positioned themselves on either side of Ochmann-Schur and both handcuffed their wrists to his. Ochmann-Schur remained silent and stared at Alex as this happened, and Alex was careful not to catch his eyes.

'Lies,' Ochmann-Schur repeated, the word more mouthed than spoken, barely audible, more of a hiss than a whisper, but something which nevertheless filled the room for hours after his departure.

29

He was woken the following morning by Whittaker, who sat on the edge of his bed and shook him.

'Dyer wants you and me at the station. They've emptied the DP camp. The happy campers are finally on their way.'

Alex rubbed his eyes. 'What does he need us for?'

'Me to give them all a clean bill of health, you and all the other mumbo-jumbo merchants to make sure they all know exactly what's happening to them, where they're going, and what bright and prosperous futures await them there.'

Alex rose and got dressed. It was not yet seven.

Following his work the previous day, he had again avoided going to see Dyer. He wasn't certain why he was avoiding the man, only convinced that the more he understood of his own compromises where Dyer and

Preston were concerned, then the less he wanted those failings openly confirmed for him in their presence.

'They emptied the camp in the night?' he said.

'Looks like,' Whittaker said. 'Something to do with the early transports. Trains. Dyer and Preston have arranged for three to come and whisk everyone away before the good people of Rehstadt awake to their own bright and prosperous days ahead.' He picked up Alex's cap from where it lay on the floor and gave it to him.

At the station, a long queue had already formed along the road leading to Paul Weiss's bar. People waited with their luggage, singly and in family groups. Most stood, as though their departure was imminent, but some sat on their cases and looked around them at everything they were leaving.

As they arrived, Alex saw Paul Weiss in the doorway of his bar. They exchanged a brief greeting. Inside the bar, a group of local men had already gathered to watch and comment on the morning's unexpected proceedings.

A line of jeeps waited at the station entrance, and Dyer and Preston sat next to each other in separate vehicles.

The town stationmaster walked along the queue, telling people to keep in line, to keep their luggage away from the road, and to prevent their children from running up and down and making a nuisance of themselves. Few responded to him.

At Alex and Whittaker's arrival, Dyer left his jeep and came to them.

'Seven, I said,' he said to Whittaker, holding up his watch. It was twenty past.

'Have we missed the trains?' Whittaker asked him, feigning concern.

'The trains are going to be late,' Dyer said. 'Apparently, the best we can hope for now is midday. They promised us eight o'clock.' He turned to Alex. 'I think you and I have a missed appointment, Captain Foster. Several, in fact.'

'What does that mean?' Whittaker said.

'I wasn't speaking to you, Doctor Whittaker. Captain Foster knows perfectly well what I mean. And if he—'

He was interrupted by a long blast of the horn from Preston's jeep. Jesus Hernandez waved to them, his hand still on the horn. Preston spoke to him, and the noise stopped and faded.

'I'll see you later,' Dyer said to Alex, and he returned to his own vehicle.

'Churchill and Roosevelt,' Whittaker said, watching as Preston gave Dyer a cigar and lit one for himself, and as the smoke from these clouded above them in the cool air. 'Speaking of which—' He indicated several lorries and another group of men at the far end of the concourse.

Alex shielded his eyes to look at these. 'Russians?' he said.

'They're wearing fur hats and passing round bottles of vodka at half past seven in the morning. It would be a good guess.'

'Why are *they* here?'

'Same reason we are? Dyer's got three trains coming – east, west and south. Half the people here are going back to what they still think of as home in the Russian sector. I imagine that will be a through train, not many unscheduled stops. The others head west or south, change, change again and then settle either where they land or where they just run out of steam.'

'Is that the idea – to keep them moving, burn their bridges, let them wash back and forth for a little longer in the hope that they just find somewhere new and settle there?'

'Unless you've got a better idea. All Dyer, Preston and the mayor care about now is demolishing the camp. While that's still standing, they'll never be rid of them. The answer to their shared problem—'

'Is to make it someone else's,' Alex said.

Ahead of them, Dyer and Preston left their jeeps and went into the station. People in the queue shouted out to them, but neither man responded to the calls. The stationmaster and his staff formed a short line and locked arms to keep a path clear into the station. Jesus Hernandez remained sitting in his jeep. Seeing what was happening, the Russians left their lorries and walked to the entrance in a group, laughing and shouting as they came.

'We'd better follow Dyer like the loyal retainers we are,' Whittaker said, yawning as he spoke.

As they'd passed Nina Lehman's flat on Usselstrasse, Whittaker had glanced up at the window. A lantern shone in the otherwise dark building. Alex guessed then that he had been there earlier, attending to Maria.

'How is she?' he asked him now, as Whittaker gathered together his cases.

'Maria?' He paused. 'Not as well as I'd hoped. She's not responding to the drugs as quickly as I'd like.'

'But surely there's *some* improvement?'

Whittaker fluttered his hand.

'Are you sure the drugs Hernandez sold you are the real thing?'

'Shout a little louder,' Whittaker said. 'Who would you suggest I ask that particular question of?'

Ahead of them, Dyer reappeared in the station entrance and beckoned to them, his impatience rising.

In the station concourse, a series of tables and chairs had been set up on the broadest of the two platforms. Alex saw Eva there, already at work with others from the Institute. She saw him arrive and waved to him.

It was Whittaker's job to examine any certificates of inoculation the departees might have, and to question them on their general health and about any treatment they had received during their time in the camp. He summarized this information on a single form and then made recommendations for further treatment on the reverse.

People were reluctant to part with old certificates and

documents, and it was part of Alex's work to persuade and reassure them, as well as to ensure that they fully understood what was being asked of them.

It was clear to both men that most of the people they questioned told them only what they thought they wanted to hear, determined not to jeopardize either their departure or their ongoing treatment. People shouted at both Whittaker and Alex that they would not be separated from their family members and their friends. Men held their wives and mothers held their children.

On the opposite platform, away from these crowds, sat a group of individual men, Dyer and Preston and several of the Russians among them.

'They're here to make sure nobody slips through their own net,' Whittaker said.

Alex considered this unlikely. 'After all this time? They'd have gone by now.'

He was distracted by a dark-haired girl of sixteen or seventeen who came to him from the head of the queue and who asked him where she was being sent. He told her that that was up to her, that she could now choose where she went.

' "Choose"?' she said. 'But I am alone.'

'Do you have friends?' he asked her.

She pointed to the family standing immediately behind her. A man, wife and two small children.

'You could go with them,' Alex suggested.

'And live with them?'

'Ask them.'

She hesitated a moment and then returned to the people behind her. She spoke to them and both the man and the woman embraced her. When she came back to Alex, the man came with her.

'We shall take her with us,' he said, his English as halting as the girl's.

Alex asked him where he and his family were going.

'Home,' the man said uncertainly. 'Bautzen. East.'

Whittaker looked up at this.

The man handed over all the necessary documents, his arm still around the girl's shoulders.

Across the tracks, on the far platform, a man started shouting in German at Dyer, and when this tirade was finished, one of the Russians ran forward and struck the shouting man hard across his face. Others in the group laughed at this violence.

Alex beckoned the rest of the man's family forward and spoke to them. He told them of their train's delay and then showed them their route on a map on the station wall.

After an hour of this work, a klaxon sounded, and in the echoing silence which followed, Preston called for everyone to take a break. His words were repeated in several languages via the station loudspeakers. The queuing people sat on the few benches, on the ground and on their cases.

On the far platform, Dyer and Preston left the Russians and followed the stationmaster into his small wooden office. A fire burned inside and the three men stood in the yellow glow of its light and looked out at everyone. The station master poured them drinks.

Alone, Alex and Whittaker sat at the edge of the platform. Eva joined them from the table where she'd been working.

'They put everyone on trucks and then started flattening the camp before people had even managed to gather up all their belongings,' she told them.

'I imagine they're all used by now to restricting themselves to what they can actually carry,' Alex said, regretting immediately how callous the remark sounded. 'I didn't mean—'

She waited for him to go on. 'Of course you didn't,' she said angrily. 'And you're right – why *should* they have any of the comforts of home without a home itself?'

'He's doing his best for them,' Whittaker told her. He took her hand and held it in both his own.

She sat with her head on his chest for a moment, then looked up at him, kissed the back of his fingers and said, 'I know he is,' turning to Alex as she spoke. Then she looked both ways along the gently curving tracks, to the distant high brick walls where the rails were lost to sight. 'Preston was saying that the trains might not now be here until two. Paul thinks even that's optimistic.'

Whittaker attempted to pull his hand free, but she held on to it.

'I saw Nina and Maria last night,' she said. 'Nina said you were going there later. She's no better?'

Whittaker shook his head.

'She knows you're doing all you can,' she said. 'Both of them know that.'

This time he nodded rather than answer her.

She was about to say something more, perhaps to reassure him further, when someone called her name. She looked up and searched around her. Alex and Whittaker did the same.

'Over there,' Alex said, seeing Kurt Remer and a group of five or six others from the barracks coming along the platform through the crowds. 'What are they doing here? Today of all days. Someone should have kept them out.'

Kurt came to where his sister sat with the two men, kicking and pushing at the people in his way. The others followed in his wake.

Whittaker withdrew his hand at the boy's arrival.

Alex looked across to the stationmaster's office, but all he saw there were the backs of three heads. He looked along the platform, hoping to see guards from the Institute, but none had yet emerged from the waiting room into which they'd gone at the sound of the klaxon.

'You and *him* now, is it?' Kurt said to Eva, nodding at Whittaker.

'Stop being stupid and go away,' she told him.

'We came to see what was happening. Who's going to stop us?' He saw the Russians on the far platform and pointed them out to the men behind him.

Eva recognized these others, boys mostly, and she called to them in greeting. They were happy to respond to her, and Alex guessed that they had accompanied her brother there reluctantly. He felt reassured by this. Eva called to several of the boys by name, asking after their families.

Kurt, angry at their response, interrupted her. 'Thing is, we heard they were leaving *our* camp alone,' he said to her. 'All they're really interested in is getting rid of this filth. And when they've done that, they're going to leave us in peace to get on with our lives.'

Few of his companions shared his conviction, though several called out in support of what he'd said.

'Of course they will,' Eva said. 'Now go away.'

Kurt looked suddenly uncertain about what to do or say next, but clearly believed, as he always believed – or so it now seemed to Alex – that he might in some way further exploit the situation.

'Take him home,' Eva called to the others.

Several of the boys urged Kurt to return to them. They wanted to leave, they told him. One of them suggested visiting Paul Weiss's bar to see what he would give them to leave there, too. This last idea appealed to Kurt.

On the far platform there was a further commotion.

This time, a group of Russians surrounded a single man, who was first knocked to the ground, then pulled upright and marched quickly away, his feet dragging along the ground as he tried to regain his balance. He was taken to the waiting lorries, where other men had already been gathered. Kurt shouted encouragement to the Russians and applauded them. This time, none of his companions followed his lead.

'He's a German they're taking away,' Eva said to him.

'So?' he said, his need to remain provocative stronger than any concern he might have felt about the cause or consequences of the man's arrest.

'Just go away,' Eva repeated. 'You only came here to cause trouble. You think they couldn't cross the tracks and grab hold of you just as quickly and as firmly, and with absolutely no right of appeal whatsoever? Just go away and stop making a fool of yourself. No one's impressed.'

'So?' he said, over and over. 'So? Not as big a fool as you're making of *your*self, sitting here like this with your two boyfriends in front of everybody, letting everybody see you for what you are.' He raised his foot, as though about to kick her.

Alex rose to his feet and stood between the two of them.

'That's right – you—' Kurt began, but was stopped abruptly by a violent push from behind.

At first, Alex thought that one of Kurt's companions,

having finally tired of the boy's posturing and aware of the danger in which he was now placing them all, had pushed him. But then he saw that Jesus Hernandez had run through the crowd at hearing the boy's raised voice, and that he was the one who had knocked Kurt to the ground.

The boy fell close to where Whittaker and Eva sat, and they both rose, leaving him alone where he lay at the edge of the platform.

'Thought I heard your big mouth,' Hernandez said, and before anyone could intervene, he kicked Kurt hard in the stomach, then again on his thigh. Kurt rolled to protect himself, almost falling from the platform to the track below. Seeing this, Hernandez kicked him again, on the chest and arm, stopping only when Eva screamed at him and began to beat on his back with her fists.

Hernandez finally stood back from the boy. 'Perhaps he should learn when to keep that big mouth of his shut,' he said, stepping quickly from side to side, the boy at his feet, making it clear to everyone that to resume kicking him remained an option.

The people waiting near by began to discuss what had just happened.

Alerted by the crowd, both Dyer and Preston emerged from the stationmaster's office and looked across the tracks. Preston called to ask what was happening.

Hernandez turned to him and held up his arms in a gesture of surprise. 'I think he fell,' he shouted.

Both Preston and Dyer looked at him and then at the boy on the ground.

'Help him up,' Preston called, and Hernandez did this, pulling Kurt Remer roughly to his feet, brushing his shoulders and his chest with his palms, and then grabbing him by his lapels and pulling his face close to his own.

'And guess what,' he said. 'When this lot of sorry excuses are gone and when everything's burned to the ground out there in the fucking woods, we're coming for you and this bunch of jokers. Me, personally, I'm going to ride a bulldozer right over your head. I'm going to flatten you, all of you, everything. And then we're going to have another little fire and I'm going to sit by that fire warming my hands and watching it all go up in smoke. I hope you're looking forward to that, kid, because I know I am.' He pushed Kurt away from him and then wiped back the hair from his face.

'Ignore him,' Eva said to her brother.

'You hear that?' Hernandez said to Kurt. 'She's telling you to ignore me. But I think you're a brighter boy than that. Are you? Are you a bright boy? Or are you exactly what all your pathetic fucking friends here already know you to be? I won't bother pointing out what that is because it would take too long and it would only embarrass you in front of everyone.' He jabbed a finger into Kurt's cheek. 'Now run along and play. And take all your friends, all these other tin-pot little soldiers with you. Christ, a full fucking year, and you still haven't seen the fucking light.' He pushed Kurt again, and the boy turned and walked slowly back to the others. 'Seems to me, this is how you always end up after our little run-ins. When are you going to learn? You push your face into mine and I have to slap it.'

Kurt rejoined his friends, who immediately pulled him into their midst and then walked with him at their centre back to the station entrance.

Watching him go, Hernandez waved again to Preston, who was still standing and watching with Dyer and the stationmaster. 'Problem solved,' he shouted. 'Just a few old soldiers who needed pointing in the right direction.'

Eva was about to respond to this, but Alex stopped her.

'Wise move,' Hernandez said to him. He flexed his shoulders and dusted down his own arms. Then he turned and left them, following Kurt and the others out of the station.

'What if he's going after him?' Eva said.

'The others will make sure Kurt keeps walking,' Whittaker said.

'You think Kurt only does what he does because he knows they will come to his rescue?' she said.

'They didn't,' Whittaker said bluntly. 'They never do. I think he does it because he can't *not* do it.'

'They're probably flattening the barracks at this very moment,' Alex said.

Neither Eva nor Whittaker responded to this.

On the far platform, Dyer and Preston had been joined by the mayor, who had recently arrived at the station with his own small delegation of local councillors.

'What's he doing?' Whittaker said. 'Come to make sure everyone gets away on time before he starts selling all those lucrative forestry permits?'

The mayor waved to the people around him, but few responded with any enthusiasm. He started to make a speech, but his voice was lost in the high space, and he quickly abandoned this.

'He's probably got a brass band lined up somewhere, ready to play when the trains eventually arrive,' Whittaker said.

'Don't worry,' Alex said to Eva, who remained anxious about her brother, her eyes fixed on the point where both Kurt and Hernandez had been lost to sight. 'Perhaps when he no longer has the barracks to keep running back to, then things will change for the better.'

She nodded once and turned away from him.

Over the public-address system, Preston announced that it was time for everyone to resume their work.

The Russians who had taken the man away returned and started to question several others still waiting there. They were again loud and violent in their actions.

Alex and Whittaker watched them, seeing Dyer and Preston move quickly away from the noisy and one-sided interrogations.

'It's probably how Dyer would prefer *us* to behave,' Alex said.

'Of course it is,' Whittaker told him, returning to his desk. He looked at the endless list in front of him, beckoned the next of the refugees forward and started singing 'Chatanooga Choo Choo'.

'He's funny,' Eva said to Alex, and she too returned to her work.

30

Alex was summoned by Dyer for a third time shortly after his return from the station. This time, the man who delivered the order said he'd been told by Dyer to wait and accompany Alex to him personally. It was eight in the evening, and the daily work of the Institute was over. The trains removing the camp-dwellers had finally arrived at five.

Alex had returned from town with a group of clerks, after parting with Whittaker and Eva outside Paul Weiss's bar. They were going together to see Maria Lehman, though it was clear to Alex that Eva was anxious to return home, hoping to find her brother there. Since Kurt's ignominious departure from the station, she had been concerned about him; alarmed, too, by Alex's suggestion about what might have been happening at the barracks in the boys' absence.

Whittaker had told her to go straight home, or to find her brother elsewhere, but she had insisted on first going with him to Nina's.

Arriving at Dyer's, Alex knocked and went in alone. The guard had remained silent throughout their short journey.

Preston was still with Dyer, and the two of them were standing at the window, drinks in their hands. They were laughing loudly as Alex entered.

'Join us,' Preston said to him. He gave Alex a glass and raised the bottle of brandy.

'What are we celebrating?' Alex asked him. The glass was in his hand and half filled before he realized it.

'What we're celebrating, Captain Foster,' Dyer said coldly, 'is—'

'Is a good day's work,' Preston interrupted, leaving Alex wondering what Dyer had been about to say to him.

Alex raised his glass. 'To a good day's work, then. To all those poor, unknowing souls on their trains to God knows where. Because, let's face it, not many of *them* know where they're truly headed.'

' "Unknowing"?' Preston said, smiling. 'To them, and to everything else here reaching an equally satisfactory conclusion. Fair exchange and no robbery and all that.' He laughed at the expression.

The remark made Alex cautious. It was clear to him that Dyer's original summons two days previously was now forgotten.

'Ochmann-Schur, you mean?' Alex said to Preston. 'Was he one of your secret exchanges at the station? Was everything else just a smokescreen?'

'Think what you like,' Preston told him, amused by Alex's continuing concern. 'They gave us our man and we gave them theirs. And you, Captain Foster, you alone continue to make considerably more of that simple transaction than it warrants.'

'And Walther?' Alex said, uncertain if Preston had heard him.

'By my reckoning, he'll be halfway across the ocean by now.'

'Who? Walther?' Alex said.

'What are you talking about him for?' Dyer said. 'Colonel Preston's talking about the man they exchanged for Ochmann. Walther's still here. Not for much longer, not now, but he's still here.'

'Halfway across the ocean and then all the way across the continent. A day, less. Imagine that.' Preston turned to Alex. 'Don't look so worried, Foster. Our man was handed over at Magdeburg at six o'clock this morning. They're happy, we're happy, everybody's happy.' He refilled his own ample glass.

'So what were the Russians doing at the station?' Alex asked him.

Preston shrugged. 'Let's just say they appreciate the opportunity every now and again to shout the odds and flex their muscles. They do it here, we do it there. Let's just say it keeps everything . . .' He trailed off and raised his glass to Dyer, who returned the gesture, but who kept his eyes on Alex.

'Is that what they were doing at the station?' Alex said. 'Flexing their muscles by beating a man up?'

'They didn't beat anyone up. Just someone who attracted their attention. They had a list. The guy looked as though he might have been on it. He wasn't beaten up, just restrained. It's how they operate. You should be used to it by now.'

'And how you operate is by standing back and letting it happen? By getting someone else to do your dirty work for you?'

The grin fell from Preston's face. 'He's catching on,' he said to Dyer. 'Your tame little soldier's finally catching on.'

Even Dyer looked uncomfortable at the remark and all it revealed.

Then Preston pointed a finger at Alex. 'Hey, and besides, Mister Moral Majority, there looked to be a little roughing-up going on on *your* side of the tracks from where I was standing.' His growing drunkenness became more apparent in everything he said.

'You can thank your driver for that,' Alex said.

'Hernandez? He's a good man. Besides, he'll be over the ocean himself in a few weeks. God alone knows why he's stayed this long.'

Alex resisted responding to this.

'Can we get to the matter at hand?' Dyer said unexpectedly. 'Gentlemen?'

'Which is what?' Preston said.

Dyer nodded towards Alex, but Preston ignored him.

'For your information,' Preston went on, 'Hernandez is a damn fine soldier. He's just been here too long, that's all. He's become too – too—'

'Too greedy? Too vicious?' Alex said.

Preston smiled again. 'I was going to say too *acclimatized*, too accustomed to a certain way of doing things. He looks on all this as his reward. This is how he gets to live after all he's been through. Hernandez is *owed*. He knows it, and that's why he does what he does.' He raised his glass. 'To Jesus. To Jesus H. Christ. To Jesus H. Hernandez.'

Dyer, Alex noticed, had hardly touched his own drink, and was becoming alarmed at the change in Preston's behaviour.

'He's here for the closing paperwork on Walther,' Dyer said to Alex. 'It should all be done, signed and sealed by now.'

'It is,' Alex said, turning to look out of the window at the men and women below him as he spoke.

'Hear that?' Dyer said to Preston. 'The paperwork on your man is all done.'

Preston came to Alex and put an arm around his shoulders. 'Of course it is. It's what Captain Foster here said would happen, and it's what's happened. My thanks and congratulations, Captain Foster. Do I mean congratulations? No. Anyhow, my thanks. We'll take Walther off your hands tomorrow. I'm sure our prosecutors will appreciate your findings and your decision on this one.'

'What findings?' Alex said. 'What decision?'

'Your decision that the guy probably has a case to answer, that he was worth another look, that he could get up in that witness box and answer personally for what he did or didn't do, did or didn't see, that there's no smoke without fire, that he was too much a part of it all for him *not* to have been involved or implicated in some way.'

'So whatever I decided, whatever I found out from Walther, the outcome was always going to be the same?'

'Pretty much. But you understood that much right from the very start. All I need now is for the paperwork to be clean and on the level.'

'And for there to be enough gaps, enough blank spaces for all that reasonable doubt to flow into and to become something more substantial?' Alex said.

'Listen to him,' Preston said to Dyer.

'I'm sure Captain—' Dyer began.

'All we need from you now, Foster, is that little rubber stamp which says you've finished with Walther and that he's ours to take away with your blessing. God save the King. I don't know what you're still worried about. If the man's innocent, if his hands truly are clean, then I'm sure the court will find that.'

'And if all else fails, then they can always find him guilty by association.'

'Hey,' Preston said to Dyer. 'What did I tell you? He's catching on.' He held out his empty glass and Dyer refilled it, sipping at his own when he'd done this.

'And as for that bastard Ochmann,' Preston went on. 'You can sleep easy on that score. You think those children were the worst of it? Think again. Directly responsible for the deaths of over four thousand people. That's *directly* responsible, Captain Foster. Indirectly, who knows? The Russians had a list of names like a New York telephone directory.'

'Then perhaps they'll try him four thousand times,' Alex said.

Preston laughed. 'Good idea.' Then he slapped his hand on the desk and lowered his voice. 'Or perhaps they drove him back to their sector, put him up against the first wall they came to and they shot him already. Hey, you know what? My money would be on option B.' He made his free hand into a gun and fired it at Alex. 'So don't *you* come running to me with tales about Jesus Hernandez,' he said. 'Because compared to these others, he's still in kindergarten. It's men like you, Captain Foster, men like you who . . . who . . .' He trailed off again, went to one of Dyer's armchairs and let himself fall back into it.

Men like me who what?

'He's just relieved today went smoothly,' Dyer said.

'The camp's gone. They're going to burn everything over the next few days and then do the same to the barracks.'

Alex was relieved to hear that this hadn't yet started.

'He's been under a lot of pressure to get the man he was after away from the Russians.'

'At the expense of what?' Alex said. 'Besides, the Russians aren't stupid: they'll already have squeezed everything *they* need out of him.'

'Perhaps, but that's not Preston's problem. Stop antagonizing him. It's not going to serve any purpose now. You did your job and—'

'No – I did what you told me to do,' Alex said calmly. 'And you told me to do it because it's what Preston told *you* to do.'

'It isn't that simple,' Dyer said.

'Really?' Alex drained his glass and put it down. 'I want to see Walther before he's taken away.'

'Is that a good idea?'

'As good an idea as you and me trying to convince ourselves that Ochmann-Schur *wasn't* taken half a mile out of Rehstadt, shot in the back of the head and then thrown into a ditch.'

Dyer searched the papers on his desk. 'Walther's going at seven in the morning. They're sending someone from the prosecutor's office at Bielefeld for him.' He took a blank sheet from a drawer and wrote on it. He folded this and gave it to Alex.

Behind them, Preston started to hum a tune.

'His son was killed at Midway,' Dyer said. 'Only child. A pilot.'

Alex turned and looked at Preston, who raised a hand to him and went on humming.

'It was a pleasure meeting you, Colonel Preston,' Alex said.

'You too, son,' Preston replied. 'You too. Pleasure meeting all of you. All the way across the continent and then all the long, long way across the ocean. The Atlantic Ocean. Take good care of yourself, Captain Alexander Foster, take good care.'

Alex left them, and then the building, and crossed the garden towards the cell blocks, showing Dyer's authorization to the guards at each of the gates he came to.

The converted prison wings were out of sight of both the Institute buildings and the hotel, and surrounded by a screen of trees which reached out like the moles of a harbour from the expanse of forest beyond.

Finally entering the cells, he was told to wait while a man was sent for to take him to Walther.

'Just tell me where he is and I'll go alone,' Alex said.

The guard looked at him and shook his head. 'No, you won't,' he said. 'You lot up there might play free and easy, but down here we have proper rules.' He turned away before Alex could respond to this.

After a further ten minutes, someone appeared and told Alex to follow him.

They descended a flight of stairs and walked the full length of a long, brightly lit corridor, both walls of which were lined with metal doors, the wall space between these no wider than the doors themselves. It was Alex's first visit to the place, and he saw what a relief it must have been for Walther and the others held there to have been brought out into the daylight and then to where they were questioned. Even waiting for hours in the corridor, handcuffed to their guards, would have been preferable to this.

Names were chalked on each of the doors, smudged marks both revealing and then concealing the identities of previous inhabitants.

'Here we are,' the guard said. He banged three times on the door marked with Walther's name and then waited a moment before unlocking it and sliding back its bolts.

When the door was opened, Alex looked into the narrow cell and saw Walther standing against the far wall, his back to them and with his hands on his head.

'Turn around,' the guard shouted at him.

Walther turned and faced them, expressionless.

'You've got a visitor,' the guard said. 'You understand me? Visitor? *Verstehen?*'

Walther nodded once.

'Good.' To Alex, the man said, 'You go in, I'll slide one of the bolts and wait here. Any trouble, you shout. When you want to come out knock three times and tell me. Anything happens, I'll hear it. He's no trouble, usually.'

Along the corridor, men had started banging on their doors and calling to each other.

Alex went into the cell and the door was bolted behind him. He signalled for Walther to lower his arms.

'I can't offer you a seat,' Walther said.

The room contained only a low, hard bed, its blanket folded at one end, and a bucket half-filled with urine. The smell from this was overpowering.

'There used to be a lid,' Walther said. 'But when the nature and extent of my depravity was suggested to the guards, they took it away.'

Alex knocked three times on the door and it was opened. 'Take that out,' he told the guard. 'Empty it, wash it, and find a lid for it before you bring it back.' It was a small improvement for Walther's final night in the cell. The guard took the bucket and then slammed the door in Alex's face.

Light in the cell came from a bright, mesh-encased bulb recessed into the low ceiling. There was no window.

'You're going to the Americans at Bielefeld in the morning,' Alex said, uncertain of how long he might now have. The guard was possibly even then calling Dyer, and perhaps Dyer was telling him to act on his own initiative.

'So soon? Still, I doubt it matters when I go. They wouldn't have wanted to wait too much longer.'

'I gave them my report,' Alex said.

'What else could you do?'

'I tried to make it clear to whoever reads it next that I didn't believe you had any direct part in what happened. I pointed out all the corroborating details, all the inconsistencies. I told them to look elsewhere for evidence. Anything they find will help you further.' He knew how unconvincing and hopeless all this sounded.

'Again, thank you. I'm sure you did all you could.'

'But you still have no faith in any of it?'

'We'll see.'

It was clear to Alex that Walther wanted to spare him his excuses. He took out his cigarettes and gave them to Walther.

'You have to blow the smoke under the door, otherwise it fills the room,' Walther explained, and then demonstrated this to him. They sat together on the bed.

'They're fair people,' Alex said. 'The Americans.'

'Not like the Ivans, you mean?' Walther reached into his shoe and took out a square of folded paper. 'Will you send this to my brother in Diepholz. It's already addressed.'

Alex took it and put it in his pocket.

'They won't search you,' Walther told him. 'Do you know what awaits me in Bielefeld?'

Alex didn't. 'More questioning?'

'Or perhaps everyone else is ready and the trial is about to begin. Do you know what other evidence they've collected? Am I to be appointed a defender?'

Alex knew none of those things.

'I told my brother not to name his unborn child after me,' Walther said. 'It might be something of a curse. What do you think?'

'You talk as though they've already—'

'I know,' Walther said. 'But – what's the expression? "All things being equal", I think it is better to prepare myself for every eventuality. Perhaps you're right – perhaps I'll be completely exonerated and released immediately. Or perhaps I'll be found guilty of a considerably lesser crime. And perhaps I'll even be given my chance to atone for everything. Or perhaps the world will suddenly right itself and all those old checks and balances will be miraculously restored and justice will once again prevail and—'

'It has to happen one day,' Alex said.

'I know. Please, ignore me.'

'I'll watch what happens,' Alex said, the thought only then occurring to him. 'I'll follow the trial. It won't be held in secret. Everybody will be able to watch, including your brother. They won't be able to find everybody equally guilty. They won't *want* to. They'll show compassion. It's how they'll want to be seen.'

Walther put a hand on his arm to stop this speculation. 'Of course they will, and I shall be the worthy recipient of that compassion, the deserving beneficiary, so to speak.'

'So to speak,' Alex said, smiling.

Despite blowing it to the bottom of the door, their smoke thickened in the room around them.

'The Russians took Ochmann-Schur this morning,' Alex said eventually.

'Then poor Ochmann-Schur,' Walther said. 'Unless, of course, you believe that knowing something with absolute certainty is preferable to living with endless doubt, confusion and uncertainty.' He paused. 'Perhaps you might . . .'

'What?' Alex asked him.

'I was going to suggest that perhaps you might add something to my letter to my brother, tell him something of the man you met here. The war changed me, Captain Foster, and latterly he saw only that changed man, not the boy he had once worked with on the farm. I'd appreciate him knowing something apart from . . .'

'I'll write,' Alex said.

They were interrupted by a sudden rapping on the door. Alex looked at his watch.

'Twenty minutes,' he said.

'It's longer than most get.' Walther rose to his feet.

The door opened and the guard stood waving his hand at the smoke which confronted him. 'Christ almighty,' he said. 'Who's on fire?'

'Thank you for coming to see me,' Walther said to Alex in German. 'I truly do appreciate having met you and having had you as my interrogator.'

'Questioner,' Alex said.

'Of course. Questioner.'

'The wall,' the guard shouted. 'Hands.'

And Walther turned to the wall and raised his hands to his head.

Alex held his shoulder for a moment and then went out into the corridor.

'Leave the door open a while,' he said to the guard. 'Let the smoke clear.' The guard was about to deny him this, still angry at having been confronted over the bucket, but then he hesitated and did as Alex asked.

It was the only thing Alex could now do for Walther, and he stood there for a minute longer, looking in at the man through the thinning smoke.

Eventually the guard said, 'Long enough,' pushed the door shut and locked and bolted it. He walked quickly ahead of Alex along the corridor towards the stairs. The other men there had smelled the smoke and they called out to Alex from behind their doors as he passed them.

'They'll be on their hands and knees,' the guard said. 'Sucking it through the gap.' He laughed at the thought of this and banged on each of the doors as he passed them. At the end of the corridor he waited at the foot of the stairs and shouted to Alex to walk faster.

31

Not wanting to return to his room or risk encountering Dyer or Preston again, Alex left the prison compound and followed the path through the grounds towards Rehstadt, hoping to find Whittaker, and perhaps even Eva, still at Nina Lehman's.

Arriving at the centre of the town, he was surprised to see the two of them sitting together in the window of one of the bars there. He crossed the cobbled square towards them, waiting outside briefly until Eva looked up from her drink and saw him.

He went in to them, sat beside Eva and looked for a waiter to order more drinks.

'Maria Lehman died an hour ago,' Whittaker said to him. He sat with his head in his hands, his small glass and cup between his elbows.

Eva put a hand on Alex's arm. 'We were both with

her. And Nina. He did all he could.'

'And she still died,' Whittaker said. 'How bloody inconsiderate of her.' His raised voice attracted the attention of the bar's other customers.

'Where's Nina?' Alex asked Eva.

She waited until the barman had set down fresh glasses and cups before answering him. 'She wanted to stay with Maria for a while, just the two of them. She's completely alone now, you see.'

Whittaker picked up his new drink and drained the glass in a single swallow.

'After that, she'll have to report the death to the hospital,' Eva said. 'The morgue's there.'

'They might even want to carry out an autopsy,' Whittaker said.

'To find out what killed her. Surely, that—'

'No – so that Herr Direktor can now completely absolve himself of all blame for having refused to treat her properly in the first place, and for afterwards having discharged her so early.' Again his raised voice attracted the attention of others, and he looked around at them, toasting them with his empty glass.

Alex picked up his own drink. 'Will that cause problems for you?' he asked Whittaker.

'Why – because I went on treating her without any real authority? Because of the drugs I used?' He lowered his voice. 'I don't know. Besides, whatever tantrums the director might now want to throw, I'll be home this time next week, beyond his reach. Anything he wants to complain about, he can do it to Dyer. I'm sure the two of them will be only too happy to brush everything under the carpet between them.'

'What happened?' Alex asked Eva.

'Maria was barely conscious for the past day or so. She seemed to be asleep when we arrived, but was very agitated, tossing and turning and mumbling to herself, and sweat was pouring off her. He gave her a sedative. It seemed to work for an hour or so. After that, she just looked as though she was sleeping more peacefully. Nina's hardly slept at all. She told us Maria had been bleeding again. Not much, but enough. And then after that hour of seemingly calm and peaceful sleep, Maria suddenly started gasping for air – or that's what it seemed like – and then she died. Nina was sitting with her. He did all he could to try and save her, but . . .'

' "He did all he could",' Whittaker repeated. 'It sounds like an epitaph. Sorry, I didn't mean . . .'

'I know,' Eva told him. 'But it's the truth. And sometimes the truth is that simple. You did what you could, and it was ten times more than anyone else ever did for her, including all those others whose *duty* it was to help her.' She spoke firmly and held his gaze as she said all this.

'She should never have gone to full term, not in her condition,' Whittaker said to Alex. 'Under normal circumstances, I doubt if—'

' "Normal circumstances"?' Eva said. ' "Normal circumstances"? When did *they* last apply to girls like Maria Lehman, to any of us here? Back home, Doctor Whittaker, back home in England, that's where your "normal circumstances" are all still safely in place and waiting for you. When did—? How—?' She pressed a hand over her mouth, shaking her head. 'Sorry, sorry,' she said through her fingers.

Whittaker reached across the table and pulled her hand from her mouth.

'I know,' he told her. He held on to her hand as she lowered it to the table.

Alex wanted to ask him if he believed Maria's death had been caused – even if only in part – by the drugs he had bought from Hernandez. But it was something he could not even suggest; something he knew Whittaker would already have considered.

'The director will perform his autopsy and announce to the world that he was right all along,' Whittaker said. 'That there was never any doubt about the outcome of all this.'

'And supposing she'd been made pregnant by some long-lost *German* soldier hero?' Eva said.

Neither of them answered her.

'I have to go,' she told them. 'I'd only intended stopping at Nina's to see how Maria was. I should have gone home hours ago. I need to find out where Kurt went after the station and what might now be happening at the barracks.'

421

Alex repeated to her what Preston had told him and she was reassured by this. He motioned to Whittaker's jeep parked outside and offered to drive her home. Whittaker said he was staying for another drink, and another one after that, and that he'd return to the Institute later.

'They definitely gave Ochmann-Schur to the Russians,' Alex told him.

'Then good riddance,' Whittaker said.

'And tomorrow they're handing Walther over to the Americans.'

Neither revelation had the impact Alex hoped it might. Eva had known neither of the men, he realized; and perhaps even Whittaker had encountered Walther only once, to treat his cuts and bruises.

'I wish someone would hand *me* over to the Americans,' Whittaker said. 'We might have felt bad about all those poor bastards this morning with their bawling kids and shabby suitcases, but at least they were going *somewhere*, at least they were *moving*.'

Neither Alex nor Eva fully understood what he was saying to them.

'Perhaps I should go to the hospital myself,' Whittaker said.

'Not a good idea,' Alex said, trying to gauge how serious he had been.

'He means it's a bad idea,' Eva said. 'A very bad idea. Leave Nina to it. The last thing she'll want now is you

422

turning up to confuse the issue. She's still angry about what happened. Let *her* confront the director, let *her* accuse him of allowing her sister to die. Let *her* do it, not you. Believe me, you won't help.'

'Perhaps you're right,' Whittaker conceded.

'She is,' Alex told him.

Whittaker waved them away from him. 'Go,' he said. 'Flee into the moonlit and starry night on your eternal quest for happiness. The keys are in the ignition. No – no keys, it's just a button. You just press it. But flee, anyway.'

'No stars,' Alex said. 'Just cloud.'

Eva put on her coat and scarf. She crouched beside Whittaker and kissed him. 'You gave Nina her sister back,' she said to him. 'Perhaps only for a few days, but you let them be sisters again. You let Nina care for her. It meant a great deal to her.'

'If you say so,' Whittaker said to her, then touched her cheek. 'No, I believe you. Thank you.'

She kissed him again and briefly held his face in both her hands, stroking her thumbs beneath his eyes.

'Under normal circumstances . . .' he said, and she kissed him again on the forehead.

Outside, it had grown much cooler. There was more traffic than usual, both in the square and on the town roads. Lorries stood in lines at the kerbs, and more waited on the broad, unpaved verges leaving the town.

They drove to the crossroads.

At the entrance of the track leading to the barracks, Eva told Alex to stop and then to turn off the engine.

'Listen,' she told him.

They heard other engines and voices coming from the direction of the barracks. Headlights showed in the otherwise impenetrable darkness of the forest.

They left the jeep and walked the short distance to the first of the vehicles, shielding their eyes against the glare. They were English lorries, filled with equipment and with soldiers Alex didn't recognize.

A man came to them and asked them who they were, saluting Alex when he saw his rank.

Alex asked him what they were doing.

'Nothing,' the man said. 'We were at the DP camp earlier, clearing and burning the wreckage. We only came here to park up the lorries and some of the equipment for a few days. We're flattening all this lot soon. Trouble is, we get here from the camp and find it still bloody occupied. Nobody told us. Not many. A couple of dozen. Old blokes and kids, mostly. They've built a barricade across the only road into the place. A bit pathetic, really. They're standing behind it as though it'll stop us going in.'

'And will it?'

The man laughed. 'It'll take about twenty seconds to sweep it away. And after that we'll be in and out in an hour. We've been told to leave them alone. We're just waiting for our transport back into town once the bulldozers and generators have been secured. Some of them even still look like bloody soldiers. What's all that about? The Americans are bringing all the heavy stuff. Two days.'

'Do you think there'll be any trouble when you finally go in?' Alex asked him.

The suggestion further amused the man. 'There will be upwards of a hundred of us. A dozen bulldozers. One for each hut. Like I said, we'll be in and out in less than an hour. A day after that, and you won't even know we were here.'

More lorries arrived behind Alex and Eva.

'You're going to have to leave,' the man told them. He indicated where the jeep was blocking the road.

Alex and Eva returned to it and drove away.

Passing the site of the DP camp, they saw the blazes there where the demolished huts were still burning. The fires were high and fierce, and a few figures still tended these, stacking and throwing on fresh fuel. Smoke from the fires rose, barely visible through the glow, up into the darkness, and sparks and burning embers floated over everything. Smaller fires burned untended at the edges of the camp.

They sat and watched all this for several minutes. The trunks and limbs of the surrounding forest were picked out in the shifting light, and shadows were thrown over the open space.

'No one will be coming back here,' Eva said.

Drifting smoke lay over the road, filling the ditches on either side like grey, flowing water.

They resumed their journey to Ameldorf.

Arriving at her home, Eva called for both her father and Kurt. Nothing of the blaze or the vehicles was visible or audible here. She went into the house and came out again soon afterwards.

'Nobody,' she said. 'My father must be in one of the sheds.'

It was past ten o'clock, and Alex heard the note of urgency in her voice.

He followed her into the yard and then the workshop. From one of the sheds came the sound of hammering, followed by her father's raised voice.

Eva ran towards the sound, and Alex followed her.

Inside the open shed, Peter Remer sat on a balk of timber and hammered repeatedly at a piece of stone on the ground between his feet. He remained oblivious to their presence, shouting and cursing with each blow he struck.

Eva called to him, and then again, until finally he heard her and stopped hammering, looking to where they stood in the doorway.

She went in to him, and Alex followed her, keeping several paces behind her.

'What are you doing?' she asked him. 'Is Kurt here? Have the pair of you been fighting?'

'Kurt?' he said. 'Who knows where he is? Who

cares? I don't know where he is. Why should I?'

She stepped back at her father's raised and angry voice. She looked at the pieces of shattered stone at his feet.

'One of your carvings,' she said, turning to glance at Alex. 'Why? What are you doing?'

Alex looked around them. Other pieces of shattered stone lay in the dim light of the shed interior. He pointed these out to her.

Eva knelt before her father. 'What's happened? Why are you doing this? Tell me.'

The old man rubbed his face hard with both hands. His hands were ungloved and pale from the dust, and bleeding in places where they had been grazed and cut by flying chips of stone.

' "Surplus to requirements",' he shouted at her.

Alex moved closer to Eva to better hear what was being said, and Peter Remer looked up at him, surprised by his presence.

'It's Captain Foster,' Eva told him. 'Alex.'

The old man said nothing in reply. The hammer he had been using stood on its head at his feet, and he kicked this away from him.

'What?' Eva said.

'The mayor came,' Peter Remer said. 'He told me to stop work on all the carving.'

'But why? You had an arrangement with the church elders, an agreement.'

Alex heard how vague and insubstantial the two words suddenly sounded.

'Did I?' her father said. 'They were verbal agreements. Handshakes between men who had known each other all their lives.'

'So what changed? How—?'

'The mayor said everything now had to be done to contract, legally, businesslike. He said the company coming to take over the forestry work possess quarries of their own, their own masons and stone yards. They'll be looking for as much work as they can get. He said he had an obligation to provide them with that work. For the good of the people of Rehstadt. They might even open up new quarries locally. Imagine that. Lots of work for lots of men. But that, of course, will only happen if they are given a clean sweep of things.'

'The church elders would never agree to him doing this to you,' Eva insisted. 'Besides, what authority does he have?' She turned from her father to Alex. 'They can't *do* this,' she shouted. 'What right do they have? He was promised. It was an agreement.'

There was nothing he could say to her, and she turned back to her father. 'But why all this? Your work, your carvings?'

The old man laughed. 'The mayor said that he regretted all the hard work I'd already done. Nine months I've been working on this.'

'I know.'

'Said he regretted it, and that, as a gesture of fairness and goodwill, he had negotiated on my behalf with this company for them to buy what I'd already carved. Whether they used it or not, they'd pay me for it. After that, he said I'd probably be able to go and work for them. No promises, mind, but he'd do his best to find me a position with them. A *position*.'

'And have they made you an offer – for your work?'

'Half of what I paid for the uncut stone in the first place. He said he'd insist that they came to collect it in their own lorries, that I'd *incur* no further expense in getting the carvings to them.'

'And you told him—'

'I told him I agreed. I told him I'd take their money and for them to send their lorries and drivers. Goodwill, see. Me and him, we were the best of friends after that. The bastards. Why do you think the camp got cleared so quickly after standing there for all that time? The company's all over this town and the forest. There's even talk of them building that power station further up the valley. Electricity. Imagine that.'

Alex went to them and crouched down beside Eva.

The old man, he saw, was now shivering in the cold night air. Lines of sweat ran through the dust and the dirt of his shoulders and arms, and the thinner tracks of his tears already traced the outline of his cheeks and chin.

'Come inside,' Eva said to her father. She reached out

to help him rise, but he pushed her away from him, causing her to lose her balance and fall backwards. He apologized immediately when he saw what he'd done, but made no attempt to help her back up or to leave his own seat. He seemed genuinely surprised by the violence of his actions.

'You go in,' he told her. 'I'll be in soon.' It was an apology of sorts.

She rose and looked down at him.

Then she left the shed, and Alex followed her.

'He won't do anything, will he?' he said. 'I mean . . .'

'I know what you mean.' She paused and looked back at her father, sitting now with his head in his hands. 'No,' she said. 'He won't do anything. Leave him. He used to sit out there with my mother on warm summer nights. Just there, that exact spot, the dead centre of his own little domain. He spent a week there when Wilhelm was killed. And then another when he lost her. It's why he's there now. When Wilhelm died, the local Masons' Guild held a ceremony of remembrance for him. They were the only ones. No one else bothered.' She smiled, then shook the sudden, unexpected memory from her head.

Alex stayed with her for a further hour, during which time Peter Remer remained where he sat amid the loss and waste of his work.

At eleven, he left her and drove back into Rehstadt. The fires still burned at the razed camp, but the men had gone now, and apart from the blazes the place was now in darkness.

Whittaker was no longer in the bar, and even as Alex considered what to do next, he knew that it was beyond him to cross the square to Usselstrasse to see if Whittaker had returned to sit with Nina Lehman beside the corpse of her sister.

And so he left the town and returned to the Institute.

32

'*Where is he? Where is he?*' Dyer pushed Alex in the chest with both palms, and repeated the same few words over and over.

'Where's who? What are you doing?'

It was half past six the following morning, and Alex stood in his room, half asleep, naked to the waist, as Dyer went on pushing him from the door back to his bed.

'Who?' Alex said again.

Dyer lowered his arms and shook his head. He looked slowly around the untidy room.

'Yes, very clever. "Who?"' His voice was now little more than a snarl. 'You know exactly who I'm talking about.'

Two more men stood in the doorway – guards. And beyond these were others. None of them followed Dyer into Alex's room.

'You get as clever as you want,' Dyer said. 'But don't get clever with me. Whittaker. Where's Whittaker? Where is he?'

Alex hadn't seen Whittaker since leaving him in the bar.

'In his room?' he suggested, guessing that he had been right the previous night, and that Whittaker had returned to keep Nina Lehman company.

'Very good,' Dyer said. 'You think I haven't looked? He's not there and his bed hasn't been slept in. So I'll ask you again – where is he? You're going to tell me sooner or later, so it might as well be now.'

'Why?' Alex said. 'What's happened? What do you want him for?'

Dyer picked up a bottle from the chair by the window and looked at it.

Alex heard others in Whittaker's room, searching it. By the time he himself had returned the previous night, every room along the corridor had been in darkness.

'I'm going to ask you one last time,' Dyer said.

Alex sat in the chair. 'I don't know,' he said. 'Shout as much as you like, I still don't know.'

Dyer looked at him closely. 'No, but you're starting to make guesses, Captain Foster, I can see that much. You're starting to put two and two together and work out exactly what kind of lies you're brave or stupid enough to go on telling me. I can see *that* much.'

One of the guards came into the room.

'Sir, no one saw or heard Whittaker come back last night. The last time anyone remembers seeing him was at the station late yesterday afternoon.'

'What?' Dyer shouted. 'Over twelve hours ago? Twelve hours? He should have been here. He should have come back here.'

'All his stuff's still in there,' the guard said. 'Including the pictures of his wife and kids.'

Dyer waved the man away. 'Are you still telling me you don't know what all this is about, Foster?' he said to Alex.

'Maria Lehman,' Alex said.

'Maria Lehman. So you do know her, then? At last, we're finally getting somewhere.'

'She died yesterday.'

'I know she died. And shall I tell you something else, Captain Foster? Something you and all those other do-gooding zealots might find hard to believe – I don't *care* that she died. I honestly don't care. What *I* care about – what matters to me now – is to know what one of my senior officers – one of *my* officers – was doing treating her illegally and against all the rules and all the advice of the proper authorities.'

'I find it quite easy to believe, actually,' Alex said, stopping Dyer in his rant.

'What?'

'I said I find it easy to believe that you don't care

434

about the girl's death.' Alex picked up his shirt from the floor and put it on.

'Don't get clever with me, Foster.'

'You've already told me that. And the reason I find it easy to believe, is because you treat everybody the same. Everybody, that is, except those people who might, in their own self-serving way, be of some use to you.'

'What?' Dyer said.

'You heard me,' Alex told him.

'You just crossed a line, Captain Foster,' Dyer shouted at him. 'I'll ask you again—'

'And I'll tell you again that I don't know where James Whittaker is.'

'But you know where he was treating that – that girl, you know *that* much.'

'And you don't? I thought you knew everything about what was happening in Rehstadt.' Alex pretended to think. 'Ah, that's right – you probably only know what either the mayor or the hospital director has so far seen fit to tell you.'

'I—' Dyer began, then stopped abruptly.

'What, you're going to deny it?' Alex said, beginning to wonder at the purpose and consequences of his own continued provocation.

'Thank Christ none of this happened yesterday,' Dyer said.

'It did,' Alex told him. 'But, yes, lucky for you that the

girl managed to hang on until the last of the trains and then good old Preston had finally gone.'

Dyer went back to the door and shouted at the men in the corridor to stop making a noise and to leave.

'They're both here now,' he said to Alex. 'The mayor and whatever he calls himself. And I want you – you, personally – to talk to the pair of them. You and Whittaker are as thick as thieves in all of this. I want you to talk to them and to sort all this out before it gets any further out of control and goes beyond my authority.'

'All what sorted out? I thought you were looking for Whittaker to find—'

'I said get it sorted out.' He looked at Alex in disbelief. 'I can be pushed only so far, Foster, only so far. Do what you're being told to do.' He paused. 'I won't bother pointing out to you that this is Whittaker's bacon you're saving. Not mine, not theirs, not your own. *His*.' He turned abruptly and left, shouting at the few remaining men in the corridor to get out of his way as he went.

Alex went to his door and watched him go.

At Dyer's departure, the men outside relaxed. Someone said something and most of them laughed.

The guard who had delivered the message returned and told Alex that Dyer wanted him to go downstairs immediately to see the men waiting there.

'What, he can't find Whittaker, so he's throwing me to them instead?'

The guard smiled. 'Looks like it,' he said. 'He said now, immediately.'

The mayor, the director and three other men were waiting in the lobby. At Alex's appearance on the stairs they all rose and looked up at him, and then behind him, perhaps expecting Whittaker to appear.

'Where is Doctor Whittaker?' the director asked him. 'Where is he? Surely he is here?'

Alex shook his head.

'You're lying. You're hiding him. He's here. In his room. Hiding from his responsibilities.'

It was then that Alex noticed Dyer waiting outside, close enough to see and overhear what was now happening, but far enough away not to be any more directly involved. A group of other townspeople stood near by.

'Do you think Colonel Dyer would lie to you?' Alex said, and both the mayor and the director looked at Dyer, who immediately turned away from them.

'Then where is he?' the mayor said.

'First tell me what happened,' Alex said.

'You *know* what happened,' the director shouted at him. 'He took it upon himself to step far beyond his authority and to administer drugs illegally to that girl.'

'Her sister finally went to the hospital,' the mayor said, resting his hand briefly on the director's shoulder, only to have it angrily shaken off by the man.

'To register the death?' Alex said.

437

'No – to storm about the place hurling her ridiculous and slanderous accusations at everyone in sight,' the director said.

'Including you?'

'Including me.'

'Especially you?'

'At everyone. Everyone. Hurling her drunken accusations and then producing a handful of phials and hurling those, too.'

The remark made Alex cautious, and seeing this, the director laughed. 'Yes, perhaps the woman *was* intoxicated, drunk, raging with grief. For having already accused everyone in sight, she then went on to tell us all that the only person who had lifted a finger to help her stupid sister was your precious Doctor Whittaker. So you are right to look concerned, Captain Foster. You know why we want to see him. You know more about this than anyone. You and that other stupid little bitch.' He paused. 'And don't think we don't know all about *her*, about you and her, about her and her pathetic little brother and her senile father.'

'Whittaker helped Maria Lehman because no one else—'

'Because no one else what? I have an Authorization of Discharge form signed by two doctors and a senior nurse,' the director said. 'Three long-serving, reliable, qualified and well-liked members of the hospital staff.'

'But not signed by you?' Alex said. 'That's convenient.

I hope *they* understand that.'

'It is hardly my job to attend to such minor details.'

Two of the town's civil policemen appeared in the doorway and came reluctantly into the lobby. They had stopped and spoken to the townspeople gathered outside to gauge the seriousness of the situation to which they had been summoned.

'At last,' the mayor said, and beckoned the men to him.

'Why are *they* here?' Alex asked him.

'To ensure that the law is upheld, of course,' the director said smugly. 'And to ensure also that every legal aspect of this is now considered. To determine that if any authority has been misused or over-reached, then the perpetrator is made to pay for the consequences. A young girl has died, remember? This is a very serious matter.'

Neither of the policemen looked happy at having all this pointed out to them by the man.

Alex glanced at Dyer, who was waiting outside. He, too, looked uneasy at the appearance of the two men, and he motioned surreptitiously for Alex to continue talking to the director.

'Have you retrieved Maria Lehman's body?' Alex asked him.

'Of course we have. How on earth did anyone imagine she might survive in her condition in such surroundings?'

' "In her condition"?' Alex said. 'But she was discharged. *You* discharged her. You just said as much.'

The director stared at him, his fists clenched by his side. 'Now you are playing games, Captain Foster. Games. But I imagine you believe that's why you are still here, still amongst us, to play your games with our lives.'

Alex couldn't follow the man's reasoning.

One of the policemen tried to placate the director, but the man pushed him away and told him to do his duty. The constable apologized, half-saluted and took several paces away from them.

'For the last time, where is he? Where's Whittaker? You think we won't find him?'

'Wait here,' Alex told him, and went outside to Dyer.

At his approach, Dyer walked away from him across the grass.

'*Do* you know where he is?' Dyer said as Alex grabbed his arm, looking at where Alex held him until he let go.

'I suspect he waited in a bar in the town square until Nina Lehman had finished at the hospital and that the two of them went back to her flat once Maria's body had been taken away.' Alex was convinced that Whittaker must have known what Nina would say and do at the hospital, and that he had done nothing to prevent her from going there and making her dangerous accusations. Likewise, Whittaker would have had neither the time nor the inclination to conceal his own involvement in Maria's treatment.

'Help him,' Alex said to Dyer, his voice low.

'How? The police are here now. It's too late.'

'Get him back here, pack his belongings, get him to Hamburg, and then home. He's due to leave in five days, anyway. Get him home, away from them, and then just let the whole thing blow over. They'll calm down and shut up soon enough. You know what they're like. They want all this to go away as much as you do.'

Dyer shook his head. 'You think this is more muscle-flexing? You're wrong. For all we know, Whittaker might have killed the bloody—'

'Maria Lehman was going to die from the moment she was kicked out of the hospital. All James Whittaker tried to do was to help her because that bastard in there was more concerned about the reputation of his precious hospital than anything else. And all he's concerned about now is the future and his place in it. The girl, Whittaker, all this, it's the past as far as he's concerned. Get Whittaker out, and *then* I'll do what I can to calm everything down, make sure everything stops here. It's in everyone's interest.'

'It's too late,' Dyer repeated absently, shaking his head.

'After all I've done for you and Preston in the past few—'

'Done for me? You did your job, Foster. You obeyed orders. Done for *me*?'

'You bastard.' Alex again clutched for Dyer's arm, but this time succeeded only in grabbing his sleeve.

'Assaulting a senior officer – *the* senior officer,' Dyer said, and Alex let him go. 'If he's at the girl's, then why haven't they found him there already?'

'The scene of his crime? By their reckoning, it's probably the last place he'd be.'

'Go back in there and tell them where he is.'

'And then what? Stand back and let them arrest him? And what if they charge him with murder, unlawful killing?'

'They won't,' Dyer said.

'They might – anything that diverts attention from all *their* failings.'

Dyer shook his head. 'Tell them. At least then we can start to make sense of all this. Whittaker's more than capable of making his own case. It might be enough. They'll probably be persuaded to turn him over to me once they've taken turns at shouting at him. And perhaps *then* I can get him home without any of them stopping me. Perhaps you're right – they don't want this blowing up in their faces any more than I – we – do.' He was starting to sound more hopeful that a solution to the situation might be found.

'What about Nina Lehman?' Alex said. 'She'll still be distraught, angry. What if she goes on making her accusations?'

'She won't, not once you make it clear to her what

they'll do to Whittaker unless she shuts her mouth.'

There was truth in that, too, and Alex considered it.

The men inside had come to the entrance and now stood looking out at Alex and Dyer. Dyer raised his hand to them.

'Get back to them,' he said to Alex. 'Take them to Whittaker. Let them think we're doing what they're pushing us to do.'

Alex looked at the two policemen and saw that they were still uncomfortable at being there, still cowed by the director.

'Just take them to him and let's see what happens,' Dyer said. 'Either we contain this here and now and get to deal with it ourselves, or we antagonize them to the point where they start insisting on handing Whittaker directly over to the civil authorities. And if that happens . . .'

Alex felt the remark like a prod in his chest. He returned to the small delegation and told them he might know where James Whittaker was.

'At last,' the director said. 'Colonel Dyer has made you see sense.' He raised his hand to Dyer, who returned the gesture.

After that, they left for the town in three jeeps. Dyer refused to accompany them. The Americans were arriving shortly, he said, and he needed to be on hand to ensure the correct transfer of prisoners. It was an excuse, and because they all understood this, no one challenged him.

Alex sat in the jeep with the two policemen. He asked them about their involvement in what was happening, and was reassured when neither man was able to answer him with any certainty. A girl had died, the mayor and director had spoken to their superiors, and so here they were. It was as much as they knew. And when Alex asked if any specific charges had been suggested to them, again neither man was able to answer him.

Arriving in the square, Alex led them to Nina Lehman's apartment on Usselstrasse.

'Here?' the director said disbelievingly. 'It's already been searched. You think either Whittaker or the woman would be stupid enough to return here? I'm warning you – if—'

But Alex refused to listen to him. He was determined to be the first to arrive at the apartment and to see Whittaker, if he was there, alone for a moment.

The door was open when he arrived, and inside the small room, Nina and Whittaker sat opposite each other at the table beside the empty bed.

At Alex's arrival, Whittaker turned and motioned for him to go in to them.

'I'm not alone,' Alex said.

'I know.' He nodded towards the window. 'We saw you arrive.'

'It's all my fault,' Nina Lehman said. Her dark hair hung over her face. She'd been crying. 'I should have kept my big mouth shut. I should have kept it shut.'

A vague outline of Maria Lehman's slender body remained impressed on the bed's single sheet.

'I just didn't think,' Nina said. 'I didn't think. I never do.'

The mayor and the two policemen arrived at the door, followed by the director, who stood for a moment to regain his breath after the steep stairs.

'He's here,' the mayor called to the man, triumphant.

In the room, Whittaker rose from the table and Nina tried to pull him back down to her.

'Time for me to go,' he told her.

She rose from her seat and embraced him. He rubbed her shoulders and then cupped her head into his chest for a moment.

Nina pleaded with Alex to do something.

'I'll sort it out,' he told her. 'I'll go with him.' He looked hard at Whittaker, wishing there was some way he could communicate what Dyer had suggested to him without all these others overhearing. Even a minute alone with his friend would have been enough. But even as he thought about this, how he might still reassure Whittaker, he knew that there was nothing that Whittaker himself wouldn't already have considered while he had waited with Nina to be found and arrested.

The director pushed into the room and then forced himself past Alex. 'There he is,' he shouted dramatically to the policemen. 'Arrest him.'

Whittaker held Nina away from him. 'Take care of her,' he said to Alex.

'I'm coming with you,' Alex told him.

'Oh no, you're not,' the director said. 'You can see him later, when the police have started their inquiries, not now.'

'Go back to Dyer,' Alex told him. 'Talk to him now that you've found Whittaker.'

The director smiled. 'I already did. Colonel Dyer and I have said all that needs to be said on the subject. I saw him before he went up to Whittaker's room, before he dragged you out of bed to listen to your lies. He guaranteed me full authority in the matter. And if not me, then the Chief of Police. You think Colonel Dyer wants any part of this stinking mess on *his* plate? The possible murder of a local girl? Or, at the very least, the theft of valuable drugs from my hospital, from your own stores? I hardly think so.'

'He didn't steal them,' Alex shouted at him.

'Oh? You seem to know a great deal about the matter.'

Alex said nothing.

'Perhaps the police will return to question you later, Captain Foster.' He turned and smiled at Whittaker as he said this.

'Just go back to Dyer,' Alex said again, aware of how futile this appeal now was; how, once again, everything had moved swiftly beyond his control or influence before he'd fully realized what was happening.

'I said arrest him,' the director shouted again at the policemen, and the two men moved to stand on either side of Whittaker, each of them loosely holding one of his arms. Whittaker allowed himself to be held like this, telling Nina to sit down, not to antagonize them any further and get herself arrested alongside him.

The director signalled for him to be taken from the room.

'Where are you taking him?' Alex said as Whittaker was manhandled past him.

'The police station. Where else?'

'I'll go back and tell Dyer,' Alex told Whittaker, who nodded once and briefly closed his eyes.

'If I – if they—'

'What?' Alex asked him.

'Ruth. The girls. I'd appreciate it if you'd let them know what's happening.'

'You'll be back at the Institute in a few hours,' Alex said.

'I know,' Whittaker said. 'Of course I will. But just in case.'

Alex nodded.

'And just consider *all* the implications of whatever you intend doing before you do it,' Whittaker said. 'Don't do anything rash.'

' "Rash"?' the director said, stepping aside as the policemen and Whittaker left the room. 'Yes, Captain Foster, don't do anything "rash". The word clearly amused him. He looked down at Nina, sitting at the table. 'Look at her,' he said. 'All this, for what?'

'For you,' Alex said, his voice low, his own eyes on Nina as he spoke. 'For this place, for this whole bloody country. That's what stinks, not what Whittaker tried to do.'

'Perhaps,' the director said, smiling. 'But even *you* must have known that you would one day have to release your grip on everything. Or perhaps only Colonel Dyer truly understands that.' He motioned to the stairs. 'And *he* certainly does, your rash Doctor Whittaker.'

He left Alex then, following the others back down to the street.

Alex went and sat with Nina at the table.

'I should have kept my big mouth shut,' she said again.

'*I* was the one who brought them here,' he said.

'So we both betrayed him.'

He shook his head at the word.

'What, we *didn't* betray him?' she said, and laughed coldly.

There were running footsteps on the stairs, and for a moment Alex imagined that James Whittaker had broken free of his guards and had come back to them.

They both turned.

Eva appeared in the doorway, looking from the empty bed to where Alex and Nina sat at the table.

'Paul Weiss told me,' she said. 'I called at the bar on my way to the Institute. Have they arrested Whittaker?' She went to the untidy bed, sat on it, and then started to cry, moving her hand over the crumpled sheet and then tracing and smoothing out the vague impression of the dead girl.

33

An hour later, Alex and Eva left Nina and went to the bar in the square.

Eva had earlier gone to the railway bar to ask for Paul Weiss's help in ensuring that her brother left the barracks without causing any further trouble there. They'd been lied to the previous night, she told Alex: the demolition men were returning to raze the barracks later that same day and not in two days' time as the soldier had told them.

Alex's mind was still full of what had just happened to James Whittaker, and he was already starting to consider what to do next to secure his release and speed up his departure. His best hope, he believed, was in contacting Preston and asking for his intervention on Whittaker's behalf. He had a vague notion of threatening to expose Hernandez as the supplier of the drugs if Preston refused to intervene or to put pressure on Dyer to act against the local authorities. He knew how unlikely his chances of success were, how quickly both Dyer and Preston might now distance themselves from the death of Maria Lehman and both Whittaker's and Hernandez's involvement in it. He saw how impotent and helpless both he and Whittaker were in all of this, and how exposed they now were to the ambitions and the capriciously wielded authority of all these others.

'Does Paul think there'll be trouble?' he asked her.

Eva seemed unconcerned by what might already be happening out in the forest, her own thoughts as confused and as diverted as his own.

'There are hardly any of them still out there,' she said dismissively. 'Like the soldier said, they'll flatten the place in minutes and that will be an end to it all. If Kurt has any sense, he'll go home and stay there until it's all over.'

He asked her how her father was.

'You can imagine,' she told him.

It was mid-morning before they left the bar, and they went together to the police station, where Alex saw one of the two constables. The man came to him and told him he would not be able to see Whittaker for at least another day.

'Are you investigating everything the director's accusing him of?' Alex asked him.

' "Investigating"?' the man said. 'I suppose so.' He exchanged greetings with Eva. 'I saw Paul,' he said. 'The barracks.' He turned back to Alex. 'I was in the Volksturm with her brother.' He held up his gloved hand, and for the first time, Alex saw that it was artificial.

Eva spoke to him for a short while and then led Alex outside. 'He'll keep me informed,' she told him. 'About Whittaker.'

He asked her if she was going to the Institute.

'Not today,' she said. 'I think I ought to go back home.'

He wanted to hold her close to him and kiss her. But he knew it was not what she wanted.

'But perhaps you should return there,' she said. 'Let Dyer get everything out of his system so he can start seeing sense and then do the right thing by Whittaker. Don't give him any more excuses to go on washing his hands of everything.'

It had been Alex's hope that he might have been there when Johannes Walther was collected by the Americans, that the two of them might exchange proper farewells. But he saw now how unlikely that was to happen. Besides, Walther had probably already gone. Another short sigh of relief for Preston and Dyer.

A chill wind blew across the square and he felt it on his face. Most of the rubble surrounding the bombed cellar had long since been cleared away, and the salvaged bricks stood in neat, geometric piles. Retrieved

452

joists had also been gathered and stacked against a nearby wall, their sawn edges vivid against the stone. In the cavern of the cellar itself, broken bricks and other waste had started to fill the empty space. There was already talk in the town of a new building rising there, and a report in the ever-hopeful local paper of the mayor's planned monument being sited close to its entrance, a headstone over the obliterated tomb.

'Dyer will want to know what's happening,' Eva told him.

'No, he won't,' he said. 'Whittaker's being sacrificed for the greater good.'

Just like Walther and Ochmann-Schur were sacrificed.

'You're not thinking clearly,' she said.

He wanted to deny this, but instead he said, 'Perhaps.' And even as he said it, the word felt like a parting between them.

'Well . . .' she said, and waited for him to leave her.

As she turned up her collar against that same cold wind, Alex heard someone calling her name. They both turned and saw Paul Weiss come into the square. He still wore his apron and carried a cloth. He ran to where they stood.

'Some of them were just in the bar,' he said, breathless, wiping his face with the cloth. 'Boys from the barracks. There's trouble.'

'What sort of trouble?' Eva asked him. 'Is Kurt still out there?'

'I think so. They weren't sure. The work started an hour ago. From what I can gather, some of them are still on the other side of their ridiculous barricade.'

The three of them ran to Alex's jeep, and he drove Paul back to his bar. Paul ran inside, called out his few customers – the boys were no longer there – and locked the door.

They drove from there to the barracks, past the smouldering ruins of the camp. They were stopped a few hundred yards from the barracks entrance by a lorry parked directly across the track. Several bulldozers stood near by. Men in blue and khaki overalls waited beside these, tending small fires, brewing tea, enjoying the delay.

'What's happening?' Alex asked the man who came to them from the lorry.

'A few old soldiers and kids thinking they can slow us down.' He grinned at the suggestion.

'Have you spoken to them?'

'No point. When we finally get the word to go in, we go in. Simple as that. They'll get out of the way fast enough then, believe me. The Yanks are up there now.' He motioned towards the barracks.

'The Americans?'

'Their equipment. They brought their own drivers. Left-hand drive. Don't look so worried. Like I said, once we get the word to go in, they'll be out like rabbits. They just want to beat their chests and shout at us. So what? Nobody's taking any of this seriously, not really.'

'Except the men at the barracks,' Alex said.

Resenting this critical and cautionary note, the man said, 'Yes, well, like I said, most of them are old enough to be either my grandfather or my kid.' It was an exaggeration on both counts.

Alex led Eva and Paul Weiss further along the track towards the huts. The smell of smoke from the burned-out camp still hung in the air, and the smoke itself showed in places through the trees.

Approaching the barracks entrance, Alex was alarmed to see Jesus Hernandez sitting there in his jeep. Other vehicles lined the track, most with their engines switched off. Ahead of him, men were unloading lorries and starting up generators, filling the air with their own distinctive smoke and noise and smell.

'Hey, look who finally turned up for the big show,' Hernandez called to Alex.

'Why are *you* here?' Alex asked him.

'Because Preston's around somewhere. Came out to see whoever's in charge of the work. He was at the Institute earlier. Crack of dawn. Him and Dyer had breakfast together before the angry villagers turned up with their burning torches, baying for blood. Where were you? Not invited? He's a happy man, Colonel Preston, a very happy man. We stopped off here on our way back home to Bielefeld. Checked on the job they'd done on the other place and then came here. Just in time for the fun and games, by the look of it. He wanted me to go in there with him. I brought along some drink on his say-so. He said if there was any trouble, then I was to go in and start handing it out before things turned nasty. Expediency, see.' He pronounced the word slowly. 'That's what all this is about. Expediency and diplomacy.' He made it clear to Alex what little faith he had in either concept.

'And are there many still in there, holding out?'

Hernandez laughed at the phrase. '"Holding out"? Jesus Christ, they're not "holding out". They were "holding out" in the Hurtgen Forest, they were "holding out" on the Rhine. This lot of idiots are just standing with their backs to closed doors and pissing themselves at the thought of what's going to happen to them. Like I told you, all Preston's bothered about now is that we don't flatten the place and then discover that we've flattened any of them with it. Bad public relations. Ask me, it's what *should* happen. Christ's sake, what do they expect?'

'They arrested James Whittaker,' Alex said.

'So?'

'They might charge him with the theft and illegal possession and use of proscribed drugs.'

Hernandez shrugged again. 'So? You think that's going to be traceable back to me? Think again. A lot of mouths going to clam shut before *my* name gets mentioned. And you think Preston's going to be happy at the thought of that? Like I said, think again.'

'You still lowered your voice to tell me,' Alex said.

Hernandez laughed. 'And the first mouth that's going to clam up will be stiff-upper-lip Whittaker's.'

'Somebody died,' Alex said. 'A girl.'

'Her and a few million others, in case you hadn't noticed. Her and twenty or thirty of my good friends. Her and three men I've known since I was in short pants.'

Alex felt Eva tug on his sleeve and he turned to her.

She indicated to where Preston had just then emerged from one of the barracks. The hut stood away from the entrance, beyond the overgrown and waterlogged parade square, and close to the surrounding trees.

'Like rabbits in a field of corn,' Hernandez said. 'And every single one of them getting ready to run. We nudge that shack and they'll all bolt for the woods as fast as their little chicken legs will carry them.'

No one responded to this.

Preston conferred with a group of men inside the camp. Several of these held rolled charts and they were clearly unhappy at what he told them. He left them and came back to the jeep.

'Foster,' he said. 'What in God's name are you doing here? You've got no business whatsoever—'

'My brother may be one of the men still in there,' Eva said.

'Kid?' Preston said. 'Dressed up like a soldier?

Holding all this up, thinking they got one last hand to play?' He did nothing to disguise his anger at the delay, or his contempt for the men responsible. Turning back to Alex, he said, 'What do you reckon, Foster, *is* this one last battle, one last rush across the Ardennes to the coast, at all cost, at any price?'

Alex ignored the remark and all it signified.

'I asked you a question, Captain.'

'I'm sure everyone will get a fair trial,' Alex said. 'It's what you Americans are renowned for, being even-handed, and shouting to the world about freedom and democracy before insisting on getting everything all your own way.'

'You got that right,' Hernandez said, not having fully understood the true focus of Alex's criticism.

Preston came closer to Alex. 'Big mistake, Captain Foster. Like Hernandez here said, you got that right. Walther and all the other murdering bastards like him will get exactly what they deserve.'

'After a fair and open trial?'

'After a fair and open trial. You forget – they're the animals in this zoo, not us.' He looked from Alex to Eva and Paul Weiss, both of whom refused to be goaded by his remarks.

'Hey, suddenly they got nothing to say,' Hernandez said.

They were interrupted by a gunshot from inside the camp.

A soldier at the entrance held up his rifle and called to them, apologizing for having fired accidentally.

Preston told the man to get away from the gate.

The soldier came to him and started to explain again what had happened.

'No one's listening, pal,' Hernandez told him. 'You should have made it a warning shot and put it through one of the windows. Perhaps that way you'd have been a hero and got things moving here.' And without any warning, he pulled out his own pistol from its holster and fired it three times into the nearby trees, causing everyone around him to duck.

When he'd finished firing, he laughed and swung the pistol in a circle above his head.

'Tell him to put it away,' Alex said to Preston.

And because this had come from Alex, Preston said nothing.

Hernandez returned the pistol to its holster and climbed from his seat on to the bonnet of the jeep. 'You want me to go in and clear the place for you, Colonel?' he shouted to Preston, half serious in his suggestion.

'You're a driver,' Preston said. 'Stay where you are. And no more firing.'

'Anything you say, Colonel.' Hernandez saluted and Preston shook his head at the gesture. 'But all of you just remember – I wasn't always a driver.'

'No,' Alex said. 'And you've probably just realized that

if you can clear the place without using your bribes, then you can sell the drink in the town and make twice as much money.'

'That was always plan A,' Hernandez said, laughing.

'Get down,' Preston told him.

Hernandez jumped to the ground.

'Paul here knows the men inside,' Alex said, beckoning Paul Weiss forward.

'How? Because he's one of them?' Preston said.

'Was,' Paul told him. 'I was their officer for three months.'

'It was a long time ago,' Preston said. 'And for all I know, you might still be on their side in all of this.'

'They trust Paul,' Eva said.

'Hey, I've got an idea,' Hernandez said. 'Send *her* in. She can pull at least one of the rabbits out by his ears and put him over her knee. The rest of them will probably be happy to follow.'

'Listen to him,' Paul Weiss told Preston. 'She's his sister. If he comes out, they might all just follow him and go home.'

Preston looked at Alex, who nodded his confirmation of this.

Just as Alex believed Preston might have been about to sanction this approach, Peter Remer appeared on the track behind his daughter and called to her.

She turned at his voice, alarmed by his unexpected appearance there.

The old man carried a stick with a carved handle, and he waved this as he came.

'Look out – he's armed,' Hernandez shouted, and then laughed when two of the nearby men cocked and raised their rifles. 'Hey, I'm joking,' he said, though unconcerned by this response.

Eva went to her father and stopped him before he reached the barracks entrance. She spoke to him for several minutes and then led him to the stump of a felled tree, where she helped him to sit down.

'What now?' Preston said, and Alex explained who the man was.

'I don't want to hear it,' Preston told him, shaking his head. 'And forget about *her* talking to the boy.' He waved to the men he'd spoken to inside the camp, making a winding motion with his hand.

And at this signal, one by one the bulldozers parked along the track started to move over the uneven ground.

Once inside the barracks, they were directed to the empty, more derelict huts, and they flattened these in minutes, driving back and forth over the wreckage of dark wood and corrugated iron until everything was broken to pieces and crushed flat into the mud. A dozen of the huts were demolished in this way, and the wreckage was then pushed and scooped into piles.

It surprised Alex to see how quickly all this happened. He expected the men in the occupied hut to emerge, but no one came out. He occasionally saw moving outlines at one of the dirty windows.

Eventually, after less than an hour, the bulk of the small barracks had been toppled and crushed, and mounded into piles ready for burning.

The men on the demolition crews switched off their engines. Small fires were lit and more kettles boiled. The men gathered in groups to smoke and talk, and to await further orders concerning the final hut.

Conscious of the likely delay after such a swift and promising start, Preston told Hernandez to go to the hut and to offer the men inside his drink. 'Tell them they all get a free ride to wherever it is they want to go, wherever it is they should have been all this time.'

Hernandez took a knapsack from his jeep and went into the camp.

'Tell him to leave his pistol behind,' Alex told Preston.

And again because the suggestion had come from Alex – and perhaps because it was something he himself should have considered – Preston ignored the remark.

Hernandez walked past the resting men and idling machinery and knocked on the hut door. It was opened and he went up the single step and disappeared inside. Few of the others waiting outside paid him any attention.

Eva returned to sit with her father, and Paul Weiss followed her.

Alex joined them, and for the first time he felt unwelcome in their company.

After a few minutes, he returned to Preston, who was sitting in the jeep. Alex sat beside him.

'I heard about Whittaker,' Preston said.

'Then you know where he got the drugs to treat the girl.'

'I don't know anything of the sort,' Preston said, looking straight ahead. 'Don't worry – everything will get sorted out. Here, there, everywhere.'

'You could have told Dyer what to do when the delegation showed up,' Alex said.

'Dyer's a spent force,' Preston said simply.

'Why? Because he's served your purpose?'

Preston pursed his lips and shrugged. 'Why did the old man come?' he asked, motioning to where Eva still sat with her father and Paul Weiss.

'He lost his wife and another son,' Alex said.

'I see,' Preston said. He closed his eyes for a moment, and Alex guessed he was remembering his own lost son. 'All the more reason to get them out of there, then, and let everybody just go home and get on with their lives.'

'You included?' Alex said.

'Me? I suppose so. Eventually.'

The two of them continued looking at the final hut.

'Whatever you think of him,' Preston said, meaning Hernandez, 'I'll miss him when he's gone.'

'You probably wish you *were* him,' Alex said, causing Preston to smile.

'You might be closer to the truth than you know.'

Although the truth, Alex then understood, was that Jesus Hernandez reminded Preston of his son, and that Hernandez, for all his faults, had become a kind of surrogate since the boy had died.

Eva rose from where she sat and came to the jeep. 'I'm going to go in,' she said. 'I'll bring Kurt out and, like Jesus says, the rest will probably follow.'

Twenty minutes had passed since Hernandez had gone into the hut. There was no longer any sense of urgency, only one of inevitability and of disappointment, like a game that had promised both a glorious victory and a crushing defeat, but which had then been badly played to its drawn-out conclusion.

'It can't hurt,' Preston told her. 'The sooner we finish off here . . .' He nodded to the wreckage. 'The weather boys forecast rain for tonight. They'll want to burn the place before then.'

Eva, Alex saw, would have entered the camp and gone to the hut whatever Preston said.

Paul Weiss and Peter Remer came to stand beside the jeep and watch her go.

Preston offered Peter Remer his hand. 'I'm sorry for your loss, Sir,' he said, and the two men shook hands and exchanged a solitary, knowing nod.

Eva crossed the waterlogged ground, her feet sticking in the mud as she approached the hut.

From inside came the sound of shouting, though whether this was the result of anger or celebration, Alex couldn't determine. It was followed by a loud clatter, as though something had been thrown against a wall. He imagined the men inside getting quickly drunk on the strong spirit Hernandez had taken in to them.

Eva hesitated at the noise, looking down at her wet legs, at the mud already splashed on her shins and along the hem of her coat. As she neared the hut, stopping a few yards away and calling in to whoever might hear her, the door opened. Both her brother and Jesus Hernandez stood there.

At first, it looked to Alex as though the two men had gone out at her summons, but then he saw that Hernandez stood with his arm across Kurt Remer's chest, raising it so that it then lay across the boy's throat.

It was how Alex had found the two of them together at the Institute entrance, and he silently cursed the boy for having again antagonized Hernandez.

'We ought to move closer,' he suggested to Preston, and the pair of them left the jeep and walked into the camp, standing beside the group of armed men there, few of whom paid any real attention to what was happening in the hut doorway.

'Tell him to let the boy go,' Alex said, and Preston shouted for Hernandez to release Kurt.

Hernandez looked up at hearing the call, hesitated for a moment, and then, recognizing Preston's voice, pushed Kurt Remer down the single step to the ground.

The boy fell badly, crying out at the impact and immediately scrambling to his feet. He turned back to the door, gesticulating and swearing at Hernandez, who laughed at him and waved him away.

It looked to Alex as though Kurt was about to retaliate, but then Eva spoke to her brother and he turned to face her, surprised at seeing her so close to him, unaware until then that either she or his father were present to witness this humiliating treatment. She continued talking to him, her voice low, and Kurt looked beyond her, to where Peter Remer now stood beside Alex and Preston.

'I should go to him before he does anything stupid,' Peter Remer said, his voice heavy with resignation.

Alex told him to wait. 'He might listen to Eva. Whatever he and the others expected to happen today, it's finished before it began, and none of them has had any real part in it.'

Peter Remer accepted this and waited where he stood.

'They're leaving,' Hernandez shouted to Preston. 'They've had enough.' He waved the bottle he held and then passed it inside to one of the others there. 'Just this little trouble-making bastard holding things up.' He took the bottle back and threw it to Kurt, who caught it and drank from it, despite a warning from Eva for him not to. Hernandez watched the boy and laughed at the gesture. The drink ran over Kurt's chin and throat. Lowering the bottle, he choked for a few seconds, regained his breath and drank again. Eva spoke to him again, and again he ignored her.

Then Hernandez called for him to hand the bottle back, and without warning Kurt threw it at him hard. The bottle missed and smashed on the door frame, showering Hernandez with broken glass and drink, and causing him to shield his head and almost fall at the suddenness of this attack. Kurt swore at him, loudly this time, finally attracting the attention and the laughter of the nearby onlookers. And again he ignored his sister's demands that he walk away from the hut and go to her.

Regaining his composure, and still angry that the bottle had smashed only inches from his head, Hernandez leaped down from the doorway, ran the few paces to the boy and grabbed him again round his throat. He shouted at him as he did this, asking Kurt over and over what he thought he was doing, why he hadn't already learned his lesson, and how many times was he, Jesus Hernandez, going to have to show him who was in charge here?

Kurt laughed at everything he heard.

Eva went to where the two men stood, Hernandez still shouting in her brother's ear, Kurt struggling to breathe through his laughter with Hernandez's arm around his throat. Eva tried to pull this away, but Hernandez was too strong for her.

Some of the nearby men saw this and called for Eva

to leave the poor man alone. Others encouraged her to continue trying to free her brother.

Eventually, Eva released her grip on Hernandez and stood back from him.

'That's better,' Hernandez told her. 'Now ask me nicely and I might just let go of this little bastard.'

Eva asked him to release her brother.

'Say "please",' Hernandez told her.

She did this and Hernandez released his hold on Kurt and pushed him hard so that he stumbled forward on the slippery surface and collided with Eva, knocking them both to the ground. Hernandez came forward to stand over them. There was now almost continuous laughter from the surrounding men.

Behind Hernandez, others started to emerge from the hut and to line up against its side. Some of them still held the bottles he'd given them. They looked to Alex like party-goers whose celebrations had been inter-rupted and who had been forced outside by the disturbance.

At Alex's urging, Preston called for Hernandez to come away from the hut and to return to him.

Hernandez heard this, but shook his head. He remained where he stood, directly above Eva and Kurt.

Eva was the first to rise, helping her brother to his feet. The pair of them were coated in wet mud. Eva's hair was plastered to her cheeks and forehead.

'Take him home and put him back in the nursery,'

Hernandez shouted at her. 'Before I really have to show him who holds all the cards around here.' He turned to the men emerging from the hut. 'Party's over, fellas.'

Most waited where they stood; a few began to wander amid the mounded ruins of their makeshift home; some went to the surrounding men and offered them the bottles they carried.

Peter Remer called for Eva to return to him and to bring her brother with her.

'Daddy's calling,' Hernandez said to Kurt. He formed a fist and jabbed it towards the boy, stopping an inch from Kurt Remer's face and laughing at his frightened response to this.

'Leave him alone,' Eva said.

The command surprised and amused Hernandez. 'Or else what?' he said to her.

Eva spoke to him in German, telling him he was a bully, and that the sooner he left them and returned home, the better it would be for all of them.

Angry that he was unable to understand or respond to this, Hernandez pointed a finger into her face and told her to repeat what she'd just said in English.

Eva refused. She stepped forward, putting herself between Hernandez and her brother. She spoke to him again – again in German – this time holding up her palm to him.

Unable to contain his anger at this continued mockery, Hernandez rushed at her and pushed her back to the ground. And as Eva fell, Kurt lunged at Hernandez and wrapped his arms around him, causing the pair of them also to fall into the water and the mud. After a few seconds of rolling and struggling together, Hernandez managed to pull himself free of the boy; he held his knee to Kurt's chest and started viciously punching him in the face.

Eva screamed for him to stop.

Kurt tried to defend himself, but was ineffectual in this, one of his arms pinned by Hernandez's leg.

Eva tried to pull Hernandez from her brother, putting her hands around his head and covering his eyes, eventually distracting him sufficiently for Kurt to struggle free of where he lay. Hernandez jabbed backwards with his elbow, striking Eva in the face and knocking her from him.

Unprepared for this sudden eruption of violence, both Alex and Preston ran forward, calling for Hernandez to stop. As they did this, a further shot was fired, surprising everyone and causing the two men to stop running and to search for who had fired.

There was yet another shot, and following this, a loud shout.

Looking up, Alex saw that Kurt Remer now held Hernandez's mud-coated pistol, and that he stood beside the man, pointing it at him.

On the ground, Hernandez scrambled away from the boy. 'I'm hit,' he shouted. 'He shot me. I'm fucking hit.'

Alex resumed running and waving his arms at Kurt Remer, calling for him to drop the gun, the same few words over and over.

Preston ran beside him and shouted the same. Then he called to Hernandez to ask him where he'd been shot.

At first, Hernandez seemed uncertain. Then he held a hand to his upper arm, where blood showed through his fingers.

Eva rose and held out her hands to her brother. She, too, told him to drop the gun and to go to her, that Hernandez was only lightly wounded, to drop the gun and to go to her, just to go to her. And as she spoke, so she moved slowly towards Kurt, again putting herself between her brother and the man on the ground.

Everyone who had a moment before been cheering and laughing at what was happening was now either crouched close to the ground or had run for the cover of the machinery.

Kurt stood with the pistol still pointed at Jesus Hernandez. And in the mud, half-hidden from the boy by Eva, Hernandez continued to scream that he'd been hit, calling now for someone to shoot the boy before he fired again and killed him.

Close to where Alex and Preston now stood, several men raised and cocked their rifles, aiming at Kurt.

'Put them down,' Preston shouted, and the men reluctantly obeyed him. 'Stop screaming,' he shouted to

Hernandez. 'I'm coming to get you. Just stop screaming. He isn't going to fire again. It isn't a bad wound. It was an accident. An accident.'

But Hernandez ignored him and went on screaming. The blood now covered his upper arm from shoulder to elbow and continued to run through his fingers where he clutched the wound.

Kurt Remer, meanwhile, stood mesmerized by the screaming, looking down at the man on the ground, the pistol still pointed through his sister's legs.

Eva continued talking to him. She spoke softly, the same few phrases, until eventually Kurt looked up at her. He lowered the pistol until it hung by his side. Eva reached forward to take it from him, but the instant she touched her brother's arm he jerked away from her, raising the weapon again and swinging it until it pointed directly at her. And then he swung it further, until it pointed towards where his father now stood with Alex and Preston. And as he swung it, so he fired it again – the shot as involuntary as the first had been – recoiling in surprise at the sudden jolt this caused him.

By the barracks entrance, one of the men who had raised his rifle aimed again and fired at the boy.

Neither Kurt nor Eva was hit; instead the bullet shattered what little remained of the glass in one of the hut windows.

Preston called again for everyone to stop shooting.

By now, others at the entrance had raised their

weapons, and this time no one obeyed Preston when he ordered them to lower them.

From beside one of the bulldozers, someone shouted for help. Kurt's wild shot had struck a man high in the chest, just beneath his throat. Unnoticed, the man had remained crouched for a few moments, and had then fallen forward gasping for breath, his face already bloody. Several of those near by ran to help him.

In the confusion of those few seconds, as Kurt still swung the pistol back and forth in a wide arc, as Eva went on pleading with him, and as Jesus Hernandez continued screaming that he'd been shot and for someone to shoot the boy, Peter Remer walked slowly forward until he stood beside Eva. He told his daughter to be quiet and then to step back. She did this, half-turning to look to where Alex still stood beside Preston, watching her. Alex saw both the uncertainty and the pleading in her eyes, but he knew that the time for him to intervene had passed.

Beside the bulldozer, someone shouted that the man who had been struck in the chest was dead.

Both Alex and Preston turned at the words. A man with a first-aid kit worked feverishly, uselessly wrapping a bandage around the wound.

Leaving Alex, Preston went to where Jesus Hernandez lay in the mud, pulled Hernandez's hand from his wound and then called for the men surrounding the corpse to go to him. He shouted again for the men at the entrance to lower their weapons. And because he now stood between them and Kurt Remer, they finally obeyed him.

Eva went to Preston and spoke to him, and he nodded several times and then lowered his head at what she said.

She came back to Alex, passing Hernandez and the two men now kneeling beside him.

At the hut, Peter Remer had reached Kurt and was standing with his hands out to his son. Kurt was no longer waving the pistol and it again hung by his side.

'It was an accident,' Eva said to Alex, looking beyond him to where a tarpaulin was already being drawn over the dead man.

'I know,' he told her. But it was no consolation to her, and they both understood this. Just as they both understood that a boundary had been crossed with the killing of this unknown, uninvolved man, and that a solitary, unavoidable path now lay ahead of all of them. He wanted to talk to her, to hold her again and to reassure her, to make impossible promises to her, and to hear her make those same impossible promises to him. But he could do none of this for her. There were no words. Nothing to express himself to her as he wanted to, and nothing she herself might now want to hear from him that would be of even the smallest comfort or reassurance to her.

She touched him gently on the arm and then turned and walked away from him.

And as she went, Alex looked beyond her to where Kurt and Peter Remer still stood, the wayward son and the forsaken father, each now finally as lost and as directionless as the other, the pistol still in the boy's hand and his hand still by his side.

Peter Remer clutched his son tight, holding one hand against the boy's back, the other cupping his head and forcing it hard into his own, their faces together, each of them looking sightlessly over the other's shoulder.

Kurt was sobbing convulsively now, asking his father in gasped and stammering sentences to tell him what he'd done, who'd been shot, who'd been killed, and what was going to happen to him. And because Peter Remer had no simple, honest answer for all his son's urgent and terrible questions, he said nothing, pulling the boy even closer to him, stroking his head and calming him, and crushing him even further into the brief, illusory sanctuary of his own broad chest.

THE END

IN ZODIAC LIGHT
Robert Edric

It is December 1922 and the aftershocks of the First World War continue to make themselves felt. Ex-soldier, poet and composer Ivor Gurney, suffering from increasingly frequent and deepening bouts of paranoid schizophrenia, is transferred to the City of London Mental Hospital, Dartford.

Neglected by the military and by his own family, and abandoned by all but a notable handful of his friends, Gurney begins a descent into the madness and oblivion which he believes has long been waiting to claim him.

Yet following his arrival at Dartford, there are still those who continue to believe in Gurney's capabilities – in his 'wayward genius'. For a brief period, it seems that he might find some calm and ease in his life, and thus achieve the status so many consider him capable of.

But few of those now responsible for Gurney realize the consequences of their hopefulness. They have no real idea of what he endured on the Western Front during almost three years of military service and the effects it had on his mind. Ultimately it is not the war but the refusal of his admirers to acknowledge the trauma of his experience that will take him further from a creative rebirth and closer to the edge of sanity that he both craves and fears . . .

'EDRIC'S WORK CONSTITUTES ONE OF THE MOST ASTONISHING BODIES OF WORK TO HAVE APPEARED FROM A SINGLE AUTHOR FOR A GENERATION'
Daily Telegraph

9780385612586

Doubleday

GATHERING THE WATER
Robert Edric

'SUPERB . . . A POWER-PACKED, STUNNINGLY
CRAFTED NOVEL'
Sunday Times

It is 1847, northern England, and Charles Weightman has
been given the unenviable task of overseeing the flooding of
the Forge Valley and evicting its lingering inhabitants.
Weightman is heartily resented by these locals, and he
himself is increasingly unconvinced both of the wisdom of
this appointment and of the integrity and motives of the
company men who posted him there. He finds some solace,
however, in his enigmatic neighbour, Mary Latimer.

As the waters begin to rise in the Forge Valley, it becomes
increasingly evident that the man-made deluge cannot be
avoided – not by the locals desperate to save their homes,
nor by the reluctant agent of their destruction, Weightman
himself.

'BELONGS WITH A GROUP OF HIS [EDRIC'S] NOVELS
WHOSE ARTISTRY AND RESONANCE CONSTITUTE ONE
OF THE MOST ASTONISHING BODIES OF WORK TO
APPEAR FROM A SINGLE AUTHOR FOR A GENERATION'
Daily Telegraph

'SUPERB...IT IS IN HIS MARSHALLING OF HIS THEMES
THAT EDRIC PROVES HIMSELF SUCH AN ACCOMPLISHED
NOVELIST'
Sunday Times

'AN ADMIRABLY SERIOUS NOVEL, WRITTEN IN PROSE AS
SPARE AS ITS SETTING. ITS LAMENT FOR THE DEATH OF
THE COMMUNITY IS SUBTLE AND POWERFUL'
Daily Mail

9780552999748

BLACK SWAN

CRADLE SONG
Robert Edric

'A REWARDING EXPERIENCE...THIS IS MURDER AT ITS
MOST FOUL, CRIME AT THE DEEP END'
Spectator

An imprisoned child murderer unexpectedly appeals his
conviction. In return for a reduced sentence, he offers to
implicate those involved in the crimes who were never caught;
providing evidence of Police corruption and, most importantly,
revealing where the corpses of several long-sought, but never
found teenage girls are buried.

Distressed at what may come to light, yet desperate to locate the
body of his own missing daughter, the father of one of these girls
approaches Private Investigator Leo Rivers with a plea for help.

Rivers' enquiries stir cold and bitter memories. Long-dead
enmities flare suddenly into violence and a succession of new
killings. Everyone involved, then and now, and on both sides of
the law, is unprepared for the suddenness and ferocity with which
these old embers are fanned back into life. As the investigation
progresses, it gathers momentum and now must speed inexorably
to the even greater violence and sadness of its conclusion.

'*CRADLE SONG* IS A SUPERBLY PACED BOOK . . . THIS IS
CLASSIC CRIME NOIR . . . EDRIC CAN ALSO PRODUCE
BEAUTIFUL PROSE AND ARRESTING IMAGES AS WELL AS
INCISIVE SOCIAL SATIRE . . . MAGNIFICENTLY ACHIEVED'
Giles Foden

'HIS NOVEL IS SOMETHING SUBSTANTIAL AND
DISTINCTIVE . . . EDRIC HAS A CLEAR, ALMOST RAIN-
WASHED STYLE, EMINENTLY SUITABLE FOR HIS HULL
SETTING . . . *CRADLE SONG* IS A STRONG AND SERIOUS
NOVEL, SOBERLY ENTERTAINING AND WELL WORTH YOUR
WHILE'
Literary Review

'HIGHLY ACCOMPLISHED . . . FANS CAN LOOK FORWARD
TO HIS USUAL SHARPLY REALISED CHARACTERS
OPERATING IN A TENSE, PRESSURED ENVIRONMENT'
Independent

9780552771429

BLACK SWAN

SIREN SONG
Robert Edric

When the luxury yacht Helen Brooks was last seen on is
found abandoned amid the treacherous marshlands of the
Humber Estuary, foul play is suspected. However, in the
absence of a body, nothing can be proven. The owner of the
yacht, ambitious businessman Simon Fowler, seems
unprepared even to offer any sort of explanation to what
Helen was doing on board.

A year later, Hull private investigator Leo Rivers is
approached by Alison Brooks, Helen's mother, to investigate
both the background to this disappearance and Fowler.
Rivers is drawn through a long, hot summer into a world of
human trafficking and governmental corruption at every
turn. In the stifling heat there are many questions and few
people prepared to offer adequate answers. Each unravelled
piece of the mystery moves Rivers further from the vanished
girl and deeper into a web of exploitation, greed,
temptation, revenge and violence, from which even he is
unable to extricate himself without unforeseen and tragic
consequences . . .

SWAN SONG
Robert Edric

'DRIPS WITH ATMOSPHERE, ABSORBING'
Evening Standard.

Hull. Private investigator Leo Rivers is at the heart of an enquiry into a string of prostitute-linked killings. Approached by the mother of the chief suspect, Rivers knows this isn't an open and shut case. Not only is the suspect not involved, but also several unconsidered and scarcely credible connections link the murders to a single perpetrator.

Heading the investigation and seeking out its glory is an ambitious, career-minded Chief of Police, who will stop at nothing to make a name for himself.

Set against a backdrop of the Humber and the long and violent destruction of Hull's once-cherished fishing industry, Robert Edric reveals a world of exploitation and ambition in an extraordinarily gripping piece of contemporary *noir*.

'READING HIS CLOSING CHAPTERS IS LIKE BEING GRIPPED BY A POLICE-ISSUE LEATHER DRIVING GLOVE'
Mail on Sunday

'A CONJURER OF STYLES AND THEMES, A VERITABLE STANLEY KUBRICK OF THE WORLD FICTION'
The Times

'EDRIC IS A TERRIFIC STORYTELLER'
Observer

9780552771443

BLACK SWAN